FAME

Also by Tilly Bagshawe

TILLY BAGSHAWE

Fame

HARPER

Harper
An imprint of HarperCollins*Publishers*
77–85 Fulham Palace Road,
Hammersmith, London W6 8JB

www.harpercollins.co.uk

A Paperback Original 2011
1

A catalogue record for this book
is available from the British Library

ISBN: 978-0-00-732652-5

Set in Meridien by Palimpsest Book Production Limited,
Falkirk, Stirlingshire

Printed and bound in Great Britain by
Clays Ltd, St Ives plc

For Viorel Rezmives
and in loving memory of Abel Teglas.

Heathcliff shall never know how I love him: and that, not because he's handsome, Nelly, but because he's more myself than I am. Whatever our souls are made of, his and mine are the same.

Emily Brontë, Wuthering Heights

You can take all the sincerity in Hollywood, place it in the navel of a fruit fly and still have room enough for three caraway seeds and a producer's heart.

Fred Allen

ACKNOWLEDGEMENTS

Thanks to everyone at HarperCollins, especially my saintly, patient editor, Sarah Ritherdon and the wonderful sales team, Oli Malcolm, Laura Fletcher and Lisa Doyle. Also to my agents Luke Janklow and Tim Glister, and everyone at Janklow & Nesbit. FAME is partly set in Romania, a country I have come to know well through our charity, F.R.O.D.O (Foundation for the Relief of Disabled Orphans). My husband Robin founded F.R.O.D.O to help improve the lives of Romania's thousands of forgotten, institutionalized children, and their work is nothing short of miraculous. Any readers who are interested can see more about our programs at www.frodokids.org. This book is dedicated to two of those children, the brave and beautiful Viorel Rezmives, and Abel Teglas, whose short life changed mine and Robin's forever and who we will never forget. I would specially like to pay tribute to the amazing Sarah Wade, who transformed the lives of these two little boys and so many others. You are a true inspiration. Finally, I would like to thank all my family for their unending love and support through a difficult year. I would be lost without you.

PART ONE

PROLOGUE

At the Kodak Theatre in Hollywood, the Eighty-Fifth Academy Awards were about to get under way.

In the hushed luxury of the auditorium, opposite the vast, 130-foot stage, designed by David Rockwell especially with the Oscars in mind, two men took their seats. Tonight, their bitter feud would be settled for better or worse. It would be settled in front of their peers, the three thousand of Hollywood's chosen sons and daughters who'd been invited to tonight's ceremony. It would be settled in front of the estimated sixty million Americans expected to tune in to the broadcast at home, as well as the hundreds more millions who would catch the Oscars around the globe. For one of the men, tonight would be a victory so sweet he knew he would still be able to taste it on his deathbed. For the other, it would be a defeat so catastrophic, he would never recover.

As the ceremony dragged on interminably – *Best Live Action Short; Best Sound Mixing; Did anybody in the universe care?* – both men kept their eyes fixed straight ahead, ignoring the smiles of well-wishers as totally as they ignored the pruriently intrusive television cameras constantly scanning their features for a reaction.

Disappointment.

Hope.

Humour.

Despair.

The cameras got nothing. Neither of the two men had got to where they were today by giving away their emotions. Certainly not for free.

At last, after almost three long hours of torture, the moment arrived. Martin Scorsese was standing at the podium, a crisp white envelope in his hand. He gave a short, pre-prepared speech. Neither of the men heard a word of it. Behind his diminutive Italian frame, a montage of images flashed across an enormous screen, clips from the year's most critically acclaimed pictures. To the two men, they were nothing but shapes and colours.

I hate you, thought one.

I hope you rot in hell, thought the other.

'And the Academy Award for Best Picture goes to . . .'

CHAPTER ONE

'I'm not asking you, Sabrina, I'm telling you. You *have* to take this part.'

Sabrina Leon looked at her manager with queenly disdain. Ed Steiner was fat, balding and past his prime (if he'd ever had a prime). In cheap grey suit trousers and a white shirt with spreading sweat patches under each arm, he looked more like a used-car salesman than a Hollywood player. He also had an intensely irritating, domineering manner. Sabrina did not 'have' to take the part. She did not 'have' to do anything. *I'm the fucking star here*, she thought defiantly. *I headlined in three* Destroyers *movies. Three! That's* Destroyers, *the most successful action franchise of all time. You work for me, remember?*

Ignoring Ed, Sabrina got to her feet and walked across the room to the French windows. Outside her room, a lush, private garden exploded with colour and scent. Bright orange, spiky ginger flowers fought for space with more traditional roses in white and yellow, and orange and lemon trees groaned with fruit beneath the perfectly blue, cloudless California sky. Then there were the views. The house was built at the top of a steep canyon, so even from the ground floor they were spectacular, across the rooftops of the exclusive Malibu Colony, home to some of Hollywood's biggest, wealthiest stars, and beyond to the endless, shimmering blue of the Pacific Ocean. If it weren't for the resolutely hospital-like furnishings in all the rooms – white metal beds, uncomfortable, hard-backed chairs – you could almost imagine you were in a junior suite at the Four Seasons, and not locked up like a prisoner at Revivals, the infamous $2,000-a-night rehab of choice for burned-out Young Hollywood.

It had been Ed Steiner who had forced Sabrina Leon to check herself into Revivals. Two weeks ago, Ed had driven round to his client's mansion off Benedict Canyon at eight in the morning, packed an overnight bag while she watched, and frog-marched Sabrina into his shining new Mercedes E-Class convertible.

'This is ridiculous, Ed,' she'd protested. Still in her party clothes from the night before, a black leather Dolce & Gabbana minidress and sky-high Jonathan Kelsey stilettos, with heavy black eye make-up smudged around her eyes, Sabrina looked even more desirable and vixen-like than the tabloid caricatures that were wrecking her career. 'I'm not an addict. There's nothing wrong with me.'

'Grow up, Sabrina,' Ed Steiner snapped. 'This is not about you. It's about your career. Your image. Or at least what's left of it. How many ratzies saw you staggering out of Bardot last night looking like *that*?'

'Looking like what?' Sabrina bristled, her sultry, almond-shaped eyes narrowing into slits, like a cat about to pounce. 'Looking sexy, you mean? I thought looking sexy was part of my job.'

Ed fought back the urge to slap his truculent, twenty-two-year-old client across her spoiled, heartbreakingly sensual face. Sabrina knew full well she had no business being in that club last night, or any club for that matter. She could be foolish, and reckless, but she wasn't stupid. He started the engine.

'Right now your job is to look contrite,' he said crossly. 'You are deeply sorry for your behaviour, for what you said to Tarik Tyler, you are addressing your problems, you are asking for privacy while you heal during this difficult time, yadda yadda yadda. You know the drill as well as I do, kid, so do us both a favour and quit playing dumb, OK?' He glanced over to the passenger seat. 'What the fuck is that?'

In the outside zip-up pocket of the overnight bag, a bottle top was clearly visible. Pulling it out, Ed Steiner found himself clutching a half-drunk bottle of Jack Daniel's.

Sabrina was unapologetic. 'Helps me sleep.'

'You think this is funny?'

'Oh, c'mon, Ed, give me a break. Rehab's boring. I'm not gonna get through it without a drink.'

'You think you're Marianne Faithfull or something?' To Sabrina's consternation, Ed flung the bottle into the rosemary bushes that lined her driveway. 'You think people are gonna forgive you this bullshit because it's so *rock 'n' roll*? Well, let me tell you something, Sabrina: they won't. Not this time. You are *this close* to being finished in this town.' He held up his thumb and forefinger, waving them inches from Sabrina's face. '*This close*. Now put your fucking seatbelt on.'

Sabrina yawned defiantly, but she buckled up anyway, slipping on a pair of Oliver Peoples aviators to shield her eyes from the sun's early morning glare. Outwardly, she continued to play the rebel – it was all she knew how to do. Inside, however, she felt her stomach flip over, a combination of last night's excessive alcohol consumption on an empty stomach and visceral, gut-wrenching fear.

What if Ed was right?

What if she really could lose it all?

No. I can't. I won't let it happen. If I have to go back to my life before, I'll kill myself.

The headlines of Sabrina Leon's rags-to-riches, *True Hollywood Story* were familiar to everyone in America. Homeless kid from Fresno gets plucked from obscurity by big-shot Hollywood producer Tarik Tyler, becomes a mega-star thanks to her lead role in Tyler's *Destroyers* movies, and slides spectacularly off the rails.

Snore.

No one was more bored by Sabrina's past than Sabrina, as she'd made patently clear in Revivals' group therapy sessions.

'Hi, I'm Amy.' A shy, middle-aged woman in a drab knitted cardigan introduced herself. 'I'm here for alcoholism and crystal meth. I pledge confidentiality and respect to the group.'

'I'm John, I'm here for cocaine. I pledge confidentiality and respect.'

'Hi, I'm Lisa, I'm an alcoholic. I pledge respect to the group.'

It was Sabrina's turn. 'What?' She looked around her accusingly. 'Oh, come on. You all know who I am.'

'Even so,' said the therapist gently, 'we'd like you to introduce yourself to the group. As a *person*.'

'Oh, "as a *person*",' Sabrina mimicked sarcastically. 'As opposed to what? A dog?'

No one laughed.

'Jesus, OK, fine. I'm Sabrina. I'm here because my manager is an a-hole. Good enough?'

Things got worse when patients were asked to talk about their childhoods. Sabrina sighed petulantly. 'Dad was a junkie, Mom was a whore, the children's homes sucked. Next question.'

'I'm sure there was more to it than that,' prodded the therapist.

'Oh, sure. There were the assholes who tried to rape me,' said Sabrina. 'From twelve to fifteen I was on the streets. Poor little me, right? Except that it wasn't poor me, because I got into theatre, and I got out. I got out because I'm talented. Because I'm different. Because I'm better.'

It was the first time Sabrina had expressed any real emotion in session. The therapist seized on it gratefully. 'Better than who?' she asked.

'Better than *you*, lady. And better than the rest of these junkie sad sacks. I can't believe you guys actually signed up for this piece-of-shit programme out of your own free will.'

Everyone knew that Sabrina Leon was not at Revivals by choice. That her manager, Ed Steiner, had staged an intervention as a last-ditch attempt to salvage her career.

Stumbling out of a Hollywood nightclub a few weeks ago, with a visible dusting of white powder on the tip of her perfect nose, Sabrina had lashed out at Tarik Tyler, the producer who'd discovered her and made her a star, calling him a 'slave driver'. Tarik, who was black and whose great-grandmother had been a slave, took offence, as did the rest of the industry, who demanded that Sabrina should apologize. Sabrina refused, and a scandal of Mel Gibson-esque proportions erupted, with outrage spewing like lava across the blogosphere. *Access Hollywood* ran Sabrina's feud with Tyler as their lead story, devoting three-quarters of their nightly entertainment roundup to a vox-pop of 'celebrity reactions' to Sabrina's ingratitude, all of them suitably disgusted and appalled. Even Harry Greene, the famously reclusive producer of the hugely successful *Fraternity* movies, emerged from his self-imposed house arrest to brand Sabrina Leon 'a graceless, racist brat'. In one, single, ill-judged night, the tide of public affection and goodwill that had swept Sabrina Leon to unprecedented box-office success – America loved a good rags-to-riches story and Sabrina had been the ultimate poor girl made good – turned so suddenly, so violently and completely, it was as if her career had been swept away by a tsunami.

And when the tide finally receded, she'd washed up at Revivals.

'There's no need to be insulting,' chided the therapist.

Isn't there? thought Sabrina

She had to get out of this place.

Two weeks she'd been here now. It felt like two years, what with the early-morning starts, the gross, tasteless health food served at every meal, the boring, self-obsessed patients. All the faux emotion of the therapy sessions, the embarrassing over-sharing of feelings, the fucking hand-holding. It made Sabrina want to throw up. Rehab was such a cliché. And, according to Ed Steiner, she still had six weeks to go.

Now, turning back from the window, Sabrina glowered at her manager defiantly.

'I'm not working for free, Ed,' she announced bluntly. 'Not in a million fucking years.'

Ed Steiner sighed. He was used to spoiled, ungrateful actresses, but Sabrina Leon really took the cake. She ought to be on her knees, kissing his hand in gratitude. Here he was offering her a life-line – not just a role, but the *lead* role in Dorian Rasmirez's much-hyped remake of *Wuthering Heights* – at a time when she couldn't get cast in a fucking Doritos commercial. And she was bitching because Rasmirez wasn't going to pay her. *Why the hell should he? Dorian Rasmirez doesn't need you, you dumb bitch. You need him. Wake up and smell the coffee.*

'Yes you are,' he said robustly. 'I accepted on your behalf this morning.'

'Well you can damn well un-accept!' screamed Sabrina. 'I decide what roles I take, Ed. It's *my* life. *I* have control.'

'Actually, according to the release you signed when you admitted yourself into the eight-week programme here, *I* have control. At least over your career and business decisions.' He handed her a piece of paper. Sabrina glanced at it, balled it up in her fist and threw it to the ground.

'And it's a good job I do,' said Ed, unfazed by this childish show of temper. 'Let's not go through this charade, OK, Sabrina? It's boring, it's bullshit, and you know I'm not buying it. You know as well as I do that you need this part. You *need* it. Right now no other director in Hollywood would piss on you if you were on fire. Sit down.'

Sabrina hesitated. In jeans and a long-sleeved navy-blue tee from Michael Stars, with no make-up on and her long hair pulled back in a ponytail, she looked about a thousand times prettier than she had the last time Ed had seen her. Healthier too, less scrawny, and with the glow restored to her naturally tawny, olive skin. *This place must be doing something right*, he thought. *All she needs is to lose the attitude*.

'Sit,' he repeated.

Sabrina sat.

'Dorian Rasmirez has had his issues,' he went on, 'but he's still a big name, and this is gonna be a big movie.'

Sabrina softened slightly. 'When does it start shooting?'

'May probably. Or June. They're still scouting for locations.'

'Locations?' Sabrina pouted petulantly. A location shoot meant months away from LA, from the clubs and parties and excitement that had become her drug of choice. 'What's wrong with the back lot at Universal?'

'Nothing,' said Ed sarcastically, 'except the fact that it's not a Universal Picture. And it's *Wuthering Heights*.'

Sabrina looked blank. She'd never been big on literature.

'*Wuthering Heights*? One of the greatest classic novels of all time? Cathy and Heathcliff? Set on wild, windswept moorland?' Ed shook his head despairingly. 'Never mind. The point is, it'll do you good to get out of Los Angeles for a while. Out of the public eye altogether, in fact. We issued your apology statement the day after you came in here, which may have helped a little. We'll probably do another one before you check out. But it's still a shit-storm out there. You need to disappear and you need to work. Come back in a year, healthy and happy and with a hit movie under your belt—'

'A *year*!' Sabrina interrupted. 'Are you out of your mind?'

Being away from the LA party scene was bad enough. But the thought of being out of the media glare for so long – of not having her picture taken or seeing her face in magazines – made Sabrina's heart race with panic. You might as well tell her she couldn't breathe, or eat. Without attention she would wither and die, like a sunflower locked in a cellar.

Ignoring her, Ed Steiner went on.

'I know they're filming some of it in Romania, at Dorian Rasmirez's Schloss. I'm told that's worth seeing,' he added, trying to strike a more cheerful note. 'Oh, and I didn't tell you the best part. It's not a hundred per cent confirmed yet, but it looks like Viorel Hudson's signing on as Heathcliff.'

Sabrina rolled her eyes. *That was the 'best part'? What was the worst part? Were they filming it naked in Siberia?* The one, the only, good thing about Dorian Rasmirez's offer was that it would be a vehicle for re-launching Sabrina back into the box-office big league. If Viorel Hudson was involved, she'd have to fight for top billing, and probably for the dressing-room mirror as well. Rumoured to be unimaginably vain, Viorel Hudson was probably the one man in Hollywood whose sex appeal, and arrogance, rivalled Sabrina's own. They had never met, but Sabrina knew instinctively that she would loathe Viorel Hudson.

Ed Steiner looked at his watch. 'I'd better go. I have a meeting at The Roosevelt in an hour.'

Rub it in, why don't you? thought Sabrina bitterly. *I have a meeting with a bunch of whining alcoholics and a 'speerchal' healer from Topanga Canyon whose last brain cell died in 1972.*

'I'll bike you over the script tomorrow. Give you something to do between sessions. How's it going, by the way? This place helping you at all?'

Serena smiled sweetly. 'Go fuck yourself, Ed.'

That night, staring at the ceiling in her hard, uncomfortable single bed, Sabrina hugged herself and said a silent prayer of thanks.

She'd played it cool with Ed, just as she played it cool with everyone. But she knew what a miracle Rasmirez's offer was. Dorian Rasmirez was one of the most respected directors in Hollywood. He'd have had actresses lining up to play the part of Cathy. Actresses whom the world wasn't unfairly branding a racist. But for some reason, Rasmirez had chosen her.

Fate, she thought. *I was born to succeed. It's my destiny.*

All Sabrina had to do now was to give the performance of her life. And to make sure she out-dazzled the smug, self-satisfied Viorel Hudson. *Still*, she reassured herself, *that shouldn't be too hard.* If all else failed, she could always seduce Hudson. Once Sabrina Leon slept with a man, her power over him was total.

Hollywood might have written her off. But Hollywood was wrong.

Sabrina Leon was on her way back.

CHAPTER TWO

'Oh my God, Vio! Don't stop! Please don't stop. Oh . . . Jesus!'

Viorel Hudson had no intention of stopping. The girl lying spread-eagled beneath him on the soft-pink bed of the Chateau Marmont's exclusive Bungalow 1 was Rose Da Luca, currently the highest-paid model in America and number one on most adult males' 'fantasy fuck' lists. Unusually for such a stunning girl, Rose was also good in bed: coy on the surface, but wildly passionate and adventurous underneath. *In fact, scratch adventurous*, thought Viorel delightedly as he felt Rose's index finger circling his asshole. *She's filthy. I think I might be in love.*

Flipping Rose over onto her knees – much more of that finger and he was going to come on the spot – he entered her from behind, slowing his pace till he could feel her writhe in delicious, agonizing frustration. Looking down at her arched back, and that famous mane of red hair spread over the pillow like a halo, he felt a familiar rush of triumph. It was the same feeling he got whenever he bedded a woman he wanted, or landed a role that he knew countless other actors coveted. For Viorel, the pleasure of any experience was always enhanced by the sense of competition. Acting was fun. Sex was even better. But *winning* . . . that was the biggest thrill of all.

Nailing Rose Da Luca was actually the final triumph in what had been a uniquely triumphant day. Not only had Viorel signed on the dotted line to play Heathcliff in the remake of *Wuthering Heights*, which meant he would be working with one of his all-time idols, Dorian Rasmirez; but to his surprise (and his agent's frank astonishment) Rasmirez had offered him five and a half million dollars for the privilege. Five million was the magic number in Hollywood, the number that separated successful film actors from bona fide movie stars. It was a rubicon that, once crossed, pretty much guaranteed you a place in the pantheon of the greats. Until your first big box-office flop, of course, at which point you could slide back down the snake into the twos, or sometimes even lower. For Viorel Hudson, however, it was a win–win situation. Despite his high public profile (last year he'd been named Sexiest Man Alive by *People* magazine, an accolade that he claimed to be embarrassed by but secretly revelled in), Viorel had never earned more than a million dollars on a movie. That was because he'd carefully chosen projects with artistic merit over blockbusters with multimillion-dollar budgets. As a result he was revered by many of his peers as an actor with integrity, an actor's actor: low-key, professional, devoted to his craft.

In fact, nothing could have been further from the truth. While it was true that Vio preferred to work with good scripts than poor ones – who didn't? – his apparently eclectic choice of movie roles was actually part of a diligently planned strategy, the purpose of which was to make Viorel Hudson as rich and as famous as possible as fast as possible. By carving out a niche and a name for himself on the indie circuit (he'd already starred in two Sundance winners and this year's runner-up at Venice), while simultaneously using his publicist to push his image as a mainstream sex symbol, Viorel's intention was always to make a sideways leap into big-league commercial movies, leapfrogging past his rivals faster than he could have hoped to had he taken a string of small parts in forgettable box-office hits. Even in his wildest fantasies, however, Vio had not imagined that he would sign a contract of this size for at least another three or four years. And to get it for a Rasmirez movie! – to be able to combine the pay-cheque he craved with the genuinely good-quality work he enjoyed – that was really the icing on the cake. He'd have accepted the part for a million, maybe even less. Rasmirez must have been dead set on casting him to have offered so much over the odds. Either that or he was secretly gay and hoping to get into Viorel's boxer shorts; which, given that Dorian had a reputation as the most happily married man since Barack Obama, was probably unlikely.

Rose Da Luca's perfect body shuddered as she finally climaxed, her taut muscles clenching and spasming gloriously around Viorel's dick. 'Oh Christ,' he moaned, exploding inside her in what was undoubtedly the best, most satisfying orgasm he'd had all year. *If only my bastard classmates from school could see me now*, he thought joyously, savouring the moment, knowing in that instant that there wasn't one of his childhood tormentors who would not have sold their souls to trade places with him.

Yes, today had made it official.

Viorel Hudson was a winner.

Shortly after midnight, Viorel was back behind the wheel of his Bugatti Veyron, driving west on Sunset Boulevard, when his mother called.

'Darling. You rang.'

Martha Hudson's clipped tones instantly made him feel tense. Incredible how in three short words, England's most celebrated adoptive mother, MP for Tiverton and a saint in the eyes of much of the British public, could convey so much disappointment. *Why the hell did I call her?* thought Viorel angrily. He was angry because he already knew the answer. He'd called because deep down he still wanted Martha's approval. And he wasn't going to get it.

He tried to keep his tone casual. 'Yes. I thought you and Johnny might like to know. I scored a huge part today. I'm playing Heathcliff in the new Rasmirez movie.'

Johnny Hudson, Martha's much older husband, was Viorel's legal father, but Viorel had never called him 'Dad', nor had Johnny ever asked him to. The two weren't close.

'Heathcliff?' Martha Hudson MP sounded disapproving. 'You mean somebody's remaking *Wuthering Heights*?'

It was eight in the morning in England now. Viorel pictured the hallway of Martha's Devon rectory – he'd never thought of it as home, just the house he came back to after boarding school: the faded Regency wallpaper, the neatly stacked pile of constituency post on the hall table next to the phone, and thought how far away it all was. Not just geographically, but emotionally. It was another world.

'Yes, Mother,' he said wearily. 'Dorian Rasmirez is remaking it. He's one of the—'

'But why?' Martha interrupted. 'The original was a masterpiece. Let's face it, my love, with the best will in the world, you're hardly going to do a better job than Olivier. Are you?'

And there you had it. Just like that, Viorel's mother had taken his triumph and squeezed all the joy out of it. Just like she always did.

The British public revered Martha Hudson for her heavily publicized fight to rescue Viorel as a baby from a horrific Romanian orphanage. Viorel's earliest memories were of strangers coming up to him and telling him how lucky he was, and what a wonderful mother he had. In reality, however, his childhood had been horribly lonely. Though he didn't want for material comforts, he knew that Martha never really loved him. It wasn't personal. Martha Hudson had never really loved anyone except Martha Hudson. But it left Viorel feeling doubly rejected, not to mention permanently displaced.

His career had driven a further wedge between him and his mother. Martha Hudson had never wanted her son to become an actor. She wanted Viorel to be a doctor. In her fantasy, he would have gone back to Romania, the country of his birth, to help the poor, orphaned children still left there – ideally his return would be documented by photographers from the *Daily Mail*, which would inevitably remind readers of Martha's own selflessness (for adopting him in the first place), and devotion to children's causes everywhere.

But it hadn't worked out that way. Viorel had selfishly decided to pursue fame and fortune instead. Martha could have forgiven him for trying. What galled her was that he had succeeded, to the point where he was now infinitely more famous than she would ever be.

'I'll be better paid than Olivier,' said Viorel. 'They've offered me five million dollars.'

Even Martha Hudson paused at this number. It was a pause-worthy number.

You're impressed, you mean-spirited cow, thought Viorel. *Just admit it.*

But of course, Martha didn't. 'Oh well,' she sniffed,

ungraciously. 'That's all well and good, I suppose. But money isn't everything you know, darling. Now look, I must run. I've got a select committee meeting this afternoon and I'm going to be late for my train.'

It was Terence Dee who had rescued Viorel from England and his mother's stifling ambitions. Martha Hudson had only ever seen her son as a PR tool, an adorable, photogenic prop with which to bolster her image as the caring face of the Tory party. But Terence saw something else in Viorel: talent.

After Eton, Viorel dutifully followed his mother's bidding and went up to Cambridge to read medicine at Peterhouse. But that was where Martha Hudson's fairytale abruptly ended. After joining Footlights, Cambridge's famous dramatic society Viorel was talent-spotted at the end of his first year by a London agent, and immediately cast in a British rom-com, *Bottom's Up*. The movie went straight to video, but Viorel Hudson's smouldering performance as a Casanova con man was good enough to get him noticed by Terence Dee, then the most powerful casting agent in Hollywood. In his mid-fifties, with a shaggy mop of dyed blond hair and a penchant for wearing pastel sweaters draped casually around his shoulders, Terence Dee was as flamboyantly gay as any Vegas drag queen, and it would be fair to say that his early interest in the edible young Englishman was not strictly professional. But clearly, Terence had no hard feelings over Viorel's *lack* of hard feelings, for his own sex in general, and Terence in particular. He swiftly found the boy both a manager and an apartment in LA, on condition that Viorel drop out of university and pursue his acting career full time.

Viorel did not need to be asked twice. After a brief, frosty farewell with his mother over lunch in London (and a longer, warmer one with his girlfriend Lucinda, his co-star on *Bottoms*

Up, and the woman who had finally relieved him of his virginity; despite his astonishing good looks, Viorel was a late bloomer), he boarded a flight to LAX and never looked back.

That was five years, six movies and countless hundreds of women ago, and in all that time Viorel had not returned to England once. Largely because of Martha, but also because he wanted to leave his shy, lonely childhood self behind. US audiences might idolize him for his Britishness: that clipped, Hugh Grant accent that for some unfathomable reason seemed to make American girls swoon, but Vio Hudson considered himself an Angelino through and through. From day one he had adored Los Angeles: the sunshine, the optimism, the gorgeous, liberated, oh-so-available women. Best of all, no one in LA had ever heard of Martha Hudson MP. And, though the US press had inevitably got hold of the story of Viorel's childhood adoption, with the help of a first-class PR team, Vio had at last managed to shake off the image of victimhood that had haunted him all his life. Yes, he was adopted. Yes, his mother was a politician. So what? All that mattered now was that he was a star, a player, a *winner*. Hollywood had offered Viorel Hudson the second reinvention of his short life, and this time, it was on his own terms.

He'd made it. And he had no one to thank for his success but himself.

After hanging up on his mother, Viorel was home in ten minutes. He had left Rose Da Luca in bed at the Chateau (but not before paying the bill in full and ordering breakfast and roses for her the next morning – no need to be a dick about these things). As much as he loved bedding beautiful women – and Rose really had been beautiful, in a class of her own – Viorel was pathological in his need to wake up alone and, whenever possible, in his own bed. By using hotels for sex, he was able to satisfactorily compartmentalize his life and protect his privacy. His apartment, right on the sand at the end of Navy, a quiet, no-man's-land between Santa Monica and Venice proper, was his sanctuary. Vio unashamedly adored the attention, glitz and glamour of Hollywood, but even he needed to know he could shut the door on the madness at the end of the day. Viorel Hudson the man was outgoing, sociable and charming. But the lonely, angry little boy he had once been still needed a fortress to retreat to.

Hidden from the street by a forbidding grey stone wall, into which was set a pair of prison-like, reinforced-steel security gates, Vio's apartment *was* that fortress. Once inside, however, the feeling of space, light and openness was incredible. In the living room, floor-to-ceiling windows provided a jaw-dropping view of the ocean, shimmering grey-blue beyond the empty, white-sand beach. Give or take the occasional cyclist, no one came by this quiet stretch of coastline. Sipping his coffee on the balcony in the mornings, Vio often forgot he was in a city at all, with nothing but the distant caw of seagulls and soft crashing of waves to break the silence. The apartment wasn't huge by movie-star standards: about two thousand square feet of lateral space. But Viorel had made it feel infinitely bigger with his simple, modern decor, the clean, geometric lines of his furniture and the calming palette of whites and greys that somehow managed to feel warm in winter and cool in summer. Had he not been an actor, he often thought he might have made a good designer, or perhaps even an architect. Every time he walked through his front door he felt a warm sense of pride, like a parent coming home to a beloved child. It was the first and only place he had ever felt completely at home, and he loved it.

Throwing his keys on the kitchen countertop, he kicked off his shoes and wandered back into the master bedroom. Dropping the rest of his clothes in a heap on the floor – Cecilia, his housekeeper, would clean up in the morning – he skipped the bathroom and crawled straight into the delicious comfort of his Frette sheets. His limbs throbbed with exhaustion, Rose had really put him through his paces, but he was too preoccupied to sleep.

Five and a half million *dollars.*

For five months' work.

God bless Dorian Rasmirez!

Viorel had yet to meet the great director in person. Today's deal had been entirely brokered through his agent. He wondered how soon he would be asked to come to a read-through, and when the locations would be finalized. Already, a bizarre aura of secrecy was growing up around the movie, with Rasmirez drip-feeding Vio's agent information on a need-to-know-only basis. Then again, every director had their little quirks. And some things, presumably, could be taken as read. Because it was *Wuthering Heights*, an English classic, most of the film would have to be shot in England. In all other respects, getting the role of Heathcliff was a dream come true, but this was a homecoming that Viorel was not looking forward to. Worse still, according to his agent there were rumours swirling around that a lot of the interior scenes were to be shot at Rasmirez's ancestral family castle in, of all places, Romania. It was an ironic twist of fate that both Viorel and his director should have been born in the same, distant, impoverished country. Although clearly, Rasmirez's family must have come from the opposite end of the social scale to Viorel's. *My ancestors probably polished his ancestors' silverware*, thought Viorel wryly. If there was one country on earth that he felt less enthusiasm for than England, it was bloody Romania. He hoped the rumours were untrue.

What was true, confirmed a couple of days ago, was that Sabrina Leon had been definitively cast as Cathy Earnshaw, his leading lady. This also bothered Viorel. Sabrina might be the hottest thing on legs (or, in her case, on back) in Hollywood, but she was also a complete liability, the biggest Tinseltown train-wreck since Lindsay Lohan. Viorel couldn't imagine what had possessed a seasoned pro like Rasmirez to hire her, especially with the flames from her most recent scandal still raging through the industry like a forest fire.

He must have got her on the cheap. Perhaps that's how he can afford to flash so much cash at me.

He could have done without England, Romania *and* Sabrina Leon. But for five and a half million bucks, they were three crosses that Viorel Hudson was willing to bear.

Fuck you, Martha.

Switching off the light, he finally drifted into sleep, dreaming of England, Heathcliff and Rose Da Luca's deliciously soft thighs.

CHAPTER THREE

'I hate you! I fucking HATE YOU, you selfish bastard, I hate this house, I hate this country and I want a goddamn fucking DIVOOOOORCE!'

Dorian Rasmirez ducked as another priceless piece of Byzantine porcelain flew past within millimetres of his left ear before smashing spectacularly against the bedroom wall.

'Jesus Christ, Christina!' he yelled. 'Calm down.'

'Calm down?' Stark naked, her small, hard apple breasts jutting towards her husband like weapons, and her cute, pixie-like features contorted into a puce mask of rage, Chrissie Rasmirez had no intention of calming down. 'Fuck you, Dorian, you self-centred cunt! You think you have the right to tell me what to do?' Scanning the room for her next missile, her eyes lit on the ornately framed oil painting above the bed.

'No, Chrissie, don't!' pleaded Dorian. 'Not the Velásquez!'

Like a panther, Chrissie turned and pounced, leaping towards the painting with her perfectly Pilates-toned arm outstretched. Acting on instinct – there was no time to think – Dorian jumped after her, rugby-tackling her down onto the bed. Dorian Rasmirez was a big man, six foot plus in his socks, and with the sturdy, solid build of a labourer. At two hundred pounds, he was also almost twice the weight of his petite, gym-bunny wife. Even so, he struggled to contain Chrissie as she writhed, bit and kicked furiously beneath him, spinning herself around to face him so that she could claw his arms and back with her newly manicured talons.

What the hell am I going to do with her? thought Dorian despairingly. Anyone watching them fight – or rather watching Chrissie fight, while Dorian struggled vainly to defend himself – would have assumed it was he who'd been caught cheating, and not *Dorian* who had walked in on *Chrissie* in soon-to-be flagrante with one of the estate carpenters. Dorian was leaving for Los Angeles today and had come home early from his little local office in Bihor to say goodbye to his wife and daughter and finish packing. Walking into the master bedroom, he'd discovered his wife already naked in their bed, and young Alexandru, a nineteen-year-old local joiner, hopelessly overexcited as he tried to free his rock-hard erection from his Abercrombie jeans. At least the boy had had the sense to make a swift exit, leaving his shirt and boots behind in his eagerness to get out of there. He was probably on the other side of the Carpathian Mountains by now. But, as always when she was in the wrong and cornered, Chrissie Rasmirez had come out fighting, hurling abuse at her husband as if he were the one who'd been caught with his pants round his ankles.

Was it any wonder she had to take lovers, when Dorian was never here?

What did he expect when he kept her locked up in this godforsaken castle like Cinder-fucking-rella, while he gallivanted off, living the good life in LA?

She hated it here. She was bored, she was trapped, she was stifled. She was practically a single mother to Saskia, their adorable blonde-headed three-year-old girl. And so it went on. Before he knew it, Dorian found himself on the back foot, apologizing, comforting, explaining. He would get her more help with Saskia. He would make sure he came home more often. The thought of his darling Chrissie being touched by that boy, that *kid*, made him want to rip the guy's throat out. But, at the end of the day, he blamed himself. *I'm the architect of my own destruction*, he thought miserably. *I'm driving away the one thing I love more than anything else in the world.*

Eventually, too exhausted to struggle any more, Chrissie went limp. Overwhelmed with anger and wildly sexually frustrated – she'd been looking forward to bedding Alexandru for weeks – she burst into tears. 'I'm sorry,' she sobbed into Dorian's blood-spattered shirt. 'It's just that . . . you never look at me like you used to. You don't *notice* me any more.'

Dorian was aghast. 'Don't notice you? That's not true! How can you say that? I adore you.'

'It *is* true,' wailed Chrissie. 'You leave me here all alone, day after day, with no life, no career, no escape. As if taking care of Saskia is all I'm good for.'

Dorian did not point out that with three full-time nannies on twenty-four-hour call, it was debatable whether Chrissie did, in fact, take care of Saskia.

'When Alexandru looks at me he sees a woman, not just a mom. He makes me feel alive, Dorian.'

Dorian winced. 'Stop.' He pressed a finger to her lips. 'Don't ever mention that kid's name to me again. Understand? Never.' His eyes flashed with jealousy, the alpha male protecting his territory.

Chrissie responded instantly, her pupils dilating, her lips

and thighs parting with naked, unconcealed lust. If she couldn't have her teenage lover, her husband would have to do. 'Show me you love me,' she murmured.

At forty-four, Dorian Rasmirez might not have his nineteen-year-old rival's Adonis-like body but, unlike Alexandru, he knew how to get his pants off in a hurry. Wriggling out of his jeans while Chrissie yanked his shirt off over his head, he was naked in seconds, thrusting himself inside her with the same passion, the same desperate, all-consuming longing he'd had for her since the first day they met. 'You're my woman,' he moaned, running his hands proprietorially over every inch of her taut, boyish body. 'I love you Chrissie. I fucking adore you.'

'Show me,' sighed Chrissie. She was already close to climax, eyes rolled back in her head, lost in some wild fantasy of her own. She'd been horny as hell for the hot little Romanian carpenter all morning. Being denied him, followed by the panic of discovery and the thrill of the fight with her husband (sparring with Dorian always turned her on) had propelled Chrissie's already overworked libido into the stratosphere. Dorian always pulled out all the stops sexually when he was scared. When he wanted to, he could fuck like an Olympic champion, playing her body like Nigel Kennedy with a Stradivarius. Right now, stroking and teasing her, bringing her to the brink time and again and then pulling back, Chrissie knew she wanted him more than she'd ever wanted Alexandru, or any of her other lovers.

When he finally came, having brought her to orgasm twice, Dorian pulled her into his strong, bear-like arms and held her so tightly she could barely breathe.

'I'll do anything to keep you, Chrissie,' he whispered. 'Anything. You know that.'

'Good,' Chrissie purred, stroking his back. 'Well, you can start by leaving me your Centurion card. I've decided to take a little trip to Paris while you're away. Distract myself with a bit of culture. Lilly can take care of Saskia for a few days.'

Dorian's heart sank. He fought back the urge to remind Chrissie that they lived surrounded by culture, and that she never showed the slightest interest in any of it. In this bedroom alone, apart from the Velásquez portrait above the bed and the exquisite Byzantine vase she'd just destroyed in a fit of temper, there were bookshelves stuffed with first-edition classics in English, Italian and French, a Dutch, hand-painted dresser that had once belonged to Marie Antoinette of France, and two framed folios of Handel's *Messiah*, signed by the composer himself. The entire castle, this 'prison' that Dorian had 'dragged' Chrissie to, prising her away from her beloved LA, was a veritable Aladdin's cave of treasures, with a collection of art and manuscripts to rival some of the greatest galleries and libraries in Europe. And it was all theirs. Not theirs to sell – the treasures could not legally leave Romania – but theirs to cherish, to appreciate, to pass down to the next generation. To Saskia, and perhaps one day – if Dorian could ever persuade Chrissie to try again – to a son, a little boy to carry on the family name.

The reality was that the only thing Chrissie Rasmirez was interested in in Paris were the overpriced clothes stores on the Avenue de Champs-Élysées. Last time she went to the flagship Louis Vuitton there she'd dropped over $100,000 in a single morning. If she tried that again this time, AmEx would demand Dorian's cards back. But he was too scared to deny her, particularly after today's close call.

'Sure honey,' he sighed, defeated. 'I'll leave the card. You go and enjoy yourself.'

Chrissie smiled triumphantly. 'Don't worry, darling. I intend to.'

Three hours later, as the Airbus A360 juddered and rattled its way up through the clouds, Dorian closed his eyes and tried to remember the relaxation techniques his therapist had taught him. *Imagine yourself on a deserted, sandy beach. Waves are softly lapping at the shore. Listen to the rhythm of the tide. Let it soothe you. Feel the warm water caress your toes . . .*

He opened his eyes. It wasn't working. Reaching into his hand-luggage bag, he pulled out a Xanax and slipped it into his mouth, knocking it back with the dregs of his pre-takeoff champagne. The pill would take a while to kick in, but the alcohol was instantly soothing, as was the knowledge that he was leaving Chrissie and their problems behind him for five whole days. Not that this trip to LA was going to be some sort of vacation. On the contrary, the *real* battles would only start once he landed. But for the next ten hours at least, he had a chance to relax. If only he could remember how to do it.

A heavy-set man in his mid-forties, with dark hair greying at the temples and a warm, open face – not handsome exactly, but appealing in a rough-round-the-edges sort of way – Dorian Rasmirez was one of the most acclaimed film directors in the world. With his intelligent hazel eyes that narrowed into tiny slits when he laughed or got angry, his strong jaw and his off-kilter nose (he broke it in a football game in high school and had never got around to fixing it), Dorian was certainly no matinee idol. Yet there was something innately masculine about him that women found compelling – and had done long before he became successful.

Dorian had been born and raised in White Plains, New York, the only, much-beloved son of Romanian immigrant parents. Both his father, Radu Rasmirez, and his mother Anamarie had suffered unspeakable horrors under Ceauşescu's hardline communist dictatorship and had arrived in America with little more than the cash in their pockets. As members of two of Romania's most prominent aristocratic families, the Rasmirezes and the Florescus, Radu and Anamarie had seen close family members arrested and shot. They had experienced first hand what it meant to lose everything: not just your wealth and privilege, but your home, your freedom, your right to live free from intimidation, imprisonment and torture. They came to America to escape the horrors of their pasts and to build a new life, and that's exactly what they did.

Radu trained as a pharmacist, eventually opening a successful chain of small stores across Westchester County. His wife gave birth to their longed-for son, and devoted herself to the traditional role of homemaking, diving in to suburban American life with unexpected enthusiasm. It was largely thanks to Anamarie's assimilation into New York culture and her love of all things American that Dorian grew up the way he did: preppy, hardworking, and blessed with a natural, quiet confidence that was the perfect complement to his impressive academic abilities. To any casual observer, Dorian Rasmirez came across as the epitome of American boyhood, from the tips of his loafers to the button-down collars of his Brooks Brothers shirts. He excelled at school, winning a place at Boston University where he majored in Dramatic Arts. By the time he graduated, he already knew he wanted to direct, and with his usual focus and determination, won a place at UCLA's prestigious School of Theater, Film and Television. But beneath the glowing, all-American CV, Dorian was his father's son as much as his mother's. Radu Rasmirez had made a point of educating his son in their family history, painting a wildly romantic picture of their Transylvanian roots, and the fairytale castle that should by rights have been Dorian's, if only the wicked communists hadn't stolen it.

'One day,' Radu promised him, 'the righteous will triumph in our homeland, and what is ours will be restored to us. When that day comes, Dorian, you will know what it is to live like a king. The honour and responsibility, the joy and the pain. We Rasmirezes will always owe a debt of gratitude to this country. But Romania remains forever in our hearts.'

Of course, to Dorian, 'Romania' was just a word, a mythical kingdom that his father had conjured up for him, from a past that the boy had never known and couldn't understand. But he *did* understand how much their family heritage meant to Radu. In later years that sense of displacement, of homesickness and longing that he saw in his father, would heavily influence Dorian's film-making.

There were other influences too. Most notably Chrissie Sanderson, the enigmatic, elfin actress whom Dorian met and fell in love with in his last year at UCLA, and whose mesmeric beauty (in Dorian's eyes at least) had entranced him ever since. By Hollywood standards, the Rasmirez marriage was considered an epic achievement. Dorian and Chrissie had been together since before Dorian became famous – five whole years before the release of *Love and Regrets*, the searing emotional drama that was to catapult Dorian to global prominence as a director. In those early days, it had been Chrissie who was the star in the partnership, with a leading role as Ali, a kooky chef, in the popular network television sit-com *Rumors*. A natural actress with a wonderful sense of comic timing, by the age of twenty-three Chrissie Sanderson was recognized across America, with a loyal, at times even fanatical, teenage fan base. Before long she was earning serious money, fifty-grand-plus an episode: a fortune in those days. It was enough to buy her and Dorian a comfortable house in Beverly Hills as well as to fund some of his early movie projects. Chrissie revelled in the limelight but, spurred on by Dorian, she also yearned for more serious critical success. In the same year that the release of *Love and Regrets* changed Dorian's life forever, Chrissie made her own debut on Broadway, as Sally Bowles in Jerry Zaks's much-hyped revival of *Chicago*. It was a huge mistake. Nervous and under-rehearsed, she flubbed her opening night performance badly. If she'd expected her status as the nation's TV sweetheart to protect her, she was rudely awakened by the next morning's reviews. The critics did not so much pan her performance as eviscerate it.

'*Laughable,*' said the *New York Times*.

'*You didn't know where to look,*' wrote *The Post*.

'*Embarrassingly wooden.*'

'*About as much sex appeal as a cold bowl of soup.*'

Dorian told her to forget it. 'What do they know? So you made a couple of mistakes, flubbed a few lines. Big deal. They're just jealous because you're a huge TV star. You know how these critics get off on bringing people down.'

But Chrissie could not forget it. Mortified at such public humiliation, she lost her nerve completely, quitting the Broadway show as soon as her contract allowed, then promptly walking off the set of her NBC show as well. For months she holed up at home in LA, refusing to attend any auditions or give a single interview about her shock departure from *Rumors*. Meanwhile, of course, Dorian's career was taking off in spectacular style, a success for which Chrissie could never quite forgive him.

After fifteen years, Dorian still spoke loyally in interviews about his 'stunning, talented wife', and was famously immune to the manifold temptations of Hollywood. His fidelity was considered all the more admirable in industry circles since for years it appeared that his wife refused to have his children. Most people viewed this as the height of selfishness on Chrissie's part. In fact, her unwillingness to become a mother mirrored her refusal to go to auditions, or to take any of the leading roles that Dorian offered her gift-wrapped in all of his movies. She was afraid. Trapped by her own insecurities in the wildly luxurious life Dorian had built for her, she complained ceaselessly about LA, how shallow it was and how being a famous director's wife made her feel empty and invisible.

Then, four years ago, three things happened. The first was that Dorian found out his wife was having an affair, with the leading man in one of his movies. The liaison was actually the latest in a string of extramarital adventures that Chrissie had used over the years to prop up her fragile self-esteem. But it was the first one that Dorian knew about, and he was utterly devastated by it. The second thing was that, at long last, Chrissie agreed to get pregnant and conceived Saskia, the Band-Aid baby that both she and Dorian hoped would repair their marriage. And the third thing was that the Romanian government contacted Dorian out of the blue, to tell him that they had begun the process of restoring pre-revolutionary property to its rightful owners. Would Dorian like to return 'home' to claim his inheritance, the Rasmirezes' historic Transylvanian Schloss, complete with all its priceless treasures?

At the time, Romania had seemed like a lifeline, the fresh start that he and Chrissie so badly needed. Chrissie had cheated on him because she was unhappy in LA and felt like a failure there. Dorian believed in marriage. His parents had managed it for the better part of fifty years under far more difficult circumstances. He owed it to Chrissie and to himself to try to repair the damage. Here was a chance to take Chrissie and their newborn daughter as far from the Hollywood madness as it was possible to go. Dorian would sweep Chrissie up on his white charger and install her as queen in his fairytale castle. Little Saskia would grow up as a princess. And they would all live happily ever after.

Or not.

If he were completely honest with himself (not always Dorian's strongest suit), becoming a father had not been the seismic, emotionally transformative event that he'd expected. The baby was sweet enough. But, after waiting so long for parenthood, Dorian began to realize that the idea of having a child was considerably more intoxicating than the exhausting, often deathly dull reality. He also realized, not without a sense of shame, that a part of him was disappointed that Saskia had not been born a boy.

For her part, Chrissie also revelled in the idea of mother-hood or, more specifically, the idea of herself as the perfect mother: devoted, selfless, instinctively maternal. It was a self-image Chrissie clung to doggedly as Saskia grew older, despite the overwhelming evidence to the contrary, and one that she demanded her husband validate by praising her mothering skills at every possible opportunity. But the truth was that, like Dorian, Chrissie Rasmirez found young chil-dren boring and her own daughter was no exception. By now a semi-professional martyr in her marriage (Chrissie had long ago convinced herself she had sacrificed her career for Dorian, and not on an altar of her own fear), her new role as tireless carer to a demanding toddler added another arrow of resentment to her ever-growing armoury.

New parenthood wasn't the Rasmirezes' only problem. Despite yearning for a fresh start, Dorian had misgivings about the move back to his homeland. Romania had been his father's dream, never his. And while he felt a sense of duty (and curiosity) about his ancestral home, unlike Chrissie, Dorian enjoyed his life in LA, and did not relish leaving it. If he was going to continue working, he'd have to get used to a gruelling transatlantic commute. The thought of having to spend time away from Chrissie made his chest tighten painfully with anxiety. But if it saved the marriage, it would all be worth it. He owed it to his father and Chrissie to go back.

Though she would rather die than admit it now, Chrissie had been very enthusiastic about the idea at first. *Transylvania!* Even the word sounded romantic. From what Dorian had told her, the house – castle! – was stuffed with wealth beyond even her wildest imagination: hundreds of millions of dollars' worth of antique crap. Apparently, the Romanian government had some ridiculous rules about all the treasures having to stay in the country, but a good American lawyer would find them a way around all that old-world baloney. If she could no longer enjoy fame in her own right, Chrissie could at least experience the thrill of being European royalty and joining the ranks of the super-rich. Plus, domestic help would be super-cheap over there, so she could have nannies and housekeepers up the wazoo. She would be Queen of the Castle, ordering around a fleet of servants, and go to bed at night draped in emeralds that had once belonged to Catherine the Great. *Not bad for a little girl from the valley.* Who knew, maybe she'd even think about trying for a second baby, and giving Dorian the son he so obviously still wanted.

Needless to say, it had not worked out like that. Almost from day one, Chrissie loathed Romania. The Schloss was as palatial as she could have wished it, the staff as slavishly obsequious, the emeralds as big and heavy as golf balls. But there was nothing to *do*. No one to *see*. Sure, the scenery was breathtaking, as lush and green and spectacular as a still from *Shrek*. Little Saskia was entranced by the Transylvanian landscape, with its wide, fast-flowing rivers, brooding pine forests and romantic, snow-topped mountains that ringed the castle like mythical, protective giants. 'Polar Express!' she would squeal excitedly every time they drove into town, pointing to the snow-tipped Carpathian Mountains with barely contained rapture. But her mother failed to share her enthusiasm. What use was it, ruling your own fantasy kingdom, if you couldn't go out to Cecconi's on a Friday night and boast about it to your friends?

Within weeks of their arrival, Chrissie's boredom was fermenting into resentment. It was all Dorian's fault, for dragging her here. He was punishing her for her affair by immuring her and Saskia in this gilded prison, while *he* jetted off to enjoy their old life back in LA, which from eight thousand miles away no longer seemed so terrible. She, Chrissie, had sacrificed her career for her husband, and what did she get in return? Neglect. Abandonment. Using the only weapon left available to her, she did a 180-degree about-face on a second baby, point-blank refusing to even contemplate another pregnancy until Dorian 'sold this dump' and moved them back home to spend the proceeds. No amount of explanation by Dorian would convince her that this was both a practical and legal impossibility; that the Schloss was theirs to enjoy, but not theirs to sell.

Moreover, unbeknownst to Chrissie, their finances back in the States were in fact in increasingly dire straits. Dorian's last film, the exquisitely shot but hugely over-budget war movie, *Sixteen Nights*, had been a major critical success. But it was box-office receipts that paid the mortgage on Dorian and Chrissie's Holmby Hills mansion and the upkeep on the Schloss, not to mention financed Chrissie's couture habit, and those had been distinctly lacklustre. Two studios had offered to come on board with funding but, unable to bear the thought of ceding creative control, Dorian had turned them down, ploughing millions of dollars of his own money into the movie instead. He'd ended up massively in the red.

To make matters worse, since the news of Dorian's inheritance, Chrissie's spending had multiplied exponentially. Nothing could convince her that they were not now billionaires – they had Renoirs in their drawing room, for fuck's sake! – and she laughed openly at Dorian's claims that the castle's upkeep was in fact bleeding them dry.

'Don't you see?' he told her, exasperated. 'That's why the Romanian government were so keen to have us back here! They couldn't afford to keep the place going themselves, and they figured we were rich enough to do it for them.'

Chrissie shrugged nonchalantly. 'Well, we are.'

No we're not! Dorian wanted to scream. But he was too frightened of Chrissie leaving him to force another confrontation, or to admit the full extent of their debts. He'd already seen her flirting with some of the younger, more attractive boys on their staff, and lived in constant dread of another affair. And Chrissie was right. He was the one who'd brought her here, brought them all here as a family. It was up to him to make it work, to dig them out of this financial hole he'd gotten them into, and to make her happy. Either that or give up the castle, which to Dorian would be tantamount to trampling on his dad's grave.

'More champagne, sir? Or something to eat, perhaps?'

The stewardess's voice brought Dorian back to the present. They were at cruising altitude now, and his fellow passengers were reclining their flatbed seats or turning on their entertainment systems, scrolling down the list of movies. Dorian had already read the in-flight guide before takeoff. Three Harry Greene movies. None of his.

Dorian tried not to mind that Harry Greene's truly terrible, derivative *Fraternity* franchise continued to go from strength to strength. But it was hard to be magnanimous when Greene seemed to have made it his life's mission to destroy Dorian's reputation, slagging him off not only in public, in the press, but also in private amongst Hollywood's power brokers. Harry Greene was an immensely powerful man in Hollywood. He was also a recluse, prone to wild fits of paranoia, especially where women were concerned. Twice he had taken girls to court: having bedded them, in the morning he'd accused them of petty theft simply because he couldn't remember where he'd left a certain coat, or a pair of cufflinks. Once he'd even tried to have his housekeeper arrested for attempted poisoning. A lamb stew had given him a stomach upset, apparently, and Harry was convinced the wholly innocent Mexican grandmother had laced the dish with arsenic.

His beef with Dorian had begun over a script. Harry had fallen out with a certain screenwriter, and the row had turned ugly. When the screenwriter came up with his next movie idea a few months later, he brought it to Dorian instead of Harry. The irony was, Dorian never came close to making the film. It was a bromance, commercial but far too vanilla for Dorian's taste. Nonetheless, Harry Greene became convinced that Dorian and this screenwriter were 'in league' against him. Over time, thanks to some shift in Harry's addled brain, the screenwriter faded from the picture, leaving Dorian as the sole target for his bizarre conspiracy theory.

It wasn't long before his professional resentment began to turn personal. For all its international influence, Hollywood remained a small town at heart, and the paths of two major producer-directors like Dorian Rasmirez and Harry Greene were bound to cross socially. After the script incident, Dorian did his best to avoid Harry. But a few years ago, for reasons that to this day Dorian had never fully understood, Harry got the idea into his head that Dorian had badmouthed him to his then wife, Angelica. And that it was Dorian's malicious intervention that had wrecked his (Harry's) marriage.

In reality, Dorian barely knew Angelica Greene, then or now, and had said nothing to her about her husband's womanizing, which was in any case an open secret in Hollywood. The only person responsible for the demise of Harry Greene's marriage was Harry Greene. But, be that as it may, in the wake of his divorce, Harry gave numerous interviews blaming Dorian, and did his best to have him ostracized by Hollywood's elite. As the *Fraternity* franchise went from strength to strength and Harry Greene's influence grew, the more difficult Dorian's life became.

He returned his attention to the stewardess, who was still hovering with her drinks tray.

'No, thank you,' he said politely. 'I'm fine.'

'OK. Well, if you change your mind, you know where to find me. I did just want to say, I really enjoyed *Sixteen Nights*. I love your work.' The stewardess blushed.

'Thank you,' said Dorian. 'You're very kind.'

She was a pretty girl, he noticed, not hard and over-made-up like so many of her profession. You could still see her creamy, natural complexion, and the tops of her full breasts jiggled invitingly beneath the white blouse of her uniform. *Sexy. But not a patch on my Christina.* 'I hope you'll go and see my new movie when it comes out.'

'Oh, I will,' she gushed. 'I certainly will. What is it?'

'Actually it's a remake,' said Dorian. '*Wuthering Heights*.'

The stewardess gasped. 'Oh my God, I *love* that book. Such a romantic story.'

Dorian smiled. 'You know it?'

'Of course,' she laughed. 'Doesn't everyone? Heathcliff and Cathy. They're like Romeo and Juliet in the rain.'

For the first time all day, Dorian felt a fraction of the tension ease out of his body. One of his concerns about his new project had been that the story might be considered too highbrow, too much of a classic for ordinary moviegoers to be interested in. Dorian had first read the book in high school and had been instantly captivated by the plot. Heathcliff, a mysterious orphan boy, is adopted by the kindly Mr Earnshaw and brought to live at Wuthering Heights, a grand but lonely house in the Yorkshire moors. Tragedy ensues when Heathcliff falls in love with Earnshaw's daughter Catherine, who also loves him, but decides to make a more socially acceptable marriage to a neighbour. The ramifications of Cathy's rejection of Heathcliff: her regret, his madness, and an ongoing saga of death and revenge, of innocent children being forced to pay for the sins of their parents, made for uniquely compelling drama, not to mention one of the most enduring love stories in English literature. But, cinematically, *Wuthering Heights* was a challenge. Whoever played Heathcliff would have to age convincingly, while remaining attractive enough to work as a romantic lead. Should original Cathy and young Cathy, her daughter, be played by two actresses, or one? How to deal with Nelly, the book's nurse narrator? And then of course there was the issue of location. In a plot where the house was as much of a character as any of the protagonists, finding the right location would be key.

A couple of the big studios had tried to warn Dorian off, as had his agent and friend, Don Richards.

'You can't follow Olivier and Merle Oberon, man. That 1939 movie is one of the all-time greats.'

'They only shot half the book,' said Dorian. 'It's half a story.'

'That's because the whole story's unfilmable. It's a fucking miniseries.' Don frowned. 'Did you see the seventies version? It blew.'

'I know,' Dorian smiled. 'That's why I'm doing a remake.'

'If you do it, you're gonna need two big names in the lead roles,' Don warned him. 'And I mean real bankable stars, none of your "respected character actor" bullshit. Oh, and Cathy's gotta get naked. A *lot*.'

'I see,' said Dorian wryly. 'Young Cathy or Old Cathy?'

'All the Cathys have to be young,' said Don firmly. 'And hot.'

'Right. So all I need is to find a major movie star who's prepared to work for peanuts *and* get her panties off for some gratuitous nudity.'

'It wouldn't be gratuitous.' Don looked offended. 'There'd be a very important point to it.'

'Uh-huh. And what might that be?'

'Ticket sales,' said Don.

Dorian had the good grace to laugh. 'OK. Well if anyone springs to mind, you be sure to let me know.'

'Actually, someone does. How about Sabrina Leon?'

At first, Dorian had assumed his agent was joking. When he realized he wasn't, he dismissed the idea out of hand. Sabrina was toxic right now, a Hollywood untouchable. Plus she was known to be a majorly disruptive influence on set: demanding, diva-ish, unpredictable. Just associating Sabrina's name with a project could be enough to kill it before they shot a single take.

'All true,' agreed Don. 'But she's still a huge star.'

Dorian held firm. 'No way.'

'Plus, everyone's watching to see what her next move will be.'

'I'm not.'

'*Plus*, she loves getting naked, on and off set. The kid's allergic to clothes.'

'I know Don, but c'mon. I need a serious actress.'

'She'll work for free.'

And that was it. Jerry McGuire had Dorothy Boyd at 'hello'. Don Richards had Dorian Rasmirez at 'free'.

Stretching his long legs out in front of him, Dorian at last began to relax. If American Airline stewardesses were fans of the story, it clearly couldn't be *that* highbrow. *It's gonna be all right*, he told himself. Sabrina Leon had signed on the dotted line. Of course, casting her as Cathy – both Cathys – remained a dangerous, double-edged sword. Dorian would have to keep a tight grip on her behaviour. But Don Richards had convinced him she was a risk worth taking. He'd just have to do the sell of his life to convince distributors that, by the time the movie was due for release, the furore over Sabrina's Tarik Tyler comments would have died down.

'Even if it hasn't, people'll still come and see the movie,' said Don.

'You reckon?'

'Sure. They like watching her. It's like slowing down on the freeway to gawk at a car crash.'

Dorian hoped he was right. Because, if he wasn't, it would be Dorian's career, life and marriage that would be the car crash. Almost certainly a fatal one.

For Dorian Rasmirez, everything depended on the success of this movie.

Everything.

CHAPTER FOUR

As Dr Michel Henri lifted the child out of its crib, Letitia Crewe watched his beautifully defined biceps rippling beneath his grey T-shirt and thought: *I have to get a grip. I'm here to play with the children, not ogle Michel like a love-struck puppy.* But it was hard. What business did a paediatrician have being that attractive? There ought to be a law against it.

Tish Crewe had come out to Romania in her year off to spend six months working with orphans in the northern city of Oradea. Five years later and she was still here, visiting hospital wards like this one, rehousing as many abandoned children as she could. It was gruelling work, and distressing at times, but it was also addictive and rewarding. Dr Michel Henri felt the same way. It was one of the things that had first brought him and Tish together, their shared compassion and sense of purpose. That and the fact they both wanted to rip each other's clothes off the moment they laid eyes on one another. Tish still felt the same way. It was Michel who'd moved on.

Watching him move purposefully from bed to bed, engaging each child with eye contact and talking to them in that deep, gentle voice of his before each examination, Tish calculated that she had been in love with him for a full year now.

Wow. A year of my life.

It felt like twenty.

Michel was so wise. So good. So capable. Tish Crewe was capable herself, very much head-girl material, and she admired this trait in others. Of course, it didn't hurt that Michel also looked like a younger version of George Clooney, complete with sexy, two-day stubble growth and smouldering coffee-brown eyes. Nor that he was so good in bed, Tish had had to restrict the lovemaking during their brief, six-week affair to Michel's apartment, afraid that she might make so much noise at home that she would wake up Abel, her adopted five-year-old son, and scare the living daylights out of him.

It wasn't Michel's fault. He'd been honest with her from the beginning. 'I don't do commitment,' he told Tish bluntly, the night they first kissed on the bridge over the Crişul Repede in Oradea's old town. 'My work is my passion. If you're looking for something serious, I'm not your man.'

Tish had assured him she was not looking for something serious. After four years of almost total celibacy, living in a city that still looked and felt as dour and grey and lifeless as it had under communism, the idea of some fun, especially the kind of fun that Dr Michel Henri was offering, sounded utterly perfect. Since founding her own children's home three years earlier, and particularly since adopting her darling Abel, Tish barely had enough time in the days to eat and shower, never mind indulge in a sex life. *I deserve some fun*, she told herself. *Why not?*

But of course she'd had to go and spoil it all by falling in love with him. *Fool*, she told herself, *but then how could one not?* When Michel took up with a pretty orthopaedic surgeon from Médecins Sans Frontières a few weeks later, Tish's heart was crushed like a bug. It had taken every ounce of her self-control to hide the worst of her anguish from Michel himself. But to everyone else who worked with her, it was painfully obvious.

'He's not worth it, you know.' Pete Klein, the head of one of the American NGOs, had been watching Tish gaze longingly after Michel's retreating back in the hospital car park a few weeks ago.

He is to me, thought Tish, but she forced a professional smile.

'Hello, Pete. How are you?'

'Better for seeing you, my dear.'

A kindly, born-again Christian in his early sixties, Pete Klein had decided to make it his personal mission to find the lovely Miss Crewe a suitable husband. She was, after all, a gorgeous girl. Not gorgeous in an obvious, long-legged, modelly sort of way. No, Tish's beauty was of an altogether more wholesome variety. Slight and naturally blonde, with a long nose, strong, aristocratic bone structure and a glorious wide, pale pink mouth that Pete had seen express every emotion from compassion to courage to delight, Tish had a natural, make-up-free charm to her that a certain type of man would give his eyeteeth to come home to every night. As Tish's schoolfriend Katie had once accurately, if tactlessly, put it: 'You're Jennifer Aniston, Tishy. Guys like Michel always go for the Angelinas in the end. You're too nice.'

Pete Klein didn't believe a person could be 'too nice'. Nor could he see what on earth wonderful young women like Tish Crewe found attractive in good-for-nothing fly-by-nights like that slimy Frenchman Dr Henri. Forget Doctors

Without Borders. Michel Henri was a Doctor Without Scruples, and he'd hurt poor Miss Crewe badly.

'You should have dinner with my friend Gustav,' Pete told Tish.

'Oh, I don't know, Pete . . .'

'Yes, yes, you must,' Pete insisted. 'Lovely young man, from a very nice family in Munich. Just started working for us. Brilliant with computers,' he added, with a wink that made Tish wonder if this was intended as some sort of double entendre. Except that Pete Klein didn't *do* double entendres. He did earnest and avuncular and kind.

So, 'too nice' to say no, Tish dutifully had dinner with 'lovely young Gustav', who was indeed brilliant with computers; though not *quite* so brilliant at either conversation or romance, judging by his clumsily attempted lunge in the back of the taxi after dinner, reeking of garlic sausage and cheap aftershave.

'What are you doing?' said Tish, squirming away from him.

Gustav looked aggrieved. 'I thought you were single?' he accused her.

'I am,' stammered Tish.

'Well, what's the problem then?' demanded Gustav. 'Everyone knows the only reason singles come out on these voluntary do-gooder vacations is for the sex. I mean, come on! We're not in Romania for the scenery, are we?'

That much, at least, was true. Tish was not in Romania for the scenery. But why *was* she still here, really? Tish was the most English person she knew and she missed home dreadfully. Not a day went by when she didn't stare unseeingly out of her car window at the bleak Romanian landscape, daydreaming about hedgerows and Marmite and *EastEnders*. It didn't get any easier. She told herself she was here for the children – both the sixteen she'd been able to permanently rescue from institutions and bring to the bright, cheerful, family-run home she'd built just outside Oradea; and for the hundreds of others she was forced to leave behind, but whom she and her staff visited regularly in their hospitals. But, gazing at Michel's strong, warm hands now as he changed a little boy's dressing, remembering the feel of them on her skin, part of her knew that she was also staying for him.

Tish was doing what all the books said you should never do. She was waiting. Hoping, praying that eventually Michel would see the light and realize that the two of them were meant to be together. He'd make a wonderful father for Abel. So noble. So dedicated . . .

'Tish!' Carl, one of her co-workers, was tapping Tish forcefully on the shoulder. 'Did you hear me?'

'Hmmm?' She blushed. 'Sorry. I was, erm . . . distracted.'

'There's a problem back at Curcubeu, Carl repeated patiently. Curcubeu was the name of Tish's children's home. It meant 'rainbow' in Romanian. 'Child services just showed up on the doorstep. They're saying Sile hasn't got all his releases signed.'

'But that's ridiculous. Of course the releases are signed. I picked up his paperwork myself.'

'Whatever, they reckon he needs something else. They tried to seize him on the spot.'

'What?' Tish placed the sleeping baby back in her crib. Sile was an adorable, curly-haired two-year-old boy, the latest addition to her happy brood at Curcubeu. He'd only been with them a week and already child services were kicking up a fuss, no doubt hoping for yet another back-hander. 'How dare they!' she seethed. 'They have no authority.'

'Yes, well, don't worry,' said Carl. 'Lucio didn't let them in the door. But they'll be back in the morning with a warrant. We need to get it sorted, today.'

Damn, thought Tish. She'd really wanted to talk to Michel today, to get his advice. Yesterday, she'd received a letter, rather a distressing letter, from home. The letter meant that she might need to leave Romania, at least for a while, an idea that filled her with such a conflicting mix of emotions that she'd barely been able to string a sentence together since she read it.

Michel will know what to do, she thought. *He's always so level-headed.* But now there'd be no time to consult him. By the time she'd sorted out this bullshit with Sile and child services, she'd have to race home in time to put Abel to bed, and Michel would already have left for Paris. He was flying home for the weekend to attend his sister's wedding. *Maybe once he sees her in a white dress, making that commitment, sees how happy and glowing she is . . .*

'Tish?'

'Yes. Sorry. I'm coming.' Tish reluctantly switched off the fantasy. 'Go down and start the car. I'll explain what's happened to the nurses and meet you downstairs in five.'

The rest of the day passed in a blur of frenetic activity and stress, with Tish and Carl breaking every speed limit in the book in Tish's ancient Fiat Punto, tearing from one government agency to the next in an effort to prove their legal guardianship of little Sile. Two bribes, a phone call to the British Consulate and countless vicious screaming matches later – Romanian Child Services did not consider Letitia Crewe to be 'too nice'; as far as they were concerned, she was a bolshy, strident, harridan who'd been a thorn in their side since the day she set foot in the country – the matter was at last resolved. 'For now,' the Child Protection Officer warned Tish sternly.

As if we're any bloody threat to him, Tish thought furiously as she finally started the drive back to her flat in the city. *As if anyone on God's earth gave a crap about that little boy until we took him in.* Sometimes, most of the time, her work was so frustrating it made her want to scream. The Romanian government were like dinosaurs, terrified of change, resentful of any 'outsider' who wanted to help. As if any of the foreign NGOs *wanted* to be there. *Don't you think we'd love it if you sorted out your own bloody country and took care of your own kids, so we could all go home?*

Home.

The word had been turning over and over in Tish's mind all day. She would have to make a decision soon, tomorrow probably, and start making some concrete plans. She'd wanted Michel's advice today, but deep down she already knew what he would have told her. *Go. Go home and do what you need to do.* There was no other way.

Home for Tish was Loxley Hall, an idyllic Elizabethan pile in the heart of Derbyshire's glorious Hope Valley. Much smaller than neighbouring Chatsworth, but widely considered more beautiful, Loxley had been the ancestral seat of the Crewe family for over eight generations. Growing up there as a little girl, Tish had never noticed the house's grandeur, not least because behind the intricately carved, exterior with its stone mullioned windows and fairytale turrets, the family actually lived in a distinctly down-at-heel 'apartment' of seven, shabby rooms, and not in the immaculately preserved ballrooms and dining halls that the public saw. What Tish *was* aware of, however, was Loxley's magic. The beauty of her grounds, with their ancient clipped yew hedges, endless expanses of lawn and deer-covered parkland beyond, punctuated by vast, four-hundred-year-old oaks. At the front of the house, beneath a crumbling medieval stone bridge, the river Derwent burbled sleepily, little more than a stream in the narrow part of the valley. As a child, Tish would sit on the bridge for hours, legs dangling, playing Poohsticks with herself or watching hopefully for an otter to make a thrilling, sleek-headed appearance. Her older brother Jago had never shared her fascination with the river, nor her romantic belief in Loxley Hall as some sort of magical kingdom. Mostly, Tish remembered him as rather distant and aloof ('sensitive', their mother called him), always playing inside with his computer games or his older, sophisticated friends from Thaxton House, the local boys' prep school. Tish's childhood playmates were her Jack Russell, Harrison, the family housekeeper Mrs Drummond, and on occasions her elderly but much beloved father, Henry.

Henry Crewe had died two years ago and Tish still missed him terribly. It was Henry's death that had set off the chain of events leading to the current crisis. Amid much familial wailing and gnashing of teeth, Henry Crewe had broken Loxley's four-hundred-year entailment and left the house lock, stock and barrel to his estranged wife Vivianna, Tish and Jago's mother. This was partly a romantic gesture. Although Vivi had left him and their children the better part of two decades ago to start a new life in Italy, visiting England only rarely, she had never actually divorced Henry. To the bafflement of all his friends, not to mention his daughter, who felt Vivianna's abandonment deeply, Henry maintained a nostalgic attachment to his wife that only seemed to intensify as the years passed. The Crewes remained on friendly terms, and Henry never gave up hope that one day Vivianna would see the light, tire of her stream of younger lovers, and return to the bosom of her family.

Needless to say, she never did. But changing the will had not solely been about Vivi. It had also been an attempt to mitigate Jago's influence over Loxley's future. The withdrawn, distant brother Tish remembered had grown up into a feckless, selfish and completely irresponsible young man. Blessed with good looks and a big enough trust fund never to have to earn a living, Jago Crewe partied away the years between eighteen and twenty-two in a narcotic-induced haze, eventually winding up depressed and seriously ill in a North London Hospital. It was after he had emerged from this self-styled breakdown that Jago had decided the time had come to change his life. He had shown no interest in 'knuckling down' at Loxley Hall, however. Pronouncing himself teetotal, Buddhist and a committed vegan, he had proceeded to disappear on a spiritual journey that had taken him around the world from Hawaii to Tahiti to Thailand (first class, naturally), spending family money like water as he tried out one spurious, navel-gazing cult after another.

Meanwhile, Henry's health had been failing. Clearly, something had had to be done. And so it was that Henry had willed the house to Vivianna, intending that she would let it out for the remainder of her lifetime, perhaps to the National Trust, and leave it on her death to whichever of the children, or grandchildren, looked like the safest bet at the time.

Things had not worked out that way. Having failed to come home for his father's funeral, or even send flowers, Jago showed up at Loxley two months later, announcing that he'd had a change of heart filial-duty-wise and had returned to claim his inheritance. Vivianna immediately made the house over to him (she never could say no to her darling boy) and retreated to her villa outside Rome, considering her duties to her former husband fully discharged and all well that had ended well.

Meanwhile, stuck out in Romania, Tish was concerned about the situation, but as a single mother with a full-time children's home to run, had problems enough of her own. Besides, as the months passed and nothing disastrous happened at Loxley, she began to relax. Perhaps Jago really had grown out of his immature, selfish stage this time and was going to make a go of things on the estate? He was still only twenty-eight, after all. Plenty of time to turn over a new leaf.

Then she got the letter.

The letter was from Mrs Drummond, the Crewe family's housekeeper of the last thirty-odd years and a surrogate mother to Tish and Jago. According to Mrs D, Jago had walked out of the house three weeks ago, announcing that he would not be returning as he intended to live out the remainder of his days as a contemplative hermit in the hills of Tibet. Mrs D, who'd heard it all countless times before, took this latest change of plans with her usual pinch of salt. But she'd been forced to view matters more seriously when Jago's wastrel hippy friends, many of them drug addicts, had refused to leave Loxley after Jago's departure. Worse, they had begun to cause serious damage.

'I called the police,' Mrs Drummond wrote to Tish, 'but they say that as Jago invited them in, and has only been gone a matter of weeks, they have no power to evict them unless they hear from Jago directly. They won't listen to me. But Letitia, they've been stealing. At least two of your father's paintings are missing and I'm certain some of the silverware is gone. I've tried to reason with them, but they can actually be quite intimidating.'

That was the part that had really made up Tish's mind. The thought of these drugged-out thugs scaring Mrs Drummond, the sweetest, most defenceless old woman in the world, brought out every protective instinct within her. She had to go back and sort out her brother's mess. How *could* he have left Mrs D to cope with all of this alone? Whenever he deigned to return from his latest self-indulgent, soul-searching exercise, Tish was going to strangle him with her bare hands.

Parking her exhausted Fiat in front of the graffiti-covered tower block she called home, Tish bolted up the staircase two steps at a time. Her flat was on the sixth floor, but the lift had long since broken, so she and Abel got regular workouts dragging their groceries and schoolbags up and down the stairs. Tish was still fumbling in her bag for her keys, trying to catch her breath, when the front door opened. Lydia, Abel's heavy-set Romanian nanny, glowered disapprovingly in the doorway.

'You're late.'

With her fat, butcher's arms, old-fashioned striped apron, and steel-grey hair cut in a blunt, unforgiving fringe, Lydia had the body of an ex-shot-putter and the face of a Gestapo wardress. She had never liked her English boss, whom she considered flighty and appallingly laissez-faire as a mother. However, she was devoted to little Abel, who in turn was very fond of her, which was why Tish had never fired her. That and the fact that Lydia was prepared to work long, often erratic hours for laughably low pay.

'I know, I'm sorry. There was a bit of a crisis at Curcubeu.' Tish forced her way past the nanny's giant frame into the hallway, dropping her bag on the floor. 'Abel! Where are you, darling? Mummy's home!'

'He sleeping,' said Lydia frostily. 'He waited long time for you. Very upset in his bath time, but now is OK. Sleeping.'

Tish looked suitably guilty. She couldn't have cared less what old iron-pants thought of her, but she hated letting

Abel down. Had he really been unhappy at bath time, or was Lydia just twisting the knife?

The old woman pulled on her coat, a thick, frankly filthy sheepskin, and a pair of brightly coloured knitted gloves. 'He need his sleep,' she told Tish sternly. 'Don't waking him.' And with this commandment she shuffled out of the flat, shaking her head and muttering darkly to herself in Romanian as the door closed behind her.

Silly cow, thought Tish, making a beeline for her son's bedroom. Inside, the low glow from Abel's Makka Pakka night-light helped her find her way to his bed. Pulling up a chair, Tish rested a hand on the warm, gently heaving Thomas the Tank Engine duvet and felt the pressures of the day evaporate. *My life's under there*, she thought. *I love him so much*. Loxley and Mrs Drummond, the children's home, even her terrible, unrequited love for Michel: they all faded into insignificance when Tish gazed down at her sleeping son. Gently peeling back the bedclothes, she stroked his soft mop of jet-black curls and bent to kiss the warm, silken skin of his rounded, still-baby-like cheek. It was hard to believe that this was the same malnourished, sore-covered baby she'd first laid eyes on in a maternity hospital outside Bucharest four years ago. Today, Abel was as healthy and chubby and rambunctious as any other little boy his age. *Much more handsome of course*, thought Tish proudly. It had been a long and arduous struggle to adopt him formally, even though Abel had lived with her since he was thirteen months old, and Tish was the only mother he'd ever known. Tish's one regret was that her beloved father, Henry, had never got to meet his grandson. Abi's paperwork had taken years to complete, and Henry had been too frail and sick to travel. Abel's passport was finally granted a month after Henry's funeral, a bitter irony for poor Tish.

Now, though, she'd have a chance to take Abel home. To show him England and Loxley and Mrs Drummond, and introduce him to his adopted culture and family. Better late than never.

Will he love it as much as I did? she wondered. *If he does, will it be hard for him to come back?*

This was something that hadn't occurred to her before, and it worried her. Because, of course, she would have to come back. Her whole life was in Romania now. *We'll be gone a month or so at most,* she told herself. *Carl can hold the fort here while I throw these vandals out of Loxley and find some suitable tenants. Then it'll be back to business as usual.*

She would tell Abel it was a holiday. It would be a holiday for him. For her, it was more complicated. Part of her was longing to see Loxley again, although after Mrs D's letter she dreaded the state she might find it in. But another part felt desolate at the prospect of leaving Michel, even for a few weeks. Before he died, Henry Crewe had implored his daughter to settle down and get married. 'Find a good man,' Henry told Tish. 'A kind man. Someone who can make you truly happy.'

That's the problem, Daddy, she thought sadly. *I've already found him. All I have to do now is get him to love me back.*

CHAPTER FIVE

Striding past the waiting paparazzi, ignoring the catcalls and boos from the gaggle of kids on the sidewalk, Sabrina Leon slipped into Il Pastaio on Beverly Drive feeling like a million dollars. In black skinny Balenciaga trousers and a figure-hugging black silk vest from Twenty8Twelve, accessorized with a vintage DVF leopard-print scarf and her trademark oversized Prada sunglasses, she looked every inch the star. After two long months climbing the walls at Revivals, it felt good to be back in the action. OK, so most of the attention she'd gotten had been negative. But at least it *was* attention. Given time – and another hit movie under her belt – Sabrina felt sure she could turn the tide. *Just as long as I'm not forgotten. Hatred's cool. It's indifference that scares me.*

Ed Steiner, her manager, waddled up to the maître d'. 'We're joining the Rasmirez party for lunch. Table eight, twelve thirty.'

'Follow me, sir. You're actually the first to arrive.'

He looks even fatter than usual, thought Sabrina, watching Ed attempt to weave between the other diners to get to the coveted table eight, the best in the house. *Nervous too*, she thought, clocking the rivers of sweat streaming down his forehead and the twitchy, rabbit-in-the-headlamps look in his beady agent's eyes. *He'd better not start fawning all over Rasmirez like we're some kind of fucking charity case.*

In fact, over the last two weeks, Ed Steiner had moved mountains trying to convince Dorian Rasmirez of his client's softer side. 'She's edgy, I'll grant you, and yes, she can be difficult. But you have to remember where she came from. Sabrina's childhood was like a Hammer Horror. Seriously. Her mom tried to sell her when she was two. Actually *sell her.* For a drug debt.'

Rasmirez was sympathetic. He was a kind man. But he couldn't afford to take on somebody else's problems, or let them spill over onto the rest of his cast. Ed had sworn blind that Sabrina had changed, that she'd learned her lesson. He just prayed she didn't undo all of his good work today.

Early signs weren't good. Coiling her long legs beneath her seat, ignoring the No Smoking signs, Sabrina lit up a Marlboro red. 'He's late,' she drawled, deliberately blowing smoke in the direction of the most disapproving-looking diners. 'If he's not here in five minutes, we're leaving.'

Reaching across the table, Ed removed the cigarette from Sabrina's mouth, stubbing it out in a plant pot by his side.

'Stop being infantile. The man only flew in from Europe a couple of hours ago. With his schedule, you're lucky he's seeing you at all.'

Serena laughed bitterly. 'Oh, yeah. I'm s*oooo* lucky. When I'm giving him a year of my time, *for free*, the tightfisted son of a bitch. You watch. He'll probably ask me to pay for lunch.'

She knew she was being childish. In part this was to try to hide her own nerves. Today's meeting was important. Rasmirez had cast her, the contract was signed; but he could easily wriggle out of it if he met her and had a change of heart. On the other hand, Sabrina was savvy enough to know that Hollywood was all about bravado. The moment she started *acting* like a failure, like she was washed up and flailing and desperate for the lifeline Rasmirez was throwing her, was the moment she knew she would sink without trace. What was Jack Nicholson's mantra? *Never explain, never apologize*. Ed had already apologized for her, so that ship had sailed. But Sabrina was determined to undo the damage by projecting nothing but A-list star quality to Rasmirez today. She did not appreciate being kept waiting.

Listening to Sabrina bitch about everything from the menu to the air-conditioning to the glare from the restaurant windows, Ed Steiner felt his self-control tanks running dangerously low. Just as he was about to lose his temper, a visibly tired and dishevelled Dorian Rasmirez walked in and was led over to join them.

'Sorry I'm late.' He addressed himself to Ed, who had stood up to greet him, and not to Sabrina, who hadn't. 'Complete craziness at my office. I've been out of town for three weeks, so I'm sure you can imagine. Have you ordered?'

Ed shook his head. 'We only just got here ourselves.'

'Oh, good,' said Dorian, who couldn't see Sabrina's furious glare behind her enormous dark glasses. He glanced round for a waitress, who materialized instantly. 'Hi there. We'll have three green salads to start, please, and just bring us a selection of main dishes, whatever the chef recommends. Hope that's OK with you.' He turned back to Ed. 'I'm on a really tight schedule today and we've got a lot of ground to cover.'

'Of course,' said Ed. 'We're grateful you could fit us in. Aren't we Sabrina?'

Slowly, with a melodramatic flourish worthy of Zsa Zsa Gabor, or a young Joan Collins, Sabrina removed her sunglasses, folded them neatly and laid them down on the table. She looked at Dorian Rasmirez, her eyes crawling over his face with disdain. It was the sort of look an empress might give to an unkempt page boy. Who the hell did he think he was, showing up late then ordering food without even asking her what she'd like? *Presumptuous jerk.* She turned to a passing waiter. 'I'll have a sour apple martini please, not too much sugar. And the lobster. And I'd like to see the menu again, please. I haven't quite made up my mind about an appetizer. You can cancel the earlier order.'

'Of course, Ms Leon,' muttered the waiter. 'Right away.'

Dorian watched this little charade with a combination of irritation and amusement. *So the stories are no exaggeration. She really is a little madam.* So much for rehab having humbled her. No wonder her manager looked as if he was one Big Mac away from a fatal coronary. Working for Sabrina Leon had clearly driven him to the brink.

The rumours about Sabrina were true in other areas too. Dorian had worked with some of the most beautiful actresses in the world, but few of them could match the electricity that positively crackled out of this girl. Electricity was good. Attitude, on the other hand, was bad, and Dorian had no intention of standing for it.

Leaning forward over the table, so that his face was only inches from Sabrina's, he said very quietly, 'You have fifteen seconds to cancel that order.'

Sabrina refused to be intimidated. 'Or what?' she taunted.

'Or you are off my movie,' Dorian smiled sweetly. 'Entirely your choice, of course. But I don't work with prima donnas.'

'Is that so?' Sabrina stood up haughtily. 'Well, it just so

happens *I* don't work with megalomaniacs. Goodbye, Mr Rasmirez.'

'Goodbye, Miss Leon.'

Poor Ed Steiner was so panicked he looked as though he were about to spontaneously combust. 'Hey, hey, come on now guys. Let's cool things down, shall we? No need to get into the Cuban Missile Crisis before we've even been introduced.' He put a restraining hand on Sabrina's arm. 'How about we start this again? Dorian Rasmirez, Sabrina Leon. Sabrina Leon, Dorian Rasmirez.'

Neither Sabrina nor Dorian moved a muscle. After a few, tense seconds, Sabrina caved first, grudgingly extending a hand. Dorian hesitated, then shook it.

'Sit down please.'

Ed shot Sabrina a pleading look. She sat.

'I'm a fair man, Miss Leon,' said Dorian. 'I have nothing against you personally. Nor do I have any interest whatsoever in your personal life.'

'I should hope not,' Sabrina bridled.

'However, I should tell you that the moment your personal life intrudes on the set of my movie, or impacts my cast and crew in any way, you will be out of that door so fast you won't know what hit you.'

Sabrina opened her mouth to speak but Dorian held up a hand for silence.

'I'm not finished. You're a good actress, Sabrina. You have potential to be a great actress. But you're also spoiled, immature, and at times breathtakingly stupid.'

Sabrina bit her lower lip so hard she drew blood. Not since Sammy Levine the youth theatre director back in Fresno had anyone spoken to her like this. All around their table, diners were straining their ears to hear her being ticked off like a naughty schoolgirl. It was mortifying.

'None of the major studios will touch you,' said Dorian. 'Nor will any of the independent producers worth their salt. You're a liability.'

'That's bullshit,' spat Sabrina, unable to contain herself any longer. 'I got offers.'

Dorian laughed brutally. 'Thank God you're a better actress than you are a liar. You have *nothing*, Sabrina. You know it and I know it. As of today, you *are* nothing. Now, if you want to become something again in this town, in this business, in this life, you'd better start by learning some humility.'

Sabrina's blood boiled, but she said nothing. Dorian continued.

'I've taken a chance on you young lady, when nobody else would. That's the reality. I don't need you. You need me. Which means that for the next year, or as long as it takes to get this movie pitch perfect, you do *exactly* as I say. You get up when I tell you to get up. You work when I tell you to work. You speak when I tell you to speak, you shut up when I tell you to shut up, and you eat whatever I put on your fucking plate. Are we clear?'

Sabrina glared at him in silent rage. He was right. She did need him. But in that moment she hated him more than she had hated anybody since the stepbrother who'd abused her as a kid.

'Are. We. Clear?' Dorian repeated, raising his voice so the entire restaurant could hear him.

'Yes.' Sabrina nodded, her voice barely a whisper.

'I'm sorry. I didn't hear you.'

'Yes,' she hissed. 'We're clear.'

'Good.' Dorian smiled broadly. 'Now go ahead and cancel your order and we can get down to business.'

* * *

Nine hours later, Dorian pulled through the electric gates of his Holmby Hills mansion utterly exhausted. *What a godawful day.*

After lunch with Sabrina, he'd had back-to-back meetings with his manager, his accountant, and Milla Haines, his casting director on *Wuthering Heights*. He'd hoped that would be a short meeting, but Milla wanted to run through an agonizingly long list of possibles for the role of Hareton Earnshaw.

'What about Sam Worthington?' suggested Dorian.

Milla attempted an eyebrow raise, not easy with a forehead-full of Fraxel. 'You can't begin to afford him.'

Stick thin, perfectly groomed and of indeterminate age thanks to decades of surgical tinkering, Milla Haines was about as sexually alluring as a bag of nails. She was, however, a first-rate casting director, not to mention a straight talker. Dorian respected her.

'Chris Pine?' he asked hopefully.

'If you wanted a solid second-tier-er, you shouldn't have blown the budget on Hudson,' said Milla.

'That was money well spent,' said Dorian firmly. 'Viorel Hudson *is* Heathcliff. I couldn't have done the film without him.'

'You wouldn't have had to,' said Milla. 'We'd have got him for *half* what you paid. Next time, let me do the negotiating.'

Dorian rubbed his eyes tiredly. 'Let's see the rest of the list.'

Years ago he used to find the early days of pre-production some of the most exciting, satisfying parts of his job, feeling his vision grow into reality beneath his hands, like a potter at the wheel. The screenwriter Thom Taylor once said that in Hollywood, 'The deal is the sex; the movie is the cigarette.' Dorian wouldn't necessarily go that far, but it was true that the deals, plural – pulling together everything from funding to distribution to merchandising – was what made a movie real. Every waitress in town had an idea for a film, a dream that had brought them to this most brutal of towns. Being a producer as well as a director, you got to make your dreams come true.

This time, however, the excitement had been replaced by unadulterated anxiety. How the hell was Dorian – was anyone – supposed to be creative with so much financial pressure? He knew Milla Haines was right. He had overpaid for Viorel. What Milla didn't know was that only two million of Hudson's salary was being paid out of the official production budget. The other three million Dorian would have to find out of his own pocket. After the disastrous *Sixteen Nights*, he needed to blow the box-office roof off with *Wuthering Heights*. If he didn't, he'd be ruined. It was that simple. He'd lose Chrissie. He'd lose the Schloss.

He tried not to think of how happy that would make Harry Greene. *Twisted, delusional bastard.* But it wasn't going to happen. He'd been burned on *Sixteen Nights*, the movie Greene had helped bury, but with *Wuthering Heights*, Dorian had a new strategy.

Step one was to shroud the production in secrecy, to generate as much buzz and curiosity as possible. He was shooting the whole thing on location, far away from the Hollywood gossip machine. (Assuming they ever found a damn location. So far the expensive scouting firm he'd hired to find them somewhere in England had come up with sweet FA.) All the sets would be strictly closed. Everyone connected with the movie – cast, crew, even the accountancy staff – had been made to sign watertight confidentiality clauses and any actor or crew member who said so much as 'good morning' to a member of the press would be summarily fired.

Step two was to wait until all the creative work was done and shooting was almost wrapped, and *then* go looking for studio investment and a shit-hot distribution deal. By then, if the work was good, and it would be good, excitement about the film should be at its peak.

We'll be fine, Dorian told himself. But his nerves persisted.

Parking his hired Prius out front (he'd had to sell the Bentley last year, a small contribution to the Schloss's first winter heating bill), he staggered through the front door to the welcoming sound of a beeping burglar alarm. Dropping his bags he punched in the code to turn it off and almost went flying on the stack of unopened mail spilling all over the entryway floor like an oil slick.

'Jesus Christ,' he muttered, reaching for the light switch. Nothing happened. The bulb must have blown. A musty smell of dust and stale air assaulted his nostrils. No one had been here for almost a month and it showed. Dorian realized sadly that the tile-hung, Spanish-style estate no longer felt like home. He wondered if anywhere would ever feel like home again, then chided himself for being so maudlin. He was dog-tired, that was all. He needed to get into a hot shower, call Chrissie and collapse into bed.

The phone rang.

'Rasmirez,' he answered crossly. Who the fuck could be calling him at this time of night?

'Wow, man, you sound like shit.'

Dorian grinned. 'Thanks, Emil. I feel like it.'

Emil Santander, Dorian's long-time friend and real-estate agent, sounded as upbeat and ebullient as ever. Emil and Dorian had been at film school together many moons ago, but their directorial careers had taken wildly different trajectories. Undaunted by his failure to become the new James Cameron, Emil had quit the business ten years ago, studied for his real-estate licence, and not looked back since, making a good, if unspectacular living selling the homes of his more successful classmates. He was just that kind of guy: upbeat, optimistic, uncomplicated. A dust-yourself-off-and-start-again-er. Dorian envied him.

'It's late, man,' Dorian yawned. 'I'm wiped out. Is this important or can I call you in the morning?'

'It's important,' said Emil. '*And*, it's good news.'

'I could use some of that,' said Dorian, wryly.

'I got you a great offer!'

'Oh.' Dorian exhaled. This was unexpected. When he first left for Romania a year ago, he'd asked Emil to 'keep his ear out' for a potential buyer for the Holmby Hills house. But having heard nothing back, he'd forgotten all about that conversation. If Chrissie had the slightest suspicion he was even thinking of selling the place, she'd have sliced his balls off with a rusty penknife. As much as she had always bitched and moaned about LA, she adored their house, and had spent a not-so-small fortune renovating and decorating it to her exact specifications. But the reality was, if Dorian could achieve a good enough price for it, he would have to sell. At the rate the Schloss was eating money, not to mention his production debts, there was no way they could afford to run such a huge house *in absentia*.

'Jeez,' grumbled Emil. 'Don't overwhelm me with enthusiasm, will you?'

'Sorry,' said Dorian. 'I'm just . . . how great, exactly?'

Part of him hoped the offer would be low enough to reject. Then he wouldn't have to broach the subject of a sale with Chrissie, who was already spoiling for the next fight. But another, more rational part prayed it would be high enough to cover his debt on Viorel Hudson's salary.

'Pretty great actually,' said Emil, unable to keep the

triumph out of his voice. 'About eight and half million bucks' worth of great.'

Dorian quickly did the math. Eight five, minus four million mortgage, minus the lien he'd raised two years ago when *Sixteen Days* was going under, minus the excess on Hudson's fee . . . he would break even, with a few hundred grand left over for a modest apartment in Santa Monica, some- where to crash when he was working. Good news indeed.

'That's awesome, Emil. Thank you.'

'You're welcome. Now just to be clear, is that "Thank you, I accept the offer"? Because I'm bringing the paperwork round first thing tomorrow morning for you to sign. The buyers want to meet you.'

Dorian's heart sank. 'Tomorrow? Oh, jeez man, I'm flat out tomorrow. Can we do it later in the week?'

'Hell*oo*?' said Emil. 'Are you hearing me here, D? I just got you eight point five for a house that you and I both know is worth six on a good day. These guys are big fans of your work and they wanna meet you. Tomorrow.'

Dorian groaned. 'OK.'

'They'd also like to move in by the end of the week. I told them that shouldn't be a problem.'

Fifteen minutes later, too tired to shower, Dorian lay back on his bed fully clothed. Feeling sleep start to creep over him, he quickly grabbed the phone and punched out his Romanian home number. He wouldn't tell Chrissie about the house sale tonight. He couldn't face the fireworks. He just wanted to hear her voice and to say good night. To tell her he loved her. And Saskia, of course.

The phone rang and rang . . . no answer.

That's weird, thought Dorian. It was early morning over there, before six, but Chrissie was usually up at this time.

She was fanatical about her sunrise yoga. He hung up and tried the line again, forcing images of Chrissie writhing naked in Alexandru's arms out of his mind.

Still no answer. *She must have gone out earlier than usual. Or maybe she's in the shower already. Can't hear the phone. I'll try again in a few minutes.*

He closed his eyes, just for a second. A movie reel of images danced through his brain.

Sabrina Leon, that beautiful, truculent child, her feline eyes glinting murderously at him across the table at Il Pastaio.

Chrissie, moaning with pleasure in some nameless lover's bed.

Emil Santander handing him wodges of hundred-dollar bills, but as soon as the notes touched his hands they crumbled into dust, staining his fingertips ash-grey.

Harry Greene laughing.

At last the anxiety dreams faded and Dorian saw a house: grey, imposing, bleak, its shuttered windows being mercilessly lashed by rain. He recognized it instantly as the Wuthering Heights of his boyhood imagination. It was a forbidding building, cold and aloof, and yet to Dorian there was something wonderfully comforting about it, and about the lulling *swoosh, swoosh* sound of the rain as it fell, enveloping everything in a cool, grey shroud.

He was asleep, the phone still clasped in his hand.

CHAPTER SIX

'Hey, Mum, guess what?' It was the third time Abel Crewe had asked this question in the last minute. 'If a dinosaur fell over, it would *die*.'

'Would it?' said his mother absently. 'My goodness.'

Tish and Abel were in the back of a taxi, on their way home to Loxley from Manchester Airport. Tish's eyes were glued to the familiar, craggy beauty of the landscape outside. She'd thought about it every day since she'd been away, but she realized now that she'd forgotten just how breathtaking the Peak District really was. This afternoon a light rain was falling, but a few pale sun rays fought their way bravely through the clouds, bathing the jutted tops of the Pennines in a soft, celestial light. With the exception of the odd crumbling farm-worker's cottage, this stretch of the Hope Valley was devoid of buildings, and seemed barely touched by man. After the ugly urban sprawl of Oradea, it was a blessed relief for Tish's senses, and she drank it in like a hummingbird gorging on nectar.

Abel, on the other hand, was far more interested in talking than sightseeing. If there were an Olympic team for not-drawing-breath, Tish's five-year-old son would surely have been appointed captain.

'Do you know *why* it would die?' he asked, not bothering to wait for a reply. 'Because dinosaurs are allergic to falling over. Like I'm allergic to mushrooms. What are you allergic to, Mum? Some people aren't allergic to anything, also some animals aren't, but some are, like monkeys. Not giraffes, though. Unless they ate a log. That would prob'ly get stuck in their necks and then . . . hey, look, another tractor! Seven! That's seven, Mum! I'm gonna be seven, after I've been six. Where's my birthday gonna be again? At home, or in In-ger-land? Can I have two parties?'

'England,' corrected Tish, who was only half listening. 'Not Ing-er-land. Try to stop talking just for a few minutes Abi, OK? We're almost there.'

The taxi took a left turn and the road narrowed sharply as it climbed and weaved its way around the hillside. Occasional farms gave way to grey stone houses, their walled front gardens bereft of flowers other than the occasional early snowdrop bravely rearing its flimsy white head above the muck. This was the outskirts of Loxley village. Tish felt her heart soar as they passed each familiar landmark: Bassets Mill, Mr Parks's farm, the abandoned dovecote that the local children used as a makeshift climbing frame-cum-treehouse. A few moments later and they were in the village proper.

A five-times-winner of Britain's Best Kept Village competition, Loxley was small but perfectly formed. It had a triangular green that was bisected by a tributary of the Derwent, which villagers had crossed for centuries by means of a Saxon stone footbridge. On one side of the green stood the post office and village shop. On the other was the perfectly preserved Norman church, St Agnes's, and on the third, the focal point of all village life great and small: The Carpenter's Arms pub.

'What do you think, darling?' Tish hugged her son excitedly.

'It's really pretty!' Abel grinned. 'It's like a picture from my book.' His sweet, snub nose was now glued to the window. Villages, apparently, were a lot more interesting than fells. 'Is it a park? When does it close?'

Tish squeezed his hand. 'It never closes.'

'Never? Cool! Can we go in that shop? Do they have M & Ms? Do they have Lego?'

The taxi continued through the village and down a gentle escarpment, Abel chattering excitedly all the while. The lane narrowed to a single car's width, hemmed in on either side by thick bushes of dog rose and briar, so it was almost like driving through a tunnel. Then suddenly, without warning, the valley opened up again to breath-taking views. A few hundred yards further and the road abruptly stopped in front of a pair of lichened wooden gates, propped open with two stone saddle stools. Through the gates, a wide, sweeping driveway wound its way into the distance, looking for all the world like the entrance to some enchanted land.

'It's a palace!' gasped Abel, his eyes on stalks. 'Who lives up there?'

'We do.' Tish laughed as the taxi pulled through the gates. 'For a little while, anyway. The house actually belongs to your Uncle Jago –' the words stuck in Tish's craw–'but he's away at the moment. Mummy's friend Mrs Drummond has been looking after it for him while he's gone, and we've come to help her.'

This seemed to satisfy Abel, who was more interested in the oak trees in the park and which of them might be most suitable for his planned Tarzan treehouse than Loxley's complex ownership structure. In-ger-land, he had already decided, was infinitely superior to Romania. He hoped his Uncle Jago's holiday lasted a long, long time.

He hoped it even more when he saw the house, a turreted, Disney fairytale that was just crying out for someone to play knights in it. While Tish paid the cabbie and struggled to drag her suitcase across the gravel, Abel raced ahead of her, bounding up the stone steps through the open front door.

A plump, elderly woman, wearing a striped apron over her gardening trousers and sweater, appeared in the hallway.

'Who are you?' Abel asked bluntly.

'I'm Mrs D,' said the woman, smiling as she wiped her floury hands on her apron. 'Who are you?'

'I'm Abel Henry Gunning Crewe,' said Abel. 'Do you like dinosaurs?'

Before she had time to answer, Mrs Drummond saw Tish lugging an enormous suitcase into the hallway. 'Darling! Let me help you.' She relieved Tish of the case, plonking it down at the foot of the stairs, and threw her arms around her former charge, enveloping Tish in a bosomy, cinnamon-scented bear hug. 'I can't *tell* you how happy I am to see you.'

'You too, Mrs D,' said Tish with feeling. 'You met Abel?'

'I did indeed,' Mrs Drummond grinned, turning to watch the little boy who was now mountaineering his way up the banisters. 'He's gorgeous.'

'Isn't he?' Tish grinned back. 'I thought he'd be tired after the flight and everything, but he hasn't stopped talking since six o'clock this morning.'

'Not to worry,' said Mrs Drummond. 'I've made some cinnamon pound cake. A couple of slices of that will take the wind out of his sails. Now, what would you like to do first, lovie? Eat? Have a bath? Unpack?'

'No,' said Tish resolutely. 'I'd like to meet our house guests.'

A cloud of anxiety descended over Mrs Drummond's kindly features. 'I don't think you should do that right away, Letitia. They're not very nice people. Wait till this afternoon and I'll get Bill and one of the other farm boys to go in there with you. They mostly keep to the East Wing, so they shouldn't bother us here.'

'Nonsense,' said Tish. 'I don't need a bloody bodyguard in my own house. If you'd take Abel and get him something to eat, I'll go and sort them out.'

'I really don't think you understand, darling . . .' Mrs Drummond began. But Tish was already marching off down the hallway towards the East Wing. *She always was a stubborn child*, thought Mrs Drummond, watching her retreating back. Perhaps she *should* call Bill Connelly, just in case.

Walking down the East corridor, past Loxley's grand, formal rooms, Tish gasped in horror as the extent of the damage wrought by Jago's 'friends' unfolded. Every few feet, dark rectangles of wallpaper revealed the places where paintings had been removed and, according to Mrs Drummond, taken to London to be sold for drugs. In the library, antique book-cases stood with their doors hanging off the hinges and an array of beautifully bound first editions spilling out onto the floor. In the grate, Tish saw torn spines and singed pages: some Barbarian had used her father's books as kindling! Everywhere there was dirt, Persian runners covered with the imprints of muddy boots, empty mugs and glasses littering every available surface, some of them growing livid green mould on the dregs of whatever vile, stagnant liquid they had once contained. The deeper Tish walked into the East Wing, once the most impressive part of the house, the more the place looked like a squat, littered with empty beer cans and overflowing ashtrays.

Finally, she approached the drawing room. There was music coming from inside – *Jimi Hendrix, if I'm not mistaken* – and raucous, male laughter. Her hand was on the door handle, but she hesitated.

Not yet, she thought. *There's something I have to do first.*

In the kitchen, Mrs Drummond watched in awe as Letitia's son inhaled his fourth, slab-sized slice of cinnamon pound cake. The child was an eating machine. And he was *still* talking.

'If you could make dinosaurs un-extinct and have one for a pet, which one would you have?' he mumbled through a fine spray of cake crumbs.

'My goodness, Abel. I've never really thought about it. I don't suppose I'd have any of them. Would dinosaurs make good pets, do you think?'

Abel looked at her pityingly. 'Of *course* they would. A T-Rex would be the most excellentest pet you could ever have, and do you know why? Because it would kill all the baddies, and eat them, but it wouldn't kill you because you'd be its owner. Pets' owners are kind of like their mum or dad. So pets actually love them. Even a T-Rex would love its owner, but you'd have to help it not to fall over, because do you know what happens to dinosaurs when they fall over?'

Mrs Drummond shook her head.

'They *die*!'

'Do they really?'

'Uh-huh. And do you know what else?'

Suddenly the clear, unmistakable *crack* of a shotgun being fired rang out.

'Good heavens!' said Mrs Drummond. A few seconds later there was another shot, then another, all of them from the direction of the East Wing.

'Was that a bomb?' asked Abel cheerfully. 'Bombs are cool.'

'You stay there my darling. Don't move.' Running into the hallway, Mrs Drummond picked up the telephone and dialled 999.

In the drawing room, a dreadlocked man in his mid-thirties stared at the petite, blonde woman in front of him in terrified astonishment.

'What the fuck?' he shouted, as his cowering companions scrambled to their feet. 'You could have killed me!'

'Indeed I could,' said Tish. She pointed her father's shotgun slowly and deliberately at the man's crotch. 'And if you and your mates aren't out of this house in the next two minutes, I probably will.'

'You wouldn't bloody dare,' said the man.

Tish cocked the gun's hammer. 'Try me.'

Henry's gun cupboard was upstairs in what had been his dressing room. Deciding it was better to be safe than sorry, and that a loaded shotgun would provide a lot more effective protection than Bill Connelly, Loxley's elderly farm manager, Tish had retrieved the key from its usual hiding place in the airing cupboard and armed herself for confrontation. When she reached the dressing room her heart was in her mouth. The squatters had evidently been here before her. Deep scratches on the thick oak closet doors documented their multiple, frustrated attempts to break it open. Tish shuddered to think what might have happened had they succeeded, high out of their minds and with poor dear Mrs Drummond in the house.

'We're guests here, you mad fucking cow,' the man snarled, stepping out from behind the Knole sofa. 'Your brother invited us to stay for as long as we liked.' His fear seemed to be receding and his aggression returning. His patchwork trousers and CND shirt suggested a peaceful, hippyish, eco-campaigner type, but the bullying look in his eyes said otherwise. *You're a thug*, thought Tish. *I've seen your type in Romania countless times: pathetic little local government Hitlers trying to intimidate the weak and helpless. You don't scare me.*

'Yes, well, unfortunately for you my brother isn't here, is he? I am. And I'm telling you to get out.'

'Fuck you. You're not gonna shoot me.' The man took two steps towards Tish, a look of cold hatred on his drug-ravaged face. For a moment, Tish experienced a stab of panic. Mrs Drummond was right. He *was* menacing. They all were. Sensing a shift in the room's power dynamics, his previously comatose friends began to rally themselves, lining up behind him like backing singers in some sinister, junkie band.

'Get her, Dan,' one of them shouted.

'Fucking posh bitch,' hissed another.

In a couple of seconds the ringleader would have reached her. Twice her size, he would easily be able to overpower her and grab the gun. There was no time to think. Switching aim from his groin to his foot, Tish fired.

For a split second there was silence. Then came the screams. 'Dan' collapsed in a heap on the floor, clutching his leg. Blood poured from his foot, seeping through his soft moccasin shoes onto the carpet. The noise coming out of him was blood curdling. His friends rushed to his aid.

'Fuck!' said the smaller, rat-faced one. 'We need to get him to hospital.'

'That's GBH, you cunt. You're looking at ten years for that.' Another of the men bared his yellowing teeth at Tish. 'I'm calling the fucking police.'

'Be my guest,' said Tish, passing him the phone with a

nonchalance she was far from feeling. 'When you're finished, I'll fill them in on your thefts of my family property. I might ask them to bring over a few sniffer dogs while they're at it. Although I doubt they'll need them. They can just follow the trail of needles.'

Dan looked up, his face white as a sheet. 'Leave it,' he whispered, through gritted teeth. The pain was clearly excruciating. 'Just get me to A and E. Get the others and let's get the fuck out of here before she kills someone.'

Tish watched as his friends scooped him up off the floor, staggering under his weight as they carried him out of the room. Once they'd gone, she bolted the drawing-room door behind them and waited, Henry's shotgun still in her hand. There were muffled noises of a commotion upstairs. After about ten minutes, Tish heard the last door slam. Looking out of the window, she saw a straggling group of eight men and women climb into their dilapidated camper van and drive off, spraying gravel noisily behind them in their eagerness to get away. It was only once they'd gone and the rumble of the van's engine had faded into silence that Tish realized her hands were shaking violently.

Forcing herself to calm down, she unlocked the door and walked upstairs, checking each room to make sure that no one was left hiding or passed out on one of the beds. If it were possible, the squalor upstairs was even worse than it was in the rooms below. Drug-related detritus littered the beds and floors, along with filthy clothes and sheets, and plates covered in rotting food. *Bastards.* Only once she was convinced they had all gone did Tish carefully replace her father's gun in the closet, lock it, and go back downstairs to check on Abel.

She found him in the kitchen, along with a visibly shaken Mrs D. And three policemen.

'There she is!' cried Mrs Drummond. 'Oh, Letitia, thank goodness you're safe! What happened? We heard the shots.'

'Is everything all right, Miss Crewe?' The senior policeman stepped forward. 'Was anybody injured?'

'Everything's fine, officer,' said Tish calmly, scooping Abel up into her arms and kissing him. 'I'm sorry to have troubled you. There *was* an accident I'm afraid. One of our unwanted visitors managed to break into my father's gun closet. I arrived in the drawing room to find him fiddling about with one of the shotguns. Damned fool. Before you knew it the thing went off and he'd managed to shoot himself in the foot. He's on his way to A and E now. His friends took him in their camper van. I have a sneaking feeling they won't be back.'

The policeman raised an eyebrow. He was no fool. 'I see. And that's the same story he's going to be telling us, is it? The injured gentleman?'

'Well, of course,' said Tish, flashing him her best, butter-wouldn't-melt smile. 'Although I'm not sure gentleman's the word I'd use.'

'And where is the weapon now, miss?'

'The gun? Oh, I put it back in the cupboard, officer, safely locked away. I didn't want to leave it lying around for my son to find.' Sensing this was his time to shine, Abel fluttered his eyelashes at the policeman and clung tightly to his mother, the picture of innocence.

'Would you like to see it?'

The policeman sighed. He'd had a long day. Unless the squatter actually reported a crime, there was no official need for him to inspect the weapon.

'Not for the moment, miss,' he said. 'I'll be in touch if there's anything else we need.'

*   *   *

Later that night, once Abel and Mrs Drummond were both in bed, Tish sank down into the Chesterfield chair in her father's old office and poured herself a much-needed glass of single malt.

What a day.

Despite Mrs D's flat-spin panic about the shooting, Tish had not been worried that Dan and his friends would spill the beans to hospital staff, or the police. They had too much to lose. If there was one thing wasters like them valued above all others, it was an easy life. As of today, Loxley Hall had become more trouble than it was worth to them. They wouldn't be back.

The bad news was that the quid pro quo for their silence about her trigger-happy antics would be that Tish could not now report them for criminal damage. She would have to find the money to make the necessary repairs and replacements herself. But, after a cursory glance at the estate's latest accounts, it was hard to see how that was going to happen. As a going concern, Loxley was losing money hand over fist. Most stately homes did. That was why you needed tenants, and/or a professional company to manage them. Had Tish's mother Vivianna done what was expected of her and put such arrangements in place, instead of handing the place to Jago on a silver platter, they wouldn't be in this mess.

It wasn't just the practical and financial recklessness of her mother's decision that had upset Tish. It also stung that Vivianna had deliberately cut *her* out of any possible inheritance. Secretly, Tish had hoped she might take over at Loxley one day, once her work in Romania was done. The estate meant far more to her than it ever had to Jago.

'But darling,' Vivianna told her at Henry's funeral, 'you've been so occupied with those waifs and strays of yours. I didn't think you'd be interested. Besides, the house would always have passed to Jago if he and your father hadn't fallen out. It's not right that Henry should be able to spite the boy from beyond the grave.'

But it's OK for you to spite me from this side of the grave? thought Tish furiously.

Behind Henry's desk, on the largest expanse of wall in the room, hung an enormous, framed photograph of Vivianna, stark naked. It had been taken in the Sixties, at the height of her youthful beauty, and mercifully had been tastefully done (Vivi had her back half turned to the camera, so only her perfect, peach-shaped bottom and half of a breast were visible). But it still had to go.

You left us, Tish thought bitterly. *You left all of us. What right do you have to be up on that wall, with your glossy black hair and your enchanting smile and your sultry black eyes, a female version of Jago?*

Vivianna Crewe had abandoned both her children, but it was only Jago that she'd ever missed. At least, that was how Tish saw it. Maybe handing over Loxley was her way of trying to make amends to him?

Whatever her motives, there was nothing Tish could do about it now. Her job was clear: to repair the estate, rescue it from total financial ruin, and then walk away and leave it all to Jago, until the next time he fucked up. It was a bitter pill to swallow, but she had no choice. Unless of course Jago really *did* spend the rest of his life as a sworn celibate in a Tibetan cave. In which case perhaps, one day, Abel could inherit as the next male in line.

But she was getting ahead of herself. Right now it was by no means certain that there would *be* an estate to inherit, for her children or Jago's. The squatters were gone, but the real work started now. They had to cut back. First thing in the morning, Tish would turn the heating off. They could all wear lots of sweaters.

On Henry's desk, her BlackBerry buzzed into life. It was a BBM, from Michel. Involuntarily, Tish's heart rate shot up.

'How was it? As bad as you thought?'

'Worse,' she texted back. *'You still in Paris?'*

'Yes. Miss you.'

Not as much as I miss you, thought Tish, her stomach lurching with hope. Did he really miss her? He'd never said anything like that before. Then another message came through. Reading it, Tish felt a skewer being pushed slowly through her heart.

'Met someone ☺ Tell you all about it when I see you. Xoxo'

Tish turned off her phone in a daze. Depression washed over her. Without even registering what she was doing, she unscrewed the top of the whisky bottle, poured herself another and drank it. Her throat burned, but she didn't care.

Michel had met someone. Someone who wasn't her. Someone who deserved him. Tish tried to picture such a woman.

She's probably a supermodel. Or a brain surgeon. You're nothing to him, she told herself cruelly. *Just some silly girl with a crush.*

Closing her eyes, she offered up a heartfelt prayer.

Please, God. Let me get over him.

In the cold, empty house, the silence was deafening.

CHAPTER SEVEN

Dorian Rasmirez's production company, Dracula Pictures, had offices on the top floor of number 9000 Sunset Boulevard, an iconic tower block marking the borderline between Beverly Hills and West Hollywood.

Parking her silver Mercedes convertible on Doheny Drive, Sabrina Leon sauntered into the building, followed by her usual shoal of ratzies, like a whale trailing pilot fish.

'Name?' asked the surly clerk on the front desk.

'You know who I am,' Sabrina snapped back.

She was right, the clerk did know who she was. But, like most African Americans, he loathed her with a passion bordering on the murderous. 'Name,' he repeated, baldly.

'Look, asshole, I don't have time for this, I'm late. Now buzz me up to Dracula, there's a good boy.'

If looks could kill, Sabrina would have dropped dead on the spot.

'I am *not* your "boy".'

Oh, shit. Wasn't there a word left in the English language that didn't have racial overtones? 'That's not what I meant.'

'No? Well what *I* mean is you can either write your name

on the visitors' list, like eeeeeverybody else–' the clerk spoke slowly, as if he were talking to a retarded child –, 'or you do not step into that elevator. Next.' And to Sabrina's fury, he turned his attention to the man behind her.

Sabrina whipped out her cellphone. 'Yeah, hi, this is Sabrina Leon. I'm downstairs. The moron on the desk won't buzz me up. Would you send someone down here, please?'

She hung up, shooting the clerk a smug smile. With any luck, he'd be out of a job by morning.

It was now more than three months since Sabrina's drunken slip of the tongue about Tarik Tyler being a slave driver, but no one seemed to want to let her move on. *If they're waiting for some kind of grovelling, Tiger Woods mea culpa, they're gonna have a long wait*, thought Sabrina defiantly. She was tired of apologizing for her existence to every black person she met in a store or on the street. *I am not a goddamn racist.*

A minute passed. Then five. Then twenty. Perched awkwardly on one of the leather banquettes in the lobby, Sabrina grew increasingly irritated. Where the hell was Rasmirez's assistant?

A buzz on her phone distracted her. It was a text from Brad, the shit-hot Australian dancer she'd spent last night with. Brad was the reason she was late this morning. Sabrina prided herself on her own sexual stamina, but male dancers were always in a league of their own. She'd spotted her latest conquest on the dance floor at Les Deux last night, gyrating his perfect six-pack abs, grinding up against the identikit blonde model he'd come in with. A friend told her he was in LA on tour with Rihanna, not that Sabrina gave a fuck. He could have been White House Chief of Staff for all she cared, just as long as he ditched the blonde, took her home and fucked her till she could barely breathe.

Since getting out of rehab six weeks ago, Sabrina had only had sex once, and that was a lacklustre performance from an ex-boyfriend whom she would never have slept with if she hadn't been drunk. Ed Steiner had pleaded with her not to go back to drinking. Sabrina had offered him a compromise – that she would only drink at home – but she was fast growing bored of her self-imposed house arrest. Playing the saint didn't suit her. And besides, what was the point if no one was going to forgive her anyway? She only had a few more weeks left in LA, before that asshole Rasmirez shipped her off to some dreary, middle-of-nowhere location in rural England. If the press were intent on crucifying her, she was damn well going to enjoy her last supper. Brad had been a quite delicious first course.

Not even he could distract her for long though. The situation was getting ridiculous. Today was the first full cast read-through of the *Wuthering Heights* script, and she was now almost forty minutes late. Damned if she was going to give the jerk on the desk her name, her first instinct was to get up and leave, but a small voice of self-preservation made her hesitate. The humiliation of her lunch with Dorian Rasmirez at Il Pastaio last month still burned in her memory, and was not an experience she wanted to repeat in a hurry. Dorian, she rightly suspected, would go nuts if she pulled a no-show.

While she sat twitchily considering her options, there was a flurry of activity outside the revolving doors. The paparazzi, who'd been loitering quietly in front of the building ever since Sabrina disappeared out of shot, suddenly sprang to life again, climbing over one another like starving animals stampeding to be fed. As always when somebody else was the centre of attention rather than her, Sabrina felt a small stab of anxiety. It grew into a rather larger stab when she saw who it was.

'Good morning.' Viorel Hudson walked casually over to the reception desk. 'I'm Viorel Hudson,' he said politely. 'I have a meeting up at Dracula Pictures. Where do I sign in?'

Dressed in a Spurr New York suit jacket over a faded grey James Perse T-shirt and dark-wash jeans, he looked relaxed and stylish. Though Sabrina was loath to admit it, he was even better looking in person than he was on screen, with his jet-black hair, strong jaw, and perfect mocha tan offsetting the deep blue of his eyes. *Too pretty*, she thought dismissively. *No edge*.

Picking up his temporary security pass, Vio turned to check his reflection in the large, lobby mirror – *vain*, thought Sabrina – and suddenly saw her sitting there.

'Sabrina.'

They had never met, but Viorel recognized Sabrina instantly. She was, after all, one of the best-known faces in America, even if it was for all the wrong reasons. He extended a perfectly manicured hand. 'Viorel Hudson. How do you do?'

Sabrina shook his hand unsmilingly. *How do I do? Who does this guy think he is – Prince Charles?*

She'd be sexy, thought Viorel, *if only she'd wipe the sneer off her face*.

'I'm glad you're late as well,' he said, ignoring Sabrina's frosty demeanour. 'The traffic on the ten was bloody awful. Shall we head up together? Safety in numbers and all that?'

Sabrina considered the options. She could hardly stay where she was now and let him go up alone. Not without having to explain the situation with the desk clerk, which would only make her look petty.

'Didn't they give you a pass?' asked Viorel, noticing she was empty handed. He turned to the desk clerk. 'This is Sabrina Leon. She's coming up to Dracula with me. Would you sign her in?'

The desk clerk positively beamed with satisfaction as he handed Sabrina the clipboard.

'Certainly. Just as soon as she writes her name, like everyone else.'

Sabrina scribbled out a signature and passed it back to him, glaring.

'You have a nice day now.' The clerk grinned.

Sabrina did not have a nice day.

In fact, the next four hours were to be some of the longest in her life.

When the double doors to Dracula's production office opened and she and Viorel Hudson walked in together, Dorian Rasmirez exploded. 'What the fuck time do you call this?' The rest of the cast, gathered around the large oval table, huddled together nervously. 'You're almost an hour late!'

Viorel at least had the decency to look embarrassed, apologizing profusely for keeping everyone waiting and assuring Dorian that it wouldn't happen again.

'Damn right it won't,' fumed Dorian, 'Or I'll want my fucking cheque back. And what the hell is your excuse?'

He turned on Sabrina, who'd quietly taken a seat at the far end of the table and appeared more interested in her cuticles than in pacifying her director. From the moment she walked into the room, Sabrina had unconsciously taken it over, shifting the centre of gravity from Dorian to herself. Even dressed down as she was today, in Love Story jeans and a plain white shirt, she dazzled. 'I called your receptionist forty-five minutes ago,' she said nonchalantly, not bothering to remove her sunglasses when she spoke to him. 'No one came to get me.'

'*No one came to get you?*' Dorian stared at her

contemptuously. 'You've got legs, haven't you? Walk to the fucking elevator like everyone else. You think my staff have nothing better to do than run after you like some spoiled child? Well? Do you?'

Sabrina dug her nails into her palm, forcing herself not to react, not to yell back at Dorian the way she wanted to. It was outrageously unfair. Viorel had arrived later than her, but he barely warranted a slap on the wrist. Clearly, Rasmirez was a sexist pig who got some sort of a sick kick out of publicly humiliating women. *Asshole.*

'I expect people to do their jobs,' she said calmly.

'So do I.' Dorian hurled Sabrina's script across the table, narrowly missing whacking her in the face. 'Read.'

For Dorian, Sabrina's attitude this morning was the straw that had broken the camel's back. The last few weeks had been breakdown-inducingly stressful.

Thanks to the location scouts' dismal failure to find him a suitable Wuthering Heights or Thrushcross Grange in England, they were still stuck in LA and running six weeks behind schedule. His intention was to shoot as many of the interior scenes as possible at home in Romania. The Schloss was more than grand enough, it would save some money, and crucially it would allow him to spend at least part of the year under the same roof as the increasingly restless Chrissie. But most of the film had to be shot in England. They ought to have been doing today's read-through on set, not crammed into his LA production office like a bunch of fucking sardines.

To add to his work stresses, things at home had gone from bad to worse in the last few weeks. Predictably, Chrissie had hit the roof when he told her about selling the Holmby Hills house. He'd made the mistake of doing it face to face, on a flying visit back to Romania last week.

'You sold *my* home in LA, behind my back?' Chrissie screeched, the sinews in her neck straining with rage, like a starving baby bird demanding food. Sprawled out on a chaise longue in one of the Schloss's myriad palatial formal rooms, wearing a coffee-coloured silk La Perla negligee and matching lace-trimmed robe, she looked every inch the pampered chatelaine. 'How dare you! I suppose now you think you can keep me and Saskia locked up here forever?'

'No one's trying to lock you up, honey,' said Dorian exhaustedly. 'I'm trying to make the best financial decisions for all of us as a family, that's all.'

'How?' yelled Chrissie. 'By selling our home to fund another one of your shitty, artistic movies? How many people actually saw *Sixteen Nights*? Five?'

Dorian winced. That hurt.

'This one'll be different,' he said quietly. But Chrissie didn't want to hear it. Another movie meant Dorian spending yet more time away from home, months on end in which she would be left to take care of Saskia alone in this dump while he gallivanted around the world enjoying himself.

'I'm not going on vacation you know, honey,' he tried to defend himself. 'For the first months at least I'll be stuck in LA, working my ass off, living in some shit-hole of a rented apartment.'

'Well whose fault is that?'

'I'll be lonely as hell.'

'Ha!' Chrissie snorted viciously. *'Lonely.* You don't know the meaning of lonely. It's Saskia and I who'll be lonely. You'll be off banging your leading lady.'

'For God's sake!' Dorian lost his temper. 'You seriously think I'm interested in Sabrina Leon?'

'Why wouldn't you be?' pouted Chrissie.

'Because she's a child,' said Dorian, 'an irresponsible child.

I'll be babysitting her, not sleeping with her. Besides, you know damn well you're the only woman for me. How do you think I feel, having to leave you here, knowing every man on this estate wants you?' Bending down over the chaise longue, he ran a hand along his wife's taut, Pilates-toned thigh. Even after so many years together, just touching her made him feel ridiculously aroused.

Slowly, Chrissie parted her thighs, allowing him a glimpse of her newly waxed pussy. She'd deliberately had a Brazilian the day before Dorian was due to leave, knowing how anxious it would make him. 'Don't go then,' she said, coyly.

'I have to go,' he whispered, his voice hoarse with longing. 'I need to do this movie, Chrissie. *We* need it.'

Chrissie sat up, clamping her legs shut like a librarian slamming closed a book. 'Fine,' she snapped. 'But don't you dare complain to me about how hard this is for *you*.'

'Come with me,' Dorian pleaded.

'And what, live in a hotel in my own home city? Schlep Saskia around some freezing-cold film set like a piece of excess baggage? No thanks. I'm not interested in following you round the world as your *little woman*.'

Dorian realized he couldn't win. He'd offered her the part of Cathy months ago, but as usual she'd turned him down flat, a mask of anger and fear falling over her face like a security grille. 'Our daughter needs at least one parent,' she'd told him bitterly. It was almost as if she *wanted* to be unhappy, but still Dorian felt like a failure. Things had not improved between them before he left for LA. He'd been in town for five days now, and Chrissie had yet to return one of his calls.

Angry and anxious, he needed a vent for his frustration. When Sabrina Leon showed up late to this morning's script read-through, he found one.

The rest of the day was not a rehearsal. It was a bullfight, a gladiatorial combat to the death, and Sabrina was the bull. While everybody else was allowed to get through their scenes, with Dorian commenting on their performance only at the end, Sabrina was picked up on every line. She was sloppy. Her delivery was too fast. She failed to react with enough emotion to Viorel's lines. She was *too* emotional.

Over and over again, Dorian hit her with the same three words, words Sabrina came to loathe like poison:

'Do it again.'

By the end of the day, even the most die-hard Sabrina-haters in the cast were beginning to feel sorry for her. Spoiled she may be, and attention-seeking and entitled. But you had to admire the stamina with which she ran back at each scene, over and over and over and over, determined to get it right, switching from her two parts as both the older and younger Catherine with consummate professionalism. As older Cathy, she'd be reading a passionate love scene with Viorel one minute, then jumping straight into a painful scene where, as the younger Catherine, she was being tormented by Heathcliff, forced to live as a common servant in her own childhood home. Even without Dorian's bullying, the emotional rollercoaster was intense.

At five o'clock, Dorian finally called time on the battle.

'All right everybody. We're done for the day. Does anyone have any questions?'

I do, thought Sabrina. *When are you going to drop dead?*

No one spoke. They all wanted to go home. Just watching Dorian shred Sabrina's performance had been exhausting.

'I have a question.' Viorel Hudson's sexy British drawl rang out through the silence. 'Do we know when filming's actually going to start?'

Dorian's eyes narrowed. 'Soon. Anyone else?'

'Is that really all you can tell us?' Viorel pressed him. 'I don't mean to speak out of turn, but I don't understand the need for all the secrecy. I mean, I haven't even been told where the location's going to be. Has anyone else?'

Everyone shook their heads.

'Whether or not you understand it, you have all signed confidentiality agreements,' snapped Dorian. 'All details – *all* details – about the production of this movie remain confidential, and logistical information will be released to you on a need-to-know basis only.

'In the meantime,' he went on, 'I hope I don't have to remind any of you that you are *all* under contract. I can call you in to work at any time, for any reason, and I will be doing so in the near future. You should expect to be asked to travel at extremely short notice, so I suggest you all go home, pack your bags and wait.' Dorian closed his script and stood up, a clear signal that the matter was now closed.

Sabrina was the first to leave – she couldn't wait to get out of there. The rest of the cast swiftly followed her lead. Only Viorel remained behind.

'Is there something I can do for you, Mr Hudson?' Dorian's tone was less than friendly. He was in no mood to be interrogated by his leading man. Considering what Viorel was being paid, he expected him to put up and shut up along with everybody else.

'I know it's not my place to say so . . .' said Viorel.

'Then don't,' muttered Dorian.

'But don't you think you were a little rough on Sabrina in there? Every time she opened her mouth, you practically ripped her throat out.'

'I did nothing of the kind,' said Dorian. 'I directed her performance. Last time I checked, I believe that was considered a key part of my job description.'

Viorel looked troubled. Dorian softened slightly. It wouldn't do to alienate all his cast before filming had even started. 'Look. I wouldn't cry too many crocodile tears over Miss Leon if I were you. The young lady can look after herself. She has a lot to learn, as an actress and in life. If my set is where she has to learn it –' he shrugged –' then so be it.'

'What if she doesn't learn?' asked Viorel. 'She might just end up hating you for it.'

Dorian smiled. 'I rather suspect she hates me already. But I'm not in this business to make friends, Mr Hudson. Are you?'

'No, sir,' said Viorel with feeling. 'I'm here to make movies.'

'As am I. In future, show up on time to rehearsals, please.'

'Yes, sir.'

'Do your own job properly, Mr Hudson, and I assure you, I will do mine.'

CHAPTER EIGHT

Tish Crewe gasped for breath as the cold water from the shower splashed onto her bare back. She'd turned the heating off at Loxley six weeks ago to save money, and only had the hot water running for an hour in the mornings. Usually, she was able to sneak a hot shower during this window, before she drove Abel to school. But today she'd overslept – after hours of lying awake, tormented by dreams of Michel and his new girlfriend – and missed it.

The girlfriend had a name now (Fleur) and a job (news reporter for Canal Plus, disappointingly impressive). Tish had seen her picture on Facebook, and been alarmed by how badly she wanted to reach into the computer and wipe the smile off her pretty, happy, accomplished face. Bizarrely, it had hurt more that the girl was not the physically perfect superwoman of Tish's imagination. Fleur was attractive, but in a very girl-next-door type of way: shoulder-length brown hair, long, slightly horsey nose, smooth skin, adorable smile. She wasn't a bimbo, or a bitch. *She's actually a lot like me*, thought Tish miserably. She felt as if she'd somehow made a terrible mistake. As if she'd allowed Michel to slip through her fingers and into this other woman's arms, by not saying quite the right thing, or wearing the right dress, or being in the right place at the right time. Worst of all, Michel had taken to calling her semi-regularly 'as a friend' and pouring out his happiness. 'I've never felt like this before,' he gushed, each word burning into poor Tish's heart like acid. 'I truly didn't think I would ever fall in love. But you were right, *mon chou*. There's someone out there for everyone.'

During the days, Tish was so busy – between the estate repairs and the finances and taking care of Abel (who'd begged to be enrolled in the village school and was having the time of his life) – that she usually managed to push Michel out of her mind. But at night he haunted her like Banquo's ghost at the feast. As the weeks passed, the cumulative exhaustion threatened to overwhelm her. At breakfast today she'd snapped quite unnecessarily at poor Abel, who once again seemed to have lost everything he needed for school, from his lunchbox to his reading book to his (*constantly* disappearing) cap. By the time she'd got him ready, dropped him off and made it back to Loxley, it was already half-past nine. By which time, of course, the water in her shower was arctic.

'Fuck!' she shivered, hopping from foot to foot and rubbing soap under her arms at lightning speed. Turning around, she let the icy jets pound down on her face before turning the water off and jumping into the nearest towel.

At least I'm awake, she thought, rubbing herself dry and feeling a surge of physical energy as her tingling limbs began to defrost. She needed something to get the adrenaline flowing. As usual, there was a mountain of work to do today.

It was May now – she and Abel had been here six weeks already – and though the weather remained cold, spring had belatedly sprung, carpeting the valley in a cheerful burst of yellow primroses and daffodils. After the daily bleakness of Oradea, it was wonderful to be able to open her window every morning and smell crisp, clean, country air, and see greenery everywhere. The sadness over Michel never left her, but she tried to take comfort in the small pleasures of life at Loxley: decent tea, bacon, McVitie's biscuits, apples that didn't taste like they'd been made out of wool. It helped that Abel had taken to English country life like a duck to water, running around Loxley's grounds building forts and camps, skipping off to school in the village every morning with a grin so wide you might have thought he was heading to Disneyland. Which, compared to the life he was used to back home, in a way he was.

Yesterday, he'd announced to Tish matter-of-factly, 'Actually, I'm going to stay here forever.'

They were up at Loxley's Home Farm, a handsome, L-shaped house with stables and outbuildings just over the top of the fell. Bill Connelly, the gruff old Loxley-lifer who had managed the farm for almost forty years, had agreed to let Abel help him feed some of the new lambs, in anticipation of which treat the little boy had worked himself up into such a frenzy of excitement he'd refused to eat either breakfast or lunch.

'Mr Connelly says I'm a excellent farmer *and* a excellent helper.'

'Well, Mr Connelly would know,' said Tish.

'He says I can stay as long as I like.'

Tish would have to have words with Bill. He meant well, of course, and hopefully Loxley would always be a part of Abel's life. But they also had a life back in Romania. They'd have to go back eventually. There were other matters she needed to broach with Bill too. Like most small Derbyshire farms, Home Farm was losing money.

But only in the last week had Tish discovered just how much it had been costing Loxley to keep the land going, and for how long. They were a mixed farm, which meant they had both arable and livestock, but because of their position and exposure to the elements, as well as the fragmented nature of the land (the entire estate was punctuated with pockets of ancient woodland, so none of the fields was of a decent commercial size), they had suffered more than other local concerns.

The Connelly family had been tenants at Home Farm since before Tish was born. There could be no question of abandoning the farm, or of asking them to move on. But with the maintenance and running costs of Loxley Hall itself easily topping eight hundred thousand a year, not including big-ticket items like roof repairs or fixing the internal damage wreaked by Jago's friends, it was hard to see just *how* they were going to support a failing farm as well. Tish's father, Henry, had already remortgaged all of the smaller properties on the estate during his lifetime, including Home Farm. Short of the not-to-be-considered sale, this left Tish precious little wiggle room. At the very least she needed to sit down with Bill Connelly and go through the numbers.

Three weeks ago, Tish had asked George Arkell, a financial advisor and family friend, to come up to Loxley and to help her devise a plan for getting the estate back on an even keel. George's prognosis was less than heartening.

'Do you want the good news or the bad news?' he asked her.

'Good news,' said Tish.

'The good news is, the National Trust will probably contribute to repairs in the public wings of the house. That could end up reducing your projected deficit for the year by as much as thirty-five per cent.'

Tish brightened. 'That is good news! So how much money is that, then?'

'Around half a million pounds.'

'George! That's wonderful!'

'Yeeess,' said George. 'Except that it leads us on to the bad news.'

'Which is?'

'You still need to find approximately nine hundred and sixty thousand pounds just to cover your current costs, interest payments on the loans, that sort of thing.'

'Oh.'

'Yes. Oh. And your projected income for the year, from visitors, farming and other revenue combined is . . .' He paused, flipping through the notes on his lap '. . . ah, here we are. Eighty-five thousand, one hundred and twenty-eight pounds and sixty-two pence. Before tax.'

Tish looked suitably crestfallen.

'You have to raise some capital,' George told her firmly. 'That means you must sell some land, property, paintings, or most likely a combination of all three. Once you've done that, we can work on consolidating your various debts. Then, with any luck, we find some reliable tenants to pay *market rates* for all of the remaining properties.'

'I can't evict the Connellys,' Tish protested.

George ploughed on. 'And finally, we come up with some sort of long-term strategy for the future. Something that will turn Loxley into a going concern that pays for itself.'

'Such as?'

'It could be tourism-based, holiday lets or what have you; it could be organic farming, conferences, shooting parties. Dirt bikes. I don't know.'

'*Dirt bikes?*' said Tish. 'Are you mad? In our peaceful little valley? The village would be up in arms, and quite rightly too.'

'I understand,' said George, who did. His own family had lost their ancestral pile fifteen years ago, casualties of the collapse of Lloyd's of London. He knew how heartbreaking it was to be the generation who broke the chain of trust, who lost it all after hundreds of years of careful estate management. Times were changing, though. All over England, estates far grander and wealthier than Loxley were going under. 'But I'm afraid if you don't find large amounts of ready cash in the coming months, and come up with a radical rethink about the estate's future, you're going to have to sell up. You know, the National Trust are cash-rich at the moment. They'd take excellent care of the place.'

'No,' Tish shuddered. 'Never. Loxley stays in private hands. In Crewe family hands, if I have anything to do with it. My God, if Daddy could hear this conversation he'd be spinning.'

'Actually,' said George, 'I suspect none of this would have surprised your father in the least. Henry knew which way the cookie was crumbling. That's why he mortgaged everything to the hilt and changed his will to cut out Jago. But he should have warned you how tough it would be.'

Tish couldn't bring herself to blame her father. He'd done his best. Day after day she sat slumped over his papers, praying for inspiration to strike, for some solution to present itself that did not involve turfing out her tenants or – horror of horrors – selling her soul to the National bloody Trust.

There must be a way to make Loxley profitable. There just must be.

Once she was dry, she pulled on the same jeans and holey red sweater she'd been wearing for the past three days, and made her way down to the kitchen. With its constantly lit log-burning stove, it was by far the warmest room in the house. As such it had become the nerve centre of Operation

Find A Miracle, as Tish now called her efforts to revive Loxley's finances, taking over from Henry's cold, draughty office, at least until the weather warmed up.

'You look terrible,' said Mrs Drummond with motherly concern when Tish walked in. 'You're no good to anyone if you don't sleep, you know. Or eat. Let me cook you a proper breakfast.'

Tish sighed, but did not protest. Mrs D's idea of a 'proper' breakfast was a fried calorie bomb so fat-drenched it could probably fatally block one's arteries just by looking at it. But feeding people up was Mrs D's vocation, and it applied as much to Tish as to Abel, who must have gained half his bodyweight since he came to Loxley, but whom Mrs Drummond still invariably referred to as 'that poor little mite' or, sometimes, 'skin and bone'.

'Not still pining over that Michael, are you?' Mrs Drummond asked, cracking three eggs into a sizzling pan full of butter.

'No,' lied Tish.

'Good. Because you know what I always say about the Frogs.'

'Yes, Mrs D. I know.'

How Tish wished she had never confided in Mrs Drummond about Michel. After a few too many glasses of red one night, it had seemed like a good idea to open her heart. But ever since then she'd been subjected to daily lectures on how one could 'never trust a Frenchman' because they were 'all cowards'. The xenophobia was entirely well meant, but Tish found it draining.

'Oh, no fried bread for me please,' she protested. 'It gives me dreadful indigestion.'

'Nonsense, lovie. You're just eating it too quickly,' said Mrs D, cheerfully dropping two battered slices of Hovis into the heart-attack pan. 'I'm going into Castleton later. Do you need anything?'

'No thanks,' said Tish. This was good news, though. She had a string of begging phone calls to make this morning to Loxley's various creditors, and was relieved Mrs D had errands to run. These things were even harder with an audience.

Just as Mrs D plopped Tish's mountainous breakfast down in front of her, the doorbell rang. Both women looked surprised.

'Are we expecting anyone?' Mrs Drummond sounded faintly accusing, as if Tish were still a teenager and had invited friends over without asking.

'Not that I know of,' said Tish, getting up. 'It's probably just a delivery.'

'Ah ah ah!' Mrs D held up an admonishing finger. 'You sit right there and eat, madam. I'll get the door. Running yourself ragged,' she muttered, shuffling out into the hallway. 'It's no wonder you look like you're half dead.'

Tish had taken only two bites of fried egg before she heard the raised voices. One was unmistakably Mrs D's, shrill and strident, the way she always sounded when she was rattled. The other was also a woman's voice, but younger, and conciliatory despite the volume. From her nasal tone, it sounded to Tish as if she might be American.

Tish moved to the door so she could hear what they were saying.

'If I could just speak to the owner,' the American girl pleaded. 'I'd only need a few minutes of his time.'

'I've told you.' Mrs Drummond was practically shouting. 'The owner is busy. And even if she weren't she would *not* be interested.'

'She? Oh, I'm sorry. I understood the house belonged to a Mr Jago Crewe.'

'Good day,' said Mrs Drummond briskly. Tish heard the front door slam. A moment later, Mrs D reappeared in the kitchen looking flustered.

'What on earth was all that about?' asked Tish.

'Oh, nothing. Some dreadful American woman.' Mrs Drummond shook her head in disgust. 'Very pushy. She's gone now.'

'Well, what did she want?'

'Want? I'll tell you what she wanted. She wanted to buy the manor! Can you imagine the cheek of it? She kept saying Loxley was "perfect" and she had to have it. As if it were a scarf she'd seen in a shop window! I told her the house wasn't for sale, and that she was trespassing, but she wouldn't take no for an answer, cheeky little thing. Kept asking to talk to . . . oh my good gracious!'

Tish followed Mrs Drummond's gaze to the kitchen window. A dark-haired girl had her face pressed to the glass. She was smiling and waving, apparently trying to get Tish's attention.

'There she is again.' Picking up a broom, Mrs Drummond waved it at the window as if she were trying to scare away a bat. 'Shoo! Get out!'

Tish giggled. She'd had precious few laughs recently, but this was like a scene from a *Carry On* film. 'I think I should go and talk to her.'

'Talk to her? Don't be silly, Letitia. The woman's plainly a lunatic.'

Watching Mrs Drummond jabbing her broom at the window, Tish thought it debatable who was the lunatic. Unbolting the scullery door, she walked out into the kitchen garden.

'Can I help you?'

The girl stepped away from the window. She was extremely

pretty, Tish noticed, with a mane of glossy, dark hair that shone like a Herbal Essences advertisement. She was also woefully underdressed for the Derbyshire spring weather, in a thin white cotton blouse, fringed suede miniskirt and bare legs. She looked like an extremely lost Pocahontas.

'Are you the owner?' she asked, extending an elegant, French-manicured hand.

'Sort of,' said Tish. 'Not exactly. It's a bit complicated. I'm Letitia Crewe.'

'Rainbow,' said the girl, shaking hands warmly.

'That's your *name*?' said Tish, realizing too late how rude it sounded. Luckily, the girl didn't seem to mind.

'I know,' she grinned. 'What can I say? My parents were Californian hippies. Still are. I actually have a sister called Sunshine, believe it or not.'

Not sure how she was supposed to react to this piece of information, Tish said nothing.

'Look, do you mind if I come in?' said Rainbow, breaking the silence. 'I've got a business proposal I'd like to make you and it is *super*-cold out here.'

Five minutes later, having convinced a deeply suspicious Mrs Drummond to go into Castleton and leave the two of them alone, Tish made a pot of Lapsang tea and sat down with Rainbow at the kitchen table.

'So, what's this all about?'

'Simple,' said Rainbow. 'I want your house.'

'Oh.' Tish looked disappointed. 'I'm sorry but, as I think my housekeeper explained, Loxley isn't for sale. It's been in my family for centuries.'

'Oh, I know *that*,' said Rainbow, taking a sip of her tea and almost gagging. It tasted like burned rubber. 'I don't want to buy it. I want to borrow it.'

Tish brightened. 'Lease it, you mean?' Though she hadn't intended on doing it so soon, it was certainly part of her plan to find a reliable, paying tenant for Loxley eventually. Admittedly, she hadn't pictured this person as a squaw-like twenty-something American hippy named Rainbow, but that was no reason to look a gift horse in the mouth.

'Not exactly,' said Rainbow. Reaching into her purse, she pulled out a business card and handed it to Tish.

'*FSL Location Scouts*,' Tish read aloud. 'You work for a film company?'

'We work for a bunch of film companies,' said Rainbow. 'Right now I'm working for one of the biggest directors in Hollywood. You've heard of Dorian Rasmirez of course?'

Tish looked blank.

'Oh, come *on*,' said Rainbow incredulously. '*Love and Regrets*? *Sixteen Days*?' In Rainbow's world, not having heard of Dorian Rasmirez was like not knowing the Pope or the President of the United States.

'I don't go to the cinema very often,' said Tish.

'Well, take my word for it, Rasmirez is huge. He's about to shoot a remake of *Wuthering Heights*.'

'Oh,' said Tish, 'I adore that book! How wonderful.'

'Uh-huh,' said Rainbow. 'His production company, Dracula, hired my company to find him a suitable location for the shoot. I think this place would be perfect as Thrushcross Grange.'

'Really?' For a moment, Tish was flattered. But reality quickly kicked in. Loxley was already in a serious state of disrepair. The last thing it needed was a film crew running around the place, lugging heavy equipment and ricocheting off the furniture. Tish remembered reading a horror story in one of the Sunday papers about the damage done to stately homes used in film shoots. Groombridge Place in

Kent had apparently taken months to restore after *Pride and Prejudice*.

'I'm not sure,' she said hesitantly to Rainbow. 'What would it involve?'

'Well, we'd need the complete run of the house. You'd have to move out. And we'd want to start filming as soon as possible, next week ideally. I know Mr Rasmirez's budget is pretty tight on this project, so the actors, cast and crew would all live here during the shoot, or as many of them as we can squeeze in anyway—'

'Let me stop you there,' said Tish. 'I'm afraid there's no way I would consider moving out.' Memories of Jago's squatter friends were still fresh in her mind. A few more weeks and the damage they caused to Loxley might have been irreparable.

Rainbow hesitated. Normally it was an absolute pre-requisite that a location be empty before filming could begin. Partly for insurance purposes, and partly because directors typically did not take kindly to having nervous homeowners getting under their feet, complaining about their work and generally making a nuisance of themselves. But in this case, it might be the lesser of two evils. Rainbow had presented Dorian with dozens of locations over the past three months, and he'd rejected all of them. He was desperate to start shooting, but his list of specifications was insanely specific and his willingness to compromise nil. Not only was Loxley literally *perfect* as the Grange, but the farm over the hill might just work as their Wuthering Heights too (L-shaped, grey stone, forbidding, isolated). Rainbow couldn't afford to let Tish say no.

'Well, we could talk about that,' she said vaguely. 'You might not have to move. Did I mention that the movie stars Viorel Hudson? I sure wouldn't mind sharing a house with him.'

She winked conspiratorially, but if dropping Vio's name had been intended as an incentive, it failed miserably.

'Viorel Hudson?' Tish struggled to place the name. 'Wasn't he that Romanian boy, the one that Martha Hudson adopted in the eighties? Is he an actor now, then?'

'Just a little bit,' said Rainbow. She tried a different tack. 'Of course, you'd be well compensated.'

This approach was much more effective.

'How well?' said Tish. In her mind she began drawing lines: She wouldn't do it for less than seventy-five thousand. It wasn't worth the risk to the building. Or maybe fifty thousand should be the cutoff?

'I'd have to talk to my client before I could give you a final number,' said Rainbow. 'But it would be somewhere in the region of a hundred thousand.'

'A hundred thousand. Dollars?'

'Sterling. Per week.'

'Per *week*?' Tish's voice had suddenly gone up an octave. 'I see. And how many, er . . . how many weeks would you, er . . . would you want the, er . . .?'

'A minimum of eight,' said Rainbow. 'Possibly twelve. Depends on a bunch of factors – how soon we could start being the main one.'

Tish struggled to conceal her elation. *A hundred grand a week, for a minimum of eight weeks!* That was almost enough to put them back in the black. She wouldn't have to sell Home Farm, not this year anyway. Even better, if they started shooting right away, she could be back in Romania by the end of the summer. The thought of returning to Oradea to face Michel and Fleur in person filled her with dread. But the longer she postponed it, the worse she knew it would get. *The kids need me*, she told herself. *I can't hide out here forever. Curcubeu won't run itself.* For the first time she realized that the girl's name was Rainbow – the same name as her children's home. *Maybe her coming here was a sign?*

Rainbow pulled out her BlackBerry and started making notes. 'Do you happen to know the name of your neighbours who own that farm over the hill?'

'Home Farm?' said Tish.

'I guess. I only saw one house over there, grey, kinda ugly? If you could convince whoever owns it to let us shoot there too, we'd pay you a commission fee over and above whatever you make on this place.'

'Actually, Home Farm belongs to the Loxley estate.'

Rainbow beamed. 'It does?'

Thinking on her feet, Tish added, 'Yes. But filming there might be a little trickier. It's a working farm, you see, with sitting tenants. We rely on them to provide a large part of our income –' *about sixty-eight pence last year* –'and the summer months are a very important time. I don't know if I'd be comfortable, what with all the upheaval—'

'We'll double the fee,' said Rainbow, not batting an eyelid.

Tish suddenly felt faint. Double eight hundred. That was one point six million.

'Interesting,' she squeaked. 'Well, I'll, er, I'll certainly think about it. Perhaps you'd better speak to your client. Mr Ramon, was it?'

'Rasmirez,' said Rainbow. *Was this girl for real?*

'Exactly. Let's see what Mr Rasmirez says. When you're in a position to make me a firm offer, we'll talk again.'

'We sure will,' said Rainbow. 'Is it OK if I take some pictures before I go?'

Mrs Drummond arrived back from Castleton just as Rainbow was leaving. They passed one another on the drive, Rainbow waving excitedly as she sped past, oblivious to the housekeeper's frosty glare.

'You got rid of her, then?' said Mrs Drummond, staggering into the kitchen weighed down with Waitrose bags.

'Mrs D!' Relieving her of the groceries, Tish picked her up and twirled her around like an excited child.

'Good heavens, Letitia. What *are* you doing?' she protested. 'Have you been drinking?'

'Not yet,' said Tish triumphantly. 'But that's an excellent idea. Do we have any champagne in the cellar?'

'Champagne?' the housekeeper frowned. 'It's one o'clock in the afternoon.'

'I know,' said Tish. Setting Mrs Drummond on the floor, she suddenly felt terribly emotional. Before she knew it, her eyes were welling up with tears.

'Darling, whatever's the matter?' Mrs Drummond put a hand on her shoulder. 'Was it that horrid American girl? Did she upset you?'

Tish shook her head. 'She saved us, Mrs D. She saved Loxley. It's going to be all right after all.'

PART TWO

CHAPTER NINE

'I'm not asking for directions again, OK? I am not doing it.'

Chuck MacNamee folded his bulging arms across his broad chest with an air of finality. A fifty-seven-year-old ex-marine, Chuck did not, as he was fond of telling his fellow crew members, 'take any shit.' He'd worked in the film business for fifteen years as a driver/set builder/security guard/jack of all trades, ever since he got out of prison (a small matter of a credit fraud and a particularly humourless judge), and Dorian Rasmirez had given him the chance that no one else would, hiring him as a runner on *Love and Regrets*. Fanatically loyal to Dorian, and generally beloved on set as a good-natured practical joker, even Chuck had his limits.

He'd spent the last four hours trying to drive an articulated lorry through country lanes so narrow they'd have been hard pressed to accommodate an overweight donkey. He'd already stopped twice to ask directions from old men with impenetrable accents, and each time he'd been sent still deeper into the wilds of rural Derbyshire. And, throughout this wild goose chase, he'd been harangued every five minutes by Deborah Raynham, a twenty-two-year-old 'cameraperson',

Christ preserve us, who kept sighing and mumbling, 'If you'd only look at the *map* . . .' under her breath.

They had now reached a T-junction in a ridiculously pretty village, tantalizingly called 'Loxley'. But was there a sign to Loxley Hall? Was there a sign to *anywhere*? Was there fuck.

'Fine,' said Deborah, flinging the crumpled Ordnance Survey map on the floor of the cab in a fit of temper. 'I'll ask then. You stay here and sulk like a five-year-old.'

Deborah was not especially pretty in Chuck's opinion: too short and pale with a snub nose and mousy brown hair that she wore scraped back in a tight bun. But when she got angry there was a certain fieriness to her that seemed to animate her features in a not-unattractive way. Chuck thought how irritated Deborah would be if she knew what he was thinking, and smiled.

'I'm glad you find this funny,' Deborah snapped, opening the passenger door and jumping down onto the wet grass of the village green. 'Let's hope Mr Rasmirez shares your *wacky* sense of humour.'

Unlike the rest of the crew, Deborah was not a fan of Chuck MacNamee. He'd sat next to her on the flight from LA, fallen instantly asleep and proceeded to snore like a fat fucking walrus for ten straight hours. No one in that cabin had got a wink of sleep. Then, once they'd arrived in England, red-eyed with exhaustion, Chuck had immediately appointed himself head of operations, ordering the camera crew around like a tyrannical ship's captain, but always saving his most patronizing asides for Deborah. Every other sentence began with: 'When you've been in this business as long as I have, missy . . .' *Missy?* The guy was a total dinosaur. And, to top it all off, he had the navigational skills of a deaf bat after one too many Jack Daniel's.

Wuthering Heights was the first feature film Deborah had

ever worked on. She was wildly excited about meeting Dorian Rasmirez, and hopefully impressing him with her work, her professionalism. But now, thanks to Cap'n Chuck, she and her crew were going to arrive so late they would almost certainly lose the first day's shooting. Directors rarely took kindly to this sort of mishap.

On the plus side, Deborah had never been to England before. She'd actually never been out of the States, although she had no intention of admitting this to Chuck MacNamasshole. It was a delight to discover that the British countryside really *was* like something out of a Beatrix Potter book. Loxley village was enchanting, with its stream and its little bridge and a brightly painted maypole with ribbons standing proud in the middle of the green. As she stepped out of the cab, Deborah heard the ancient church clock strike three. Closing her eyes, she breathed in the intoxicating smell of newly mown grass and fresh, floral summer air, and said a silent prayer of thanks that she'd landed this job. It was hard to believe that twenty-four hours ago she'd woken up in smog-ridden Culver City.

'Afternoon, my love. What can I get for you?'

The old woman behind the counter at the village shop was fat and friendly. Her hair was blue – literally blue, as bright and bold as an M&M, which was a little disconcerting – but her accent was intelligible, to Deborah's great relief.

'I'm looking for Loxley Hall. I wondered if you might be able to direct me?'

The old woman's face lit up. Marjorie Johns had run Loxley Village Stores for the last thirty-five years, and the most exciting thing to happen in all that time was when Des Lynam had popped in one Sunday morning for his paper, back in 1987. But this? This was something else. An American accent in Loxley could only mean one thing: this girl must be one of the film people. From Hollywood! Word that Tish Crewe was hiring out Loxley as a film set had inevitably got out in the village. For the last three weeks the talk in The Carpenter's Arms had been of little else.

'I can do better than that, my darling.' Bustling out from behind the counter, Marjorie shooed her one other customer out of the shop with a brusque, 'Not now, Wilf', turned the sign on the door to 'CLOSED' and positively beamed at Deborah. 'I can take you up there myself.'

Deborah Raynham would probably have been relieved to know that, less than three miles away, Dorian Rasmirez was having an equally trying time locating his location.

'Fuck!' Slamming his fist down on the dashboard of his rented Volkswagen Golf, Dorian cursed the British for their obsession with gear sticks. Was the whole country stuck in the fucking Dark Ages? 'Fuck, fuck and double fucking FUCK.'

The Hertz office at Manchester Airport had had no budget or mid-range automatic cars available when Dorian showed up this morning. His choice had been to pay fifteen hundred a week for a luxury automatic sports car he didn't need, or two hundred for a 'reliable' dark green manual Golf GTI. He'd taken the Golf, smugly congratulating himself for his thriftiness, and proceeded to stall the damn thing approximately every five minutes on the apparently endless drive out to Loxley Hall. No one had thought fit to warn him that rural Derbyshire could only be navigated by means of single-lane roads about the width of your average drinking straw, many of them set at gradients at which one would usually expect to use crampons. Nor had he been prepared for the baffling lack of signposts (one sign per five junctions seemed to be the policy), or the thick accents of the two locals from whom he had misguidedly asked directions.

Leaning back in the driver's seat, he took a deep breath

and willed himself to calm down. OK, so he was hours late, on his way to a location he'd paid well over the odds for, despite having only seen it in photographs. *Why? I must have been mad!* But at least the scenery was beautiful. This time his car had spluttered to a halt at the top of a rise, right where the narrow lane opened onto a gloriously wide vista. Below Dorian, the Hope Valley spread out like an emerald carpet, criss-crossed with the glinting silver threads of the river Derwent and its myriad tiny tributaries. The landscape was an intoxicating mixture of the bleak and wild, up on the fells themselves, and the rich, pastoral milk-and-honey beauty of the valley floor, with its gold stone villages, lush farmland and pockets of ancient woodland, a tapestry of old England.

Dorian had arrived in England two days ago, and spent most of his waking hours since then meeting with his London bankers, Coutts, trying to get them to increase the already very substantial loan they'd made him a few months ago. He'd been booked on the early flight to Manchester this morning but, thanks to a fraught dawn phone call with Chrissie in Romania, he'd missed the plane. Saskia had a low-grade fever, apparently, and Chrissie was demanding that Dorian fly home to join her at their daughter's bedside.

'But honey,' Dorian protested, 'you just told me the doctor said it wasn't dangerous.'

'Not *yet*,' said Chrissie darkly. 'What if she takes a turn for the worse?'

Dorian bit his lip and counted to ten. 'By the time I land she'll probably be over it. I'll have to turn around and come right back again. It doesn't make sense.'

'Oh, I see.' He could hear the resentment in Chrissie's voice. 'So what you're saying is your work is more important to you than your child.'

'No! Of course not. Saskia's far more important—'

'So come home.'

'Honey, be reasonable. Today's the first day of set-up on location. I have twenty crew arriving. My cast'll be here in a week, and you know how much there is to get done before we can start rolling. I can't just come home on a whim every time there's a problem.'

In retrospect, his use of the word 'whim' had probably been a mistake. In any event, he was already exhausted by the time he finally landed in Manchester, with Chrissie's screams still ringing in his ears. The subsequent three hours spent chasing his tail round the Derbyshire countryside had done little to improve his temper.

Pulling up on the handbrake, he looked again at the crumpled map on the passenger seat. According to this, he was practically on top of Loxley Hall. He prayed that when he finally got there the owner wouldn't want to chew his ear off about taking care of the place, or lecture him about his crew remembering to take their boots off when they came inside. They were saving money by staying at the house, rather than pitching camp in local hotels, an arrangement that would also make it easier to keep a lid on the inevitable production gossip. Even the actors would be sleeping on site. Unfortunately, however, the owner had made it a condition of the deal that she too be allowed to remain on the property throughout the shoot, a proviso that made Dorian's heart sink.

Letitia Crewe. That was her name. It sounded like something out of an Agatha Christie novel. Dorian could picture Loxley's chatelaine now: a meddling old bag in twinset and pearls, bossing everybody about like the Queen while her hunting dogs chewed up his expensive equipment.

He turned dejectedly back to his map. *One problem at a time*.

* * *

Back at the house, Tish was having a difficult morning. Rainbow, the sweet girl from the location company, had told her not to worry about the film crew's arrival.

'You won't know we're there,' she assured her. 'Two reps from my firm will be on site, plus another two from Dracula Productions. We'll do everything: set up the catering vans and portable washrooms, inspect the trailers, plumb in the showers . . .'

'You're bringing your own showers?' said Tish.

Rainbow laughed. 'Of course. And laundry facilities. This is a sixteen-man crew, plus nine live-in cast. Trust me, a private house cannot deal with that amount of laundry.'

Tish was to provide beds in the house for Dorian Rasmirez and four of the film's main stars, including Viorel Hudson and the infamous Sabrina Leon. Everyone else would sleep, eat, bathe and generally exist in a makeshift gypsy camp in the grounds. Apparently, half the crew were still lost somewhere in the Derbyshire countryside but, true to her word, Rainbow had shown up at Loxley at the crack of dawn with the other half, hammering and drilling and installing like a troupe of whirling dervishes. Unless one were deaf, or blind, or ideally both, it was hard to see how exactly one was supposed not to notice them. Or how one was supposed to relax, when an important and no doubt irascible Hollywood director one had never met was about to turn up on one's doorstep, there were no clean towels anywhere in the house, and one's son was tearing down the hallways shrieking with excitement and yelling, 'Ben Ten Alien Force! Jet Ray!' at anyone who came within ten feet of him. Thank God it was only Mr Rasmirez arriving today, thought Tish. Abel would need a shot of horse tranquillizer before the actors turned up.

'Oh my goodness. I think it's him. Is it him?'

Tish was upstairs in the blue bedroom, one of Loxley's

less shabby, vaguely more presentable guest suites, plumping up the pillows for the third time in as many minutes and driving Mrs D mad with last-minute requests – wouldn't a Hollywood director expect a soap dish without chips on it? Did Mrs D think it wise to leave a dyptique Figuier candle by the bed, or was that a blatant fire hazard? Through the open window, she saw a dark green Golf pulling up, its gears screaming for mercy before the engine finally cut out with an unhealthy sounding 'pop'.

'Whoever it is, they're a rotten driver,' said Mrs D, smoothing down the Liberty bedspread and shooing Tish out of the room. Mrs Drummond had come to terms with Tish's decision to allow Loxley to be 'invaded', as she put it, by a swarm of ghastly Americans. She understood the economic rationale. But she didn't have to like it.

'Would he drive a hatchback, do you think?' asked Tish. 'I'd rather imagined a red Ferrari.'

The doorbell rang. Embarrassed at herself for being so flustered, Tish patted down her flyaway hair and hurried downstairs to answer it.

Standing outside the door, on flagstones that looked as old as the surrounding hills, Dorian gazed up in wonder at the house. It was even better close up than it had been from the end of the drive, and a thousand times better than it had looked in Rainbow's pictures. It was grander than the Thrushcross Grange of his imagination, with its picture windows and turrets and exquisite, sweeping expanse of oak-dotted parkland but. from a cinematographer's point of view, it was utter perfection. He couldn't have asked for a more romantic house, a more English house. As you drove into the garden proper, you crossed a wide, dancing silver river by means of a positively Shakespearean stone bridge (*what scenes could I shoot there, I wonder?*). Even the yew hedges were a gift:

dark and brooding and so thick they must have been planted when the house was built. From the second he saw Loxley, Dorian was in love. Suddenly last night's row with Chrissie and the frustrations of his journey seemed to melt away, like stubborn pockets of snow in the spring sunshine.

No one had answered the doorbell. He pressed it again, picturing Loxley's cantankerous elderly owner hobbling to the front door, a curse on her pursed, cat's-arse lips. Moments later the door flew open. Dorian found himself face to face with a ravishingly pretty girl.

'Hello,' the girl smiled. 'You must be Mr Rasmirez.'

'That's right.' Dorian smiled back. He was glad to see the maids here were not expected to wear uniform. All that stuffy British upper-class posturing made him break out in hives. Indeed, if this girl's clothes were anything to go by, Loxley Hall's dress code made California look formal. In her late twenties, slim and petite, with a natural, tomboyish beauty that effortlessly outshone the surgically perfected look of LA girls, she was wearing cut-off jeans and espadrilles, and a faded pink T-shirt with some charity logo on it that reflected the pink of her cheeks and her incredible, wide, palest pink mouth. She wore no make-up, and her wild blonde hair was tied back with what looked suspiciously like a scrunched-up pair of panties. Tendrils kept escaping across her face, so that she was constantly blowing and swatting them away as she spoke.

'Is Mrs Crewe at home? Letitia Crewe? I'm afraid I'm a little later than I anticipated. I—'

'I'm Tish Crewe,' said the girl, cheerfully extending an unmanicured hand.

Dorian was so surprised, he half expected to hear the anvil-like clang of his jaw hitting the floor, in true cartoon style. This *girl owns* this *house*? It took a good ten seconds for the WI battleaxe of his imagination to fade to black, and for him to regain the power of speech.

'Hi,' he stammered, dropping his battered suitcase and shaking Tish's hand. 'I'm Dorian Rasmirez.'

Trish looked at him curiously, and he realized he must have been staring. 'I'm sorry,' he said awkwardly. 'You're not exactly what I expected.'

'Nor are you,' said Tish, grinning. 'I thought you'd be driving a Ferrari.'

Just then, a battered-looking lorry rumbled through the gates, clattering its way over the bridge and pulling up behind Dorian.

'Hey, boss, sorry we're late.' A burly-looking man jumped out of the cab, followed by an exhausted-looking young girl and . . . *wasn't that Mrs Johns from the village shop?* 'Our sat-nav lost the will to live somewhere north of Manchester.'

'Don't worry,' said Dorian. 'So did mine. Miss Crewe, I'd like you to meet Chuck MacNamee, my crew director.'

Tish extended a hand. As she did so a small human missile appeared out of nowhere in the hallway behind her and flew directly into Dorian's stomach, winding him and almost knocking him off his feet.

'Oh my God,' Tish gasped, 'I am so sorry! Abel! Apologize to Mr Rasmirez this instant.'

The missile looked up sheepishly. For the second time in as many minutes, Dorian did a double take. *Jesus. It's Heathcliff.* The little boy had jet-black hair and wary, watchful blue eyes.

'Sorry,' Abel said, a tad unconvincingly given his broad, cheeky smile. 'I was being Ben Ten and you were the Alien Force.'

'I do apologize.' Tish blushed, as the boy spun around and ran off down the hall.

'That's quite all right,' said Dorian. 'We invading aliens are tougher than we look, you know.'

After Chuck, Deborah and the others had been introduced and driven round to the back of the house to join the rest of the crew, Tish took Dorian inside.

'Sorry again about my son. He's been terribly overexcited about all this,' Tish explained. 'I think the whole village is, to be honest. Heaven knows how Marjorie Johns managed to hijack your lorry already. Come on in.'

Dorian followed her into the hallway. It was considerably less grand inside than the façade of the house suggested. The floors were of the same, rough-hewn stone, more appropriate to a farmhouse than a stately home, and the staircase, though broad and sweeping, was visibly scratched and its runner stained. Kid-related detritus was everywhere: a three-wheeled scooter propped against an antique chest, a pair of muddy Wellington boots kicked off in a hurry into opposite corners, diecast trains lined up carefully at the foot of the stairs then abandoned for a more interesting game. Dorian thought of Saskia's neatly ordered playroom at the Schloss. Chrissie had colour-coded every toy to within an inch of its life, no mean feat when everything was in varying shades of pink.

'Sorry about the mess,' said Tish, reading his mind.

'Not at all,' said Dorian, adding truthfully, 'you don't look old enough to have a son.'

'I feel old enough, believe me.' Tish rolled her eyes.

'I noticed his accent,' said Dorian. 'Your husband . . .?'

'Oh, no,' said Tish. 'I'm not married.' Unbidden, an image of Michel and Fleur skipping down the aisle together hand in hand popped into her mind. She forced it aside.

'Is he adopted?'

It was a very direct question from a total stranger, but, for some reason, Tish found it didn't bother her. Something about Dorian's manner, so respectful and gentle and not at all what she'd expected, put her at ease.

'He is, yes.'

'From Romania?'

Tish looked taken aback. 'I'm impressed you could tell. Most people say he sounds Italian.'

Dorian shrugged. 'I spend a lot of time in Romania, so I know the accent well.'

'You're joking?' Few Americans outside the charity world had even heard of Romania, let alone spent time there. 'How come?'

Dorian grimaced. 'It's kind of a long story.'

'Sorry,' said Tish, misinterpreting his facial expression as boredom. 'Listen to me, wittering on about nothing when you've travelled halfway across the world to get here. Please, follow me. I'll show you to your room.'

The rest of the afternoon passed in a whirlwind of activity. Tish struggled to get through Abel's normal routine of weekend homework, supper and bath, while all through the house and grounds strange men and women tramped around with cameras and light meters and sound machines, politely but completely disrupting everything. Occasionally, Rainbow's apologetic face would pop up at a window, assuring Tish that they were 'nearly done' and should be out of her hair 'momentarily', only to be distracted by Chuck MacNamee and Deborah Raynham arguing loudly behind her. Meanwhile, Mrs Johns from the village shop was still hanging around as dusk fell, in the hope of bumping into Viorel Hudson or Sabrina Leon, despite being told repeatedly by both Mrs Drummond and the crew that no actors were expected till the following Tuesday. It wasn't until after Abel was in bed at eight, and Mrs Drummond had finished complaining for the umpteenth time about the house being like 'Piccadilly Circus' that Dorian Rasmirez reappeared, having not been seen since lunchtime.

Tish was in the kitchen, reheating yesterday's kedgeree, when he walked in.

'Hi there.'

Tish spun around. He'd changed out of the jeans and sweater he'd been wearing earlier into what Tish could only presume was an American's idea of English country attire: green corduroy trousers, with matching green shirt, waistcoat and sports jacket, all topped off with a green-and-brown tweed flat cap. In one arm he held a Barbour jacket that still had the label attached, and in the other a pair of (green) Hunter wellies. *Kermit the Frog goes stalking*, thought Tish, stifling the urge to giggle.

'You wouldn't have a pair of scissors I could borrow, would you?' Dorian gestured to the label on his coat. 'Figured I might need this tomorrow. We'll be doing test shots up at the farm all day. It's beautiful up there by the way. You have an amazing property.'

'Thanks.' Tish opened a drawer and handed him some kitchen scissors. She contemplated explaining that Loxley wasn't really her property at all, but then decided that a potted history of Jago's various self-serving disappearing acts would only confuse things.

Dorian snipped off the tag and slipped the jacket on. 'How do I look?'

Ridiculous, thought Tish, trying to think of a response she could say out loud. Eventually, she came up with, 'Warm.'

'Not really me, huh?' Dorian smiled sheepishly, taking it off. 'No offence, but is it supposed to smell like that?'

Tish turned around. 'Shit!' She'd forgotten all about the kedgeree on the hob. A mini-mushroom cloud of black, fishy smoke now hovered ominously over the frying pan. Pulling it off the heat with one hand and opening the window with the other, she looked down at the sticky blackened mess. 'Oh well. Beans on toast, I suppose.'

'I've got a better idea,' said Dorian. 'Why don't I take you to that quaint little public house I saw on my way up here? It's the least I can do after all your hospitality. The Woodmen or something, I think it was called.'

'The Carpenter's Arms?' said Tish. 'We can't go there.'

'Why not?'

'Because the minute anyone hears an American accent and sees you with me, you'll be mobbed. I don't think you quite appreciate just how little goes on in Loxley. Your film is the most exciting thing that's happened here since the Norman invasion.'

'Well, where then?' said Dorian. 'I'm starving. And, no offence, but I'm not sure how much faith I have in your cooking skills.'

Tish frowned but did not defend the indefensible. 'Fine,' she said, grabbing her car keys from the hook above the Aga. 'I'll ask Mrs D to watch Abel. Follow me.'

The King's Arms in Fittleton was about ten miles from Loxley, a low-beamed, cosy village pub with squashy dog-eared sofas and a log fire that was constantly burning, even on summer evenings.

'This is cute,' said Dorian, nabbing an open table close to the fire. A few of the locals glanced round in mild curiosity when they heard his accent, but they soon resumed their interest in the tense game of darts going on to the left of the bar.

'I haven't been here in years,' said Tish, 'but the food's supposed to be good.' Dorian noticed that she pronounced the word 'yars'. In movies he'd always found the upper-class

British accent grating, but on Tish's lips it was oddly charming and seemed quite unaffected. She ordered a fish pie from the blackboard. Dorian went for the moules marinières, and insisted on an expensive bottle of Sauvignon Blanc for the two of them. He ought to be exhausted. Starting with Chrissie's five a.m. rant this morning, it had been a hell of a day. But for some reason he felt excited and revived. Both Loxley and Tish had been a pleasant surprise.

'So. Tell me about your family,' he asked. 'You live in that incredible house on your own?'

'I'm not on my own,' said Tish, sipping her wine, which was delicious and tasted of gooseberries. 'I have Abel and Mrs Drummond. And now all of you lot. It's a veritable commune up there.' She explained that she spent most of her time in Romania, and gave him the condensed version of her mother's bohemian life in Rome and Jago's latest Tibetan adventure.

'A cave? He lives in a *cave*?' Dorian cocked his head to one side.

He's attractive, thought Tish. *Not handsome, like Michel, but sort of* joli-laid. *An American Gerard Depardieu.*

'Would you care to elaborate?'

'I'm not sure I can, much,' said Tish. 'My brother's choices have never made a lot of sense to me. But you know, running an estate is hard work. I'm afraid that "incredible house" I live in has an incredible appetite for money. You wouldn't believe how much it costs to run.'

'Oh, you'd be surprised,' said Dorian, biting a chunk out of the warm bread the waitress had left on the table. He gave Tish a brief potted history of his own Romanian background, and how he'd come to inherit the long-lost family Schloss. Tish noticed the way his eyes lit up when he spoke about the castle and its treasures, and the way the light faded when he mentioned his wife, and how hard Chrissie had found the transition to life in Transylvania.

'She's an actress, you know, so she has that temperament.'

Tish didn't know, but nodded understandingly anyway.

'There's a part of her that still craves excitement and adventure,' explained Dorian. 'The Schloss is indescribably beautiful, but it can be lonely, especially when I'm away and Chrissie's on her own with Saskia.'

'Saskia?'

'Our daughter.' Dorian picked up the last remaining mussel from his bowl and sucked it out of its shell. 'She's three.'

Tish thought it odd that they'd been talking about his family life in Romania for fifteen minutes, and this was the first time he'd mentioned a child. 'You must miss her.'

'Sure,' he said, shifting uncomfortably in his seat. Reaching in his wallet, he pulled out a photograph and handed it to Tish. She expected to see a little girl's picture, but instead it was a professional headshot of an attractive blonde woman with tough, slightly angular features. To Tish's eyes, the woman in the photograph looked cold as ice, but maybe it was just a bad picture.

'Chrissie,' said Dorian proudly. 'Stunning, isn't she?'

'Gorgeous,' lied Tish, wondering if Michel carried Fleur's picture around in his wallet and showed it to every stranger he encountered. *I have to stop thinking about Michel.*

'Tell me about Curcubeu,' said Dorian, abruptly changing the subject. 'What exactly is your work there?'

'Anything and everything,' said Tish. 'There's so much need.' And she was off, waxing lyrical about the failings of the Romanian government and the shameful neglect of the country's abandoned children.

'That's incredibly impressive,' said Dorian when she'd

finished, ordering a sticky toffee pudding to share and a second bottle of wine, despite Tish's protests. 'Not many girls your age would give up a life of privilege back home to go and do something like that.'

Tish frowned. 'You mustn't think me some sort of saint. I like the work. Oradea's a dump, but Romania's got some strange magic to it, something that keeps drawing you back there – despite the corruption and the bureaucracy and the godawful winters. But I imagine I don't need to tell you that.'

'No.' Dorian smiled.

'Strange, isn't it, our paths crossing like this?' said Tish. 'And both of us having a Romanian connection?'

They talked solidly for another hour and a half, about Romania, life and literature – Tish had almost as encyclopaedic a knowledge of the Brontë sisters' work as Dorian did, and could practically recite *Wuthering Heights* and *Jane Eyre* – and about Viorel Hudson and Sabrina Leon, Dorian's Heathcliff and Cathy.

'Viorel has a Romanian connection too, doesn't he?' asked Tish.

'You might not want to bring that up when you meet him,' warned Dorian. 'I tried, but Hudson has a low opinion of the motherland.'

Tish, who spent her life in Romanian orphanages like the one she assumed Viorel Hudson had been dumped in, didn't blame him.

'I'll say this for him, though: he's a terrific actor,' said Dorian. 'The minute I thought about doing this movie, I knew I wanted to cast Viorel. He was born for the role.'

'And Sabrina?' asked Tish. 'I've only ever seen her in gossip magazines, so I don't know if she's a good actress or not, but she doesn't look like an obvious choice for Cathy.'

'Not looks-wise, perhaps. But if you want someone as wilful and spoiled and frankly insane as Catherine Earnshaw, Sabrina's your girl.'

'Catherine wasn't insane,' protested Tish. 'She was sensible. She chose a decent man over a wicked one.'

Dorian looked at Tish quizzically. 'You admire that, do you? Being sensible rather than passionate?'

Tish blushed. 'I think passion can be overrated.' Suddenly the conversation seemed to have taken a rather personal turn. 'But I suppose, in an ideal world, one wouldn't have to choose.'

There was an awkward silence. Tish changed the subject. 'Is she as pretty as she looks in the pictures?'

'Sabrina? About a hundred times prettier,' said Dorian truthfully. 'That's part of the problem. For Sabrina and Cathy.'

'What do you mean?'

'Just that when you look like that, no one ever says no to you.'

By the time they left it was almost midnight.

'I'll drive if you like,' said Dorian.

Remembering the sound of his gear-changing when he'd arrived this morning, not to mention the fact that the drive from Manchester had taken him three and a half hours, Tish declined the offer.

'That's OK,' she said. 'You drank all that second bottle so you're definitely over the limit.'

They made it back to Loxley without incident. Tish took them home the back way, via Home Farm, which looked even dourer, bleaker and more soul-wrenching by moonlight. Dorian's heart leapt at the sight of it. *That's my Wuthering Heights*. He'd been dreaming this movie for two years now. Today, he'd felt as though he was walking into his own dream. Tomorrow, he would spend all day up at the farm, measuring light and distance and planning the exterior long-shots with Chuck and the camera crew. He couldn't wait.

'I'm sorry about all the disruption,' he said to Tish once they got back to the house. 'There'll be a few days of crazi-ness, but once the cast get here next week and we start shooting on a regular schedule, everything should calm down. We'll try not to get under your feet too much.'

'You mustn't worry about me,' said Tish. 'Abel and I are quite used to chaos, believe me. Besides, you've paid for the house. For the next eight weeks you must consider it yours.'

'Thank you,' said Dorian, kissing her on the cheek. 'Good night.'

Ten minutes later, tucked up in her own bed, Tish reflected on how strange life could be. The very fact of someone coming to Loxley Hall to shoot a film in the first place was unlikely enough. But that that person should turn out to be a Romanian . . . how small-worldy was that? She didn't really believe in fate. And yet it did seem uncanny that Dorian Rasmirez should have found his way to Loxley and, in a very real sense, saved them from falling into the abyss. *My knight in shining armour.*

Wriggling her toes under the blankets, luxuriating in the warmth of her bed, she thought about Dorian's kind, animated face, the odd mixture of anxiety and love with which he'd spoken about his wife, and his strange detachment from his daughter. After weeks of worrying what he'd be like, she was relieved and surprised to find that she liked him.

Perhaps this summer wasn't going to be such an ordeal after all?

CHAPTER TEN

Sabrina Leon adjusted her new Prada aviators and arranged her hair into tousled, rock-chick perfection. Heathrow was Sabrina's second favourite airport in the world after LAX. There was always a scrum of paparazzi waiting for her when she walked through the electric double doors at terminal three, reminding her that she was still famous, still relevant, still alive. If anything, the Brits worshipped celebrity even more than the Americans, although they certainly delighted in seeing the mighty fallen. Sabrina was prepared for the inevitable heckles, and the pasting she was certain to get at the hands of the British tabloid press. In fact, she was looking forward to it. After three weeks of 'lying low', as her agent called it (*playing dead, more like it*), immersing herself in Sacha Gervasi's brilliantly written screenplay till she was so gorged on Cathy Earnshaw she could have barfed out her lines, Sabrina was ready for some attention. At Heathrow she knew she would get it, and she wasn't about to walk through customs till she was sure she looked like a total fucking vixen.

Write what you want about me, you bastards, but you're not getting a bad picture.

'You got everything?'

Billy, Sabrina's Irish bodyguard of the past tumultuous four years, nodded from behind a trolley piled high with Louis Vuitton suitcases. Sabrina had brought two bodyguards with her to England: Billy, who was really more of a friend and had been a total rock since her life turned to shit earlier this year; and Enrique, an enormous hunk of Hispanic muscle who had the brain power of a special-needs rabbit and the quick reactions to match, but who looked good in photos and could always be relied upon to act as an impromptu human dildo should Sabrina find herself in need of one. She usually travelled with at least four guards, as well as Camille and Sean, her two closest hangers-on (officially her 'stylist' and 'personal advisor'), but she knew Rasmirez would have a fit if she brought anything resembling an entourage onto his set. The guy was so tediously holier-than-thou about keeping things low-key, not to mention obsessed with secrecy and having as few bodies as possible on the production. 'Fewer people means less chance of leaks,' he'd told Sabrina endlessly, like the world's preachiest parrot. He'd only divulged the movie's location to his actors forty-eight hours ago, expecting them to drop everything and get on a plane like a bunch of lemmings.

'All set, ma'am.' Billy's gentle brogue was reassuring. 'You sure you're ready for this, now? D'you want me to go in front?'

'No,' said Sabrina, her dark eyes glinting with a combination of fear and excitement. 'I can handle it.'

As it turned out, she couldn't.

The arrivals hall was complete insanity. A zoo of photographers and reporters literally trampled people underfoot, knocking their cameras into mothers and children and elderly people in their desperation to get to Sabrina. Meanwhile, from all sides, reporters screamed out inflammatory questions, desperate to get a reaction that they could spin into a story.

'Is it true you've come to Britain because no American director will work with you?'

'Dorian Rasmirez *is* American, asshole,' Sabrina shot back.

'What were you in rehab for, Sabrina?'

'Exhaustion.'

'Are you an alcoholic?'

'No. Are you a moron?'

'Is it true you were being treated for sex addiction? How many men have you slept with?'

'Six thousand. That's why I was exhausted.'

A few of the reporters did at least laugh at that.

'Have you anything to say to the black community of this country, after your offensive remarks about slavery?'

The press pack was moving in closer. Suddenly Sabrina felt panicked. There were no police, no security at all to protect her. Billy and Enrique were the only things standing between her and being torn to shreds, or at least that was how it felt. Her heart rate quickened and her palms began to sweat.

'Fuck off,' she snarled, edging closer to Enrique, who wrapped a tree-trunk-like arm around her tiny shoulders. A cacophony of cameras whirred into action: *click click click.*

Meanwhile, Billy moved forward, using the luggage trolley as a defensive shield. 'Give her some space please, guys.' A seasoned professional, he knew that firm politeness worked a lot better than aggression in these circumstances, and wondered if Sabrina would ever learn to keep her mouth shut. The sad thing was that – for all her stupid outbursts – she wasn't actually a bad kid. Just scared and insecure as hell, like most actresses.

Finally, they made it outside the terminal building, where

a blacked-out limo was waiting for them. Enrique bundled Sabrina inside, lifting her up one-handed and stuffing her into the back seat like a rag doll, simultaneously pushing back two photographers with his other hand. Sabrina put her head down between her knees and waited for all the banging and shouting to stop. Even once the car pulled away, with Billy in the front seat shouting 'Go, go, go!' at the driver like a marine heading into battle, she looked up to see grown men chasing after them like a pack of slavering hyenas, the flashes on their cameras hopelessly *pop-pop-popping* as the car gained speed.

Only once they'd reached the motorway did Sabrina sit up and take a breath.

'Well that was fucking crazy.'

Billy turned around and gave her a disapproving look. 'You shouldn't have said anything, you know,' he said. 'They'll use it against you.'

'They were attacking me!' protested Sabrina. 'If you guys hadn't been there they'd have torn me limb from fucking limb. You saw it.'

'Yeah. We did. But whoever sees those pictures in tomorrow's papers won't have seen it. All they'll see is you lashing out and swearing. Is it *really* that hard to put your head down and say nothing?'

Yeah, thought Sabrina. *It is. For me it is. I've always been a fighter. If I hadn't fought back, I'd still be in Fresno, pumping some shit into my arm and getting molested by assholes who knew they could get away with it.*

Leaning against Enrique's chest, she felt comforted by the size and smell of him. The awareness of his strength and closeness, combined with her own wildly pumping adrenaline, suddenly gave her a rush of desire. If only they were alone, she'd pull over somewhere and have him take her right there on the back seat. Screw all the fear and tension out of her head.

But sadly they weren't alone. They were with Billy who, as usual, was right. She shouldn't have said anything to the reporters. This movie was her chance, her comeback, her lifeboat back to adulation. She'd already agreed to spend the entire summer holed up in Butt-Fuck Nowhere England with a director who clearly hated her and Vain-o-rel 'you're in my light' Hudson as a co-star, for *no pay*. So the idea that she might have screwed things up for herself before she'd even reached the set filled her with frustration and dread.

'How long till we get there?' she asked morosely.

'According to the sat-nav, three hours,' said Billy. 'Here.' He threw a pillow into the back seat. 'Put Mr Muscle down for five minutes and try and get some sleep.'

'What do you think?'

Viorel looked across Loxley's deer park to the house in the distance. It was still early morning, and a low, dawn mist hung over the grass like a gossamer shroud. In the air he could smell scents at once deeply familiar and long forgotten – wood smoke, mown grass, rain, honeysuckle – smells of the English countryside. It felt bizarre to be standing here next to Dorian Rasmirez, of all people, with the director holding out his hand like a proud father, as if the exquisite Elizabethan manor were his home and not some movie location he'd rented by the hour.

'I think it's perfect,' said Vio. 'Quintessentially English. Merchant Ivory couldn't have dreamed this place up.'

He'd arrived from LA very late last night and gone straight to his room to crash. The housekeeper who'd shown him where he'd be sleeping was a real blast from his boarding-school past, a bossy, no-nonsense matron type who could not have been less impressed by Viorel's movie-star status.

'Clean towels are in the cupboard,' she said brusquely. 'Sheets are changed on Mondays, and if you want a cooked breakfast you need to be down by half-past eight.' She was gone with a swish of her tartan dressing gown before Viorel had a chance to ask her her name, let alone where breakfast would be served, or whether she had such a thing as an alarm clock. As it turned out, he didn't need one. After a fitful night's sleep on a bed that seemed to have been fashioned out of a solid slab of granite, he woke before dawn to the sound of rooks cawing in the trees and had to pinch himself in order to remember that this was *not* in fact 1996, he was *not* in his bedroom in Martha Hudson's Dorset rectory, and that his fabulous LA life, fame and success were *not* merely a beautiful dream from which he had just woken up.

After a cold shower (no hot water till seven, he later learned), he pulled on a pair of vintage Levis and a blue silk Armani sweater and headed downstairs in search of the kitchen and a cup of coffee. Everyone else was asleep, so the house was quiet and gloomy. It took Vio a while to get his bearings. The place was enormous, a veritable maze of corridors, with servants' staircases popping up in unexpected places and leading you into another section of the rabbit warren. Vio had been in hundreds of similar houses growing up: grand, old, down-at-heel. Hundreds of bedrooms, no bathrooms. Everyone living in the kitchen. But his memories of England had not been happy ones, and the familiarity of Loxley Hall made him more queasy than it did nostalgic.

Once he found the kitchen, however, he perked up. It was cheerful and bright, with a large jug full of daffodils on the table and a child's scribbled artwork Blu-tacked to the cupboards. There was real coffee in the fridge, and bacon, and someone had helpfully left a sliced white Hovis loaf and a frying pan out on the table. Two bacon sandwiches and a mug of coffee later, feeling infinitely revived, Vio was just about to explore outside when he ran into Dorian, another early riser. They agreed to take a walk together.

'Wait till you see the farmhouse,' said Dorian excitedly. 'It's like they designed the thing to Brontë's exact specifications. You'll love it.'

Vio followed him down a steeply sloping sheep track.

'You can cross the river at the bottom,' Dorian panted over his shoulder. 'Then it's up the other side and over the hill.'

'What are the family like?' asked Vio, making conversation as they trudged along. 'They're living here for the duration, I gather? That's a bit unorthodox, isn't it?'

'It was cheaper,' said Dorian frankly. 'We've got to save money somewhere if we're going to pay your fee.'

Viorel grinned. 'Touché.'

'Anyway, as it turns out, it's only one girl and her son,' said Dorian. 'Tish Crewe. She's terrific actually.'

Terrific? Vio's ears pricked up. 'How old is she?'

'Mid- to late-twenties, I guess. The kid's five.'

'Cute?'

'Oh, adorable. Five's a great age for a boy.' Dorian tripped over a bramble and almost went flying.

'Not the kid,' Vio laughed, helping him to his feet. 'The girl.'

Dorian frowned. 'She's attractive. Not your type though.'

'Meaning what?' said Viorel. 'I don't have a type.'

'Sure you do,' said Dorian. 'I've seen your press. The girls on your arm are glamazons. Tish isn't glamorous. Besides,' he added, 'she's in love with some French doctor.'

Viorel raised an eyebrow. 'Wow. You've really got to know

this woman. She's confiding in you about her love life already?' He nudged Dorian in the ribs. 'Maybe she likes you.'

'Grow up,' said Dorian crossly.

'Maybe you like *her*?' Viorel teased. 'Am I getting warm, Il Direttore?'

'No, you are not getting *warm*. I'm a happily married man.'

This was stretching a point at the moment, but it was true that Dorian had zero romantic interest in anyone other than Chrissie. Tish Crewe was charming and kind and, if he were honest, Dorian probably was a little star-struck by her family background. He might have inherited what Chrissie would insist on describing as a 'fuck-off castle', but the Crewes clearly sprang from a far more ancient and senior branch of the aristocratic tree. None of which amounted to Dorian 'liking' Tish Crewe, at least not in Viorel Hudson's sense of the word.

'We've been thrown together in the same house for a week,' he said defensively. 'Of course we're going to talk. And yes, I do like her. Just not in the way you mean.'

Viorel looked sceptical but said nothing. They'd reached the river now and began the short but gruelling climb up the other side of the fell. It was still only eight o'clock, and walking in the shade you could feel a distinct chill in the air.

'What time are the others arriving?' asked Viorel, changing the subject.

'Sabrina and Lizzie should be here later this morning,' said Dorian. 'Jamie and Rhys both got in yesterday.'

Lizzie Bayer, a well-known American television actress, was playing Isabella Linton, Heathcliff's wife. Jamie Duggan, a Scottish theatre actor, was playing Catherine's husband, Edgar Linton. And the unknown Rhys Evans had been cast as Hareton Earnshaw, the young Catherine's love interest at the movie's end. Along with Viorel and Sabrina, Lizzie, Jamie and Rhys made up the core cast.

'I'm starting with you and Sabrina, though, first thing tomorrow. You know that, right? Heathcliff's return-from-exile scene, outside Thrushcross Grange?'

'Absolutely,' said Vio. He hoped Sabrina would arrive on time and in a fit state to run through the scene with him privately before the morning. He'd tried to contact her numerous times in LA since the read-through, offering to work on their joint scenes together, but she'd blown him off each time. 'I work better alone,' she told him arrogantly. 'If you're nervous about your scenes, talk to Rasmirez. I'm sure he'd *love* to hear from you.'

Vio was perplexed. 'Have I done something to offend you?' He'd been sweetness and light to Sabrina at the read-through, even sticking up for her afterwards with Dorian. What the fuck was with her attitude?

'You're not important enough to offend me,' said Sabrina rudely, and hung up.

Mind games, thought Vio, fighting down his anger. *She's trying to provoke me so I'll lose my shit on set. Make a dick of myself in front of Rasmirez and take some of the heat off her.*

Too bad, sweetheart. At least one of us knows how to be a professional.

He hoped he'd be able to translate some of the hostility between them into sexual tension on camera. But, after weeks of waiting, he was getting increasingly jittery about how they would play together. This was his five and-a-half-million-dollar lead role, the biggest break of his career. He wanted to get started.

'Whoah.'

After five minutes of climbing, they had reached Home Farm. Vio was suitably impressed. 'I see what you mean,' he said, marvelling at the L-shaped building with its weathered grey stone. Even the thick front door could have been lifted directly from the pages of the novel. 'It's exactly what I pictured. Except . . .'

'Except what?' said Dorian.

'Is it a little small, maybe?'

'Small? I don't think so,' said Dorian, sounding a tad put out. In fact, he'd thought the same thing himself when he first saw the farm eight days ago, and spent much of the last week working on long-angle shots to create a better illusion of size, but it irritated him to have Viorel confirm his doubts. 'We won't be filming inside. I'll show you some of the rushes we did last week of the exterior. It's workable.'

But Viorel was no longer listening.

The front door of the farmhouse had swung open and a figure had emerged, covered from head to toe in thick black soot. Looking up, Dorian saw it too.

'Tish?' he asked tentatively. 'Is that you?' He walked towards the figure. An amused Viorel followed behind.

'Oh, er, hello. Yes.' Flustered, Tish attempted to brush the worst of the coal dust off herself, but it stuck fast, like iron filings to a magnet. She'd been up since seven, trying to rescue a nest of birds from the Connellys' chimney shaft, and had not expected to see Dorian or any of the film people up at the farm at such an early hour.

Leaning forward, Viorel whispered in Dorian's ear. 'Am I imagining things? Or is she naked?'

Disappointingly, he saw as they drew nearer that Tish wasn't naked. At least not quite. Beneath her sooty disguise she was barefoot and wearing nothing but a pair of knickers and a skinny-ribbed vest. *Definitely not a glamazon*, thought Viorel, remembering Dorian's arbitrary description of his 'type'. *Terrific legs though. My goodness.*

'I was . . . we were . . . having a bit of trouble,' Tish babbled nervously, suddenly aware of how ridiculous she must look. 'The chimney sweep's coming this morning, you see, and there's a family of swallows nesting . . .'

She stopped talking. From behind Dorian's familiar, bear-like form, the most divine-looking man Tish had ever seen in her life suddenly emerged like an apparition. A vision in blue, his floppy black hair gleaming like a raven's feathers, he stood there, staring at her. Of course, no one could ever hope to compare with Michel, not in terms of the overall package. But it could not be denied that on looks alone – when it came to regularity of features, proportionality of limbs, or any other objective standard of male beauty one might care to put forward – this toffee-tanned, blue-eyed Adonis took some beating.

The Adonis smiled at her wolfishly.

'I'm Viorel Hudson. You must be Tish Crewe.'

'Hmmm?' Tish seemed to have temporarily lost the power of speech.

'A pleasure to meet you,' said Viorel, delighted by the effect he seemed to be having on her. 'You won't mind if I don't shake your hand.'

'Hmmm?' said Tish again. She seemed to have developed late-onset autism. 'The soot,' Vio explained.

'Oh!' Tish looked down at her ape-black hands. 'Of course. Sorry.'

It was only at that moment that it occurred to her that she was, to all intents and purposes, naked. She blushed so violently she was surprised Viorel wasn't scorched by the heat coming off her cheeks.

'Here.' Dorian stepped forward, wrapping his Barbour around her. 'You must be freezing.'

'Spoilsport,' said Viorel. Dorian glared at him.

138

'Thank you,' said Tish gratefully. 'My clothes are inside. Everything got so caked with coal dust, you see. I could hardly move, so I . . . I assumed . . . I didn't think there'd be anyone up here so early.'

'Please, don't apologize on our account,' said Viorel, who was starting to enjoy himself. It was hard to get a good look at the girl's face through all the grime, but the combination of her gloriously displayed figure and all-too-evident embarrassment was seriously endearing. As was the fact that she'd got up at seven to pull a bird's nest out of a chimney. *Who did that?*

After a few more stammered apologies, Tish bolted down the hill to the manor, pulling Dorian's oversized jacket around her tiny frame like a shield as she ran. Still grinning like the Cheshire Cat, Vio opened his mouth to speak, but Dorian cut him off.

'No,' he said firmly.

'What do you mean "no"? I never said anything.'

'I mean "no". Not with her.'

'All right,' said Vio, amused. 'But, just out of curiosity . . . why not?'

'Because she's our hostess.'

'So?'

'So it will cause tension on my set,' said Dorian. 'And because she's a nice girl who doesn't need your bullshit. And because I say so,' he added stubbornly. 'There's a village full of eager young women on the other side of those gates. If you have to get your rocks off, go do it with one of them.'

'OK, boss,' said Vio, still smiling. 'Whatever you say.'

The next time Viorel saw Tish was at lunch. Mrs Drummond had laid on a welcome spread for the actors. Walking into Loxley's impressive, wood-panelled dining room in jeans and a plain white T-shirt, her newly washed, still-damp hair tied back in a ponytail, Tish blushed scarlet when she saw Viorel standing there.

'My, my,' he teased, enjoying her discomfiture. 'Don't you scrub up well?'

'Ignore him,' said Dorian, introducing Tish to the rest of her temporary house guests. 'Lunch looks spectacular, by the way. You shouldn't have gone to so much trouble.'

The long mahogany refectory table had been set with white bone china and silverware, and a variety of estate-grown food laid out on large platters in the middle. There was a side of venison, fresh tomato and basil salad, a whole poached salmon and various vegetable dishes, including a mouthwatering stack of asparagus dripping in butter, which Mrs Drummond proudly informed everyone had been churned at Home Farm from Loxley cows.

'The fish is out of this world.' Rhys Evans, a stocky, curly haired Welshman with a reputation as a practical joker, tucked into the salmon with unconcealed delight.

'It's all delicious. Very generous of you, Miss Crewe,' said Jamie Duggan, wiping a yellow stream of liquid butter off his chin. Jamie was better looking than Rhys, blond and regular featured, but Tish found herself thinking how utterly devoid he was of sex appeal. She tried to picture him as Edgar Linton, making love to Sabrina Leon's Catherine Earnshaw. It wasn't easy.

'Please, call me Tish,' she said. 'And I'm afraid I can't take credit for lunch. It's entirely Mrs Drummond's hard work.'

Viorel watched Tish as she chatted to everyone in the room, playing the interested hostess like the well-brought-up lady of the manor that she was. She swapped Scottish reeling stories with Duggan, a dreadful, pompous bore in Vio's opinion, smiling at all his weak jokes, and tried valiantly to engage Lizzie Bayer in conversation, not easy given that the girl had the attention span of a concussed goldfish. Vio had tried to chat Lizzie up himself in LA after the read-through. Classically pretty in a large-breasted, Scandinavian, *FHM* sort of way, she'd looked as if she'd be worth having a crack at. But looks could be deceiving. In fact, Lizzie Bayer had about as much spark as a decomposing kipper. All she wanted to talk about was her deathly dull TV show and its ratings.

'*Variety* named me as one of NBC's "faces to watch" this year,' she had told Vio for the third time, preening vacantly in the Veyron's rearview mirror.

Really? thought Vio. *I'd have named you one of their 'faces to slap'. Talk about self-obsessed.* In the movie, Lizzie was to play Isabella, the trophy wife who Heathcliff relentlessly abuses and humiliates. Viorel was looking forward to it already.

Looking round the room at his cast-mates, Vio swiftly decided that Rhys was by far the best of the bunch – funny in a cheeky-chappie, naughty-glint-in-his-eye sort of way that gave Vio hope that he might become a mate. He was flirting with Tish outrageously but quite hopelessly, each elaborate compliment flying over the girl's head like so much wasted shrapnel.

Aware of Viorel's eyes boring into her, Tish was starting to feel unpleasantly hot. The effort of not returning his stare was giving her a headache and making it hard to concentrate on what Rhys Evans was saying. It was relief when the phone in the hallway rang and she was summoned away to take the call.

Two minutes later she returned to the table looking white.

'Is everything all right?' asked Dorian.

'It's my son,' said Tish, her voice a monotone. 'He's had an accident at school. They've called the local GP. Apparently, he's concussed.'

'Oh my God. What happened?'

'He fell out of a tree. He and another boy were playing *Alvin and the Chipmunks* or something . . . the doctor says he's fine, but he's been asking for me. I have to get down there right away.'

'Of course,' said Dorian. 'Do you want me to drive you?'

Tish looked at him blankly for a moment, lost in her own anxiety. She was sure she'd read somewhere that people often seemed fine after a head injury but then haemorrhaged and died hours later.

'Tish?'

'Hmm? Oh, no, thank you. I'm fine to drive.'

'Are you sure?' Dorian looked concerned.

'Positive. Excuse me,' she said to the room at large, running out at a jog.

Tish was already in the car and starting the engine by the time Viorel caught up with her. He opened the driver's door. 'Scooch over.'

'What?' Tish looked flustered.

'I'm driving.'

'But—'

'It wasn't a question,' said Vio firmly, nudging her over to the passenger side. 'I'm driving. You need to focus on your son.'

By the time they got to St Agnes's primary school, Abel had got over his teary, 'I want my mum' stage and was thoroughly enjoying being the centre of attention.

'I nearly died,' he told Tish cheerfully, pointing proudly to the cold compress strapped to his forehead with Dennis the Menace bandages. 'If I'd died, Michael would have had to go to prison until he was a hundred years old.'

'No I wouldn't,' said Michael, without glancing up from

his colouring-in. 'It was a accident, wasn't it, Miss Bayham? No one goes to prison for a accident.'

Miss Bayham assured Tish that it had indeed been an accident, and that Dr Rogers had said there was no need to get Abel's head X-rayed.

'I'll drive you to A and E, just in case,' said Vio. He couldn't take his eyes off Abel. *The kid looks exactly like me.*

'Who's he?' asked Abel, noticing the dark-haired man staring at him as Tish carried him across the playground. 'Is he a taxi driver?'

Tish looked embarrassed but Viorel laughed. Dorian was right: the kid was seriously cute.

'I'm Viorel,' he said, offering Abel his hand to shake. 'I'm a friend of your mother's.'

'Viorel who? I've never seen you before.'

Vio grinned. 'Viorel Hudson. Why, how many Viorels do you know?'

'Two,' said Abel, 'at my old school.'

Vio's eyebrows shot up. 'Really? Where was your old school?'

'Romania,' said Abel.

Vio felt the hairs on his arms stand on end. *No wonder he looks so like me. And nothing like his mother. I wonder if he's adopted?*

'My long name is Abel Henry Gunning Crewe,' said Abel, abruptly changing the subject. 'What's your favourite dinosaur?'

'Therizinosaurus,' said Vio, not missing a beat. 'What's yours?'

Abel looked at Tish, wide-eyed with admiration. Most grown-ups were embarrassingly ignorant on the giant reptiles of the Mesozoic Era. Mummy's new friend was cool.

'Mine's Ceratosaurus, but in a tie with Fukuisaurus. My

mum likes T-Rex, but that's just because it's the only one she knows.' He rolled his eyes.

Vio nodded in sympathy. 'That's girls for you.'

'Tell me about it.'

In the car on the way to the hospital, Tish told Vio, 'You're good with children.'

He smiled. 'You sound surprised.'

She shrugged. 'I suppose I am, a little.'

'Why? Because I'm an actor?'

'I don't know. Maybe, yes.'

Lifting his hand off the gear stick, Vio rested it casually on Tish's leg. 'Don't judge a book by its cover, Miss Crewe. I'm actually good with all sorts of things.' Slowly, infinitesimally slowly, he began stroking the ball of his thumb up and down the fabric of her jeans.

It was a definite come-on. Tish felt a rush of blood to her groin that she hadn't experienced since Michel. *Oh Lord*, she thought. *He's incredibly sexy. But he's a film star. Do I really want to be another notch on his bedpost?*

'I'm sure you are.' Gently she removed his hand.

'But . . .? I'm sensing there's a "but".'

'But I'm afraid I'm off romance at the moment,' said Tish. 'Sorry.'

'Ah, yes. The frog doctor,' said Vio dismissively. 'Dorian mentioned it.'

Tish looked mortified. When she'd spoken to Dorian about Michel, she'd assumed it was in confidence.

'Oh come on, lighten up,' said Vio, seeing her face fall. 'For one thing he's French. You can't possibly want to date a Frenchman.'

'Oh, really?'

'Yes, really. And for another he's an idiot. Any man who let you slip through his fingers is, by definition, an idiot.'

Tish softened slightly. 'You've got all the chat, haven't you, Mr Hudson?'

'I try,' Vio grinned.

The hospital trip took forever. As predicted, Abel was fine, as evidenced by his ceaseless chatter in the waiting room and quizzing of each doctor who examined him on the minutiae of *Ben 10: Alien Force*. By the time they left, Viorel's jet lag was starting to kick in, so Tish offered to drive them back to Loxley.

Abel talked for fifteen more minutes in the back seat before finally running out of steam and falling asleep, his little dark head slumped against the window. Tish thought Vio was asleep too, when he suddenly yawned loudly beside her.

'So what happened?' he asked her. 'With your French doctor?'

Tish sighed. She might as well tell him. Perhaps saying it out loud would help? 'He met someone else.'

'I'm sorry,' said Vio.

He sounded sincere. Tish thought, *He's a nice man. A flirt and a player and everything I don't need in my life. But a nice man, nonetheless.*

'Is that why you left Romania? Abel mentioned he used to go to school there.'

'No, no,' said Tish. 'It was nothing like that.' She filled him in briefly on her life in Oradea. Her work with the orphans, how she'd come to adopt Abel and the PG-rated, synopsis version of her doomed affair with Dr Michel Henri. Finally, she told him about Jago and the squatters who had forced her home to Loxley.

Viorel thought, *This is quite a woman.* It was a lot of life and responsibility to have packed into twenty-seven years.

'So you're really off men then, are you?' he asked her. 'You're sure about that? No dating at all?'

'For now I am,' said Tish. 'But it's nice to be asked. Thank you.'

'My pleasure.'

'And thank you, for today. With Abel I mean.'

'He's terrific,' enthused Vio, then suddenly shouted, '*Jesus H. Christ!*'

Tish jumped out of her skin. Out of nowhere a recklessly speeding limousine flew around the corner and came within a hair's-breadth of hitting them. Only thanks to Tish's quick reactions were they able to swerve onto the grass verge and avoid a smash.

'What the fuck was that?' asked Vio as she slammed on the brakes. 'Are you OK?'

'I think so.' Tish was still shaking. She turned to the back seat. 'Abi darling, are you all right?'

Wide awake again after all the commotion, Abel stared after the long black car as it disappeared into the distance. 'That was *so cool*!' he declared breathlessly 'How fast do you think it was going, Vio? As fast as a jet?'

'It was going much too fast,' muttered Viorel. 'Ridiculous on a little country road. We could have been killed.'

'As fast as a rocket?' asked Abel. 'How about a jet-pack? Hey look! It's coming back.'

To Tish and Vio's astonishment, they saw that the car was indeed coming back, marginally more slowly this time. Perhaps the driver had realized he'd run them off the road and was coming back to check that they were OK. As the limo came closer, it slowed down and stopped. Tish wound down her window, composing her features into what she hoped was a sternly disapproving attitude, and waited for the other driver's grovelling apology.

Instead, it was the rear passenger window that opened. The woman's face was almost entirely obscured behind giant sunglasses, but her voice was imperious. 'Loxley Hall,' she barked. 'I don't suppose you know where the fuck it is?'

Tish was livid. 'Do you have any idea what speed you were doing just now? You actually forced me off the road! If I hadn't swerved, you might have killed us.'

'But you did swerve, didn't you?' The American accent was clearer this time, as was the arrogance. 'Now do you know where this house is or not? I haven't got all day.'

Viorel leaned forward. He'd have recognized that voice anywhere.

'Sabrina?'

'Vio. Thank God.' Sabrina took off her sunglasses and smiled at him sweetly. Tish looked at the slanting, feline eyes, high cheekbones and wide lips that had made Sabrina Leon a star and temporarily forgot her indignation. Her beauty was disabling, like a stun gun. What was it Dorian had said? *'When you look like that, no one ever says no to you.'*

'I take it *you* know the way to this godforsaken location?' Sabrina purred at Viorel. 'We've been driving around for hours. I'm losing my mind.'

'Sure.' Viorel's earlier anger seemed to have melted away like an ice lolly in the sunshine. 'Tish and I are on our way back there now. Why don't you follow us?'

'Was that a princess?' asked Abel to Tish's irritation as she backed onto the road. 'She's *really* pretty. And she's got a cool car. With cool windows.'

'That is not a princess,' snapped Tish. 'That is a very rude woman. And you wouldn't think her car was so cool if it had hit us. Why didn't you say something?' she added crossly to Viorel. 'She shouldn't be on the roads.'

Viorel clocked Tish's angry, tense expression and thought: *She's jealous. How endearing. She didn't like me being nice to Sabrina.* 'I'll have a word with the driver later,' he said soothingly.

He hadn't been looking forward to this shoot. He'd already spent far too much of his life in the English countryside, and had always found it deadly dull. But perhaps Derbyshire would be the exception?

There was hope in the Hope Valley after all.

'No! No way. They're not going to a fucking hotel.'

An hour later and Sabrina Leon's screams could be heard the length and breadth of Loxley Hall.

'Well they're not staying here, Sabrina.' Dorian Rasmirez's voice was ten decibels lower but every bit as firm. 'I told you before. No entourage.'

'*Entourage?*' Sabrina's yelling shot up an octave. 'In what alternative fucking universe are they an entourage? They're my bodyguards. I need them for protection. How are they gonna protect me if they're in a hotel?'

'They aren't, because this is bullshit,' said Dorian. 'Self-important bullshit. No one else brought bodyguards. What do you need protection from?'

'The press!' shrieked Sabrina. 'Who do you think? You should have seen them at Heathrow, like a pack of fucking hyenas.'

'Perhaps you should try being polite to them?' said Dorian. 'They're always very respectful to me.'

'They're not interested in you,' said Sabrina bluntly. 'No one else brought bodyguards because no one else sells newspapers the way I do, OK? It's that simple.'

Dorian was unmoved. 'You can shout all you like. Those neanderthals are *not* staying on this set and that is my final word on the subject.'

'Fine. Then I'll check into a hotel with them.'

'No you will not. You will stay here. You're under contract.'

At that point both the decibel level and the language got so bad that Tish had to abandon Abel's bedtime story and come downstairs to confront them. 'I'm sorry, but I have a small boy sleeping upstairs. If you can't have a civil conversation, please go and shout at each other somewhere else.'

'Sorry,' said Dorian sheepishly. 'I forgot you guys were home.'

Abel, looking more adorable than ever in his white cotton Peter Rabbit pyjamas, appeared on the staircase behind his mother. 'Guess what?' he said brightly to Dorian.

'What?' said Dorian, ignoring Sabrina and focusing all his attention on the boy.

'I nearly died today.'

'Did you, now?'

Abel nodded solemnly. 'Uh-huh. Twice.'

'Don't exaggerate, Abel,' said Tish.

'I'm not!' Abel insisted. 'Once when Michael pushed me out of the apple tree, and once when that lady tried to crash into our car.' He pointed at Sabrina.

Dorian's eyes narrowed. 'Is this true?'

'No!' said Sabrina.

'Yes,' said Tish simultaneously. 'She ran us off the road. Or at least her driver did.'

'That's crap,' said Sabrina. 'She was driving like an old lady. We passed her and she panicked. Tell him, Viorel.'

'Oh no. Don't look at me.' Walking down the stairs, Viorel stopped behind Abel, scooping the boy up into his arms.

'Hello, Abel Henry Gunning Crewe.' He beamed.

'Hello, Viorel Hudson.' Abel beamed back.

Sabrina said what everyone was thinking. 'Holy crap, you two look alike.'

'*Language!*' hissed Tish. But she was really annoyed with

herself for feeling so flustered now that Viorel had turned up. He'd changed out of the jeans and sweater he'd been wearing earlier into a pair of white linen Paul Smith trousers and an open-necked Gucci shirt in racing green that made his eyes positively glow. *This is ridiculous*, thought Tish, as another rush of blood made its way towards her cheeks. *If he's going to be living under my roof for the next two months, I'm going to have to stop blushing like a schoolgirl every time we're in the same room.*

'Look,' snapped Sabrina, irritated that for a full minute attention had been diverted from herself. 'I don't have time for this. I'm tired and I need to get this shit resolved about my security guys so I can get some rest.'

'It's resolved,' said Dorian. 'They go. You stay.'

Sensing things were about to kick off again, Viorel stepped in, snaking one arm around Sabrina's waist and lifting her suitcase with the other. 'You must be shattered, darling,' he said smoothly. 'Tish has already shown me where your room is. Let me take you up.'

'I'll help!' said Abel, leaping onto Sabrina's Louis Vuitton trunk like a squirrel monkey. 'I've got super-strong muscles. Look.' He flexed his nonexistent biceps at Viorel.

'I don't think so.' Tish stepped forward to retrieve her son. 'You've had enough injuries for one day.'

'But I want to,' Abel moaned. 'I want to help the lady who tried to run me over with her car.'

Viorel roared with laughter.

'For God's sake,' said Sabrina, 'I did not try to run him over.'

'I didn't mind,' Abel assured her. 'It was a really cool car. You're very pretty.'

Even Sabrina had to be charmed by that. 'Thank you. Abel, is it?'

'Abel Henry Gunning Crewe.'

'Well, thank you, Abel. But I think you'd better go upstairs now. Your mommy looks mad.'

Doesn't she just? thought Vio mischievously. Tish was a gorgeous girl, and sweet with it, but he knew which side his bread was buttered. Rasmirez had warned him off in so many words, and heartbroken chicks were usually more trouble than they were worth anyway. Not as much trouble as Sabrina Leon, perhaps, but then Vio had already decided he wasn't going to screw Sabrina. As Terence Dee, the agent who discovered him, had once memorably said about the perils of sleeping with one's co-stars: 'Even dogs don't shit where they eat.' If eight weeks of celibacy proved too much, Vio would simply have to take Dorian's advice and get his rocks off with a local girl.

Pity.

A few hours later, Tish collapsed into bed exhausted. What a day it had been! From her crack-of-dawn expedition up the Home Farm chimney and mortifying first encounter with Viorel Hudson, to Abel's hospital trip and their near-death run-in with Sabrina Leon, the arrival of the actors seemed to have raised the stress levels at Loxley by a factor of about a hundred.

Viorel's flirting was flattering. But Tish was a sensible girl. Men like him were in it for the chase, for the game. As soon as one slept with them, they lost interest and were off to the next girl. Even Sabrina's arrival today had turned Hudson's head, like a dog suddenly seeing a squirrel.

I have enough drama in my life without all that nonsense, Tish told herself, turning out her bedside lamp. *Especially after Michel.*

And that was when she realized.

Today was the first day in over a year when she had not thought about Dr. Michel Henri once.

CHAPTER ELEVEN

Harry Greene lay back against his purple velvet pillows and scrolled down the options on the giant screen in front of him.

Lisa
Twins 1: Sandy and Dee
Twins 2: Keisha and Joanne
Clara

The list ran to over twenty, but Harry always ended up picking from the same three movies. He'd basically given up commercially produced porn. Ever since he'd started filming himself having sex, over two years ago now, he found his home-made collection infinitely more arousing. For one thing, the girls were better looking. For another, he got to direct them exactly the way he wanted: thighs wide, lips parted, eyes always open and straight to camera. Other producers had Hollywood at their feet. Harry Greene had Hollywood on its knees, sucking his dick. Clicking on *Keisha and Joanne*, he threw the remote onto his Chinese silk bedspread and slipped a hand under the waistband of his Turnbull & Asser pyjamas, already hard with anticipation.

At thirty-nine years old, Harry Greene truly was the man who had everything. His *Fraternity* movies were the most successful comedy franchise of all time. As a result, he was not only wealthy beyond his own wildest dreams – his main residence, in Beverly Hills, was a 30,000-square-foot palace that made Versailles look poky, but he kept life interesting by maintaining fully staffed mansions in every habitable continent of the globe, for the rare occasions when he felt like a change of scene – but he was also worshipped by his peers in the movie business as little less than a god. Women fell into Harry Greene's bed like ripe apples from a never-exhausted tree. Studio executives fell over themselves to make deals with him. In Los Angeles there was no party to which Harry Greene was not invited, no club of which he was not a member, no luxury known to man of which Harry was not able to avail himself, day or night, whenever he chose.

And yet Harry Greene was not a happy man.

Born into a stable, loving, middle-class family in a swish suburb of San Diego, Harry had always been blessed. Smart, charismatic and good-looking, he was popular at school and a natural success with women. By the time he met his wife Angelica, at a valley party when he was twenty-four, he was already a relatively successful producer, with two profitable indies under his belt and a reputation as an up-and-comer in the industry. This modest success was more than enough to earn him ready access to all of Hollywood's many temptations. Having never denied himself in the past, Harry saw no reason to do so now, simply because he had moved one woman under his roof. He loved Angelica. She was smart, stunningly beautiful, loyal and undemanding. Harry had repaid her with a five-carat diamond, a new surname and an unlimited platinum AmEx card. With these gifts, he considered his spousal duties to be fully discharged.

It was a shock, therefore, when, after five years of marriage characterized by unfettered philandering on his part, Harry's wife left him, suing for divorce on the grounds of his adultery.

'I don't understand it,' Harry complained bitterly to the business acquaintances that he mistook for friends. 'I gave her everything she wanted. I never said no to her. *Never*. How could she stab me in the back like this?'

For the first year, he was so bitter about Angelica's blatant betrayal that he refused to speak to her at all, restricting all contact to terse exchanges between their respective battalions of attorneys. But eventually, being the magnanimous soul that he was, Harry met his ex-wife for lunch at one of his ex-houses, and it was here that she'd dropped the bombshell.

'When did I first find out? Jeez, Harry, I don't know. I think the first time someone said something to me was at Bob Grauman's Halloween party. Some guy dressed as Richard Nixon was gossiping about you and Farrah James. I was in a werewolf mask at the time; I don't think he even knew who I was. Anyway, after that I did some digging . . . you've only yourself to blame you know. More Chablis, honey?'

Harry Greene did not blame himself. Nor, any longer, did he blame poor Angelica. He blamed some loose-lipped cunt in a Richard Nixon mask. That shit-stirring little fucker, whoever he was, had ruined a perfectly happy marriage. In a town where marriages were considered a success if they outlived milk, Harry Greene considered himself to have been seriously hard done by, wantonly robbed of something rare and precious, something that was his – that should have been his – for life. He did some digging of his own. And lo and behold, his nemesis had a name! A name that Harry

Greene had come to loathe over the years with a passion bordering on the pathological: Dorian Rasmirez.

So stealing my scripts wasn't enough for you, eh? Or turning my writers against me? Oh no. You have to take my wife from me too? My wife!

What stung the most was that Dorian's own marriage remained a Hollywood paragon. Of course, everyone knew Rasmirez's wife was a slut, a middle-aged, over-the-hill TV actress who fucked everything with a pulse under thirty in a sad attempt to keep her husband's attention. Yet Dorian stood by her, besotted, proclaiming his cuckolded love for her from the rooftops. Harry Greene wanted to destroy Dorian Rasmirez's marriage, to take away his wife the way that Dorian had taken away Angelica. But the Rasmirezes remained tighter than ever, a fact that ate away at Harry like a flesh-rotting virus.

He'd tried to numb the pain by hurting Dorian professionally, using his immense influence with studios, distributors and the media to damage his rival's movies. Harry liked to think that by deliberately moving the release date of the most recent *Fraternity* film so that it coincided with Rasmirez's dull and worthy war flick, he'd put the final nail in the coffin of *Sixteen Nights*. 'He'll be lucky if it runs for fourteen nights,' Harry told a reporter from *Variety*, in a quote that made headlines across the industry – and turned out to be an accurate prophecy. The film bombed. But the satisfaction it gave Harry to know that Rasmirez had lost money was fleeting. Money could always be replaced. A marriage, on the other hand, once destroyed was destroyed forever.

On the screen in front of him, two girls were giving each other head. One was black, the other Asian. Both were perfect physical specimens, narrow-hipped and boyish, the way Harry liked them, but with outlandishly large, round breasts stuck to their ribs like two soccer balls. Every couple of seconds they looked up from each other's pussies and stared into the camera, while Harry whispered obscenities at them. As always it was the look in their eyes that made him come. So desperate, so wholly under his control. Harry Greene liked things being under his control. It made him feel that life was as it should be.

Grabbing a tissue from the box by the bed, he cleaned himself up and reached for the phone. It was midnight in LA, but the person he was calling was in Europe and would have been up for at least two hours. They picked up immediately. Just hearing their voice on the line gave Harry a thrill far stronger than the orgasm he'd just finished.

'It's me. Harry. Listen, I need to talk to you. Uh-uh, no, in person. How soon can you be on a plane?'

He hung up two minutes later, suffused with a feeling he hadn't experienced in years: contentment. Dorian Rasmirez was shooting his *Wuthering Heights* remake somewhere in England. Everyone knew that. Everyone also knew that he'd paid way over the odds for the Hudson kid and been left so broke he'd been forced to cast Sabrina Leon as his female lead. The details of the production itself were shrouded in secrecy. Some saw this as a deliberate attempt by Dorian to create mystique, to get everybody talking about his big 'comeback' movie. But Harry Greene saw it differently

He's hiding from me, he thought, smugly. *He's running scared. And so he should be.*

Harry Greene had a secret of his own.

He was about to blow Dorian Rasmirez out of the water.

CHAPTER TWELVE

Sabrina awoke gripped with fear. A familiar fear: her bedroom door was rattling. It was him, Graham Cooper, the foster 'brother' who'd abused her as a kid back in Fresno, coming to 'cuddle' her, as he called it. Already she could smell the foul excitement on Graham's breath, see his sallow, twenty-year-old cheeks flushing as he slipped under her bedclothes, telling her not to make a fuss, that he loved her, that she was lucky to have a roof over her head.

'No!' She sat up in bed, her heart thudding against her ribcage like a trapped animal. 'Get out!'

'Come on, Sabrina. It's almost five. If you don't get to wardrobe on time, Dorian's gonna skin both of us alive.'

It took a few seconds for Viorel's gravelly English voice to register. He wasn't Graham Cooper. This wasn't her childhood bedroom in Fresno. And she wasn't a helpless, twelve-year-old nobody any more. She was Sabrina Leon, movie star, on the set of her latest film. And oh my god she was already late!

Pushing back the covers with a groan, Sabrina got up and walked to the window, opening the curtains. It was still dark

157

outside, with only the faintest shards of dawn light pushing their way tentatively over the horizon. Sabrina's room looked out over parkland at the rear of the house. In the half-light, she saw a family of deer sleepily getting to their feet beneath a sheltering oak, brushing against one another in the early morning mist. *It looks so peaceful*, Sabrina thought, with a pang. Like many people addicted to the thrills of city life, she wished she had the ability to switch off and enjoy nature without feeling so anxious all the time, as if life were somehow passing her by, leaving her behind in a trail of dust. *I guess if you grew up somewhere like this, you'd learn how to do it. How to be at peace.*

Tish Crewe had grown up here, of course. Maybe that was why she looked so annoyingly *hearty*? The girl positively radiated wholesome, rural goodness. Their paths had crossed for only a matter of minutes yesterday, but Sabrina had already taken a strong dislike to Loxley Hall's mistress. Tish's accent was so cut-glass it couldn't possibly be genuine; besides which, Sabrina made it a rule never to trust a woman who didn't wear any make-up. *Look at me*, they seemed to be saying, *I'm so artless*. Of course, Rasmirez had lapped it up. Sabrina could see at a glance how enamoured her director was of Tish Crewe, with her doe eyes and her cute kid and her whole motherly schtick. It was enough to make you want to throw up.

Dorian probably thinks she's a lady. Unlike me.

Viorel Hudson seemed to like the girl too. Or maybe it was just the child he was interested in? Last night, when he'd shown Sabrina to her room, he'd been waxing lyrical about little Abel – how funny he was, and how smart. Sabrina's own maternal instinct had been surgically removed years ago, along with her tonsils, but it was sexy to see a man being fatherly. At least, it was sexy when Viorel did it.

'Are you up?' Right on cue he stuck his head round the door. He looked revoltingly refreshed at such an early hour.

Sabrina stretched her arms into a long, cat-like yawn. 'I'm up, I'm up,' she sighed. 'I'll see you down there.'

The *Wuthering Heights*' wardrobe and make-up departments consisted of two basic mobile-home-style trailers parked next to Loxley's stable blocks. Along with the crew's accommodation, catering vans, an editing suite and a temporary structure housing bathroom and laundry facilities, they made up what was known as the 'Set Village' – the hub of the production. Viorel was already in costume by the time Sabrina walked in. In a pair of high-waisted breeches, riding boots and a ruffled shirt, torn open at the chest, he ought to have looked quintessentially English. In fact, thanks to his dark colouring and three-day growth of beard, he looked more like a pirate who'd lost his cutlass.

Sabrina, by contrast, looked a thousand per cent LA in Victoria's Secret pink pyjamas, a Juicy Couture silk puffa jacket and a pair of Ugg boots, her entire face hidden by a YSL leopard-print scarf. All that was visible above it were her eyes, puffy with tiredness and narrowed resentfully at the fact they were expected to be open at such an ungodly hour.

Viorel looked her up and down. 'Well, well. If it isn't Aurora, Goddess of the Dawn.'

'Fuck off,' said Sabrina, but Vio could see the smile in her eyes. 'Thanks for waking me. I think I slept through, like, six alarms.'

'My pleasure.' After all her tantrums and standoffishness in LA, he was delighted that Sabrina seemed to have decided to cease hostilities between them. Dorian had given her such a hard time at the read-through, and again yesterday, sending her bodyguards packing, she probably needed an ally. Given that they'd be spending the next three months of their lives together, day in, day out, both here and in Romania; and that the only other female company available was the brain-dead Lizzie Bayer or the lovely-but-off-limits Tish Crewe, this was a relief.

'Excuse me, darling.' Maureen, the fat, motherly wardrobe mistress shooed Viorel out of the way. From the back of the trailer she dragged out a wooden folding screen.

'You can undress behind here,' she told Sabrina. 'Give you a bit of privacy.'

Sabrina's outfit, an intricate blue-and-yellow embroidered crinoline with hooped skirts and multiple lace petticoats, had been laid across two chairs next to where Viorel was standing. It was huge, taking up a good half of the available space in the trailer.

'That's OK,' said Sabrina, 'I don't need it. Just bring the dress over here and I'll step into it.' Viorel watched as Sabrina slipped off her coat, boots and pyjamas. In seconds she was standing in front of him in nothing but a minuscule pair of thong panties. Her hands covered her nipples, but everything else was visible – the large, firm, perfectly rounded breasts, the boyish bottom without a hint of cellulite that was as tanned and smooth as the rest of her, the perfectly flat stomach defined, Viorel suspected, by genetics rather than hours of crunches in a gym. *She's magnificent*, he thought, *and gloriously unselfconscious. Although who wouldn't be, with a body like that?*

In fact, Sabrina was entirely conscious of what she was doing, and delighted by the effect it seemed to be having on her co-star. She'd resented Viorel when they first met in LA, because he was getting five and a half million dollars for this movie and she was getting nothing, and because she feared he'd steal her attention, and perhaps even make a play for sole top billing on the credits. Certainly, he was ambitious enough to try it – *he's almost as hungry as I am* – and might even get away with it. Ed Steiner had the spine of an amoeba when it came to defending her interests, and Rasmirez had plainly already decided which of his two lead actors he favoured.

But seeing him again yesterday, Sabrina decided she'd changed her mind about Viorel Hudson. Not only was he fully fuckable, but he seemed genuinely eager to be friends. He hadn't needed to wake her up this morning. He could have let her sleep in and face Rasmirez's legendary temper, but he didn't. At this point in her life, Sabrina needed all the friends she could get. *Plus*, she thought happily, *if he likes me now, just think how much more he's going to like me once I take him to bed.* She was going to need something to do in this sleepy little corner of England, especially now that Dorian had confiscated Enrique.

'Here you are.' Maureen and her assistant carried the enormous dress over to Sabrina, rolling down the bodice so that Sabrina could step into the hooped skirt. 'Hop in there before you catch hypothermia.'

Sabrina did as she was asked. Reaching down to pull up the dress, she let go of her breasts, deliberately giving Viorel a full frontal view. 'Oops.' She looked him in the eye and smiled.

Vio smiled back. *Careful*, he thought. *She's delicious, but she's trouble.*

'I'll go and get us some coffee.'

'And a bagel for me,' said Sabrina, not breaking eye contact. 'I'm staaaaarving.'

So am I, thought Viorel, his dick hardening at an alarming rate beneath his skintight breeches.

Make-up took forever. Even though it was only the two of them in this morning's scene, and neither of them needed to be aged or scarred or otherwise transformed, the process seemed to drag on and on.

'You want to run through it?' asked Vio, closing his eyes as yet another shade of base was applied to his lids. 'We may as well do a line check while we're stuck here.'

Sabrina, who was still fruitlessly trying to bring her BlackBerry Pearl to life, was about to say 'no'. They were very different actors. Viorel seemed to want constant reassurance and ad hoc rehearsals, whereas she preferred the adrenaline rush of jumping blind into the first take. But, in the interests of their newfound friendship, she relented.

'OK,' she said, wincing as her hair was pinned tightly into her bonnet. 'Hit me.'

As they ran through the scene, Vio felt the tension he'd been carrying around since the read-through drain out of him like pus from a lanced boil. Sabrina had shown promise at the read-through, but she'd been flustered, no doubt by Dorian's bullying, and the dynamic between the two of them had never fully gelled. This was *Wuthering Heights*. The love–hate relationship between Cathy and Heathcliff was not just the most important part of the movie. It *was* the movie. Viorel knew that Sabrina's performance could make or break his own, and that her reputation for making scenes difficult for her opposing actors was horrific. So it was wonderful, miraculous to hear how far she'd come since that day in LA, how much she had to give him. Her voice, her attitude, that precarious combination of arrogance and naiveté – it was Brontë's Cathy to a tee. Vio responded in kind, finding a depth to his Heathcliff that he knew he hadn't reached before, that he knew he couldn't reach without Sabrina to help him.

TILLY BAGSHAWE

Sabrina was happy too, aware of the chemistry between them. So much rested on this job, she'd found it hard to think of it as anything other than that: a job, an ordeal that had to be gone through in order for her to win her life back. Now, for the first time in a long time, she remembered what it was she loved about acting. The escape. The release. The passion.

The door to the trailer flew open. Dorian Rasmirez loomed in the doorway with a face like fury, waving the morning copy of *The Sun* like a weapon.

'What the *fuck* do you think you are playing at?' he roared at Sabrina, so loudly she felt as if her hair were being blown back, the way it did when baddies yelled in a cartoon. Her pulse raced unpleasantly as the fear welled up within her, but outwardly she managed to keep her cool.

'I take it that's a rhetorical question?'

'You fucking idiot,' said Dorian, opening the paper to page four and shaking it in front of Sabrina's nose. When she read the headline, her stomach lurched.

'*RACE ROW ACTRESS TELLS BRITAIN'S BLACKS TO F*** OFF.*'

Beneath the bold, black lettering they'd run a picture of her at Heathrow yesterday looking glamorous and starry, walking beside a mountain of Louis Vuitton luggage. Her face was set in a hard, uncompromising attitude that Sabrina remembered as fear, but that in print looked horribly like arrogance.

'Read it,' commanded Dorian. 'Read it out loud.'

Sabrina took a deep breath. '*Controversial Hollywood actress Sabrina Leon, the woman at the centre of a bitter Hollywood dispute after branding African American director Tarik Tyler a "slave driver", yesterday astonished Britons by making a second ugly slur, this time against our own black community. When asked by our reporter if she had any message for black people in Britain who*

163

may have been offended by her original remarks, Miss Leon, who is in this country to film a remake of the British classic Wuthering Heights, *replied that they could "f*** off".'*

'That's not true,' said Sabrina, lowering the paper. 'I never said that.' There was a silence you could have cut with a knife. Then she added, 'I mean, I did tell the *guy* to fuck off. The reporter.'

'Jesus.' Dorian shook his head in disbelief. 'Why? Why did you say anything?'

'Because he was crowding me!' said Sabrina. 'The whole pack of them. It was intimidating.' She looked to Viorel for support. 'You know what it's like, right? It's frightening.'

Vio nodded, but Dorian was having none of it.

'Read the copy, Sabrina. They've got quotes from a whole bunch of witnesses, all of whom apparently heard you insult the entire black population of this country.'

'Well, the witnesses are lying!' Sabrina shot back. 'I was talking about him, the reporter. I told *him* to fuck off, not anybody else. Why would I? You think I want to reopen this can of worms? You know, if you hadn't been so damn high-handed and sent them away, you could have asked my bodyguards. They were there. They'll tell you.'

'Oh, great,' snarled Dorian. 'And are they gonna tell the ten million people who read *this* over breakfast this morning?' He snatched the paper back from her. 'All you had to do was keep your mouth shut.' Turning on his heel, he stormed back out, slamming the trailer door behind him so loudly that everyone jumped.

For a moment, Sabrina just stood there, stock-still. Vio saw the tears in her eyes, saw the struggle as she fought to contain them. Then, after a few seconds, she sat back down in the make-up chair, her face as blank and unreadable as an empty screen.

'You OK?' he asked her.

'I'm fine,' she said briskly. Turning to Maureen, she asked: 'How much longer?'

'Not long, lovie. Five minutes, tops.'

Chuck MacNamee knocked on the door. 'Ready on set when you are, Mo.'

'Come on,' said Sabrina to Viorel. 'Let's finish reading through the scene. Your line, I think. From "Does it really matter, Catherine?"'

You're a good little actress, thought Vio. But he could see how scared Sabrina was. He hoped Dorian would ease up a bit once they started filming.

Dorian didn't.

The morning shoot was long and gruelling. It was a hot day, a good ten degrees warmer than it had been the day before, and by eleven Sabrina was roasting in her heavy meringue of a dress. But Rasmirez didn't seem to care, keeping her standing for hours under the glare of the lights, refusing her a chance to sit down or grab a glass of water, and rolling his eyes when Sabrina insisted on a break after three straight hours on set.

'Either I go to the bathroom, or I pee right here on the ground,' she said defiantly.

'Go,' Dorian growled. 'You have two minutes.'

'Come on,' said Viorel, once she was out of earshot. 'Give her a break. My horse is getting better treatment.'

Dorian glanced across at Heathcliff's skewbald pony, contentedly gorging itself on a bucket of oats behind camera two. 'Yeah, well. Your horse hasn't single-handedly alienated the entire British press.'

'It's her first day,' said Vio.

'And she's already fucked up.'

'It was a mistake.'

'Yes it was. A big one. Look,' said Dorian, sensing Vio's disapproval, 'she has to learn. Actions have consequences. Of course the press were hounding her. What did she expect? Of course they were pushing her, trying to get her to lose her temper. That's what they *do*. But that's all the more reason to keep a lid on it. If people are trying to trip her up, if they want to think the worst of her, she's only herself to blame for that.'

Sabrina was coming back. Vio dropped his voice to a whisper.

'Fine,' he said. 'But just ease up a little, OK? Let her finish the scene. She won't be able to give much of a performance if she drops dead from heat exhaustion. And neither will I.'

At four o'clock they wrapped for the day. Dorian headed straight for his room. There were bound to be a thousand emails and voice messages wanting his response to Sabrina's latest blunder, and he needed to get some sort of statement out there before tomorrow.

On his way back to the house, he bumped into Tish. She'd been out to a local theme park with Abel. When she saw Dorian she flashed him the kind of megawatt, grid-lighting smile that forced you to smile back yourself.

'How was your first day of filming?'

'Awful. But thanks for asking. How was Thomas the Train Land?'

'Oh, you know. Hell on earth,' shrugged Tish. 'Abel enjoyed himself.' She turned around to look for him, but he'd already scampered off somewhere. She hoped it was for a slice of cake with Mrs Drummond, and not to pester the actors or film crew. At breakfast this morning he'd already coloured three cards: one for Deborah Raynham, the camera girl who always gave him sweets, one for 'Princess Sabrina' and one for Viorel – a therizinosaurus.

Dorian followed Tish into the house.

'Would you like a cup of tea?' she asked him. 'I bought milk and biscuits on the way home.'

'I can't,' said Dorian. As they walked to the kitchen, he explained briefly about *The Sun*'s article and the problems Sabrina had caused. 'I should have dealt with it this morning, but it was such a great day, I didn't want to lose the light.'

'I'm sure she didn't mean it the way it came out,' said Tish, wondering as she switched on the kettle why she was defending Sabrina, who – if yesterday's behavior was anything to go by – was a loathsome little madam. 'Our papers do have a way of twisting things.'

Dorian rolled his eyes. 'You sound like Viorel.'

Tish made herself a cup of Lapsang and asked casually, 'How was he today? I hope we didn't tire him out too much yesterday, with the hospital and everything.'

Dorian watched in silence as Tish put far too much tea into the pot, lost in her own thoughts. 'Might that not be a bit strong?' he asked, after the seventh heaped spoon of tea leaves.

'Oh!' Tish blushed. 'Sorry. I was, er . . . I was miles away.'

Damn it. Dorian frowned. *Why couldn't Hudson have left the girl alone?*

'Listen,' he said, taking the stewed tea and emptying it into the sink. 'Viorel's a great actor and a nice enough kid. But he's young. He's looking for a good time, not for anything serious.'

Tish looked taken aback. Was it really *that* obvious she found Viorel attractive?

'I know it's none of my business and I'm probably over-stepping the line here,' said Dorian. 'But you're a nice girl. I wouldn't want you to get burned.'

Tish contemplated getting angry. It was none of his business. But she knew that Dorian meant the advice kindly. She also knew he was right.

'Actors are a difficult breed,' he told her. 'Moody. Unpredictable. Trust me, I'm married to one. One minute you're the hero, the next you're the villain, and no one ever gives you the script in advance.'

'It sounds exhausting,' said Tish.

Dorian thought of Chrissie. Since his refusal to fly home to Romania for Saskia's 'Temperature-gate' they were barely on speaking terms.

'It is. But you know, when you love someone, you'll put up with anything, right?'

'Well, hopefully not *anything*,' said Tish. 'You have to know where to draw the line.'

For a split second, Dorian wondered how different his life might have been if he'd married someone like Tish – sensible, reasonable, self-assured – and not the wildly needy Chrissie. He hoped Tish's level head extended to her own love life and that she steered clear of Viorel Hudson.

'Don't worry,' she said, reading his mind. 'I like Viorel, and Abel adores him. But I have no intention of making my life more complicated than it already is.'

'You forgive the meddling?'

'Of course,' said Tish, adding a touch sadly, 'My own father died last year. It makes a nice change to have someone looking out for me.'

Jeez, thought Dorian. *She looks on me as a father?* Working with Sabrina Leon must have aged him even more than he thought.

On her way up to her room, Sabrina passed the kitchen and saw Dorian sitting at the table with Tish, laughing it up, as relaxed and avuncular as Santa Claus. *Of course he's sweetness and light with wholesome Lady Letitia*, she thought bitterly. It hadn't escaped her notice yesterday, the way that Dorian had automatically taken Tish's word over Sabrina's about that stupid non-incident with the car. To see the two of them now, so companionable and touchy-feely, you'd think they were lifelong friends. Or maybe it was more than that? *Maybe Dorian patron-saint-of-marriage Rasmirez isn't as squeaky clean as he makes out?*

Trudging up the back stairs to her room, Sabrina tried to put her bastard director out of her mind and focus on the evening ahead of her. After filming, Vio had offered to take her out to the pub for supper and she'd jumped at the chance. She was under contract not to touch a drop of alcohol, but she was still looking forward to it. With any luck, tonight would mark the beginning of a beautiful friendship with her sexy co-star. Unless Rhys or the dreadful Jamie Duggan decided to join them – or, worse, Lizzie Bayer, who'd already been nicknamed 'Mimi' by Chuck MacNamee and his crew because she talked about herself so much. Sabrina thought this was hilarious, but had no intention of joining in the general cast banter or becoming 'one of the gang' on set. That wasn't what stars do. Stars remained aloof, fraternizing only with others of their own status. In this case that meant Dorian Rasmirez or Viorel Hudson. Sabrina knew which of those she preferred.

It'll be just the two of us, she thought happily. *Viorel and me for the whole summer, with no competition and no distractions.* A summer affair was just what she needed to lift her spirits. That and for the movie to be a hit. But it would be. Having hot sex with one's co-star off set invariably made for better love scenes once the cameras rolled. If Dorian Rasmirez was determined to make her life on this movie a misery, which if today was anything to go by he quite plainly did, then Viorel Hudson could be her consolation prize.

Starting tonight.

Back in her room, Sabrina crashed for a couple of hours, exhausted after the traumas of the day. When her alarm went off at seven, she was so out of it that it was a struggle to open her eyes, but the prospect of a night out with Viorel propelled her up and into the shower, and after ten minutes beneath the pounding hot jets, she felt fully revived. Opening her still-unpacked trunk, she pulled out a sexy new pair of white Fred Segal trousers and a floaty chiffon blouse from Chloé. The trousers were skin tight, but the overall look was casual and effortless. It wouldn't do to let Hudson think she'd tried. *To heel or not to heel*, she thought, holding up a pair of hot pink Manolo sandals and some simple Fendi ballet pumps. *Fuck it.* She pulled on the heels. One could take this low-key shit too far.

Rough-drying her still-damp hair, she spritzed herself with Gucci Envy, dusted a little bronzer across her cheekbones, and opened her bedroom door. On the floor in front of her was a folded note with a set of car keys on top. Sabrina picked up the note and read it.

'Sorry Angel. Terrible migraine. Gone to bed. I left you the keys, in case you still fancy getting out of Dodge tonight. Will make it up to you soon, promise, V xx.'

The disappointment hit her like a punch to the stomach. She was angry with herself for caring so much. After all, it was only one dinner. And it was only Viorel Hudson who, if Dorian had let her keep Enrique, she probably wouldn't be bothering to try to seduce in the first place. Even so, standing there in her sexy pants and heels, it was hard not to feel a bit like Cinderella at midnight. She also wondered whether Vio really had a migraine, or whether this was some sort of petty power game he was playing to get her attention. He'd been fit as a fiddle all day on set. It had certainly come on very suddenly.

Pocketing the car keys, she was about to change back into flip-flops and wander down to the kitchen – most of the actors skipped Mrs Drummond's buffets and ate supper in the catering trailer with the crew, but Sabrina had no interest in making small talk with cameramen – when she suddenly changed her mind. Sabrina had never been to a British pub, and although the thought of dinner alone was not exactly appealing, it was better than spending the night here making conversation with Tish Crewe and her house-keeper, or, worse, getting cornered again by Rasmirez. She was pretty sure she remembered the way down into the village.

Fuck it, she thought. *I'll go.*

The Carpenter's Arms in Loxley was a low-beamed, medieval building, built in the same warm stone as the rest of the village, but covered almost completely at the front by blos-soming violet wisteria. It had an old-fashioned swinging sign, a pretty beer garden overlooking the village green and, on a warm, late spring evening like this one, it was packed.

Sabrina didn't even have to step out of the car for people to turn and stare. Just the sight of Vio's rented Mercedes SL 500 pulling into the car park was enough to set tongues wagging, and see pint glasses being set down warily on wooden picnic tables. When Sabrina actually walked in, you could have cut the silence with a knife.

'Table for one?' she asked the barman, nervously. What had felt like a casual outfit back in her room now seemed ludicrously over the top. Everyone else here seemed to have at least one item of clothing held up with string. Perhaps this had been a mistake.

'We're a bit busy at the moment, love,' the barman began, but he was interrupted by his wife, a stocky woman with wobbly, butcher's arms and a distinctly lesbian haircut, who grabbed Sabrina's hand and pumped it vigorously, as if she were a fruit machine in a Vegas casino.

'*Busy?* Course we're not *busy*, Dennis,' she said, smiling ingratiatingly at Sabrina and revealing a row of half-rotten teeth. 'Table for one, was it? Follow me. I'd expect you'd like somewhere nice and private, would you?'

'Thank you. That'd be great.'

The landlady led Sabrina to a recessed corner of the room, where an old man was nursing the dregs of a pint of bitter. 'Let me clear that away for you, Samuel,' she said briskly.

'But I'm not finished,' the old man protested, as she physically prised the glass out of his gnarled hands.

'You are now. We need the table. Lady's having dinner.'

'Oh, please, you mustn't disturb your customers on my account,' said Sabrina, embarrassed. Insisting on special treatment at Hollywood clubs was one thing, but she wasn't in the habit of turfing harmless seniors out on the street, especially not in a little village joint like this one. 'I can wait.'

'Nonsense,' the landlady laughed nervously. 'Sam doesn't mind.'

'Yes, I do,' muttered the old man with an air of hopelessness as he was dragged from his cosy corner and propelled towards the snug bar.

'There now,' said the landlady, ignoring him and turning back to Sabrina. 'You make yourself comfortable. Dennis'll be over with a menu in two shakes of a lamb's tail.'

Feeling more awkward than she had since high school, Sabrina sat alone at her stolen table, cursing Vio Hudson. What the hell was she doing here? Grateful for the low lighting, she slunk back as far as possible into the corner and, a few moments later, hid herself behind the large, leather-bound menu. Deciding that as she was here, in a British pub, she ought at least to do the thing properly, she ordered steak and kidney pudding and chips. She was contractually forbidden to drink, but no one was here except for the locals, and they could barely see *her* in the gloom, never mind the contents of her glass, so she ordered a double vodka and tonic, following it swiftly with a second. By the time she'd finished that, and eaten the chips (she took one bite of the pudding and almost gagged), she found she was feeling less awkward and, for the first time since arriving in England, relaxed.

'You're that actress, aren't you?' A young girl having supper with her parents approached Sabrina's table. She looked to be about eleven, with braces on her teeth, and wearing a low-cut pink top that revealed nothing at all but which she clearly thought of as teenage and cool. 'Can I have your autograph?'

'Of course,' Sabrina beamed. She used to resent autograph hunters. In the States they were like locusts, they'd swarm you anywhere – at the doctor's office; while you were on the phone. But she realized with a twinge of panic that this kid was the first person to ask for her autograph since before she went to Revivals, over four months ago now.

'What's your name?'

'Michaela,' said the girl shyly.

Running her pen across the back of the cardboard coaster, Sabrina felt a rush of pleasure like a heroin shot in the arm.

'There you go, Michaela. It was a pleasure to meet you.'

The child skipped away happily, clutching her treasure. Sabrina was gazing after her, basking in her own magnanimity, when she felt a tap on her shoulder.

'I sincerely hope that was a mineral water.'

Dorian Rasmirez was towering over her, holding her empty glass in his enormous, fat-fingered hand. He was wearing corduroy trousers and a chunky knit fisherman's sweater, which only added to his already substantial bulk, and he was smiling, the first time Sabrina had ever seen him do so. *He's happy because he's caught me out*, she thought dully, but she was too tired to care. She felt like an exhausted salmon about to be eaten by a bear.

'Of course,' she lied, wearily. 'Ask at the bar if you don't believe me.'

'I don't believe you,' said Dorian, pulling up a chair and sitting down opposite her. 'Luckily for you, however, I don't care. You're entitled to a drink after today.'

Sabrina's eyes narrowed. Was this a trick?

'Why are you being nice to me?'

'Would you rather I wasn't?'

'What are you doing here anyway?' She eyed him suspiciously. 'Did you follow me?'

Dorian laughed, a deep, throaty laugh that shook his whole chest and made people turn around to look at him. 'I have better things to do with my evening. Like trying to undo the shit-storm you caused with your little impromptu press conference at Heathrow yesterday.'

'Look, I've said I'm sorry,' said Sabrina, who felt the beginnings of a migraine coming on herself.

'Did you?' Dorian raised an eyebrow. 'I must have missed that.'

After three tense hours on the phone, pacifying everyone from the British Institite of Race Relations to the American Screen Actors Guild, he'd walked the forty minutes into Loxley village to try to clear his head. Stopping at the pub had been an afterthought, but he was glad he'd had it. The landlady waddled over. Dorian ordered a malt whisky for himself and 'the same again' for Sabrina, who instantly tensed.

'For Christ's sake, relax. If I didn't fire you for this morning's papers, I'm not going to fire you for having a drink. Just don't make a habit of it.'

The drinks arrived. Dorian raised his glass. 'To our movie.'

Cautiously, Sabrina did the same. 'To *Wuthering Heights*.' After a short pause, she added, 'I'm not a racist, you know.'

'I believe that,' said Dorian, truthfully.

'That's why I didn't want to apologize to Tarik Tyler. I know I should have. It made me look so much worse, not saying anything for so long. But it would have been like I was admitting I said something I never said, you know? Like I viewed people a certain way because of their colour. It's bullshit. So what if his grandmother was a slave? My grandmother was a crack whore, but you don't hear me banging on about it.'

After months on the wagon, the alcohol was quickly going to her head. Not only was she babbling, but she found herself staring at Dorian in a way she never would have if she'd been sober, examining his features closely for the first time. When he wasn't scowling, or shouting, he was actually quite attractive in a rough-and-ready, Sean Penn kind of way. Of course he was old, and certainly not handsome in the way that Sabrina liked her men – no one was going to sign Rasmirez up to model Calvin Klein underwear any time soon, that was for damn sure. But there was definitely something about him.

'So why are you here?' she asked him.

'Same reason as you. I had a shitty day, I needed a drink, and this is the only pub in town. Plus, a friend told me *not* to drink here, which of course made me curious to try it.'

'A friend? You mean Tish Crewe?' Sabrina asked archly.

'Yes, as it happens.'

'You like her, don't you?'

'I do,' said Dorian, either missing the insinuation or choosing to ignore it. 'I like you too, Sabrina.'

This was too much for Sabrina, especially delivered with such a straight face. She laughed so hard she choked on her drink, spraying vodka and tonic all down the front of her blouse and narrowly avoiding giving Dorian an impromptu shower.

'Really?' she spluttered, cleaning herself up with a napkin. 'I'd love to see how you treat actresses you *don't* like.'

'I treat them exactly the same,' said Dorian. 'I'm not in the business of favouritism. If Viorel or Lizzie or Rhys had been all over *The Sun* this morning, I'd have yelled just as hard at them.'

Sabrina looked at him sceptically.

'It's true. You personalize everything, Sabrina. I'm not your enemy. If it's an enemy you're looking for, try the mirror.'

Sabrina opened her mouth to argue with him, but decided against it. She was too tipsy to defend herself properly, and anyway it made a nice change to be having a semi-civil conversation.

'Tell me about yourself,' said Dorian, taking a long slow sip of his whisky. It was delicious.

'Tell you what?' said Sabrina. 'The sob story? Rags to riches? Doesn't everybody know that already?' She put on her best whiney, facetious voice: 'I'm Sabrina Leon, and I'm from a *bwoken home.*'

Dorian just looked at her, arms folded. Waiting.

'You really wanna know? OK fine.' Sabrina jutted out her chin defiantly. 'My mom was a heroin addict. Dad was a petty thief and general, all-round douche bag, or so I'm told. I never met him. I first got taken into care when I was eighteen months old.'

'First? You went back to your parents?'

'To my mom, twice. The first time she left me with "friends", who tried to sell me to pay off a drug debt.'

'Shit.' Dorian had heard this story from Sabrina's agent, but had assumed it was apocryphal.

'The second time the neighbours called the cops after I almost died climbing out of a second-floor window. Mom's boyfriend was hitting her round the head with a frying pan. I thought I was gonna be next.'

'How old were you then?'

Sabrina took a sip of her drink. 'Three.'

Saskia's age.

'By five they made me a permanent ward of the state. Which pretty much saved my life, although after that I was constantly on the move, bouncing around from one foster home to another.'

'What were they like, your foster parents?' asked Dorian.

Sabrina smiled. 'Which ones? There were the Johnsons. They were nice. I lived with them for a year and a half until their older daughter got fed up with sharing her bedroom and they dumped me back on the doorstep of the children's home like an unwanted Christmas puppy.'

Dorian winced.

'Then there were the Rodriguez family. The dad, Raoul, believed in "old-fashioned family values". That basically meant beating me with a bamboo cane across the backs of my legs when I was late home from school, or left food on my plate.'

'Jesus Christ,' said Dorian.

Sabrina smiled. 'Yeah. It wasn't the Waltons, but it was better than the next place. The Coopers.'

'What happened there?' asked Dorian.

'Their son, Graham . . .' Sabrina began, then broke off suddenly. 'You know, I don't really wanna talk about it.

Anyway, it doesn't matter 'cause I ran away and spent the next two years on the streets. Which actually wasn't as bad as it sounds.'

'How old were you then?'

'Twelve,' said Sabrina matter-of-factly. 'I got off the streets at fourteen, but I learned a lot in those two years.'

I'll bet you did, thought Dorian.

'Such as the fact that men are assholes who only want one thing,' Sabrina went on. 'Luckily, they're also mostly idiots, so if you're smart you can use that filthy, one-track mind of theirs to your advantage.'

It was an unusually frank confession. Dorian could imagine just how many men in Hollywood Sabrina Leon had manipulated over the years to claw her way to the top. Now he knew where she'd learned her skills.

'It was acting that really saved me,' Sabrina continued. 'A guy named Sammy Levine ran a youth-theatre company on the outskirts of New Jack City, where I was living at the time. I loved Sammy.' Her eyes lit up at the memory. 'He was passionate about theatre, passionate about kids. He was gay, and kind of flamboyant, and he could be tough as old nails when he wanted to. I remember he made me audition four times before agreeing to give me a part in *West Side Story*. And it was a fucking walk-on! Can you believe it? *Rosalia*.'

'You remember the name of the character you played?' Dorian was impressed.

'Of course,' said Sabrina, surprised. 'I remember all my parts. They're part of me. Anyway, I was so mad at Sammy. I thought I should have been Maria. Fuck it, I *should* have been Maria. I was the best.'

'If you do say so yourself,' Dorian grinned. Like everyone else in Hollywood, he knew the rest of the story. Tarik Tyler heard an NPR programme on the radio one morning about Levine's Theatre and drove up to Fresno to take a look. He saw Sabrina, cast her, an unknown, as Lola, the lead in his first *Destroyers* movie. And the rest, as they say, was history.

'So drama got you off the streets,' said Dorian. 'But what about now?'

'What do you mean?'

'I mean what motivates you, today. Why do you act?'

Sabrina shrugged. 'Because I can, I guess.'

'Oh, no no no, I'm not buying that.' Dorian leaned forward and looked her right in the eye. 'What do you *feel*, when you walk out on stage or in front of a camera?'

Sabrina had been asked the question before. Every good director wanted to get inside her head, to find out what made her tick so they could draw it out in her performance, get the maximum emotional bang for their buck. With Dorian, however, she sensed that his desire to understand came from somewhere deeper. It wasn't just artistic. It was personal.

'I feel fear,' she said honestly.

'Of what?'

'Of it ending. Of failure. Of going back to where I started.'

Dorian asked her the million-dollar question. 'So why did you turn on your mentor, the man who helped you more than anyone? It doesn't make sense.'

'You mean Tarik?' said Sabrina dismissively. 'Firstly, I didn't turn on him. It was a throwaway remark. *He* turned on *me*. Second of all, everyone says it was Tyler who discovered me and I guess that's true in Hollywood terms. But Sammy Levine was the one who really changed my life. Sammy showed me the magic. He showed me how to do it.'

'Do what?' asked Dorian, quietly.

Sabrina's answer was unequivocal.

'Escape. I act for the same reason I drink. And fuck around and shoot my mouth off at airports. I act to escape.'

It told Dorian everything he needed to know. As a kid, Sabrina was escaping from others, from the grim reality of her life. Now she was escaping from herself, from the fears that still so evidently drove her. *She's so like Cathy*, he thought. *Part of her wants to fit in, to be accepted and loved. But another part of her wants to escape, to be wild and passionate and free. I was right to cast her.*

'Come on,' he said gently. 'I'll drive you home.'

They walked out to Viorel's car, Sabrina swaying like a ship in the breeze in her Manolos, fumbling in her Hermès Birkin bag for the keys. 'They're definitely in here somewhere,' she kept muttering to Dorian. At some point in the last two hours, the sky had grown dark, and the throng of drinkers crowding the beer garden had thinned to a die-hard trickle. Dorian was gazing upwards, marvelling at the clearness of the starry sky, and wondering if his darling Chrissie was admiring the same view in Transylvania, when a belligerent young man approached them.

'Oy. You!' He was talking to Sabrina, but she was too preoccupied in her car-key search to notice him. This seemed to enrage the man more. 'Oy, bitch. I'm talking to you. Are you deaf or something?'

Dorian stepped forward. 'Hey.' He put a hand on the man's shoulders. 'Easy.'

The guy was shorter than Dorian, and slightly built, but he was young and fit and had an air of aggression about him that made Dorian wary. His hair was cut army-short and he wore drainpipe jeans and a shiny red Manchester United football shirt, from which his tattooed forearms protruded like two white, freckly twigs.

'Easy?' he snarled, shrugging off Dorian's hand. 'D'you

180

know who she is, mate? She's a fucking racist. Don't you read the papers?'

The man looked like such an unlikely champion of Great Britain's black community that Dorian assumed he was simply drunk and looking for trouble. Unfortunately, by this time, Sabrina had realized what was happening, and appeared quite happy to oblige him.

'Excuse me,' she said haughtily, brushing past him to hand the Mercedes keys to Dorian. 'You're in our way.'

'Don't you push me, you cow!' The man lunged forward. Without thinking, Dorian grabbed him by the shirt. He spun around and threw a punch, narrowly missing Dorian's left eye.

'Get in the car,' Dorian told Sabrina, still struggling to keep his would-be opponent at arm's length.

'Why?' said Sabrina defiantly. 'You think I'm scared of this pathetic little prick?'

'You what?' The man turned around again, his face like fury. Sabrina was on the passenger side of the car now, but a couple of strides and the man would be within striking distance. '*I'm* a prick? You think you own the whole fucking world, don't you? We don't want scum like you in this country. You make me sick.'

'Sabrina!' Dorian shouted. '*Get* in the *car*! NOW!'

Sabrina did as she was told, but not before hissing 'asshole' at the tattooed man, forcing Dorian once again to have to grab him and manhandle him down the lane before running back and scrambling into the driver's seat himself. He hit central locking and started the engine. As they drove away, he could see a furious red-shirted figure sprinting after them, hurling obscenities.

He turned to Sabrina, who seemed blissfully unconcerned in the passenger seat.

'For God's sake,' he snapped. 'Why do you engage them? Can't you see it only makes things worse?'

'Oh, so this is *my* fault now?' said Sabrina. Dorian noticed that her features had reset themselves to their default position of belligerent defiance. Was this what Saskia was going to be like when she got older?

'You called him a prick.'

'He was a prick.'

'Maybe. But people are angry, Sabrina,' Dorian said sternly. 'You *must* take some responsibility for that. You're in a position of great privilege, you lead a life most ordinary people can only dream of, and you've abused that privilege.'

'Give me a fucking break,' muttered Sabrina under her breath.

'No,' said Dorian hotly. 'I will not give you a break. What do you think would have happened if I hadn't been there just now to help you? To keep that man from attacking you.'

'I'd have survived.'

'Like hell you would.'

'Well, if you hadn't gone all Lord Capulet on my body-guards yesterday, I would have had some protection.'

'And if you would learn to walk away occasionally, you wouldn't need it,' said Dorian, exasperated. 'That's the last time you leave Loxley Hall unaccompanied.'

'*What?*' Sabrina exploded. 'You can't do that! I'm not your fucking prisoner.'

After all the shit Dorian had had to deal with on Sabrina's behalf today, not to mention just saving her ass from Mr Man United, this was the last straw. Slamming on the brakes, he skidded to a halt just outside Loxley's gates, leaned across Sabrina and opened the passenger door.

'You're right. You're not my prisoner. If you want to walk, walk.'

'What?'

'Now's your chance. Go back to LA and see if you can find someone else prepared to work with you. Go on. Go!'

The two of them sat glaring at one another in the darkness. For a few awful seconds, Dorian thought Sabrina was going to call his bluff and get out of the car. When she didn't, he was relieved, but it was a relief tinged with regret. He could tell just by looking at her that she had completely shut down again. He'd lost her. All the progress they'd made this evening had been for nothing. Reaching across her again, he pulled the door closed. Sabrina shrank back against her seat, as if his arm were a rattlesnake about to sting her.

They drove on.

So much for the entente cordiale.

When she finally got back to her room, Sabrina slammed the door and sat down on the bed, shaking with anger. *What the fuck?* She felt betrayed, humiliated. Rasmirez had tricked her, playing 'good cop' so she'd open up to him, which stupidly, *stupidly* she had, then putting his preachy, you-do-as-I-say hat back on the minute they got in the car. As if it were *her* fault some yob had attacked her! And what was she supposed to do, sit there and take it while guys threatened and harassed her, accusing her of things she'd never done?

Angrily, she kicked off her shoes and pulled off her clothes, flinging them in a heap at the foot of the bed. There was a knock at the door. Sabrina ignored it.

Rasmirez, come to deliver round two of his lecture. Well he can kiss my ass.

A second knock was louder and more insistent. Furiously,

Sabrina walked over and opened the door in her underwear, lips curled and nostrils flared in defiance. 'What now?'

Vio stood in the hallway in sweatpants and a T-shirt, admiring Sabrina's semi-naked body for the second time that day. Her bra and panties were both made of sheer lace, so he could see the faint pink outline of her nipples and the dark border of neatly trimmed fuzz between her legs. He smiled appreciatively. 'Hi.'

Following his eyes downwards, Sabrina blushed. 'Sorry. I thought you were Rasmirez.'

Viorel's eyebrow shot up. 'That's how you'd open the door to Dorian?'

Realizing belatedly how it must look, Sabrina blushed even harder. 'Jesus, no! I mean, it's not like that. Nothing like that. I thought you were in bed, that's all. Sick.'

'I was. I heard the door slam. Thought I'd check if you were OK.'

'I'm fine.'

Indeed you are, thought Vio with a sigh. Three paracetamols and a few hours' sleep had done little to take the edge off his migraine, but the sight of Sabrina's deliciously voluptuous body appeared to be working wonders. Locking on to his lust like a missile finding its target, Sabrina stood on tiptoes and reached her arms around his neck.

'D'you wanna come in?'

She pressed her lips to his and felt her libido release like an opened dam, all the anger and frustration of her evening with Dorian flooding out of her. Clearly, Vio felt it too, kissing her back passionately, his tongue hungrily darting between her lips, his hands warm and rough as they roamed over her skin. They staggered inside, locked together, and fell back onto the bed. Sabrina closed her eyes and inhaled the scent of him, a heady combination of aftershave, sweat and a faintly minty smell of mouthwash. She could feel his rock-hard erection beneath his sweat pants – *at last, some good news!* – and slipped a hand beneath his waistband, coiling her fingers slowly around his dick, one by one.

Vio groaned. Then, with every last fibre of his willpower, he removed her hand, pulling it back up to his mouth and kissing it. 'We can't.'

Sabrina looked at him, surprised. 'What do you mean? Sure we can.'

Vio sat up and ran a hand through his hair. He frowned, annoyed at himself. 'No. We can't. *I* can't.' He shook his head, like a dog drying itself off after a swim, as if he could somehow physically 'shake off' his desire for her.

Sabrina pouted. 'You don't want me?'

'Of course I do,' said Vio truthfully. 'You're so fucking sexy it hurts.'

Mollified slightly, Sabrina gave him a quizzical look. 'So what's the problem?'

'You're my co-star,' said Vio. 'I never get intimate with co-stars. Not till after we wrap, anyway. It's a policy.'

'You're kidding?' Sabrina looked astonished. She tried to think if she'd *ever* had a co-star she hadn't fucked. No one came to mind. 'Why on earth not?'

Viorel shrugged. 'It's distracting. It affects the dynamic on camera.'

'But we're lovers on camera,' said Sabrina. 'Shouldn't that help?'

'Frustrated lovers,' Vio corrected. 'Unrequited lovers. Heathcliff sleeps with Isabella, remember? Not Cathy.'

'Oh. So you'd rather fuck Lizzie, you mean?'

Vio shuddered. 'No. Good God no. Look, it's not just the professional thing. You know as well as I do, on-set romances can get complicated. Someone always ends up wanting more.'

'Not me,' said Sabrina, truthfully.

'I'm not good at monogamy, even in short bursts.'

'Perfect. Me neither.'

Vio hesitated. He didn't doubt that sex with Sabrina would be fantastic. Certainly, there was no one else at Loxley he had the remotest interest in sleeping with, other than Tish Crewe, whom he wasn't allowed near. None of the make-up or prop girls were even vaguely attractive; the one camera girl, Deborah, looked like a librarian and Lizzie Bayer was borderline retarded. But he knew that the instant they slept together, his relationship with Sabrina would change irrevocably. Whatever she said now, she would end up wanting more from him than he knew how to give. Women always wanted more. It was embedded in their DNA.

'I should get back to bed.'

Sabrina hesitated. She had zero experience of sexual rejection. *What did one do in these situations?* On the one hand it was agonizingly frustrating to have to sleep alone tonight. But on the other hand, the prospect of a challenge was novel and exciting. Viorel Hudson had thrown down the gauntlet. *Policy, indeed!* She would seduce him eventually, of that she had no doubt. And how satisfying it would be when she finally got to watch that vaunted willpower of his crumble.

'Fine.' She smiled sweetly, unhooking her bra and letting it fall into her lap, cupping her magnificent breasts admiringly, as if she'd never seen them before. 'I'll see you bright and early tomorrow then. Be a darling and turn the light off on your way out, would you?'

It was all Vio could do not to whimper. He walked to the door and turned off the light.

'Goodnight, Miss Leon.'

'Goodnight, Mr Hudson,' Sabrina whispered. 'Sweet dreams.'

CHAPTER THIRTEEN

Chrissie Rasmirez stretched out her lithe legs on the sun-lounger and sighed contentedly, glancing around for the handsome waiter she'd seen earlier. She was at the rooftop pool of the chic SLS Hotel in downtown Beverly Hills. It was almost noon, the June sun was blazing down, scorching its way through Chrissie's Lancaster factor-30 sun cream and, just as soon as she got her second vodka lime and soda, all would be right with the world.

She'd flown out to LA two days ago to spend five gloriously childfree days in town, shopping, catching up with friends, and of course doing her bit for charity. Linda, a girlfriend from *Rumors* days, had invited Chrissie to the Starlight Ball, an impossibly ritzy fundraiser and the closest thing that Beverly Hills' ladies-who-lunch got to the Oscars.

'The economy's so bad, our ticket sales are way down this year,' Linda complained to Chrissie over the phone last week. 'We need you, honey.' At the time, Chrissie had been elbow-deep in playdough, helping Saskia make yet another princess castle for her collection of plastic dogs, and quietly losing the will to live. It was a hundred degrees in Bihor, with a hundred per cent humidity, but of course Chrissie wasn't allowed to sell off any of their mountains of antique silverware to pay for air-conditioning.

'It's not ours to sell,' Dorian repeated for the umpteenth time on one of his rare calls from his movie set in England. 'And, even if it were, they wouldn't let us install air-con, not in a historic building like ours.'

What was the point of living like a queen when you spent your days cooped up in a stifling playroom, sweating like a pig? Especially when one's friends on the other side of the world 'needed' one, and for such a worthy cause too.

Linda had offered Chrissie a room in her 'little guesthouse,' actually a mini-Versailles at the southern end of her palatial estate off Benedict Canyon, but Chrissie preferred to stay at a hotel. It gave her more freedom, plus she didn't want anyone to think she was in need of Linda's charity. (After a few short years of acting, Linda Greaves had married well and divorced even better, retiring into alimony-funded luxury at the grand old age of thirty-four. She was generous with her money, in the manner of people who have never had to earn it, but she *did* enjoy lording it over her less fortunate friends; those scraping by on their last few million, like Chrissie.)

A shadow fell across Chrissie's sun-lounger. 'Can I help you, ma'am? Is there anything you need?' The exquisite specimen who'd waited on her earlier was back, biceps bulging through his dark blue linen shirt, perfectly straight teeth gleaming, blinding white against the mocha tan of his skin. Chrissie put him in his late twenties, and a classic 'strug'. (Strug was short for 'struggling actor' and was the term used to describe all the film-star handsome staff in LA's upscale hotels.)

'I'd love another drink, please.' She uncrossed then

recrossed her legs in as inviting a manner as possible, sucking in her nonexistent stomach.

'Of course,' he smiled. 'And is that all?'

Chrissie looked him up and down, like a farmer considering a fattened calf for slaughter. 'For now.'

It was almost a month since Dorian had left for England, and longer than that since he and Chrissie had had sex. She had been so angry with him the last time he'd deigned to come home, she'd refused to share his bed. Under normal circumstances, she'd have distracted herself while he was away with one of the boys who worked in the grounds, or even a kid from the village. But ever since he'd caught her with Alexandru, Dorian had become crafty. She knew he had staff watching her, spying on her. Between the beady, resentful eyes of the servants following her everywhere, and Saskia's ceaseless demands for attention – despite three full-time nannies, the little girl constantly moaned for her mommy – Chrissie had begun to feel more like a prisoner than ever. Linda's phone call was like someone throwing a rope ladder into her tower. Chrissie had grabbed the chance to escape with both hands.

Needless to say, Dorian had bitched about it.

'The Starlight Ball? Isn't that, like, ten thousand bucks a ticket?'

'Fifteen,' Chrissie deadpanned. 'So what? It's for a good cause.'

Not as good a cause as our bank balance, thought Dorian. He also doubted very much whether Chrissie knew *what* cause the ball was raising money for. But he let it go.

'If you want to get away, why don't you come here? I miss you, honey.'

'Yeah, right.' Chrissie laughed bitterly. 'That must be why you've made so many trips home.'

'Come on,' sighed Dorian. 'We've been through this. I'm working.'

'Exactly. Why would I want to fly to some shitty, rainy film set in the middle of nowhere so you can ignore me for a week while you focus on your all-important *work*?'

Dorian was silent. She had a point.

'I don't like Linda Greaves,' he said eventually. 'She's a gold-digger.'

'It's LA,' shrugged Chrissie. 'If they threw out all the gold-diggers it'd be a ghost town. Anyway, you don't have to like her. *I* like her. And I need a break.'

Tonight's ball was at six, at the Regent Beverly Wilshire. Chrissie had bought her dress yesterday, at one of the boutiques on Robertson, a backless, knock-'em-dead D&G number in gunmetal grey sequins, to match her new six-inch Jonathan Kelsey stilettos. In an hour, she'd have one of the hotel's drivers whisk her up to Ole Henriksen on Sunset to get her nails and eyebrows done, then it was back to Melrose for hair at Ken Paves and finally back to her suite to have Betty help her into the dress and do her make-up. When they lived in Holmby Hills, Chrissie had had beauty treatments daily. In Romania, a week could go by without her so much as washing her hair. What was the point, with no one there to see it?

In the new, acid-green Madison beach bag by her side, Chrissie's cellphone started to ring. Lost in a particularly enjoyable sexual fantasy involving the strug waiter, a camera and a bottle of baby oil, she answered bad-temperedly.

'This is Chrissie.'

'Oh my *God*, honey. How *are* you? Are you *okaaaay*?' Linda still tended towards the melodramatic in her phone manner, a hangover from her soap-star days.

'I'm fine,' said Chrissie, admiring the strug's ass in his

tight white shorts as he bent low to deliver a drink to another guest. 'Grabbing some lunch before the spa at Sunset Plaza. Why wouldn't I be?'

'Oh my *Gaaaaad*!' said Linda again. 'You haven't heard, have you?'

'Heard what?' asked Chrissie, still only half listening. Linda could open a sentence with that kind of drama and end it with a remark about the weather.

'Dorian. And that tramp Sabrina Leon. It's all over *E!*, honey.'

Chrissie's blood ran cold. She watched as the downy hairs on her forearm stood on end one by one, like tiny, frightened dominoes. '*What* is all over *E!*, exactly?'

She'd given Dorian a hard time about Sabrina last time he came home, but that was only because she was mad at him for leaving her again, and for enjoying his life while she couldn't. Never for a moment did she actually believe he would cheat on her, with Sabrina Leon or any other woman. Dorian was so fucking faithful and devoted, he could make a puppy look disloyal.

'Pictures, honey!' panted Linda, who was now clearly enjoying herself. 'Pictures of the two of them *togeeeeether*. They ran them in some British newspaper. Oh my God. Like, *what* are you gonna *do*? I've already had reporters calling my house. It's crazy!'

'Why would they be calling your house?' asked Chrissie, realizing immediately after the question had passed her lips that there could only be one reason: Linda had tipped off the media that Chrissie would be coming by later, and that they'd be going to the ball together. *Publicity-hungry bitch.* But Linda wasn't important now. She had to get to a TV.

'Are you still coming tonight?' The note of panic in Linda's voice was unmistakable. Without Chrissie, she wouldn't be the centre of attention in front of the whole of Beverly Hills society. *And* she'd look like an ass to all the TV stations she'd already spoken to.

'Probably,' said Chrissie. 'Yes. I need to talk to Dorian.' She hung up.

'Here you go, ma'am. One fresh vodka lime soda. And was there anyth—'

'No,' Chrissie barked, downing the drink in one long gulp till the soda bubbles stung the back of her eyes. Suddenly the waiter's bland, regular features and Ken-doll body had lost all their appeal. If Dorian really had cheated on her, if it were true, she would have nothing to live for. Not because she loved him. But because *he* loved *her*. Her famous husband's devotion was the last remaining prop holding up the withered remains of her self-esteem. Without it, she'd be nothing: another scorned Hollywood ex-wife, replaced by a younger, more beautiful model. She'd be like Linda, only poorer. No one would invite her anywhere. All their friends would stick by Dorian and the new bimbo – that was simply the way it was. The only men who'd want to sleep with her would be strugs and plastic surgeons. *No!* She couldn't bear it.

She forced herself to calm down, gathering up her things and hurrying inside. There was a TV in her room that played *E!* 24/7.

It's not true. It can't be true, she told herself. *Not Dorian.*

'Cut!' Dorian shook his head, disappointed. 'Come on, Sabrina. Heathcliff's betrayed you. You're angry with him, you're furious.'

'I know,' said Sabrina, smiling playfully up at Viorel. 'This is me being angry. What do you want me to do? Hit him?'

'I want you to quit smirking and play the goddamn scene,'

snapped Dorian. 'And *you* can stop encouraging her,' he added tersely to Viorel.

It was two weeks since his run-in with Sabrina at The Carpenter's Arms, and since then her on-set behaviour had deteriorated sharply. She could still deliver a pitch-perfect Cathy when she chose to. The more he saw of Sabrina's acting, the less Dorian doubted her innate ability. But she seemed more interested in flirting with Vio Hudson, or deliberately attempting to get under his skin, than in showing Dorian what she was capable of. The attention-seeking was both blatant and wearing.

The girl needs a father, Dorian found himself thinking, over and over again. *Someone to draw her a line in the sand.*

Before that idiot had come along that night outside the pub and provoked an argument, Dorian had felt as if he were finally getting closer to Sabrina. At her core she was still a frightened little girl, hungry for love and acceptance. Though she professed to loathe him, it hadn't escaped his notice how quickly she became jealous whenever his attention was diverted elsewhere – helping Lizzie Bayer with a scene, for instance, or chatting with Tish Crewe once the cameras stopped rolling. Tish, in particular, seemed to bug Sabrina, perhaps because she was the one other female with whom Viorel Hudson spent significant time.

To Dorian's relief, the early signs of flirtation he'd noticed between Tish and Vio seemed to have melted away, and the two had formed a genuine friendship. After filming, Vio would often spend hours playing computer games with Tish's little boy, Abel. Tish had learned that as long as she steered clear of contentious subjects, like Romania, which she loved and Viorel loathed, and Sabrina Leon, about whom their opinions were reversed, Viorel could be great company: warm, funny and intelligent. It pleased Dorian to watch the two of them together, bringing out the best in each other. Around Hudson, Tish was less serious, less old-before-her-time. And around Tish, now that the sexual tension was gone, Viorel seemed to grow up and step out of the shadow of his own ego. The truth was, Viorel had never had a real friend before, someone who wanted nothing from him, who enjoyed his company purely for its own sake. He loved it.

But Sabrina hated it. She never missed an opportunity to put Tish down, making fun of her accent, which Sabrina could mimic perfectly, and rolling her eyes affectedly whenever she passed by the set.

'Take four,' Dorian shouted into the wind. 'Places.'

Viorel started back up the bank, to the spot where he entered the scene, but Sabrina grabbed his hand, pulling him back and talking at him animatedly, ignoring Dorian's instruction. In a boned, lavender crinoline that showed off her spectacular breasts like two scoops of vanilla ice cream on a plate, and emphasized the tininess of her waist, she looked even more ravishingly beautiful than usual, flicking her hair back and laughing coquettishly at her dashing co-star. *She's mesmerizing*, thought Dorian.

Last night, worried by the tight, club-of-two atmosphere developing between her and Viorel on set, Dorian had asked Vio outright whether they were lovers. He had denied it vociferously.

'Absolutely not. We're friends, but I would never cross that line. Not while we're working, anyway.'

Something about his tone had made Dorian believe him. But watching the pair of them flirting outrageously now, he felt his doubts creeping back.

'Sabrina!' he said, irritated. *She's deliberately defying me*. Knowing that she wanted him to lose his temper, Dorian struggled not to, but it was hard. He was growing mightily tired of Sabrina's time-wasting games, and so were the rest of the crew. Chuck MacNamee had already complained to Dorian about her diva-ish antics and outright rudeness to his staff. The sun would set in an hour or so, and everyone wanted to call it a day. Scenes with Rhys and Lizzie were a dream by comparison. Dorian would have to take Sabrina aside again later, a thought that depressed him more than he cared to admit. *It's as if she gets off on conflict, on making me the bad guy.*

'Hello.' Tish appeared at the top of the rise, with a large thermos flask in one hand and little Abel clasping the other. 'We bought you all some soup. Mrs Drummond's famous mulligatawny. You haven't lived till you've tried it.'

Abel squealed with excitement like a puppy when he saw Viorel, rushing straight across the set into his arms like an affection-seeking missile. Vio lifted him onto his shoulders and walked back down the hill towards Tish.

'For me?' He nodded towards the thermos.

'For all of you,' said Tish, her cheeks reddening.

In plain white shorts and a striped Boden T-shirt, her make-up-free face flushed from the walk, she looked sweetly adorable, the proverbial breath of fresh air.

Sabrina flounced over, all breasts and fury, looking neither sweet nor adorable, but breathtakingly sexy. 'Some of us are trying to work here, you know,' she snapped at Tish.

Chuck MacNamee and his lighting crew laughed out loud.

'Really? And which ones of us might that be, I wonder?' Chuck's stage whisper was audible to the whole set. To Sabrina's intense irritation, the laughter spread.

'OK. Take a break guys,' said Dorian. 'Five minutes.'

Sabrina stormed off in a huff, followed by Viorel, with a thoroughly overexcited Abel bouncing up and down on his shoulders. Dorian and Tish were left alone.

'Any trouble today?' he asked her. 'At the gates?'

Since the piece in *The Sun*, Loxley's location was no longer a secret, much to Dorian's dismay. Protesters had started congregating outside the gates, waving placards demanding for Sabrina to be sent home and jeering at any traffic that went in or out. They were a pretty tame bunch all in all. Other than one incident with an egg thrown at Dorian's car, there'd been no violence, and Sabrina herself had wisely not ventured out of the grounds. Though she resented Dorian's stipulation that she not leave Loxley unaccompanied, especially as Viorel and the others were out every night at The Carpenter's Arms, lapping up the attention of the adoring locals, even she could see that in the current climate it was probably in her best interests to lie low.

Tish shook her head. 'All quiet. I took some soup out there too, but they must all be at home, polishing their pickets.'

Sitting down on the bank, Dorian took a sip of the proffered soup. It was delicious, warm but not too spicy, the onion, curry and ginger melding miraculously in his mouth the way that only fresh, home-made ingredients ever seemed to. He thought disloyally how much better it was than his wife's efforts, then found himself missing Chrissie with an unexpected pang.

'Penny for them?' said Tish. 'You look like you're miles away.'

'Oh, not really,' lied Dorian, forcing a smile. He didn't know why, but he didn't want to talk about home. 'I'm a little stressed, I guess.'

'Sabrina?'

Tish looked over to where Sabrina was standing. Viorel was playing with Abel, holding him by the feet and twirling him around while he squealed with laughter. You could see Sabrina's pout from here.

'Partly,' admitted Dorian. 'She's been difficult today. But she's not my only problem. It bothers me that people know where we are now. The location's already been compromised. How long before other information gets out?'

Tish knew a little of Dorian's strategy, to keep the details of *Wuthering Heights* a secret in order to tempt investors once filming was complete. She wasn't sure she fully understood the logic, but presumably Dorian knew his own business and he seemed to feel that secrecy was vital. So much so that last week he'd arbitrarily got rid of all the TVs in the cast and crew's quarters and banned newspapers from the set, figuring that the more cut off they were from the outside world, the less chance of damaging leaks. Unfortunately, he didn't have the same powers of censorship when it came to Sabrina's bad press.

'The actual work is good. What we've shot so far,' he told Tish. 'I was looking at the rushes last night.'

'There you go, then,' said Tish encouragingly, wondering whether she should step in and tell Viorel to go easy on the twirling. Abel was still giggling but he'd turned a worrying shade of green. 'That's all that matters, isn't it?'

'I wish,' said Dorian. 'Sometimes I feel like King Cnut, trying to hold back the tide. Only Sabrina's not so much a tide as a tsunami. I've never known an actress who can generate so much bad publicity out of thin air. Hopefully, things will get better once we get to Romania. If she plays me up there, I can lock her in the dungeon.' He grinned.

In his jeans pocket, his cellphone rang.

'That's weird. I thought I turned it off.' Pulling out the offending object, his heart gave a little jump. The screen flashed: *Chrissie LA Cell.*

Despite all the rows, Dorian had missed Chrissie this past month, and regretted the distance that had grown up between them. He knew that her current trip to LA had been intended at least in part to punish him for leaving her, playing on all his insecurities about her fidelity, not to mention her spending. So the fact that she was calling him, unsolicited, was an unexpected surprise. A thaw in the permafrost at last.

'Honey! What's goin' on?'

Tish watched the way Dorian's eyes lit up when he took the call. Then she watched the light die, replaced by abject panic.

'What pictures?' He spluttered. 'I have no idea . . . *Sabrina*?' His eyes widened. 'That's ridiculous! Trust me, honey, that is so far from the truth it's hilarious . . . No, I didn't mean it like that . . . no, Chrissie, I don't think it's funny. I am not bullshitting you! We're totally isolated here, I haven't seen anything.'

He held the phone away from his ear. Though no one could make out the words, Chrissie Rasmirez's hysteria could be heard at forty paces.

Deborah Raynham whispered to the head cameraman, 'Sounds like trouble in paradise.'

'Poor Dorian,' said the cameraman. 'Surrounded by angry women everywhere he turns.'

Sabrina, who could smell a drama like a shark smelled blood, hurried over.

'Who's he talking to?' she asked Tish imperiously.

'His wife,' said Tish curtly. 'Not that it's any of your business.'

'At that volume I'd say it was everyone's business,' sneered Sabrina. 'Oh dear oh dear. Has our saintly director been caught playing away? Who's the unlucky girl?'

'You are, apparently,' said Chuck MacNamee.

'What?' The sneer died on Sabrina's lips.

'Sounds like someone's run pictures of you and Dorian getting cosy. Who's been a naughty girl, then?'

Tish's eyebrows shot up. *Dorian and Sabrina? Surely not.*

'Don't be preposterous,' Sabrina snapped at Chuck. 'I wouldn't sleep with Dorian Rasmirez if he were the last man left on earth.'

'Perhaps you'd better tell that to his wife?' said Chuck, glancing over at Dorian. He'd stepped a few feet away from the set in the hope of some privacy, but his body language was clearly that of the condemned man pleading for his life.

'Come out here, honey,' he begged Chrissie. 'Please. Come see for yourself. There's nothing going on. Less than nothing. I know when those shots must have been taken. Some local idiot was giving Sabrina a hard time and I was saving her ass, as usual. Come on Christina. She can't compare to you.'

Hearing these last words, and knowing that Chuck and the others had heard them too, Sabrina felt a jolt of annoyance. She'd seen pictures of Dorian's wife. The woman was positively ancient.

'I wonder if she'll come out,' said Chuck.

'Who?' Viorel had finally joined the throng, handing Abel back to his mother.

'Frau Rasmirez,' said Deborah Raynham. 'She's on the warpath, apparently. She seems to be under the impression that Dorian's been having his wicked way with Sabrina.'

The crew giggled. Even Tish couldn't resist a smile.

'Come on. That's ridiculous,' said Vio.

'*Thank* you,' said Sabrina with feeling. At least someone was prepared to stick up for her.

'What's a "wicked way"?' asked Abel. 'Can I have one?'

'All right, young man,' said Tish briskly, sensing that the conversation might be about to turn distinctly X-rated. 'Let's get you back to the house.'

'If Chrissie Rasmirez does fly over, we're all gonna need hard hats,' Chuck MacNamee warned, once Tish had gone. 'That lady generates on-set tension faster than a wasp in the undershorts.'

'Oh, I don't know,' mused Sabrina. 'Maybe if Dorian gets some action he'll be less of an uptight asshole to work with. What do you think, darling?' She snaked an arm around Viorel's waist. 'Do you think a good fuck might ease the tension around here?'

Vio felt a rush of blood to his groin. Sabrina would have been delighted if she knew how hard he was finding it, keeping to his vow of self-denial. Every day he wanted her more.

'After we wrap,' he said hoarsely, rubbing a hand against the small of her back.

'Uh-uh.' Sabrina shook her head, walking away in the direction of the wardrobe trailer. Dorian was still glued to the phone. Clearly, they weren't going to do another take this evening. 'If you leave it till the wrap party, I'll turn you down.'

Vio laughed arrogantly. 'No, you won't.'

Sabrina quickened her pace, skipping away from him down the hill. 'Watch me!' she called back over her shoulder.

Later that night, Tish carried a sleeping Abel back to his bedroom. He'd wet the bed four times in the last two weeks, a regression that Tish could think of no explanation for. She'd started lifting him for a pee at ten o'clock until he got over it.

In a way, she was glad. She loved the feeling of his warm,

sleep-heavy body in her arms, and the way he clung to her instinctively as she tucked him back into his bed. At Loxley, he slept in the same bed she'd used as a small child, a tiny continuity that somehow seemed poignant and meaningful to Tish. *So much has changed since then*, she thought, a little sadly. Soon, filming would be over. Dorian and the others would leave, first for Romania and then for Los Angeles and their 'real' lives. Tish would finish the repairs, install new tenants, and take Abel back to *their* real life, to Curcubeu and the children, to her apartment and disapproving Lydia, to Michel and Fleur . . .

'Mummy?' Abel's voice brought her back to the present. He opened his eyes sleepily as Tish laid him back in his bed.

'It's late, darling,' she whispered. 'Go back to sleep.'

'Mummy, next term it's gonna be football and Viorel says I'm so excellent about football I could definitely *definitely* be on the team.'

'Shhh, Abi,' said Tish. 'Next term we'll be back home.'

A cloud of anxiety passed across Abel's sweet, five-year-old face. 'But Viorel said.'

'I'm sure you're very good at football,' said Tish soothingly. 'When we get back home you can play with Vasile and Radu and the other boys. Show them how great you are. Now go to sleep.'

'But . . .'

'Good footballers need their sleep.'

After a bit more negotiation, she settled him down and tiptoed out of the room, closing the door behind her. It was time to have a little chat with Viorel.

She found him in the library, whisky in hand, flipping through her father's collection of Romantic poetry.

'Can I have a word?'

Viorel snapped shut the leather-bound copy of Wordsworth's *Intimations of Immortality*. 'Of course.' Tish was wearing a faded pair of Snoopy pyjamas and a man's dressing gown riddled with holes. She had her hair tied up in a bun and, as she came closer, she smelled strongly of toothpaste and talcum powder. 'You look like you're ready for bed. What brings you down here so late?'

'It's Abel,' said Tish. 'He's wet the bed again. I think he's starting to feel anxious about the future.'

'He is,' said Vio seriously, leaning back against the corner of Henry's desk. 'I meant to talk to you about it actually.'

'The important thing is not to confuse him,' said Tish. 'I know you meant well, but you really mustn't put ideas into his head about staying at Loxley. Once you lot all leave, Abel and I will be going home.'

Viorel frowned. 'Isn't this home?'

'Romania is where our life is,' said Tish. 'My work. Abi's cultural heritage.'

Vio stiffened. His own mother used to bang on about his 'cultural heritage' all the time. Martha Hudson never tired of reminding him how lucky he was to have been adopted, and how important it was that he become a doctor and return to Romania one day, to 'give back'. He hated it.

'Don't you think you're being a little selfish?'

Now it was Tish's turn to stiffen. 'I'm sorry?'

'I mean, you've adopted the kid. You've brought him here to England, shown him how the other half live, put him in a village school where he's happy as a clam. And now you want to uproot him again, take him back to that hellhole of a country, just because you like playing Florence Nightingale? I don't think you're seeing this from Abel's perspective.'

Tish struggled to control her anger. 'With respect, Viorel, I think I know my own son a little better than you do.'

'Then you know he wants to stay at Loxley,' said Vio stubbornly. 'More than anything.'

'He's five,' said Tish, as authoritatively as possible for someone wearing a pair of Snoopy pyjamas. 'He also wants to live in an underwater kingdom and eat chocolate buttons for every meal. That doesn't mean it's a good idea.'

'Now you're just being facetious,' snapped Vio. The whisky was fuelling his temper. That, and his own memories of growing up with a mother who put her charitable work before the interests of her own son. He tried to remind himself that Tish wasn't Martha Hudson. And that Abel wasn't him. But the thought of the little boy being torn away from all he held dear made Viorel's blood boil.

'I'm his mother,' said Tish. 'I know what's best for him.'

'What's best for you, you mean,' muttered Viorel.

Tish had no idea where this sudden hostility was coming from. Certainly, she'd done nothing to deserve it. There was a meanness to Viorel tonight, a self-righteous arrogance that she had never seen before. *Thank God, I never fell for him*, she thought with a shiver.

'I'm sorry you feel that way,' she said frostily. 'But I'm not here to debate. Abel is my son, and I am *telling* you not to upset him any further with this nonsense. Understood?'

'Fine.' Turning away from her, Viorel poured himself another whisky and reopened his book. He felt angry, but also helpless on Abel's behalf. What right did Tish have to let her own Mother Teresa fantasy blight the boy's life? It was a powerlessness that Viorel Hudson hadn't felt since boarding school. It frightened him.

Walking back upstairs to bed, Tish also felt shaken by their encounter. *How dare Viorel question my parenting! What the hell does he know about it, or about our life in Romania? Judgemental wanker.*

She tried to focus on her anger. But a small, questioning voice in her head made it difficult.

Am I being selfish? Am I putting myself before Abel?

She hoped not. *Wuthering Heights* had been Loxley Hall's saviour. Tish was glad she'd come back and let them make the film. But the sooner they left and life got back to normal, the better. For all of them.

Outside the Regent Beverly Wilshire, a legion of paparazzi lay in wait for the glamorous attendees of tonight's Starlight Ball, like a shoal of piranhas scenting blood.

In the back of Linda Greaves's chauffeur-driven Bentley Continental, Chrissie Rasmirez positively throbbed with excitement. It was a long time, years, since she'd been the object of so much media attention. Of course, she was used to having her picture taken. As the wife of a Hollywood winner, she'd been snapped on Dorian's arm at countless awards ceremonies and exclusive industry parties. But always as an appendage, a plus one. *Tonight*, she told herself, *I'm the star. It's me they've come to see, not Dorian.*

The fact that they were here because of Dorian's alleged infidelity did slightly take the edge off her triumph. But only slightly. For one thing, after speaking to her husband today and hearing the utter desperation in his voice, Chrissie was certain that Dorian hadn't, in fact, cheated. He wasn't going to leave her, for Sabrina Leon or anybody else. For another thing, if there was one role that Chrissie knew how to play to perfection, it was the role of the victim, the wronged wife stoically standing by her man. *Make that wronged, drop-dead gorgeous wife*. Her backless Dolce & Gabbana number looked even hotter on her tonight than it had in the store. Or perhaps it was Chrissie herself who was hotter, flushed with pleasure at so much unsuspected attention?

'You OK, honey?' asked Linda as they pulled up outside the hotel. 'You're sure you wanna do this?'

Chrissie looked at her friend, and felt her confidence swell still further. In a red Valentino sheath, with half of Siberia's annual diamond output round her neck, Linda looked rich, glamorous and *old*. Too much Fraxel had frozen her once-beautiful face into a bland, featureless mask. Her hair was too blonde, her tits too big and her smile too desperate. She was the perfect date.

'I don't *want* to do it,' Chrissie lied, arranging her face into an expression of fragile vulnerability. 'I have to. I can't let malicious gossip ruin my marriage.'

The popping of flashbulbs and calls of 'Chrissie! Chrissie!' as she stepped out of the car were almost enough to give her a small orgasm on the spot. Clasping Linda's hand, head down in a perfect Princess Diana pose, she walked slowly into the building, making sure the photographers got plenty of time to catch her sexy back-view before disappearing inside.

Tonight, she decided, was going to be a lot of fun. And it was. Friends old and new flocked around her, drawn to the drama like junkies to a dealer.

'Of course it isn't true,' Chrissie repeated to all of them, with practised, sorrowful dignity. 'Dorian's tried to act like a father to that troubled girl. He's too generous for his own good. Everyone knows Sabrina Leon's addicted to the press. It wouldn't surprise me if she'd planted the story herself.'

'Aren't you mad?'

Cue modest, forgiving head-tilt. 'I try not to waste energy on anger. Not when I have so much to be thankful for.'

By the time dinner came around and they all sat down for the auction, Chrissie was thoroughly enjoying herself. She'd had just enough glasses of champagne to loosen her up, been flirted with by at least two men who were better-looking than Dorian and another three who were richer, *and* she'd seen on the table plans that she'd be sitting next to Keanu Reeves, on whom she'd always had a mini-crush.

'Hello, Mrs Rasmirez. You're quite the belle of the ball tonight.'

Through her semi-drunken haze, it took Chrissie a few moments to recognize the immaculately dressed, handsome blond man who'd sat down beside her. Not until he'd kissed her hand and chivalrously pulled out her chair did it come to her.

'Harry Greene.' She giggled coquettishly. 'I don't think I'm allowed to talk to you.'

'Says who? Dorian?' Ignoring the dirty looks from his fellow guests, Greene pulled a cigarette out of a vintage silver case and lit it. 'Don't tell me you're the kind of girl who takes orders from her husband. I couldn't bear the disillusionment.'

'It's not a question of taking orders. It's a question of loyalty,' said Chrissie. 'And that's somebody else's seat.'

'Not any more it isn't. I'm afraid I wanted you all to myself, so I told Keanu he was moving.' Harry waved across the room to table nine, and a familiar dark-haired man waved back. Chrissie was torn between annoyance and gratification. She'd been looking forward to flirting with Keanu, but it was flattering that Harry Greene had singled her out, and sexy that he had the power to tell major movie stars where they could and couldn't sit. Chrissie had always been turned on by power.

'You know, your husband's a fool.' Harry leaned back in his seat, languidly blowing smoke rings into the air. 'Fooling around with Sabrina Leon when he has a woman like you at home.'

'He hasn't been fooling around with her,' said Chrissie stiffly. 'It's just the tabloids, stirring up trouble.'

Harry raised a perfectly groomed eyebrow, but said nothing.

Chrissie looked irritated. 'I trust my husband.'

'Is that why you're flying out to his set next week?' Harry asked wryly. 'Because you trust him so much?'

Chrissie cocked her head to one side, curious. 'How did you know I was going to the set?'

'I know a lot of things,' said Harry. He took another deep, satisfying lungful of nicotine and looked at her appraisingly, the way a trainer might examine a racehorse. Locking eyes with her he said: 'If you were my wife, I wouldn't let you out of my sight.'

Chrissie felt a rush of pleasure course through her. Of course, she knew that Harry Greene had it in for Dorian, and that he was probably flirting with her so outrageously to settle some kind of score. She'd never entirely understood Harry's beef with her husband – something about his ex-wife and a screenplay – but she knew he had damaged Dorian professionally. Not that she gave a shit about Dorian's precious career. No, what Chrissie cared about was the look of pure lust in Harry Greene's eyes. That was something that could not be faked.

This is what I've missed, she thought, *stuck out in Romania, running after Saskia all day like the hired bloody help. I've missed being adored.*

'Sure you would.' She played along. 'You're all the same, you directors. You're workaholics.'

'It's true I love my work,' admitted Harry, leaning in closer. 'But not as much as I'd love spreading your legs and licking you till you come and come and come.'

Chrissie gasped. 'You can't say things like that!' But she

was so turned on, she felt her eyelids getting heavy and her lips instinctively beginning to part.

'I can say whatever I like,' said Harry.

Chrissie squirmed helplessly as his hand began caressing her thigh under the table.

'I can do whatever I like. I'm a god in this town, sweetheart. I don't have to run around with a begging bowl every time I want to get a movie made, like your husband. You know what I heard?' His hand was creeping higher.

'What?' Chrissie breathed heavily, so aroused now she felt as if she'd been hypnotized.

'I heard all this bad press swirling around Sabrina Leon is killing interest in his movie. Withering *Heights*, they're calling it.' He laughed, stubbing out his cigarette. 'The film's dying on the vine.'

'That's not true,' said Chrissie, trying to block out the sensations in her groin and focus on what Harry was saying. 'If you must know he's had a lot of early interest from the big studios.'

'Like who?' Harry tried to keep his voice casual.

'Like Paramount,' said Chrissie smugly, 'among others.'

'And what "others" might those be?' asked Harry.

Chrissie opened her mouth to tell him, when something made her hesitate. It was as if the hypnotist had suddenly clicked his fingers and awoken her from the trance. *I'm being played*, she thought, furiously. *He's not interested in me. He's just pumping me for info on the damn movie*. Removing Greene's hand from her thigh, she cleared her throat. 'Nice try,' she said tersely. 'But if you want information about my husband's business, you're going to have to fish for it elsewhere.'

Turning her back on him, she engaged the man on her other side in conversation, and proceeded to ignore Harry Greene for the rest of the night. Irritatingly unfazed,

Harry focused his attentions on the pretty blonde to his right, 'helping' her to bid for a number of items at the charity auction, including a delicate Fred Leighton emerald necklace that Chrissie coveted wildly and a six-night stay at the Post Ranch Inn, which just happened to be Chrissie's favourite hotel in the entire world.

They didn't speak again until they were leaving. Reunited with an out-of-her-mind-drunk Linda Greaves, Chrissie was waiting at the coat check for her borrowed vintage mink when she felt someone come up behind her and slip a hand around her waist.

'You're right,' Harry whispered in her ear. 'I did want information. But I wanted you more.'

Before Chrissie had a chance to say anything, he planted a kiss on the back of her neck that made every hair on her body stand on end.

'Next time,' he murmured, and disappeared into the night with the blonde trailing in his wake.

CHAPTER FOURTEEN

Two days after Chrissie Rasmirez's arrival on the *Wuthering Heights* set, Chuck MacNamee opened a book on who would be the first to snap and murder her with their bare hands. Rhys Williams had put his money on Lizzie Bayer, whom Chrissie had audibly refered to as 'middle-aged' on day one. But most of the cast had bet on Sabrina.

On a good day, Chrissie was merely distracting, interrupting Dorian mid-take to offer suggestions on how this or that actor might play the scene better, or how a certain camera angle 'wasn't working'. On a bad day, she would deliberately rile an already overwrought Sabrina, ordering her around as if *she* were the director, criticizing everything from Sabrina's stance to her delivery to the way she wore her period dresses. ('Amazing how that girl can manage to look like a slut in anything.') She was only fractionally less overbearing with the rest of the cast, the one blatant exception being Viorel, for whom Chrissie quite plainly had the hots.

Off set, if possible, her behaviour was even worse. Used to being waited on hand and foot at the Schloss, Chrissie treated Tish like a maid, complaining about everything from the softness of her and Dorian's towels to the creaking of the water pipes at night.

'Can't you get that fixed? How's my husband supposed to be creative when our bedroom sounds like a sinking ship?'

When Tish pointed out that Dorian had made no complaints about the room until Chrissie arrived, Chrissie cut her off mid-sentence with a curt, 'Well, he's complaining now,' before demanding a taxi be ordered to take her into town to collect her prescription allergy medicines. 'This place is so dusty, I'm surprised you haven't all asphyxiated.'

Her most abominable rudeness, however, was reserved for Mrs Drummond, whom she seemed to view as some sort of indentured slave. After one particularly grizzly incident, when Chrissie had tried to insist that Mrs D hand-wash her period-stained underwear ('It's La Perla. I'm not trusting it to that clapped-out old washing machine') Dorian had taken her to one side and attempted to smooth the waters.

'This is not our home, honey,' he remonstrated gently.

'Thank God!' said Chrissie.

'And it's not a hotel either.'

'For heaven's sake, Dorian. You've paid for the location, haven't you?'

'Yes, of course. I'm just asking you to be sensitive, that's all. You'll be gone in a week, but the rest of us have to live and work together here for another month.'

'Oh, I see,' said Chrissie petulantly. 'Counting the days till you can get rid of me already, are you?'

Dorian sighed. It was hopeless.

Sunday was a day off filming, the first in seventeen straight days, and a much-needed break for everyone. Half the crew decamped en masse to the pub in Loxley. The other half retreated to their trailers to watch downloaded American football or indulge in the backgammon craze that had swept the set over the last two weeks. (Viorel was in the lead, although Deborah Raynham was giving him a good run for his money.) Sabrina announced her intention of spending the entire day in bed. By noon, she appeared to have kept her word. No one had seen her. Rhys Evans and Lizzie Bayer, who'd recently started sleeping together ('Any port in a storm,' as Vio had wryly observed to Sabrina), left early to spend the day at Alton Towers. Jamie Duggan, officially the most boring man on set, had pleased everyone by taking himself off on a cultural tour of the local Saxon churches.

All of which meant that Mrs Drummond's mouthwatering buffet lunch was attended by only a skeleton crew of five: Tish and Abel, Dorian and Chrissie, and Viorel.

'This chicken pie's yummy!' Abel mumbled appreciatively, spraying pastry crumbs all over the table, his cheeks stuffed full like a chipmunk's. 'Canniavanothslice?'

'No,' said Tish. 'You haven't even finished what's in your mouth yet, greedy grub.'

'Let the kid eat,' said Viorel contemptuously, sending his own plate of pie flying across the table like an ice-hockey puck in Abel's direction. 'He's a growing boy.'

'Cool!' said Abel, catching the speeding plate and giving Vio a big thumbs-up sign before cramming the third slice into his mouth.

Dorian observed this little exchange with a growing feeling of unease. Something was up between Tish and Vio. Up until about a week ago, they'd been the best of friends. But now there was a tension you could have eaten with a spoon.

'Use your knife and fork,' said Tish to Abel, deliberately not challenging Viorel and giving him the fight he was so obviously spoiling for. *I've got nothing to prove to him*, she told herself angrily. *Certainly not my love for my son*. But somehow, ever since their run-in in the library, Viorel had an uncanny knack of making Tish feel as if she were on the back foot. It was infuriating.

'I've always believed you should let young children eat whatever they like.' Chrissie Rasmirez fluttered her eyelashes at Viorel. 'That's our policy with Saskia. Kids know what their bodies want instinctively.'

'Exactly,' said Viorel, with a triumphant glance at Tish.

Chrissie looked good today, he thought. Her frayed, white denim miniskirt and faded green T-shirt from Fred Segal showed off her tanned, fit body to perfection. More surprisingly, she looked relaxed, skin glowing, eyes lacking the telltale bags that her husband sported, symptoms of the stress and exhaustion involved in shooting a movie.

Tish also noticed how well Chrissie was looking. *You're beautiful*, she thought. But there was still something hard-edged about her, something cold. Once again, Tish wondered how a man as warm and emotional as Dorian Rasmirez could have chosen such a bloodless woman to share his life with.

Spearing a gherkin on her fork and slipping it into her mouth suggestively, Chrissie's green eyes locked onto Viorel's lapis-blue ones. 'I'm a big believer in listening to my body's needs.'

'So am I,' Viorel grinned, revelling in the attention. He wasn't particularly attracted to Chrissie. But since his run-in with Tish he'd been feeling a growing sense of frustration that increasingly needed an outlet. With Sabrina off limits, his options were slim. The flirtation with Chrissie was a welcome distraction. 'I'm religious about it actually.'

Tish felt embarrassed for Dorian and wildly disapproving of Viorel. The flirting was shameless. But when she looked up she saw that Dorian hadn't noticed anything. Eating mindlessly, eyes on his food, brow furrowed, he was clearly miles away, lost in worries of his own.

'What are your plans this afternoon?' Chrissie asked Viorel. 'My husband's going to be working, as usual.' She rolled her eyes.

Dorian glanced up. 'What? Working? Not the whole afternoon I'm not, honey. I need to look at some of the rushes of Rhys's scenes, that's all. It shouldn't take more than a couple of hours.'

'Yeah, right, and pigs might fly,' muttered Chrissie. 'I thought maybe Viorel could give me a tour of the local countryside. Show me some of the sights.'

'I'd love to.' Vio smiled wickedly.

The air was so thick with innuendo, Tish almost felt like covering Abel's ears. She certainly wished she could cover her own.

'But I'm afraid I already have plans. I'm taking a young lady into Manchester. We thought we'd do a spot of shopping this afternoon, then grab dinner.'

'A young lady? Who?' Tish heard herself asking. She didn't know why, but the idea that Vio might have scored himself a date seemed to rankle.

'You know her, actually,' said Vio nonchalantly. 'Laura Harrington.'

'Laura?' Tish choked on her Perrier water, sending a stream of frothy bubbles shooting out of her nose. 'The girl who came to babysit Abel the other night?'

'That's her.' Vio smiled.

Last Thursday had been Mrs Drummond's bridge night, and Tish had arranged dinner with an old schoolfriend. Laura was the teenage daughter of the local vicar, and had offered her babysitting services for eight pounds an hour. All Tish could remember about her was that she had terrible grammar, and that Abel had been wildly impressed with her 'princess hair'. Clearly, he wasn't the only one who'd noticed her charms.

'But she's a child!' Tish looked at Vio, horrified.

'She's eighteen actually,' said Vio. 'And very mature for her age.'

'*Mature?*' Tish scoffed. 'Please. She was carrying a Miley Cyrus backpack! She gave Abel two chocolate cream eggs in an egg cup for supper.'

'Did she?' Vio beamed. 'I like her even more.'

'He was sick all over his bed.'

'Yes, well, happily I'm blessed with a strong stomach.'

Tish's glare intensified.

'It's only dinner,' said Viorel. 'I'll drop her back home afterwards.'

After what? thought Tish furiously. Boy, had she misjudged Viorel Hudson. Being a flirt was one thing, but using his celebrity to lure an innocent local girl into bed? He should be ashamed of himself.

Chrissie Rasmirez obviously felt the same way, if her epic pout was anything to go by.

'Don't worry, Mrs Rasmirez,' Mrs Drummond piped up cheerfully. 'I'll have a word with Bill Connelly. Bill knows Derbyshire a lot better than Mr Hudson here. I'm sure he'd be happy to show you around until your husband's free.'

Momentarily forgetting their mutual disapproval of one another, Tish and Vio locked eyes and smiled. Chrissie looked as if someone had just squirted lemon juice in her eyes.

'Thank you,' she said sourly. 'I wouldn't want to be any trouble.'

'You should go, honey. Bill Connelly won't mind,' said Dorian, scoring himself no points with his wife whatsoever. 'If the forecasters are right, we could be in for some heavy rain in the next few days. Maybe even enough to hold up shooting.'

'Yay!' said Abel, jumping down from the table and disloyally settling himself down in Viorel's lap. 'That means you can play with me more, right?'

As ever, Abel's sunny, trusting little face brought out the lion in Viorel. He still couldn't get his head around the fact that Tish was planning to drag the boy back to some ex-communist dump in a few short weeks. If he could, he'd have stuffed Abi in his suitcase and brought him back to America.

'Of course.' He ruffled Abel's hair. 'We can play computer games and eat Hula Hoops till our tongues fall off.'

Tish shot him a thunderous look. She was so easy to wind up, there was almost no sport to it.

Yesterday, Vio had walked in on a conversation between Tish and Mrs Drummond. Tish was droning on about her bloody charity work, again.

'A lot of it's about training the local staff on the ground,' she was telling the housekeeper earnestly. 'When we first came to the children's hospital in Oradea, we saw seriously malnourished babies. The nurses were trying to spoon-feed them while they lay in their cots. Well, you can't swallow lying down. It's impossible. So that's the sort of basic thing we teach them.'

'I see, dear.' Mrs Drummond nodded sagely. 'That sounds marvellous.'

'Except that it's bollocks,' drawled Viorel. 'I know at least six girls in LA who can *definitely* swallow lying down. Perhaps I should send them out there, to train the kids?'

The look on Tish's face had kept him smiling all night long.

Laura Harrington was a disappointment.

Notwithstanding her tender years, the vicar's daughter had clearly been around the block a time or twenty. Having nixed the shopping plan ('I can think of better things to do, can't you?'), she'd taken Viorel out to a secluded part of Loxley's idyllic ancient woodland, and slipped out of her clothes before he'd had time to blink. Indeed, her whole been-there-done-that, business-like approach to proceedings left Vio feeling deflated and – odd as it might seem in the circumstances – used.

Lying back, he closed his eyes and tried to enjoy the painting-by-numbers blow job that Laura was giving him. No doubt she would be cataloguing it in graphic detail on her Facebook page later – *blow by blow*, he thought, laughing quietly to himself. He tried to turn himself on by imagining it was Sabrina's tongue darting around his cock, and not that of some chubby village slut with big tits and the IQ of a fossilized dog turd. But strangely, the Sabrina fantasy wasn't working either. After weeks of denial, perhaps he'd come to associate her with frustration?

Laura looked up. His erection was still strong – a blow job was a blow job, after all – but she could sense his lack of enthusiasm. 'What's the matter?'

'Nothing,' he lied.

'Would you rather just shag?'

Vio raised an eyebrow. And he'd thought Hollywood chicks were fast! 'You don't beat around the bush, do you?'

In answer, Laura straddled him, barely giving him time to slip on a condom before she lowered her pale, freckled thighs over his hips and slipped his cock inside her. She rocked back and forth, her melonous breasts juddering like water balloons, eyes closed in concentration more than ecstasy. Lifting her up, Vio turned her around so he wouldn't have to look at her mooncalf face. Closing his own eyes, he tried to focus on Laura's oversized boobs and not the sizeable arse that came with them.

At least I'm pissing off Tish Crewe, he thought, increasing the pace of his thrusts as he tuned in to his anger. Before he realized it, he found himself fantasizing that it was Tish naked on all fours beneath him; Tish's back arching in silent pleasure as he pushed deeper inside her; Tish's breasts he was squeezing and kneading like two balls of softest dough. The fantasy repulsed and excited him in equal measure. Part of him wanted to stop, but Laura was clenching her muscles more tightly around him, bucking wildly in response to his own increased arousal, and he knew he was too far gone to turn back.

When he came it was Tish's hair he was grabbing, pulling it painfully, wanting to hurt her as much as he wanted to satisfy her, wanting to punish her. But for what exactly? For taking Abel back to Romania, or for his own unhappy childhood? He didn't know any more.

'Ow! That hurts,' Laura complained. 'My hair. Let go of my hair!'

'Sorry.'

Viorel released her, like a man coming out of a trance. He slumped back on the blanket feeling frustrated and dirty, aware that behind the confusingly erotic images of Tish, a different woman's face hovered ghostlike in the background. He hated the idea that Martha Hudson could still get to him. That even now, after all his success, it was his adoptive mother who had moulded his relationships with women, sowing the seeds of self-destruction and distrust into his sexuality like a cancerous gene. He hadn't contacted his mother since he came to England, nor had Martha made the remotest effort to contact him. But clearly his falling out with Tish, and the connection he felt with Abel, had raked over feelings in his subconscious that he would rather not have been reminded of. Feelings of loneliness, of

abandonment and rage. What was that Philip Larkin poem?
They fuck you up, your mum and dad.

Was Tish going to fuck Abi up, the way Martha had him?

'Let's eat.' Laura's grating voice broke the spell. 'I'm famished. Where are you taking me?'

The thought of having to sit in a restaurant making small talk with this half-witted girl depressed Vio even further. But he supposed the least he owed her was a meal, and the alternative – heading straight back to Loxley Hall – was even less appealing.

'Where would you like to go?'

'Somewhere posh.' The girl was unequivocal. 'Harvester?'

It was late by the time Viorel got back to Loxley. In the clear night sky, a full moon bathed the house's fairytale turrets in a gossamer haze of softest silver, with no sign of Dorian's predicted storm clouds. *With any luck, we'll be shooting again tomorrow*, thought Vio. *I should get some kip.* The few lights left on in the East Wing gave the house a warm, welcoming glow and, as he crunched across the gravel to the front door, Vio was surprised by how much affection he'd come to feel for the place. Behind him he heard the rushing of the River Derwent as it skipped and danced its way through the valley floor. Above him, trees swayed gently in the night breeze, the rustling of their leaves soothing and rhythmic, like waves lapping on a shore.

Part of me will be sad to leave, he admitted to himself. *Sad to leave Loxley. Sad to leave Abel.*

A couple of weeks ago, he realized with a pang, he would have added Tish Crewe's name to the list of people he would miss. Was he being foolish, maintaining this feud? Perhaps he should try to build bridges. But then again, why should he be the one to make the first move?

Once inside, he closed the door gingerly behind him, hoping not to wake the sleeping household. He was halfway up the dark stairs when a figure in a dressing gown emerged from the shadows.

'You're late.' Sabrina's voice sounded low and throaty.

'Jesus.' Vio jumped. 'You scared me.'

'So how was the date with your teenage dream? Did you have fun?'

He sighed. 'Since you ask, no, not really.'

'But you fucked her anyway, I suppose.'

'Come on, angel,' said Vio placatingly. 'Don't be like that.'

'Like what?' snapped Sabrina. 'Pissed, you mean? That you can go out and get laid while Rasmirez has me stuck here like frikkin' Rapunzel, twiddling my thumbs?'

'Is that all you were twiddling?' Vio teased. But Sabrina was in no mood to see the funny side.

'I'm serious. I need to get out of here. I'm climbing the walls.'

'So go out.'

'How?' Sabrina laughed. 'Dorian's spies are everywhere. He'd eviscerate me, and the Countess Dracula would have my entrails for breakfast.'

'Poor baby,' said Vio, hugging her. 'If it makes you feel any better, the sex with Laura was terrible.'

'It doesn't make me feel better,' said Sabrina, pulling away and tying her robe more tightly around her waist like a knight fastening his armour. 'I hope you sleep like shit.' She stalked off, slamming her bedroom door behind her.

Wearily, Vio continued up the stairs.

'You should be ashamed of yourself, you know.'

That was all he needed. What was Tish doing up? Judging by the look of withering disapproval on her face, he assumed she'd overheard him talking to Sabrina about Laura.

'Give it a rest, Mother Teresa,' he said crossly, trying to erase the mental picture he'd had a few hours ago of Tish naked and desirous beneath him. 'We're not all gunning for a sainthood.'

Tish said nothing. She didn't have to.

The contemptuous look in her eyes said it all.

The following morning the whole house was woken by the rain. The storm that had seemed so invisible last night had arrived with a speed and force that shook the ancient glass in the windowpanes and battered the trees in the park till they were bent double. Water pounded against glass and stone relentlessly, a wild cacophony of drumbeats accompanying the tortured howling of the wind. It was the kind of dawn in which you almost expected to see Cathy Earnshaw's ghost at the window, her wrists bloodied on the jagged, broken glass, tormenting her beloved Heathcliff.

Dorian Rasmirez certainly awoke tormented. Half of the set village had flooded, with trailers containing not only people but also valuable equipment sinking feet deep into the mud. Chrissie, who'd taken a sleeping pill after they made love last night, was dead to the world. But Dorian had pulled Wellington boots on over his pyjamas and headed out into the torrent shortly after four a.m., to help Chuck and the crew with the salvage effort. Rhys had helped out too, God bless him, and some of the extras, but it was still an uphill struggle. At six thirty, exhausted and soaked to the bone, Dorian crawled back to bed, but the pounding rain made it impossible to sleep. There was no way they could film in this, and it might last for days, a delay they could not begin to afford.

I'll go to London, he thought. *See if I can wrangle a third loan out of Coutts. At least that way I won't waste the day.* He'd assumed

Chrissie would be delighted at the prospect of a trip up to town. She was due to fly back to Romania on Wednesday (it was two weeks since she'd last seen Saskia) and had been complaining ceaselessly that Dorian never made time for her, never took her anywhere, and that her visit had been a grave disappointment. But over breakfast she surprised him by turning down the chance of a London jaunt.

'I can't face going out in this weather,' she moaned, carefully removing all traces of yolk from her boiled egg before eating it. 'It's too depressing. I'd rather stay here and read.'

'Are you sure?' asked Dorian, a little ashamed by how much his spirits lifted at the prospect of going alone, but knowing he'd get far more done. 'I thought we could catch a matinée or something, after my meetings.'

'I'm fine,' said Chrissie. 'I have a new novel. And I never get time to read when I have Saskia with me. Really. You go. I'll stay.'

'Can I stay home too?' asked Abel, missing his mouth with a piece of Nutella-covered toast and smearing chocolate sauce across his cheek. He and his mother were also downstairs early, as was Viorel after a fitful night's sleep. Abel was dressed for the weather in a plastic Togz rain-suit and rainbow-coloured boots, over which he'd thrown a chain-mail knight's outfit complete with shield and visor. 'Viorel can play knights with me. Or Dinosaur King.'

'No,' said Tish firmly. 'You have a play date with Jack today. We're leaving straight after breakfast.'

'We can play when you get back,' said Viorel, ignoring the disapproving looks he was getting from Tish. He regretted sleeping with Laura, but he didn't need Tish to keep rubbing his nose in it.

'Viorel doesn't have time to play, I'm afraid, Abel,' said Dorian, folding away his newspaper and looking at Vio. 'You and Sabrina need to work on Cathy's ghost scene. Friday's effort was pitiful. As soon as this shitty weather lightens up, we're re-shooting it.'

'I'd be happy to,' said Viorel, 'although I can't vouch for Sabrina's willingness to rehearse with me. I'm afraid I'm not top of her Christmas-card list at the moment.'

'Really?' Chrissie visibly cheered up. She disliked Sabrina Leon intensely, just as she disliked all women who were better-looking than she was, and was jealous of her tight relationship with Vio. 'Why's that?'

'I have no idea,' said Vio, poker-faced.

Tish practically choked on her Earl Grey. 'Come on, Abi,' she said, hustling her son out of the room. 'We need to make a move.'

Dorian looked at his watch. 'Me too . . . I'll try and make it home for dinner tonight,' he said to Chrissie. 'We'll go out. Somewhere romantic.'

Chrissie smiled. 'Sounds nice.' She looked happier and more relaxed than Dorian had seen her all week. He hoped she was on the verge of forgiving him for the whole media storm about Sabrina.

I wonder if the bank will be equally understanding?

The weather was no better in London. But whereas in Derbyshire there was a certain romantic grandeur to the rain, in the city it was merely dirty and damp and depressing. Dorian sat in the back of a black cab, watching the raindrops chase each other down the windowpane, a game he'd played as a boy, fighting back his own dark thoughts.

What have I done? he brooded miserably, as they crawled along the Embankment. His meeting at Coutts had been a disaster. Not only were they not going to recommit more money to the movie, but they'd read him the riot act about his outstanding loan.

'You're four months behind on interest payments, Mr Rasmirez.'

Dorian did his best to rationalize this failure. 'This is the movie business. It's a long lead. Once the film's wrapped and I hook a big studio partner, you'll get all your interest and more.'

'Ah, but *will* you find a studio prepared to back you?' Hugh Mackenzie Crook, the Old Etonian head of the private banking team, fixed a beady eye on his errant client. 'You promised us you'd keep Sabrina Leon under control. Recently, her press has been worse than ever. Ever since she set foot in this country, it's been one gaffe after another, and now there are these rumours about the two of you—'

'All nonsense,' said Dorian. 'Completely fabricated.'

'Doesn't matter. Those stories are toxic, as you well know. If Sabrina's the star draw of your film, she needs to *be* a draw. Right now she's a turn-off. People'll pay *not* to see her.'

'I disagree,' said Dorian. 'The reason they're still running stories about her is that she still sells newspapers. She still sells.'

'Yes, but the film business is different, is it not? No one shows up to see an actor they dislike.'

'When you see the rushes, you'll know why they're gonna show up,' insisted Dorian. 'Sabrina's magical on film. Believe me, she'll blow you away.'

His confidence about Sabrina's performance was the real deal. And not just Sabrina's. Under his direction the whole cast, Rhys and Lizzie and Jamie, and of course the sensational Viorel, had delivered some of the best work of their careers. And Loxley had proved to be the perfect location, even more atmospheric and romantic and Gothically compelling in celluloid than it was in reality. He still had about a third of the film to shoot once he got to Romania. But he already knew that *Wuthering Heights* would be the critical triumph he'd dreamed of.

What he doubted was whether they could survive Sabrina's bad press. He'd tried to control it, to control *her*. But the shit kept flying. The truth was, Hugh Mackenzie Crook was right. Dorian was by no means certain that moviegoers wouldn't boycott his film, and big studios disliked risk. One more piece of negative PR, and his chances of hooking a white knight might well disappear completely.

'I'm afraid any further loan is out of the question until we receive our back interest on your outstanding debt,' said the banker, closing his lever-arch file with a distinctly final *click*. 'Good day, Mr Rasmirez.'

The taxi pulled up outside Rules restaurant, one of Dorian's favourite places to eat when in London. The Coutts meeting had been brutal but mercifully swift. At least now he'd have time for a proper sit-down lunch.

In the cosy, candlelit atmosphere of the restaurant, settled into a squishy leather booth with a perfectly steamed steak and kidney pudding and a restorative glass of claret, Dorian felt his bedraggled spirits start to revive. OK, so he hadn't secured any new money. But he had just enough left to finish the film in Romania, as long as he made a few cutbacks (and continued defaulting on his interest). And at least Hugh hadn't actually recalled the original loan.

There were other things to be thankful for too. His marriage had survived the vicious tabloid rumours. Chrissie would go home in a few days. Hopefully then some of the tensions on set would ease. If they caught a break in the weather, Dorian would be flying out to join her in a couple of weeks. He was determined to do a better job as a husband when he got home. *I'll pay Chrissie more attention. And I'll take up some of the slack with Saskia.* Aside from a few unsatisfactory Skype calls, Dorian realized guiltily that he hadn't laid eyes on his daughter in two months. *She's still only three,* he told himself. *I have time to put things right. To build a real bond with her, like the one Tish has with Abel.*

Tish brought his thoughts back to Loxley and what was happening on set without him. He hoped Viorel and Sabrina were working and not wasting their creative energy on some silly squabble. In the early weeks of filming, the sexual tension between them had at least been creatively productive. But inevitably, as Sabrina's frustration mounted, it had started to turn sour. On one level, Dorian instinctively revolted against the idea of Sabrina becoming another notch on Viorel Hudson's bedpost. For all her tantrums and spoiled, selfish behaviour, there remained something incredibly childlike and vulnerable about the girl that brought out all his protective instincts.

His phone rang, earning him dagger looks from all the other diners – pompous elderly Brits to a man. 'Sorry,' said Dorian, getting up to take the call outside, acutely aware all of a sudden of the Americanness of his accent. On the street the rain was still lashing the pavement, making it hard to hear. He cupped the phone to his ear. 'Hello?'

There was a crackle on the other end of the line, followed by some muttered cursing. At last he heard a familiar voice demand, 'Can you hear me?'

It was Sabrina. She sounded agitated.

'Yes, I can hear you. What's up?'

'I thought you said you could hear me? I already told you what's up. I'm in a fucking police cell in Manchester, that's what's up. I need you to come pick me up.'

'You're *what?*' Dorian exploded. 'What the hell . . .? What *happened*, Sabrina? What are you even doing in Manchester in the first place?'

'Look, I don't have time to chat about it,' Sabrina replied tersely. 'This dickhead cop's trying to get me off the phone.' There was another muffled altercation. It sounded as if someone were physically trying to pull the receiver out of Sabrina's hands. Occasional choice words cut through the crackle in Sabrina's strident American voice. 'Just get here, OK?' she barked at Dorian. Before he could say anything further, the line went dead.

For a few seconds, Dorian stood in the rain, silently contemplating his options. If he raced up to Manchester, there was a chance he could sort out whatever mess Sabrina had got herself into before the press got wind of it.

Who am I kidding? he thought miserably. *The local rag's probably already there.* Still, he had to try.

Racing back inside, dripping with water like a dog after a swim, he signalled for his bill. The waiter looked crestfallen.

'No pudding, sir? Are you sure? One really shouldn't go out into weather like this on a half-empty stomach.'

Dorian thought about the mountain of suet he'd just eaten and almost smiled.

Goddamn Sabrina.

Tish fastened Abel's seatbelt with gritted teeth. Outside the car, icy rain was soaking the lower half of her body so her jeans clung to her legs like a wetsuit. Inside, Abel continued to bounce his newly won stegosaurus toy through her hair, simultaneously wriggling around on his booster seat so it was almost impossible to click the belt into its holster.

'For God's sake, Abi, stop!' Tish snapped. It wasn't often she lost her temper with him, but Abi's behaviour today had been beyond trying. The planned day at Jack's house had been a disaster. Jack's mother, Monica, the yummiest mummy at the village school, was not the most involved of parents at the best of times. Today, she seemed to be even more in her own, self-absorbed little world than usual, dragging Tish off to look at her newly bought Fendi dresses while the two boys ran wild, having flour fights in the kitchen, almost setting fire to themselves in the drawing room, and finally coming to blows in a particularly testosterone-fuelled game of pirates played on Jack's bunk beds. After that, Monica had placated both boys with Kit Kats and Cadbury's Mini Rolls, adding sugary fuel to the fire, and plonked them down in front of *Ben 10: Alien Force*, a cartoon that never failed to transform Abel into a blood-thirsty little thug within about fifteen seconds. At home, Tish could have imposed order with a quiet word or, if push came to shove, by invoking the dreaded naughty carpet. But here, egged on by Jack and already resentful about being dragged away from Viorel, Abel's behaviour got progressively worse. In the end, Tish had been forced to take him home hours early.

'Do it one more time, Abi, and that dinosaur goes in the bin,' she said, finally strapping him in and squelching around to the driver's seat.

'You're mean,' muttered Abel.

'Probably,' said Tish grimly, heading out of the village.

'When we get home, I'm going to play with Viorel and not you.'

'You're not going to play with anyone, I'm afraid,' said Tish. 'You're going to tidy up that playroom, and then you can help me and Mrs Drummond make some soup. What are you doing?'

'I'm using "the force",' muttered Abel, ominously.

In the rearview mirror, Tish watched her son trying to

strangle her with Darth Vader's death grip, sweaty little fingers outstretched, eyes narrowed in malicious concentration. He seemed quite baffled that it wasn't working.

Despite herself, Tish laughed aloud.

'Come on, darling,' she said. 'Let's not argue. How about you tidy up your toys, and then we'll play Connect Four?'

They were still negotiating when they arrived at Loxley, but as soon as Mrs D came out with a tray of home-made shortbread biscuits, the tension evaporated. 'We'll tidy up the toys together,' she whispered conspiratorially, leading him off to the playroom. 'I'll race you.'

Exhausted and soaked to the bone, Tish followed them inside, heading straight for her room and a change of clothes. When she reached the landing, she heard the first noise. It sounded like a muffled scream. Heading down the corridor, she turned the corner to see one of her father's favourite Victorian lamps had been knocked off a side table. All the bedroom doors were open. A few feet further on, a broken vase lay between discarded articles of clothing.

Oh my God, thought Tish. *We've been burgled. In the middle of the day!*

A second scream, not muffled this time but audibly a woman in distress, rang out from the direction of Dorian and Chrissie's bedroom.

And the burglar's still here.

Arming herself with the fallen lamp (its heavy resin base would make a perfect blunt instrument), Tish ran towards the screams, adrenaline pumping.

'I've called the police!' she shouted. 'Whoever you are you can get the hell out of here, now!'

She burst into the bedroom and froze. It was hard to tell who was the more shocked: Tish, Viorel or Chrissie Rasmirez. Chrissie was naked and spread-eagled at the foot of the four-poster bed, with both arms tied to the wooden posts with what looked like ripped pieces of shirt – Dorian's shirt, unless Tish's eyes deceived her, which at this point she could only pray that they did. Chrissie's body looked even thinner naked and with arms outstretched, her breasts an insipid pair of fried eggs spread across jutting ribs, her hip bones grotesquely prominent.

Viorel was also naked but, lying flat on his back on the bed, he was mostly concealed by Chrissie. Unfortunately for all of them, Chrissie's enthusiastic bucking and yelping had only stopped when she registered Tish's presence, a full three seconds after Tish had in fact walked into the room. Three seconds that would be burned in Tish's memory for the rest of her life.

'You're back early.' Viorel's languid, arrogant voice was the first to break the silence. If he was embarrassed, or guilty, he didn't show it. 'I would say "this isn't what it looks like", but I'll admit I'm hard pressed to come up with an alternative explanation. Would you buy "experimental yoga"?'

But Tish was in no mood for banter. She turned and fled, unable to bear the sight of the pair of them a second longer. She felt sick, physically sick, and violated, as if Viorel had deliberately lured her into his obscene little peep show. Sitting down on the bed, she put her head between her knees, willing the nausea to pass.

There was a knock on the door.

'Go away,' said Tish.

'Can't, I'm afraid.' Viorel, who'd got dressed back into his black jeans and James Perse sapphire-blue shirt stood sheepishly in the doorway. 'We need to talk.'

'No, we don't.' Tish could still barely bring herself to look at him.

'We do,' said Vio. 'I need to know what you're planning to do. Are you going to tell Dorian?'

Incredible, thought Tish. *Even now, all he cares about is saving his own skin.*

'I don't know. I don't know what I'm going to do.'

Ever since their stupid falling-out about Abel and her plans to take him back to Romania, Tish had clung to her anger, convincing herself that her feelings hadn't been hurt by the loss of Viorel's friendship. Now she realized fully just how much she'd been deceiving herself. It was Viorel who had made her forget Michel. OK, so nothing romantic had developed between them. But his affection, the way he looked at her, sought out her company and advice; all that had restored Tish's self-confidence. She missed the person she'd believed Vio Hudson to be. She missed her friend, the one who had brought her back to life.

Viorel closed the door behind him and took a seat on a Liberty-print armchair in the corner. 'Come on,' he said. 'Don't drag it out. Are you going to spill the beans to Rasmirez or not?'

Tish turned on him furiously. Unable to handle her own hurt feelings, she focused on Dorian's. 'How could you? You know how much Dorian loves her.'

'What he doesn't know won't hurt him,' said Viorel.

'And that's an excuse, is it? You aren't even attracted to her.'

'Aren't I?'

'Well, are you?'

Viorel ran a hand guiltily through his hair. 'All right, no. Not really.'

'So why?' asked Tish. She was embarrassed to find that her voice was shaking.

'I don't know.'

231

A hundred possible answers to Tish's question played in Viorel's head, but none of them sounded good.

Because she was there.

Because I was bored.

Because I have to prove that every woman in the world wants me, to prove my mother wrong.

Because I'm an asshole.

He knew his own inadequacies. But Tish Crewe seemed to have the power to make him feel them in a way that no one else did.

'Look. Dorian's a good man,' he said. 'Please don't tell him. He'd be destroyed by it if he knew and he doesn't deserve that.'

'I know he doesn't bloody deserve it,' snapped Tish. 'You've put me in an impossible position.'

'Funny,' Vio quipped. 'Mrs Rasmirez was saying the same thing a few minutes ago.'

'This isn't funny! Don't you have any shame? Any moral code at all?'

Vio bridled. He knew he was in the wrong, and he hated to have Tish think so badly of him. Despite everything, he cared about her good opinion, probably more than he ought to. But he reacted instinctively against her preachiness. She sounded so like his mother sometimes, it was unnerving.

He stood up. 'I didn't come here for a lecture. I'd like to know what you're going to do. So would Chrissie. That way at least we can be prepared.'

'I don't care what you and Chrissie would *like*,' said Tish indignantly. 'You make me sick, the pair of you.' Her wet jeans clung to her thighs like a poultice. She shivered. 'However, as it happens, I'm not going to tell Dorian.'

'Thank you,' said Viorel grudgingly.

'Don't you dare thank me,' said Tish. 'I'm not doing it

232

for you. Or that bitch of a wife of his. I'm doing it for him.'

Vio scanned her face, trying to read the range of emotions there. The rage was clearly visible, flashing in her eyes like a lightning storm. But there was something else too. Sadness. Disappointment. Pain.

'I'm sorry,' he mumbled. And he was. He wished he could be the man she wanted him to be. But not everyone found self-sacrifice as easy as Tish seemed to.

Turning her back on him, Tish gazed out of the window at the rain falling in grey sheets over Loxley's park. She was horrified to find herself fighting back tears. 'Just get out.'

Sabrina Leon stared at the concrete ceiling above her head and tried to stay angry. If she didn't stay angry, she'd start crying. And if she started crying, she wouldn't be able to stop.

Why do these things always happen to me? Why?

After a fitful night's sleep tormented by dreams of Viorel having sex with the fat babysitter, she'd woken up to the sound of battering rain against her windowpane. Real *Wuthering Heights* weather, but clearly they weren't going to be able to shoot in such a downpour. Equally clearly, Sabrina knew that if she didn't do something to engage Viorel's sexual attention and make him jealous soon, she was in danger of losing every shred of power in their relationship. She was Sabrina fucking Leon, for God's sake, the most lusted-after woman in the world. And here she was, tolerating being rejected in favour of a local teenage moron.

With Dorian distracted in London, she'd never have a better opportunity to defy her house arrest and slip away for a little fun. It wasn't as if she intended anything too drastic. She'd wear shades and a headscarf under her raincoat and head into the city incognito. Then, after a little shopping, she'd lose the disguise, hit one of the local bars or clubs and flirt up a storm. Someone would inevitably photograph her with a good-looking man, just as they always did in LA. Tongues would start wagging and, with any luck, Viorel self-satisfied Hudson would be forced to sit up and take notice.

It should have been so simple. But of course, it wasn't. Despite her best efforts at concealment, she was recognized within a few minutes of arriving at Harvey Nichols in Exchange Square. An angry Tarik Tyler fan confronted her in the lingerie department (Sabrina was stocking up on her favourite Elle Macpherson bras, which were like gold dust in the States). Sabrina defended herself robustly, but within minutes the woman had been joined by a number of other shoppers, some of whom began to get physical, jostling and heckling and blocking Sabrina's path when she tried to leave. Eventually, to Sabrina's great relief, security arrived. But instead of rushing to her aid, they proceeded to try to escort *her* out of the store! As if *she'd* been the one making threats and causing trouble! As soon as the guard laid a hand on her arm, Sabrina lashed out instinctively, kicking and biting at him like a wildcat, demanding that he let her go.

After that, the rest was a blur. There were many more guards, and the crowd of hecklers swelled as people came to join in the action from other floors and departments. Eventually, the police arrived, and were even less sympathetic to Sabrina's plight than the store staff had been, bundling her into a van as if she were some sort of drug dealer, and now locking her up in this cold, windowless six-by-eight-foot cell.

'It's for your own good,' the staff sergeant told Sabrina. 'If we held you in one of the open cells, someone'd have a pop at you. And if we give you a window, there'll be a camera lens pressed against it before you can say "How's your father".'

Sabrina had no idea why she might want to say 'How's your father', or even what such an expression might mean. What she did know was that she had committed no crime, had not been charged, and therefore had every right to demand immediate release, something she did vocally, repeatedly and in increasingly colourful language, until a superintendent arrived, told her she could make one phone call, but that if a single further obscenity passed her lips in his station he would remove the phone and send her straight back to her cell to 'cool off'. Which, during her short but heated exchange with Dorian, he duly did.

That had been more than five long hours ago. It was evening now, and still no sign of Dorian riding to her rescue. Lying on her bunk, with nothing to do but brood, Sabrina's emotions seesawed from anger – at the crowd for attacking her; at Dorian for not getting off his ass and sorting this mess out; at fate for putting her, yet again, in such a hideous position through no fault of her own – to fear, depression and ultimately panic. Perhaps she had to face it. Perhaps her career, her reputation, would never be saved. Perhaps the moviegoing public, in their fickleness and cruelty, would never forgive her. She thought about Ed Steiner, the manager with whom she had battled for so many months back in LA. She could hear Ed's voice now: *I'm not asking you, Sabrina. I'm telling you. You have to take this part. Rasmirez just offered you a lifeline. It's your last chance.*

But Ed was wrong. Coming to England to play Cathy had not been Sabrina's last chance. That had already been and gone, so swiftly she hadn't even registered its passing. No one was going to give her a chance now, no matter how hard she tried, or worked or prayed. Not back home. Not here in this depressing, rainy little island, crawling with gutter press like a pelt full of lice.

There was a commotion outside the door. Voices, a clanking of metal. A bolt being drawn back. Sabrina sat up hopefully. *Dorian?*

'Come with me.'

No. It was only the staff sergeant.

Despite herself, Sabrina's stomach lurched unpleasantly with fear. She hadn't been in a police cell since her Fresno days, and it was not an experience she'd ever hoped to repeat. They were obviously going to charge her, with disturbing the peace, or affray, or some such archaic bullshit. They must be taking her to an interview room to make it official. Of course, she'd get off in the end. She hadn't done anything. But by then it wouldn't matter. A criminal charge would be the final nail in her career coffin, not to mention the death knell for *Wuthering Heights*. She'd fucked things up for herself, for Vio, for Dorian. It was all so unfair.

The sergeant was leading her down some stairs at the rear of the station, past what looked like the interview rooms. At the bottom was a long corridor with a fire door at the end. It almost looked like some sort of service entrance.

'What's this?' asked Sabrina. 'Aren't you going to charge me?'

The sergeant turned and looked at her. 'No, love. You're going home.' He smiled, and suddenly Sabrina felt her eyes welling up with tears. She could have stood anything in that moment apart from someone being kind to her. He opened the fire door. On the other side was an enclosed courtyard. An unmarked Nissan Altima was waiting, its engine idling. The windows were darkened. The front passenger door swung open.

'Get in.'

Dorian's voice sounded neutral. *At least he's not yelling*, thought Sabrina. *Not yet, anyway.* She got into the car and closed the door. Immediately, double electric gates in the rear wall opened, and they drove slowly out into the night. All the press were outside the front of the station, so they escaped without incident. It took Dorian fifteen minutes to navigate his way out of the city and onto the motorway, fifteen minutes in which neither he nor Sabrina spoke a single word. For Sabrina, the silence was torture, her mind running through every possible scenario:

She'd be fired.

She'd be sued.

She'd be fired *and* sued.

She wasn't sure whether her unauthorized jaunt to Manchester was officially a breach of contract or not. But it was certainly a breach of trust, Dorian's trust. As always when she felt guilty, Sabrina came out fighting.

'You took your time,' she complained as they eased into the slow lane of the M6.

Dorian kept his eyes on the road.

'I sweated it for five hours in that stinking cell.'

Silence.

'Not that I expect you to give a shit about *me*; about my false imprisonment, my being assaulted, any of that.' Sabrina flicked back her long dark hair dismissively. 'But I figured the media attention might have persuaded you to put your fucking foot down and get me outta there. Wrong again. What were you doing? Let me guess. Shopping with your *lovely* wife?'

'Are you finished?' said Dorian quietly.

'I guess.' Sabrina, who'd been expecting an immediate firestorm, suddenly felt stupid and chastened.

'Good,' said Dorian. 'Firstly, for what it's worth, I agree with you. You should never have been held. From what the police told me, you were clearly the innocent party.'

Sabrina was so shocked she was speechless.

'Of course, you should never have been in Manchester in the first place. You know you're not supposed to leave the set.' Sabrina opened her mouth to protest, but Dorian gave her a look and she swiftly shut it. 'But I understand your frustration, cooped up in that house for so long.'

'You do?'

'Of course.' Dorian smiled at her astonished face. 'I know things between you and Viorel have been . . . tense. I'm not an ogre, you know, Sabrina. I do have some inkling of the pressures you're under.'

'Do you?' Sabrina raised a sceptical eyebrow.

'Believe it or not,' said Dorian, 'I've been trying to protect you from them. To protect you from situations like this.'

'Protect your investment, you mean. Your precious movie,' said Sabrina, horrified by her own hostility, but apparently unable to stop herself lashing out. It was as though she had some bizarre form of Tourette's, a voice in her head telling her to self-destruct.

'No,' said Dorian quietly. 'That's not what I mean at all.'

Sabrina looked across at him, suddenly aware of how physically close they were in the confined space of the car. Dorian was so big that he seemed stooped in the driver's seat, and his knees appeared to be in constant danger of bashing against the underside of the dashboard. He looked tired too, she noticed, the grey hairs at his temples in keeping with the heavy bags under his eyes, and though he'd shaved for today's meetings, there was no disguising the pallor of his skin, despite weeks spent filming outside.

He needs someone to take care of him, thought Sabrina. *Someone other than that whingeing harridan of a wife.*

The combination of the darkness outside and the torrential rain slamming against the windscreen and roof heightened the sense of being in a cocoon: warm, insulated and safe, together. Impulsively, Sabrina reached across and stroked Dorian's cheek.

It was a small, tender gesture, but the sexual jolt it sent through both of them could have rebooted the national grid. Dorian reached up to remove her hand but found himself gripping it tightly, his fingers entwining themselves with hers. Suddenly it was hard to breathe, let alone drive. He pulled over onto the hard shoulder and turned to face her.

'Sabrina,' he began falteringly, barely trusting himself to speak. 'I . . . we can't.'

She leaned forward and kissed him full on the mouth. Not a long kiss, but passionate and hungry, a taste of the wildness inside her. Dorian kissed her back, but it was he who pulled away first.

'We can't,' he said again. 'Really.'

He said it so gently and with such kindness, Sabrina found herself nodding in agreement. 'I know. Of course we can't. You're right.'

Outwardly, she sounded calm. But inside she was still in shock, horrified by how much she'd wanted him in that moment. *Still*, she told herself, *it was just a moment*. An animalistic connection that flared up for a second between them and was gone.

'I don't know what I was thinking.'

'Nor do I.' said Dorian. 'A gorgeous young woman like you oughtn't to be wasting your time with a stuck-in-the-mud old man like me. You could have anyone you wanted.'

'You're not old.' Sabrina laughed, relieved that the tension had been broken. 'And besides, I can't have any man I want. I can't have Vio.'

After that it all came spilling out: her increasing longing for Viorel, her frustration at his rejection, her anger and despair about his screwing around, knowing she had no option but to sit by and watch.

'I came to Manchester to make him jealous,' she admitted, shaking her head with embarrassment. 'Pathetic, isn't it?'

Dorian put a reassuring arm around her shoulder. 'Not pathetic,' he assured her. 'Not the smartest move in the world, perhaps – I dread to think what the papers are gonna do to us in the morning – but not pathetic.'

'Oh God, the papers,' groaned Sabrina. 'I've fucked it up for all of us. Again.'

'Yes, well. It's not an ideal state of affairs,' admitted Dorian.

Sabrina eyed him suspiciously. 'How come you're being so calm about it?'

'I'm like a swan,' Dorian grinned. 'I look serene, but under the waterline my feet are paddling like crazy. Look, the truth is there are some golden rules in movie-making. And one of them is, if the director panics, the ship goes down. Studios want to see confidence. One sign of weakness and you're finished.'

Sabrina remembered how desperate she'd been to act confident in front of Dorian the first time they'd met, terrified that if he saw how much she needed it he'd take the part away. How embarrassingly cocky she'd been at that lunch in Beverly Hills.

'Thanks for bailing me out,' she said meekly.

'You're welcome. Shall we get going?'

Sabrina nodded and Dorian turned on the ignition.

Easing back into the sluggish traffic, he said, 'I do love my wife, you know.'

'Of course you do,' said Sabrina. 'I never doubted it for a second.'

Who's he trying to convince? she wondered silently. *Me or himself?*

CHAPTER FIFTEEN

For the next three days, until Chrissie left for Romania, Tish felt as if she were living in some sort of play. Everybody was acting, and nothing was what it seemed. *I suppose I'm as guilty as the rest of them*, she thought, watching Chrissie lavish affection on Dorian, hugging and kissing him at mealtimes and making a big deal about holding his hand on set. *I'm playing the detached, gracious hostess, behaving as if nothing's wrong. I'm part of the charade.*

Dorian had been in a strange mood ever since he'd got back to Loxley with Sabrina, who'd managed to get herself into even more hot water in Manchester. The headlines the next morning had been predictably awful, but Dorian seemed unfazed, pressing on with the shoot thanks to an early break in the weather. In two weeks, most people working on the film would be heading home to join their families. Only a skeleton crew and the five lead actors would be coming out to Romania to shoot the final interior shots at Dorian's Schloss. As a result, the end-of-term atmosphere was palpable. Once Chrissie left and the sun returned in earnest, the mood on set became even more positive. The work they'd done at Loxley had been worth all the effort. At last, they were on the home straight.

Only Tish found it difficult to share in the celebratory mood. Try as she might, she couldn't get the awful image of Viorel and Chrissie in bed together out of her mind. Every time she saw either of them, she felt sick. To make matters worse, the day after she'd walked in on them, she received a phone call from Carl at Curcubeu. One of the kids from Tish's children's home had been taken seriously ill with suspected liver failure. They'd had to empty the home's bank account to pay for the little boy's treatment. As a result, none of the carers had had their wages paid for a week, and two had threatened to quit. Tish had wired emergency funds right away, but Carl had made it clear this wasn't enough.

'The staff need to see you here, Tish. Morale's as low as it's ever been. People are starting to say that maybe you aren't coming back.'

'Of course I'm coming back,' said Tish, irritated. 'I was always going to be gone over the summer. Nothing's changed.'

'Well it has here,' said Carl bluntly. 'We're broke and exhausted. Child services know you're in England and they've been on our backs harder than ever. You know they want to reopen Vasile's custody case?'

Tish didn't know. She felt terrible. She'd been so caught up in all the drama at Loxley, she realized she'd pushed everything else out of her mind, even the children who counted on her. But at the same time, Viorel's criticism still bothered her. Was taking Abel back to Romania selfish? Or was staying here selfish? Whichever way she turned, she was wrong. Irrationally, she blamed Viorel for this.

'I'm damned if I do and damned if I don't,' she complained to Mrs Drummond one evening, sorting through a vast pile of Abel's laundry on the kitchen table. 'I feel like I'm being pulled three ways. There's Loxley, there's Curcubeu and there's Abel. And I can't let any of them down.'

'You aren't letting any of them down,' said Mrs Drummond matter-of-factly. 'Thanks to you, Loxley Hall's future is looking rosy.'

'I wouldn't go that far,' said Tish.

'I would. We've got that nice family moving in in October, haven't we?'

This was true. To Tish's delighted relief, Savills had found long-term tenants for the hall who were prepared to take occupancy in the autumn, once the shoot was over.

'Yes, that's a start.'

'And the last third of the film money's still to come. As for your children's home, you've paid the bills and you'll be back before they know it. And Abi will be happy wherever you are, my lovely. Don't let that jumped-up Hudson lad or anybody else tell you different.'

Mrs D's encouragement meant a lot. But Tish still felt depressed and overwhelmed. Since catching him in flagrante with Chrissie, living under the same roof as Viorel had become virtually unbearable. She couldn't wait for him to leave, yet at the same time she dreaded Dorian's departure and how empty Loxley was going to feel once they'd all gone.

One bright Thursday afternoon, Tish found herself with that rarest of luxuries, some time on her hands. Abel had gone out riding with old Bill Connelly, and was going to spend the night sleeping up at Home Farm in a tent, an event of almost indescribable excitement. Bill had found himself somewhat out of favour with Abi since Viorel's arrival, but with Vio now keeping his distance and focusing all his energies on the final few days of filming, the elderly farmer was once again proving a draw.

'Lavender and I'll take good care of him,' Bill assured Tish, unnecessarily. Conscious that their time in England was running out, she wanted Abel to squeeze every last ounce from his Derbyshire summer.

After two blissful hours hiding in the library window seat, lost in her book, Tish could no longer resist the lure of the late-afternoon light dancing across the woods and parkland, and decided to go for a stroll. Heading down to the bridge where she'd spent so many happy hours as a child, she felt quite overcome with nostalgia. Henry's presence was everywhere, in the cawing of the rooks overhead, the burbling rush of the stream, the dappled glow of the sunlight filtering through the leaves. *I've made my life in Oradea*, thought Tish. *But if home is where the heart is, Loxley will always be home.*

She sat there musing and soaking up Loxley's magic for longer than she'd intended. All of a sudden she felt cold and, looking up, realized it was dark. The night had crept up on her. Hurrying inside, she found most of the downstairs lights were off. It must be even later than she'd thought. A dim glow drew her towards the kitchen. There were bound to be some leftovers in the fridge and she realized suddenly that she was starving.

Not until she'd pulled the remnants of a cold roast chicken out of the fridge and turned on the hob to fry up some onions did she sense she wasn't alone. She didn't hear anything exactly, or see another body in the room. But she felt a presence behind her, so strongly that she didn't think to question it. She also sensed its malevolence. *Mrs D wouldn't sneak up on me like that,* she reasoned. *Nor would the film crew. They'd announce themselves. It must be an intruder.* Gripping the saucepan more tightly, Tish prepared to swing around, steeling herself for confrontation, when a familiar voice froze her to the spot.

'Hello, Tishy. Made enough for me?'

Tish turned around slowly.

'Jago.'

It was almost two years since Tish had last seen her brother in the flesh. He'd grown a beard since then and lost weight but, even in his current lean, angular state, Jago Crewe was preposterously good-looking. With his raven-black curls and sensuously full lips, he was so like their mother, Vivianna, it was disconcerting. Standing in the kitchen doorway now in an open-necked hemp shirt and flowing linen trousers, with various beads and talismans hanging from his neck and wrists, Tish thought he looked like a Hollywood version of Jesus.

'What are you doing here?'

Jago pouted, instantly ruining the beatific effect. 'Well, that's not very welcoming. What about, "How are you, Jago?" or, "Nice to see you, Jago"?'

Tish turned back to her cooking, mindlessly chopping at an onion.

'So what happened to Tibet? The life of a hermit started to pall, did it?' She made no effort to keep the sarcasm out of her voice. Tish loved her brother, but sometimes his selfishness was really too much. As for his faux spirituality, it had always stuck in Tish's craw. Especially as every time he committed himself to a new cult he abandoned his responsibilities without a backwards glance, leaving others to pick up the pieces. 'You're all caved-out, I suppose?'

'You know, that's always been your trouble, Tishy,' said Jago, walking up behind her and rubbing her stiffened shoulders. 'You're so quick to judge things you don't understand.'

'I understand that you buggered off and left Mrs Drummond at the mercy of your drugged-out bloody friends!' Tish said furiously, shrugging him off. 'I had to leave my home and my work to fly back here and get rid of them, but not before they'd trashed the place. They sold Dad's paintings, you know. Oh, no, sorry, you *don't* know. You were too busy trying to stick your head up your arse in some Tibetan fucking ashram!'

Jago shook his head pityingly. 'You see, there you go again. So materialistic. What's a painting, Tish? Some coloured marks on a bit of canvas, that's all. Let them go.'

'That's all very well,' snapped Tish, 'but some of those coloured marks were Staithes Group originals. We lost over a hundred thousand pounds, Jago! It's not about materialism, I don't want to rush out and spend the money on a bloody necklace. It's about preserving Loxley for the next generation. When I got here, we were days away from bankruptcy. *Days.*'

'I'm assuming that's why you sold your soul to Mammon,' said Jago, disapprovingly. 'I saw the film trailers parked outside. They're *American*, I assume?' He said the word as if it were code for 'vermin'.

'If it weren't for those Americans, you wouldn't have a home to come back to,' said Tish.

'Even so, you might have asked me,' grumbled Jago, helping himself to a Braeburn from the fruit bowl. 'You know I loathe Hollywood. The crap they churn out's all propaganda for the fascist, capitalist globalization movement. Loxley shouldn't be supporting that.'

It was all Tish could do not to hit him. 'I couldn't ask you,' she said through gritted teeth, 'because you weren't here. If you remember, you did tell Mrs Drummond and anybody else who'd listen that you wouldn't be coming back.'

'Yeah, well, life's a journey, isn't it?' said Jago. 'Things change. Now be an angel and give me a plate of that chicken, would you? I've been travelling for two days straight; all I want to do is eat and crash.'

'You're staying, then?' asked Tish despairingly, thinking of the tenants she'd lined up for October and all the hard work she'd done wrenching the estate's finances back from the brink.

'I dunno,' said Jago. 'I'll see how I feel. One step at a time, eh, Tishy? You gotta live for the now.'

The unexpected return of Loxley's prodigal son created ripples of excitement among the *Wuthering Heights* cast and crew.

All of the make-up and wardrobe girls pronounced Jago Crewe 'gorgeous' and took to hanging around the set in hot pants and barely there vests in an attempt to gain his attention. Poor Deborah Raynham could barely utter a syllable in Jago's presence, much to the irritation of Rhys Evans, who'd been quietly trying to woo the girl for weeks. Rhys wasn't the only male whose nose was out of joint. Viorel, who'd had the same effect on the girls when *he* first arrived, but who had rapidly lost his appeal once his on-set vow of celibacy became common knowledge, was wildly jealous.

'Personally, I don't see what the big deal's about with Jago Crewe,' he complained to the odious Jamie Duggan, who played Edgar Linton, Sabrina's on-set husband. Normally, Viorel wouldn't have stooped to chat with Jamie, who was a crashing bore, but he was fast running out of friends on set. Sabrina and Tish were both still barely speaking to him, and he avoided Dorian's company for obvious reasons.

'I agree,' said Jamie Duggan, tongue in cheek. 'A rich, landed aristocrat who looks like a Calvin Klein model . . . they're ten a penny, aren't they?'

'That's what I told Debbie,' chipped in Rhys Evans. '"It's a Welshman you want," I says to her. "Size isn't everything, you know." But does she listen?'

Vio frowned. 'He isn't that attractive.'

'Oh, come *on*.' Rhys nudged him in the ribs. He liked Vio, but he found his vanity hilarious. 'He's not exactly Quasimido, is he? Anyway, look on the bright side. Lizzie Bayer's so smitten with Lord Jago she's finally stopped boring everybody's tits off about her bloody career.'

'That's true,' Vio smiled thinly. Any relief he felt that Jago had captured Lizzie's vacuous attentions was more than counterbalanced by the effect he seemed to be having on Sabrina.

The morning after Jago arrived, he strode onto the set in the middle of a take and, completely ignoring everybody else, including Viorel and a furiously gesticulating Dorian, introduced himself to Sabrina.

'I loved *Destroyers*,' he said, taking her hand and kissing it. Sabrina was so taken aback, she actually blushed.

'Thank you.'

'You were so beautiful on screen, I didn't think it was possible you could be any lovelier in the flesh. But here you are. Jago Crewe.' He released her hand. 'A pleasure to meet you, Miss Leon.'

'Likewise,' said Sabrina, smiling broadly, ignoring the death stares from everybody else on set. 'And please, call me Sabrina.'

'Er, excuse me!' shouted Dorian irritably through his loud-hailer. 'We're in the middle of a scene here.'

Jago ignored him. 'I understand you've been here for

some weeks already, Sabrina. But if you were interested, I'd adore to give you a full tour of Loxley and her grounds.'

'I'd love that,' said Sabrina.

'Great.' Jago's face lit up. 'I need to reconnect with the place myself. I've been doing a lot of inner work recently, you know, following the call of the Spirit? But hopefully, I can bring a more centred energy now that I'm back.'

'Uh-huh,' said Sabrina, trying to keep her focus on Jago's chiselled bone structure and not the unadulterated drivel coming out of his sensuous, full-lipped mouth.

It was all getting too much for Vio. 'For God's sake,' he snapped. 'Can we get on with the fucking take?'

Delighted to have finally made him jealous, Sabrina deliberately reoffered Jago her hand for another lingering kiss.

'Till next time,' Jago murmured flirtatiously.

Sabrina was elated. *Put that in your pipe and smoke it, Viorel Hudson. Looks like you're no longer the only show in town.*

As the days passed, Sabrina's flirtation with Jago intensified. Apart from being a diverting way to pass the long, boring hours at Loxley, it had the added advantage of irritating both Viorel and Tish, who was annoying Sabrina at the moment more than ever. Her cliquey little friendship with Viorel now appeared to be well and truly over, thank heavens. But Tish's bossy, head-girl wholesomeness continued to rub Sabrina up the wrong way. She got particularly irritated by the way that Dorian continually leaped to Tish's defence.

'Give her a break,' he'd say, whenever Sabrina made some cutting remark or joke at Tish's expense. 'She's a nice girl, and a great mom. At least she's trying to make a difference.'

'So am I,' said Sabrina indignantly. 'You don't have to open a frikking Romanian orphanage to do good in this world, you know. I'm making *art*.'

She tried not to be put out by Dorian's hearty guffaw.

Since Manchester, Sabrina had grown closer to Dorian. The kiss was never mentioned and never would be. But the communication barrier between them finally seemed to have been broken. If only Tish Crewe weren't always around him like a bad smell, laughing and joking and talking about things that made Sabrina feel excluded, like politics and Romania and literature, intellectual things, Sabrina and Dorian might have really connected. As it was, Sabrina felt yet again as though she were playing second fiddle.

Tish acts like she owns him, she thought bitterly. *Like she's the only one who gets him. She's not even in the movie business. What does she know about his life?* It bothered Sabrina hugely that Dorian seemed so impressed by Tish, in awe of her even, because it played on her own deep insecurities and feelings of inadequacy. Around Tish Crewe, Sabrina felt like the little girl from Fresno again. She hated it. But Jago's arrival was a gift. Correctly surmising that by flirting with Jago she could strike back at Tish where it hurt, Sabrina wasted no time returning Jago's interest.

You try and take over my world, honey, and I'll try and take over yours. See how you like it.

Not that flirting with Jago Crewe was too difficult a sacrifice. True, he wasn't the sharpest knife in the drawer. Sabrina heard enough of all that New Age, spiritualist bullshit in California, but somehow it seemed even more vacuous delivered in a posh British accent. And true, he lacked sex appeal. Despite his undeniable good looks, there was something deeply vanilla about Jago. Like Viorel, he was vain, but Jago's vanity had none of the sharp, predatory edge of Vio's. However, one shouldn't look a gift horse in the mouth, particularly after so many months in a parched sexual wasteland. Jago was handsome, rich and quite openly smitten with Sabrina. In the wake of

Viorel's rejection, his lust alone was enough to draw Sabrina to him like a junkie to a needle.

Five days after Jago's return, he invited all the actors out to dinner at the new French restaurant in Castleton, Fait Maison.

'I see you've got over your moral objections to capitalist film-makers, then.' Tish looked up from behind a giant stack of filing on Henry's desk. Even now, with her return to Romania imminent, there was a lot to be done.

'You invited them, so they're here now. It'd be churlish not to behave graciously,' said Jago sanctimoniously. 'Besides, poor Sabrina's been cooped up at Loxley like a chicken for the last God-knows-how-many weeks. Rasmirez sounds like a total bastard, locking her up like Lord Capulet or something. I can't think why she puts up with it.'

Dorian had flown out to LA that morning on a suddenly scheduled three-day trip. The rumour on set was that he was in Hollywood doing some early scouting around for a distribution deal. But, as always with Dorian, information was thin on the ground.

'Dorian's lovely,' said Tish loyally. 'Trust me, "poor" Sabrina would try anybody's patience. Anyway, I thought you and I were going to sit down tonight and go over the finances?'

Jago sighed dramatically.

'You've been putting it off ever since you got home,' said Tish, 'but we have to talk. It's not my idea of fun either, you know.'

'Fine,' said Jago with a shrug. 'Come to the dinner. You can show me your precious pie charts while we eat.'

Now it was Tish's turn to sigh. Dorian and Rhys were both away, reducing the prospects for a jolly evening to nil.

Jamie Duggan and Lizzie Bayer, temporarily reunited since Jago had fixed his sexual attentions so firmly on Sabrina, would have eyes only for each other. Which meant that Tish would be left making small talk with Viorel while her brother drooled over Sabrina like a starving puppy.

On the other hand, she had to pin Jago down about Loxley. She hoped to convince him to hire a full-time financial manager after she'd gone. Soon she'd be back in Romania, and the thought of all her hard work going to waste – of Jago letting the estate slip back into the abyss – was enough to bring her out in hives. A least at a restaurant, he'd be trapped. She could force him to look at the numbers.

'OK,' she said. 'I'll be there. But I'm bringing the files with me. And you *must* look at them.'

'Give it a rest,' grumbled Jago. 'I said I would, didn't I?'

Tucked into what had once been a medieval millworker's cottage, Fait Maison was a cosy, candlelit gem of a restaurant, but very much designed for romantic dinners for two. The 'table for six' to which the owner proudly led Jago was tucked under the eaves and looked as if it had been made by elves.

'We're six people,' said Viorel. 'Not six eggs. There's barely room to breathe, never mind eat.' Happily, while he was still remonstrating with the owner, Jamie Duggan texted Sabrina to say that he and Lizzie had decided to stay at home and 'rest up' before shooting tomorrow.

'There, you see?' said Jago brightly. 'It's yin and yang, man. Everything balances out in the end. Now let's stop with all the negativity and have a beautiful evening, shall we?'

The quaint elfin table had benches on either side rather than chairs, upholstered in the same cheerful red gingham as the tablecloth. Viorel squeezed his six-foot-plus frame into one of the benches, narrowly missing whacking his head on a low beam as he sat down. Tish quickly made a beeline for the opposite bench, sitting as far away from him as possible, but she was still so close she could have held his hand across the table. She didn't understand why part of her still wanted to. To her right, Jago was pressed against her like a giant sardine in a tin.

'Are you all right?' he asked Sabrina. 'Not too squashed?'

'I'm fine, thank you. Very comfortable.'

Perched opposite Jago on the end of the bench, next to Viorel, Sabrina was so slim and tiny she had somehow contrived to surround herself with space. *She and Vio look like two magnets repelling each other*, thought Tish. Vio was dressed casually in jeans and a T-shirt and hadn't bothered to shave, but Sabrina had clearly made an effort in a white lace Marc Jacobs sundress and a pair of delicate Louboutin sandals in palest coral pink. Unusually for her, her long hair was tied up in a ponytail and she wore a simple single-pearl pendant at her neck, enhancing the youthful innocence. Even Tish had to admit she looked stunning.

Viorel, on the other hand, looked tired and irritable, and as if he wanted to be there even less than Tish did, if that were possible. His arms were folded defensively, and his face set into a petulant scowl as he glared at the menu.

As Jago and Sabrina chattered away, focusing wholly on each other, the silence on Tish and Vio's end of the table was becoming oppressive.

'The food's supposed to be good here,' said Tish, forcing herself to at least be polite.

'I hate French cuisine,' said Viorel.

Oh, fuck you, thought Tish. Out loud she said, 'That's a bit sweeping, isn't it?'

'No.' Viorel looked sullenly up from his menu. 'It's fussy and pretentious. It's up its own arse. I hate all that classist, snobby crap. It's one of the many reasons I prefer America to Europe.'

'Really?' said Tish. Clearly, they were no longer talking about the food. 'Well, of course I can imagine that snobbery must feel totally alien to you, coming as you do from such a simple background.'

Viorel's eyes narrowed. 'What do you mean?'

'The son of a minister, Eton, Cambridge, Hollywood . . .' mused Tish. 'I'm not surprised you're overwhelmed by the pretensions of Castleton.'

Viorel looked furious. That was definitely fifteen-love to Tish.

'Should I ask Henri to make you up a plate of egg and chips? I'm sure he wouldn't mind.'

'Don't be childish,' snapped Viorel. 'Must you make an argument out of everything?'

Tish was too gobsmacked by the hypocrisy of this to say anything at all. Silence resumed until the first course arrived, a giant pot of moules marinières to share between the table. Viorel picked at his helping, but managed to sink two large glasses of wine. Meanwhile, Jago made a token effort to include him in conversation, asking him some dull questions about playing Heathcliff and whether he was looking forward to the last leg of filming in Romania.

'I know you're itching to get back there, aren't you, Tishy? My sister's an honorary Romanian,' he stage-whispered to Sabrina. 'Can't get enough of the place.'

'I'm not there because I like it,' said Tish, more defensively than she'd intended. 'I'm there because I'm needed.'

Vio, whose head was becoming distinctly fuzzy, thought back to the countless interviews his cold and distant mother had given to the *Daily Mail* when he was a boy, about how Europe's orphan children 'needed' her. Never mind that her *own* child needed her. He looked at Tish with renewed bitterness.

'Of course. Where would all the poor abandoned kids be without you? Saint Letitia of Loxley.'

Sabrina and Jago both sniggered. Tish gripped her fork more tightly. God, she hated him.

'Well, *I'm* not looking forward to going to Romania, that's for sure,' said Sabrina. 'The only reason we're doing the interior shots there is to save Dorian money. There'll be nothing to do.'

'There's nothing to do here,' mumbled Viorel. 'But I agree, Romania's a drag. The sooner we get back to LA, the better as far as I'm concerned.'

'I hear Rasmirez's wife is a bit of a cow,' said Jago, trying to lighten the mood.

'That's an understatement,' said Sabrina. 'She was here for a week before you showed up and I swear we all wanted to top ourselves. She's got a face like a bulldog chewing a wasp. God knows how Dorian can sleep with her. It must be like sticking your dick in sandpaper.'

Despite himself, Vio laughed. He instantly regretted it.

'I'm surprised you find that funny.' Tish's voice was like ice. 'I got the *distinct* impression you and Chrissie rather liked each other when I came home last Monday.'

Sabrina's ears pricked up. You could have cut the tension round the table with a knife. She looked at Vio accusingly. 'What's she talking about? I thought you hated Chrissie.'

'I . . . no,' said Vio awkwardly. Would Tish stick to her word, or would she blurt out the truth to spite him? His palms began to sweat. 'I didn't hate her, exactly. She certainly had her issues, but I mean . . . she was OK.'

'*Issues?*' Sabrina looked at him uncomprehendingly. 'She was a fucking nightmare. Anyway, what happened last Monday?'

Viorel waited an agonizing few seconds for Tish to say something. When she didn't, he said brusquely, 'Nothing happened. She was asking my advice about some interior design ideas, if you must know.'

'Interior design?' Sabrina's eyebrows arched sceptically. But Vio was deadpan.

'Yes. It's a hobby of mine, design, architecture. You should see my Venice apartment some time. It would blow your mind.'

For a split second, the crackle of sexual tension was almost audible. Then Sabrina pointedly returned her attention to Jago.

'Yes, well, interior designed or not, the thought of living under Chrissie Rasmirez's roof for a month is about as appealing as going back to rehab. But at least it means getting out of Loxley. No offence, darling, but I think I've had just about as much of rural Derbyshire as I can stomach for one lifetime.'

Tish thought '*darling*'? *Good grief.*

Under the table, Jago slipped off his shoe and caressed Sabrina's bare calf with his foot. 'Don't say that,' he said smoothly. 'I haven't given you the full tour yet. At least give me a chance to change your mind.'

'Gladly,' purred Sabrina.

Both Viorel and Tish said silent, unheard prayers to Scotty to beam them up.

'You know, when I first inherited Loxley, I rebelled against it,' mused Jago. 'It was like, this represents *so* many things that I'm, like, *so* not about: wealth and privilege and, like, the class system and everything. But after some time away,

I realized, you know, maybe I was born into a family like mine for a reason.'

'Sorry,' Sabrina interrupted, a slow smile of appreciation spreading across her face as the full implications of Jago's admission dawned. 'You mean Loxley Hall is actually *your* house. Not Tish's?'

'It's a family house,' said Tish stiffly.

Sabrina laughed. 'Wait a minute, let me get this straight. All those earnest conversations you've been having with Dorian about the *pressures* of running a stately home; all your grand plans for Loxley Hall and the future after we wrap; and you're actually just a tenant, like the rest of us?'

'Loxley's my home,' said Tish, fighting to keep the emotion out of her voice. 'I came back to run it because Jago couldn't be bothered.'

'How very noble of you.' Sabrina took a slug of her wine. Turning back to Jago she said, 'But now you're back.'

'Now I'm back.'

'And Loxley belongs to you? The entire estate?'

'For my sins, yes,' said Jago, delighted by how impressed Sabrina seemed to be at this information. 'I suppose I'm a lucky man.'

Viorel looked at Tish's stricken face and part of him wanted to reach across the table and take her hand. But what would be the point? She'd only shrug him off and make him look like a dick for trying to be nice. She was impossible.

Sabrina, on the other hand, couldn't have looked more delighted if she'd won the lottery. She looked ravishing tonight in that demure but somehow super-sexy white dress. But by God she could twist the knife when she wanted to. Maybe she and Jago deserved each other, although the thought of that Anglo-Italian gigolo touching Sabrina made Vio want to rip Jago's handsome head off with his bare hands.

Dinner limped on. Tish and Vio had both lost their appetites and waited impatiently for the bill to arrive, while Jago and Sabrina drank and flirted happily. There was no way Tish could talk finances with Jago now. Sabrina would have a field day at her expense if she pulled out the financial files she'd brought with her, and in any case Jago was too drunk and love-struck to concentrate on the figures. The whole night had been a wash-out. Judging by the sour look on his face, Viorel felt the same.

When they got back to Loxley, Tish went straight to her room. Vio followed suit, much to Sabrina's chagrin. It was hard to make someone jealous when they refused to stick around and watch you doing it.

'Is Hudson always this miserable?' asked Jago, pouring Sabrina a large glass of Laphroaig from the bar in the West Wing library. It was a glorious room, especially at night with its dark wood panelling glowing in the candlelight like a newly polished conker. Sabrina wondered how she'd managed to spend two months at Loxley without ever noticing it before. 'I've had more enjoyable evenings on an operating table.'

'Not always.' Sabrina smiled, allowing her fingers to brush Jago's as she took the glass. She would never have accepted a drink if Dorian were here, but while the cat was away . . . Moving towards the window, she said. 'I guess his nose is out of joint since you came along.'

'Me?' Jago feigned ignorance.

'Sure.' Sabrina sipped her whisky. It was so long since she'd had spirits, the liquid burned her throat, but it was a delicious burning. All the more so for being forbidden. 'All the girls on set think you're hot. It drives Vio crazy.'

'*All* the girls?' Jago had moved up behind her. Slipping a hand around her waist he pressed his lips lightly to the back of her neck. Sabrina closed her eyes and let the arousal course through her. It was so long since she'd had a man, just the light pressure of Jago's lips felt wonderful.

'How about that tour I promised you?' he whispered. His warm breath made the hairs on Sabrina's neck stand on end.

'Sure,' she said huskily. 'You're the Lord of the Manor. Impress me.'

Jago thought for a moment. Though he'd have liked nothing more than to rip Sabrina's clothes off there and then and fuck her on the library floor, he didn't want to blow it. Sabrina Leon was a film star, after all, used to having men bend over backwards to please her. He had to think of something romantic, impressive, unique. Suddenly, it came to him.

'I know,' he said excitedly. 'The folly. Has anyone taken you across the lake yet?'

Sabrina looked at him blankly. 'What lake?'

'Perfect.' Jago grinned. 'Follow me.'

Fifteen minutes later, Sabrina found herself lying back on a pile of old blankets in the back of a rowing boat, gazing up at the stars. It was almost midnight now and there was a chill in the air, but wrapped up in two of Jago's sweaters and a heavy woollen overcoat of Henry's, and with the warmth of the liquor still in her chest, she felt cosy and safe and quite preternaturally happy.

The lake itself was a revelation. It was so close to the house – a short wooded path behind the stable yard led you straight there – and yet neither Sabrina nor anyone else on the movie had ever found it, as far as she knew. And it was big. Once you emerged from the path, the velvety water spread out before you apparently endlessly, like a giant sheet of silver baking foil. In the middle of it, sticking up like a strange, Gothic pie funnel, was a redbrick tower straight out of *The Lady of Shalott*.

Jago rowed towards it, prattling on about Buddhism and Tibet and what a perfect spot the tower was for transcendental meditation. Sabrina tuned out his voice, focusing instead on the rhythmic lapping of the oars against the water, and the way Jago's impressively sculpted biceps rippled with each new stroke. Above her, the stars shone comforting and familiar. She suddenly remembered looking up at them in Fresno, one particularly clear night when she was sleeping rough, and shivered to think how far she'd come. *Too far to slip back?* She wasn't sure sometimes.

'Are you cold?' asked Jago.

'I'm OK.'

'We're almost there. I'll warm you up once we get inside.'

They hit the shore with a gentle bump, and he dragged the boat up onto the grass, lifting Sabrina out and setting her down gently beside it. Looking up into the smooth planes of his face with its strong jaw, full lips and flawless olive skin, she wondered what it was that made him so much less appealing than Vio, then smiled to herself because the answer was obvious.

Viorel plays hard to get. I only ever want what I can't have.

Misinterpreting her expression, Jago smiled back. 'Your tower awaits, my lady.'

'I sure hope so,' Sabrina grinned, staring unashamedly at the bulge in Jago's corduroy trousers.

Walking up to the tower, she rattled the door. 'So does this thing open, or what?'

'Locked,' said Jago. 'Happily, I have the key.' Reaching into his pocket, he pulled out a heavy brass key, unlocking the thick wooden door with a satisfying click. Inside, slightly disappointingly, an electric light switch glowed in the dark. Jago pressed it, illuminating a narrow, winding staircase that seemed to swirl above them into infinity.

Freud would have a field day, thought Sabrina, starting to climb. But for the first time in a long time, she was actually having fun.

'What's at the top?' she called back over her shoulder. The stairs were steep and relentless and she was already becoming out of breath.

'A trap door,' said Jago. 'You'll see. Just push it, hard, and it'll open.'

A few seconds later, Sabrina saw it. As he'd asked, she braced herself against it with both hands and pushed. 'Wow,' she gasped. 'This is amazing!'

At the top of the tower was a small, circular room, with one enormous mullioned window facing the lake and the ghostly, moonlit turrets of Loxley Hall beyond. In daylight, Sabrina imagined, one must be able to see for miles. But at this time of night the view was limited to the hall's few, orange-bright windows glowing warm and inviting through the trees. Inside, the room had been simply but beautifully decorated in white, with cotton cushions and soft lambswool blankets scattered over the sanded wooden floor and a quaint, white-painted rocking chair facing the window. It was feminine, but not at all fussy: sparse and yet comfortable at the same time. Sabrina was delighted. Taking off her heavy overcoat and Jago's sweaters, she lay them on the rocking chair and twirled around like a little girl, the skirts of her Marc Jacobs sundress billowing up like a musical-box ballerina's. 'It's like heaven.'

She turned around and immediately found herself wrapped in Jago's arms, being pulled ever more tightly against the hard warmth of his body. 'You're like heaven,' he murmured. Reaching behind her, he expertly undid the zipper of her Marc Jacobs dress with one hand while the other caressed her cheek. 'You're the most perfect thing I've ever seen.'

Sabrina shifted her weight slightly onto one hip so that her dress slipped off her body onto the floor. Beneath it, she was completely naked.

Jago stepped back and caught his breath. He'd slept with countless beautiful women over the years, but none of them could hold a candle to Sabrina. With her full, high breasts, long, supple legs, and most of all with that face, so angelic and yet so utterly, defiantly wanton, only a nymphomaniac God could have created her.

Reaching up, Sabrina released her hair from its elastic band, never taking her eyes from Jago's as the slick chestnut mane spilled over her shoulders like molten chocolate.

Jago tried to speak but his throat was so dry, the words came out a strangled croak.

'Tell me what you like.'

'I like everything,' said Sabrina truthfully. *It's been a long time.*

Taking this statement as a metaphorical starting pistol, Jago began tearing at his own clothes as if they were on fire. Within seconds, he too was naked and had thrown Sabrina down quite roughly onto some of the cushions, positioning himself on top of her so that the tip of his enormous erection brushed the top of her thighs. *Good*, thought Sabrina. She wasn't in the mood for foreplay. Closing her eyes, literally squirming with excitement and anticipation, she imagined Viorel watching them, seeing another man take all the pleasure in her body that he'd so determinedly denied himself. *This'll teach you to ignore me. To think that you can lead me on, then walk away.* It was a delicious fantasy, so intoxicating that she found it hard to hold herself back from coming. Desperately, she reached around Jago's hips, trying to pull him inside her, but Jago pulled back.

'Uh-uh,' he whispered, teasing her. 'Not yet. You don't say when. *I* say when.'

It was like flicking a switch. Sabrina's eyes widened, her pupils dilating like a junkie after a hit. Jago slid his body downwards, parting Sabrina's thighs wider, slipping one hand under each of her taut buttocks. He bent low so she could feel his breath between her legs. Suddenly she no longer cared about Viorel. She was here in the moment, arching herself up towards Jago, her body begging him to give her what she needed, one animal to another. But again he made her wait, his tongue darting everywhere but where she wanted it, caressing her legs, her hips, her belly, tantalizingly close.

'No!' she moaned. It was agony: ecstatic, exquisite agony. She felt close to tears.

'No?' Again his voice was soft and controlled, relishing the power he held over her. 'You want me to stop?'

'NO!' It was a shout this time, and it spurred Sabrina to action. She sat up, pushing against him with all her strength, kicking, punching, grabbing at his hair like a wildcat. 'Do it!' she yelled. 'Do it now. NOW!'

Jago laughed, wildly turned on himself but determined to give Sabrina a night she would remember. Extending his forearm, he lifted her a few inches off the ground and held her wriggling at arm's length like a worm on a hook. 'Do what, now, exactly?'

'Fuck me!' commanded Sabrina. It was almost a snarl. Jago released her. Lying back, he pulled her on top of him, cupping one magnificent breast in each hand. Sabrina grabbed his cock hungrily, but yet again Jago denied her.

Raising his back and chest off the ground, his stomach muscles tightening into sculpted rock and his dark, Italian curls falling forward across his face, he said slowly, 'Please. Fuck me, please. If you really want it, sweetheart, you're going to have to ask me nicely.'

Sabrina lost it, lashing out again, but this time she was really trying to hurt him. 'I hate you!' she screamed, sinking her teeth into his shoulder. If she was trying to make him lose his cool, it worked. Jago yelped in pain. 'Bitch!' Sabrina lunged, trying to do it again, but he was too quick for her. Flipping her over onto her back, he pinned her down and drove himself inside her like an industrial drill, each thrust so violent that they shot across the floor.

Sabrina shrieked with pleasure. 'Harder,' she goaded him. 'More.'

Jago was a revelation. Who'd have thought Tish's vain, idiotic brother would turn out to be such an Olympian in the sack? His dick was like a goddamn tree trunk – almost as big as his ego – but it was more than that. Sexually at least, Jago knew how to press all of Sabrina's buttons. She was no longer thinking about Viorel, but as she raced towards climax, an image of Tish's disgruntled face at dinner tonight popped into her mind.

How much would Dorian's Little Miss Perfect hate it if she could see me with her brother right now?

'Oh fuck, Sabrina, I can't hold it,' Jago panted above her. 'I'm coming!'

'Me too!' gasped Sabrina.

As they exploded into one another, a second, even more intoxicating thought came to Sabrina.

What if I married him?

Dorian was so impressed with Tish's breeding and the Crewe family name. He made out that he only admired Tish for her charitable work and for being such a good mom, but Sabrina recognized the snobbery inherent in their friendship. She was also convinced that Tish looked down on her socially, that she saw through the movie star to the white-trash reject underneath. The thought struck Sabrina now. *Is that why I hate her so much? Because I think she'll make Dorian and Viorel see me the same way?*

If Sabrina were to become Mrs Crewe, all that would change. She wouldn't need a comeback movie to 'be' someone. She would be someone by right. Viorel Hudson could kiss her aristo ass!

'What are you thinking?' Jago cuddled up to her. He still could not quite believe that he, Jago Crewe, had just made love to Sabrina Leon. And that, unless Sabrina was a very fine actress indeed, she'd loved every minute of it.

'Nothing,' sighed Sabrina. 'Only that I'm happy you decided to come home.'

Me too, thought Jago. Life at Loxley Hall had just become considerably more interesting.

CHAPTER SIXTEEN

For the next ten days, Sabrina and Jago were inseparable. Whenever Sabrina wasn't working, the pair of them wandered around the house hand in hand, apparently unable to stop kissing and touching one another, and totally unconcerned about who might be watching their PDA-fest. Tish in particular seemed to bear the brunt of it. It seemed as if everywhere she turned she bumped into the two of them entwined and giggling. After one particularly gruesome breakfast, where she'd had to ask them to stop canoodling in front of Abel, she'd confided her worries to Dorian.

'Do you think it'll burn itself out?' she asked nervously, helping Mrs Drummond clear away the dirty cereal bowls.

'I hope so,' said Dorian, who didn't enjoy watching Sabrina and Jago crawling all over each other any more than Tish did. 'It's bound to. Sabrina will be in Romania soon and too busy to think about a long-distance love affair. Then she'll be back in LA, so it can't last. Unless . . .' a hideous thought just occurred to him, '. . . you don't think your brother's planning to come with us, do you?'

'Oh, no. He can't!' said Tish, aghast. 'He hasn't mentioned anything like that, has he?'

Dorian shook his head, but they both looked worried. Tish's concern was Loxley Hall. Despite her pleading, Jago still hadn't sat down to go through the finances with her, nor had he made a single decision since he got back: on the new tenants, on keeping up the farm, on anything. He was totally consumed by Sabrina.

Dorian's worries were more complex. On the surface, they were all professional. When Sabrina was filming, Jago would moon around the set like a lovesick puppy, and his very presence was proving divisive and distracting. More importantly, the chemistry between Sabrina and Vio seemed to have evaporated, and the atmosphere on set was becoming increasingly toxic. Not good with two of the key Cathy-and-Heathcliff love scenes still to be shot. No, Jago must not be allowed to disrupt things in Romania.

But Dorian's concern ran deeper than a director's professional anxieties. He disliked Jago Crewe quite intensely. He'd behaved horribly selfishly towards poor Tish, but beyond that there was something Dorian found instinctively untrustworthy about him. The last thing Sabrina needed in her life right now was another good-looking charlatan to distract her from her work and recovery. Especially a self-indulgent, hedonistic one like Jago.

'Isn't she luminous?'

It was late afternoon in Loxley's deer park and Jago was gushing to the sound engineer between takes about his 'girlfriend', as he now referred to Sabrina.

'Uh-huh,' said the sound engineer, pulling on his headphones so he wouldn't have to endure any more of Jago's drooling. 'Luminous' wasn't the first word that sprang to

mind when the sound engineer thought of Sabrina Leon –
'late', 'spoiled' and 'rude' all had more of an authentic ring
to them – but he wasn't in the mood to debate the point
with Lord Snooty.

'Fabulous energy, darling!' Jago called to Sabrina. 'I can't
take my eyes off you.'

Sabrina smiled and blew him a kiss. Next to her, Viorel
failed to conceal his irritation.

'How long are you planning to keep up this charade?' he
hissed through clenched teeth as the make-up girl
re-powdered his forehead. '*Fabulous energy*, indeed. You can't
possibly be attracted to that idiotic hippy.'

They both looked at Jago. Wearing an open-necked hemp
shirt with prayer beads strung around his neck and an orange
bandana tied around his forehead, Sabrina had to admit that
his dress sense did err on the alternative side. The headband
made him look like a Buddhist tennis player. But even whilst
doing his best John Lennon impression, he was still
improbably good-looking. And Vio knew it.

'Can't I?' Sabrina fluttered her eyelashes innocently. 'Why
not? Just because you've taken a vow of celibacy, honey, it
doesn't mean the rest of us have to. For your information,
Jago's one of the best lovers I've ever had. Why, only last
night he—'

'Take Three!' Dorian's voice boomed out through the
loudhailer.

Thank God for small mercies, thought Vio. For the last six
nights he'd been forced to listen through the wall to Jago
and Sabrina's highly vocal and athletic lovemaking. Hearing
Sabrina gasp in pleasure at another man's touch was
torturous, and at the same time disconcertingly arousing;
like getting a lap dance from a gorgeous stripper you know
you can't touch. As much as it pained Vio to admit it, clearly

Tish Crewe's moronic lug of a brother was doing something right in bed. Sabrina was a good actress, but nobody was *that* good.

Reciting his lines mechanically, Viorel was distracted by an extra running across the corner of the set and lost his thread. After a sleepless night and frustrating day, this was the last straw.

'What the fuck?' he exploded.

Dorian made the signal to cut the take.

'Hey, you!' Viorel shouted, advancing menacingly towards the culprit. 'Kid! Are you blind?'

The extra turned around, looking confused. He was only about sixteen, and Viorel Hudson was one of his heroes.

'Sorry, sir,' he mumbled, embarrassed. 'I didn't realize we were rolling.'

'You didn't *realize*?' bellowed Viorel. 'You just walked right through my fucking shot, you moron.'

It was so unlike him to lose his temper, the whole set turned around to stare. 'Go easy on the boy,' said Chuck MacNamee, but Viorel shot him down with a withering glance.

'What's your name?' he asked the boy.

'M-M-Michael,' stammered the extra. 'Michael Lega.'

'Well, Michael Lega, you are a fucking prick.' Vio reached out his hands and pushed the boy in the chest, making him stagger backwards.

'All right, that's enough.' Dorian walked over and broke the two of them up. 'Mike, go get us some coffee. We're taking a break. We'll shoot again in five.'

'No, screw that,' said Vio angrily as the extra scurried away. 'I don't want him back on set. He's a fucking liability.'

Dorian grabbed Viorel roughly by the arm and pulled him to one side. 'What the fuck is the matter with you?'

'What do you mean? Nothing's the matter with me. The kid fucked up my shot.'

'Bullshit,' said Dorian. 'I'd have cut the scene anyway. I've seen better acting from a goddamn waxwork.'

Viorel grimaced. He knew Dorian was right.

'What's going on with you?' Dorian went on angrily. 'You've been like this for days now.'

'I don't know,' said Vio, not meeting Dorian's eye. 'I'm not sleeping.'

'Yeah, well, you and me both,' said Dorian. 'Less than two weeks till we leave for Romania, and my Heathcliff's decided he's got nothing better to do than take out his shit on the set hands.'

'Sorry.'

For once, Viorel looked it.

'Good,' said Dorian. 'And you can apologize to that poor kid when he gets back. Now let's please make this our last take, OK? Get your head in the game.'

Vio nodded and walked glumly back to Sabrina, who was now perched on Jago's lap, stroking his hair the way one might pet a well-behaved dog. 'Temper, temper,' she goaded Viorel.

He ignored her.

'You know, anger is one of the three poisons that prompts samsara,' said Jago, his voice taking on the sanctimonious lilt he preferred when delivering such nuggets of spiritual wisdom. 'Samsara means rebirth. We need to cleanse ourself of poison before we can progress our journey towards the truth.'

'Fascinating,' said Vio sarcastically, determined not to give Sabrina the satisfaction of losing it a second time. 'You're quite the font of wisdom, Jago.'

As soon as they wrapped tonight, Vio decided, he was

going to ask Dorian for a week off to go home to LA. He shot his last moorland scene tomorrow, and the thought of hanging around Loxley like a spare part with nothing to do but watch the Sabrina and Jago show was more than he could stomach.

The only thing holding him back was Abel. With things so strained between him and Tish, Viorel had seen less of the boy than he would have liked over the past few weeks. He'd promised Abi they'd spend more time together once his scenes were over, and he didn't relish seeing the inevitable look of disappointment on the boy's sweet little face when he told him he was leaving.

But it couldn't be helped.

If he didn't get out of here soon, he was in danger of losing his sanity.

The next day, Tish took Abel into Manchester to shop for some new winter clothes. They'd be back in Oradea soon, where the winters made Derbyshire look like the Costa del Sol, and none of his warm things from last year came anywhere close to fitting him now.

It was a trying trip. Like most small boys, Abel detested shopping, unless it was for a Ben 10 omnitrix or anything 'dinosaurish'. He whined and moaned his way through the boys' department of Marks & Spencer, complaining about everything. Every shirt Tish picked out was 'girlish'. Every sweater was itchy, every pair of shoes too tight. Tish tried hard not to lose her temper with him. He was having a tough enough time dealing with Viorel's imminent departure.

Vio had told Tish last night that he was leaving early and he had broken the news to Abel today.

'I'll be sorry to leave him,' Viorel told Tish, and on this

point at least she believed him. 'But there's a bunch of stuff I need to deal with back home.'

He'd come to find her in her father's study, which somehow felt even more like Tish's home turf and put him even less at ease. The last time the two of them had been alone together had been the afternoon Tish caught him in bed with Chrissie Rasmirez. Then he'd felt like a naughty, inadequate schoolboy. He felt the same way now, as though he'd been sent to the principal's office, complete with desk and globe and wood-panelled walls.

'Of course,' Tish nodded. 'I understand.'

Although, the thought struck her that in fact she understood almost nothing about Viorel Hudson. He adored her son but loathed her. Or did he? They were friends; then they weren't. It was all very confusing. At times, Tish still felt a connection to Vio, an echo of the attraction they had both felt that first day when she'd met him half dressed and covered in soot. But whatever it was that drew them together then seemed destined to repel them now. Perhaps, in the end, they were just too different to get along? Vio clearly found her preachy and self-righteous, that much was clear, and it was true Tish disapproved of him wildly. Sleeping with your friend's wife was pretty shabby in Tish's book, and Dorian and Viorel were friends of a sort. Then there were his more general faults, his arrogance and his vanity. And yet there were flashes of real goodness in Viorel, his love for Abel chief amongst them. The man was a mess of contradictions. He claimed to despise the English upper classes, yet he radiated public-school poise and confidence, and gave Tish a hard time for taking Abel away from a life of privilege at Loxley. None of it made any real sense.

'I'd like to keep in touch with him,' Viorel said to the floor. 'If that's all right with you.'

'Of course,' said Tish. She was surprised by his hesitance. He was usually so arrogant around her, around everyone, but tonight he seemed nervous. 'He'll be sad to see you go, you know,' she heard herself saying. 'He loves you.'

Viorel looked up suddenly, like a driver with whiplash. For a split second, Tish caught a glimpse of anguish in his eyes. He *almost* looked as if he might be about to cry. But then he turned away, mumbling a hurried 'thanks' and something about packing as he hurried out of the door.

Back in Marks & Spencer, Tish tried to put Viorel Hudson out of her mind.

'What about this one?' She held up a puffa jacket covered in flying ace badges and with zips in the shape of aeroplanes. 'Shall we try it on?'

Abel shook his head. 'I want to go home,' he said morosely. 'I want to say goodbye to him.'

'Oh, darling.' Tish looked at her watch. It was already almost four. An unpleasant feeling of nervous tension crept over her. Were they too late? 'I think Viorel will have left for the airport by now. You said goodbye to him this morning, remember?'

Abel looked crestfallen.

'Cheer up, chicken. He promised he'd write to you, didn't he? And call, when we're back home in Oradea. Who knows, he might even come out and visit.'

'He won't,' said Abel, bitterly. 'He hates Romania. I hate Romania, too.'

'Abi.' Tish looked pained. 'Don't say that, darling. That's not true.'

'It is,' said Abel. 'I want to stay at Loxley forever. Why can't Uncle Jago go away again? Why does *he* get to stay there and we don't? Everyone I don't like is staying, and everyone I do like is going, and it's ALL YOUR FAULT!'

He burst into tears. To her shame, Tish found she was close to tears herself. Though she didn't want to admit it, the idea that she might never see Viorel again was almost as painful to her as it was to Abel.

She hesitated for a moment, not sure what to do. Then she put the jacket back on its hanger and took him by the hand.

'Come on,' she said gently. 'Let's see if we can catch him.'

'So I'll see you on the fifteenth.' Dorian stood on the gravel drive outside Loxley's grand front door, watching Viorel load cases into the boot of his car. It was a warm day and both men were in shorts. Pairing his with a checked Abercrombie shirt and Oliver Peoples aviators, Vio looked as if he were already in California.

'Absolutely. I'll be there. I appreciate you giving me the time.'

'Just make sure you get some rest in LA. Smoke some joints, get laid, do whatever you gotta do, but I want to see you in Romania refreshed and relaxed. No more yelling at my extras.'

'Yes, boss,' said Vio. Watching Dorian walk back towards the set he felt a pang of guilt. Rasmirez was a good guy, a better guy than he was.

Viorel had hated saying goodbye to Abel this morning, and his difficult interview with Tish last night had to rank as one of the least enjoyable five minutes of his life. Sabrina had pointedly not bothered to come and see him off, but he didn't really care. Now that he was finally packed and ready to go, he felt enormous relief. He needed an injection of reality, away from Sabrina and Jago, away from Dorian, whose kindness and good humour were starting to make him feel seriously uncomfortable. He was dreading the last few weeks of filming in Romania. Being in his 'home' country, seeing Chrissie again, living under Dorian's roof, it couldn't help but be a strain. But it *was* only a few weeks.

After that I'll be back in LA for good, five and a half million dollars richer and with enough beautiful girls on tap to push Loxley Hall and Tish Crewe and Sabrina Leon out of my head for good.

It was always like this on location, Vio reminded himself. Your world shrank to become one place, one small, incestuous group of people. One woman. *Two women?* No wonder his head was a mess.

A loud beeping made him look up. It was Tish, driving at a hundred miles an hour, leaning on the horn and spraying gravel everywhere as she skidded to a halt in front of him. Despite himself, Viorel thought how sexy she looked when she was flustered, with her face flushed and strands of hair flying everywhere. Before she'd even turned the engine off, Abi was out of the car, sleek black head down, arms and legs pumping, running into Viorel's arms and clinging on to him like a monkey.

'Don't go!' he sobbed, burying his head in Vio's open-shirted chest.

Vio bit his lip. 'I have to go, mate,' he said, hugging the child tightly. Before this movie, he'd never thought of himself as remotely paternal. Now he wondered how on earth he was going to cope having his own kids, if it felt this terrible to be leaving someone else's. 'We'll see each other again, though. I promise.'

'When?' wailed Abel. Tish had got out of the car and walked around to join them. Viorel tried to read her face. There was pain in it for sure. But was she upset because her son was upset or because he was leaving?

'I don't know exactly,' Vio said to Abel, floundering. 'Soon, I hope. I'll have to ask your mother.'

'Mummy likes you,' announced Abel out of nowhere, wiping his eyes on his sleeve. 'She acts like she doesn't, but she does.'

Viorel raised an eyebrow, but didn't dare look at Tish. 'Really?'

'Yes,' said Abel. 'Even though you're extremely irri . . .' He frowned, trying to remember the word Tish had used.

'Irritating?' offered Viorel.

'No, not that.'

'Irresistible?' Vio tried hopefully.

'Abel,' Tish did her best to sound authoritative, not easy with her heart beating nineteen to the dozen. 'Viorel needs to catch his plane.'

'I know!' Abel grinned as it came back to him. '*Irresponsible!* Even though you're extremely irresponsible, my mum does actually like you. So please come and visit us.'

Viorel looked at Tish. If ever there were a chance for them to patch up their quarrel and part as friends, this was it. But both of them were too stubborn to make the first move. Tish gave the briefest of nods and said, 'Of course. You're always welcome.'

'See? And when you come you can sleep in my mum's bed,' said Abel brightly.

Tish went puce. '*Abi!* Really, darling, you mustn't say things like that.'

'Why not?' asked Abel. 'You've got a big bed. There's a space in it. He can sleep next to you.'

Viorel grinned. Tish's blushes had always been one of her most endearing habits. 'We'll work it out,' he said to Abel. 'Now, I really have to go, kiddo, or I'm gonna miss my plane. I'll call you from America. After your bedtime, so you'll have to stay up late. That's how we irresponsible grown-ups roll.' Setting Abel down, he got into the car. Watching him go, Tish was mortified by how terrible she felt, how empty. But she pushed the feelings aside.

'Wait!'

Sabrina, still in costume from an earlier scene, came running down the hill from the set with skirts billowing, holding onto her bonnet like Scarlett O'Hara racing to see Ashley off to war. Above the boned bodice of the dress, her breasts jiggled precariously, as if they might be about to break for freedom at any moment, and her glorious long dark hair streamed behind her like the tail of some dark comet.

'Wait for me!' She arrived at the car panting, looking as flushed and wanton and desirable as Viorel had ever seen her. She was also smiling broadly, and seemed thrilled to have caught him before he left. *And I'm only going for a week,* he thought, smugly. *She does care after all.* Somehow it was doubly gratifying to receive Sabrina's unexpected show of affection in front of Tish.

'Sorry, angel,' he said suavely, kissing her on the cheek. 'It was nice of you to come and see me off but I've really gotta fly.'

'Oh, that's OK,' said Sabrina. 'I actually wanted to show all of you.' Letting go of her bonnet, she held out her left hand, beaming with pride. On her fourth finger, a diamond the size of a small frog glinted dazzlingly in the sunshine.

'Isn't it wonderful?' she panted, looking triumphantly from Viorel to Tish. 'Jago proposed to me this morning. We're getting married!'

CHAPTER SEVENTEEN

'Viorel, over here!'

'Vio, Vio, this way!'

'Is it good to be home, Mr Hudson?'

'Very good, thank you.' Viorel pushed his way through the throng of paparazzi and staring tourists that stood between him and the restaurant. The Malibu Country Mart was a well-known pap-trap, but Vio never really minded being photographed. In fact, after weeks stuck in England, it felt good to be back in the game. Besides, today was *definitely* a day for a little lazy lunch at the beach. For the first time in months, he'd woken up in his own bed in Venice and to the sort of Saturday morning that only Los Angeles ever really seemed to be able to conjure up: sunny, cloudless and blue skied, with a gentle breeze taking the edge off the eighty-plus-degree heat, and a palpable sense of energy and possibility in the air.

Carlos from the Bugatti dealership had delivered his beloved Veyron back to the apartment so, after a leisurely breakfast on the terrace gazing out over the Pacific, Vio had taken it for a spin, shooting down the coast almost as far as

La Jolla before turning around and flooring it back up Pacific Coast Highway all the way to Malibu, feeling like Tom Cruise in *Jerry Maguire*.

This is good, he thought, feeling the engine's immense power at his fingertips, drinking in the sunshine and the acacia trees and the majesty of the swaying palms that lined the familiar streets. *This is where I belong.* Speeding along the magnificent, winding coast road, he could almost believe that the past summer had been a dream. All of it: Tish and Abel, Dorian and Chrissie, Sabrina and the ludicrous Jago Crewe.

Although he'd been careful not to show it when he left Loxley yesterday, Sabrina's shock engagement had annoyed him more than he cared to admit. All the way to the airport, he'd found himself wrestling with an anger that made no sense when he analysed it rationally. *Sabrina wanted me*, he told himself. *I was the one who said no to her. So I can hardly bitch about her finding somebody else.* But marriage? To Jago?

He realized it was embarrassingly egocentric, but ever since Sabrina had got together with Tish's brother, Viorel had convinced himself it was a ploy to make him jealous. Not an entirely unsuccessful ploy, but a ploy nonetheless. But no one got *married* to someone just for the attention, not even Sabrina. The idea that she might actually be in love with Jago; that she honestly, genuinely *preferred* Jago to him, shook Viorel's ego profoundly.

Happily, waking up in LA had turned out to be exactly the tonic he needed. *Fuck Sabrina Leon. Fuck Tish Crewe. Fuck the lot of them.* Loxley's on-set politics wasn't real life. *This* was.

Sidestepping the last of the persistent photographers, he made his way into Tony's Taverna. Instantly, every female head turned to look at him. Vio felt his confidence returning like the tide.

'Mr Hudson.' The maître d' approached him, smiling warmly. 'It's been a long time, my friend. Your usual table?'

'Thank you, Carlos.'

Vio sat down and took off his sunglasses. The food at Tony's hadn't changed in ten years, and he always had the same thing anyway – tiger shrimp salad washed down with an ice-cold glass of retsina – but he reached for the menu on autopilot. As he lifted the stiff, white card, an exquisite blonde at the bar turned and made eye contact. Vio smiled and mouthed *Hi*. In white cotton hot pants and a tie-dyed vest, her long, tanned legs dangling from the bar stool like two sticks of toffee, she was a little bit generically Californian, but nonetheless sexy for that. He was about to go over and introduce himself – she was bound to know who he was, but to assume that she did might make him look like an asshole – when he suddenly stopped. A small boy with jet-black hair came running out of the bathroom and wrapped himself around one of the toffee legs. 'Mommy, Mommy, guess what they have in the boys' room?' he breathed excitedly. 'Magic faucets! You put your hands underneath, and the water shoots out by magic!'

The girl smiled and bent down to respond to him, but Vio was no longer interested in her. It was the boy. From behind, he looked so like Abi, it was uncanny. All of a sudden a dark cloud descended. The good mood Viorel had so carefully cultivated all morning was gone in a flash, like a candle flame snuffed out in the breeze. In its place, all the churning emotions of yesterday returned: anger, anxiety, unease, guilt. He missed Abel. But it wasn't just the boy. It was Abi's mother, too. He'd never had a real friend before. Tish was the first and he'd blown it spectacularly. He pictured her now as he'd last seen her, driving like a bat out of hell through the gates at Loxley, her cheeks flushed and her hair flying everywhere. Objectively, she wasn't nearly as beautiful as the girl at the bar. But Viorel seemed to have lost his objectivity somewhere over the Atlantic Ocean, at least as far as Tish Crewe was concerned.

'May I bring you something to drink, sir?'

A pretty brunette waitress was hovering at Viorel's table. Her cleavage was right at his eye level, but he barely looked up.

'Yes. No.' He frowned, irritated at himself. Two minutes ago he'd known exactly what he wanted. Now, whatever he ordered he knew it would be a glass half empty.

'I'll leave you to think about it,' said the girl, smiling sweetly. 'No rush.'

Ah, but there is a rush, thought Viorel. *I want my life back.* He was sick of feeling guilty all the time. His mother had often made him feel like that as a child – inadequate, lesser, disappointing. Tish Crewe seemed to have the same ability, to shame him with a look or a word, to make him feel like a naughty schoolboy when by rights he ought to be feeling like the King of the World. Landing the role of Heathcliff had been the biggest break of Viorel's career. Even if the film bombed, he would wind up a rich man. *So why aren't I happy?*

'Excuse me,' he called after the brunette. 'I'll have a retsina, please.'

She nodded. 'One glass of retsina coming up.'

'You know what?' said Vio grimly. 'Make it a bottle.'

He turned to look at the yummy mummy and her son, but they were gone.

'For God's sake, Jago. You can't!'

Tish closed her eyes and pressed her hands to her temples, counting slowly backwards from ten. She was in the kitchen, leaning back against the cool enamel of the switched-off Aga, and her head was pounding with a tension-induced headache that was starting to feel like a brain tumour. Jago was sprawled out in the armchair at the back of the room, with Sabrina coiled in his lap like a beautiful snake. *Beautiful and deadly*, thought Tish. *That girl is pure poison.*

'Of course he can,' Sabrina drawled, yawning dramatically to indicate her boredom at the circuitous debate they'd been having for the past ten minutes. 'It's his house. He can do what he likes with it.'

'With respect, Sabrina,' said Tish frostily, 'you don't know what you're talking about.'

'Don't talk to Sabrina like that,' said Jago pompously.

'Loxley isn't "his house",' Tish told Sabrina, ignoring him. 'It doesn't belong to any one person. It's been left to Jago in trust for the next generation.'

'So you keep saying.' Sabrina's green eyes positively shone with mischief. 'But as the next generation are going to be *my* kids, then *I* say where they're gonna be raised. And it's not gonna be in this godforsaken corner of nowhere, that's for sure. It's gonna be in LA.'

'Fine,' said Tish exasperated. 'Then let the tenants move in and keep Loxley on a long-term lease.'

'You're not listening.' Sabrina sat forward, like a cobra about to strike. 'We don't *want* to lease it. OK? Read my lips. We want to sell it and use the money to get a fuck-off estate in Beverly Hills. Legally, Jago has every right to sell.'

'And morally, he has *no* right! Inheriting a house like this is an enormous responsibility.'

'Yeah, Jago's responsibility,' said Sabrina. 'Not yours.'

Tish looked to her brother for support. Neglecting his responsibilities at Loxley was one thing, but blatantly cashing in on his birthright, on hundreds of years of Crewe family history? That was a new low, even for Jago. A month ago, not even he would have contemplated selling their ancestral home. But already Sabrina's pernicious influence had changed him for the worse. Perched on top of him now in a pair of skintight black Fendi suede trousers and a ribbed Gucci vest, she looked as tiny and fragile as a nymph. Yet it was crystal clear who called the shots in the relationship. If Sabrina had told him to douse himself in kerosene and light a match, Jago wouldn't have batted an eyelid. It was hopeless.

Too exhausted to talk any more, Tish left the room. Thank God Abel was out on the farm with Bill Connelly, so she could retreat to her bedroom and down some Nurofen in peace. If possible, Abel was worrying her even more than Jago. Since Viorel's departure a few days ago, he'd been so down that Tish hadn't been able to interest him in anything. So desperate was she to cheer him up, she'd even offered to play *World of Warcraft* with him on the office computer, a game that he had played with Viorel for hours. Tish loathed computer games, especially violent ones but, thanks to Vio, her son was utterly hooked. But even this concession had been met by the same, monotone 'no thanks' that Abel had given to every proffered treat since Viorel left, from chocolate ice cream at breakfast, to a trip into Castleton arcade to win some new Dinosaur King cards. When Bill had offered to take him for the day, Tish was appalled at how relieved and grateful she felt.

She'd reached the foot of the stairs when Dorian came through the front door. In a plain white T-shirt and khaki shorts, he looked well, Tish thought, tanned from so much outdoor filming and visibly happier now that his return home to Romania was at hand.

'Have you seen Sabrina?' he asked, looking around the

hall as if she might be hiding behind the umbrella stand or crouched under the stairwell. 'She's late for wardrobe, again.'

'She's in the kitchen.' Tish sighed.

'Everything OK?' asked Dorian, picking up the weariness in her voice.

'Not really.' She told him about Sabrina and Jago's latest bombshell, their plan to put Loxley on the market. 'I don't know how serious they are. A few days ago, Sabrina was banging on about how great it was going to be to be mistress of Loxley, and how she was going to rip out all the original features and spray-paint the place gold or some such rubbish. Maybe this is just her latest attempt to wind me up.'

'Maybe,' said Dorian.

'Well, if it is, it's working,' said Tish. 'On a purely practical level, if Jago doesn't sign the tenancy agreement this week, we'll lose the renters I lined up, even if he later changes his mind about a sale. Which, please God, he will.' She closed her eyes again as the throbbing returned. 'It's not that easy, you know, finding a family willing to take on an estate this size. And I can't keep coming back to fix Jago's messes. I have to get back to Curcubeu, to the kids. I have a life of my own.'

Dorian nodded understandingly. 'Sabrina's in the kitchen, you say?'

Tish nodded wearily.

'OK. Let me see what I can do.'

Sabrina and Jago were kissing with all the passionate intensity of a couple of teenagers. Sabrina had turned around in the chair and was straddling Jago, who had slid both hands up underneath her vest, and whose lips were clamped over hers as if he were trying to revive her after a near drowning.

With their perfect bodies entwined and their tangled dark hair flying everywhere like wildly spun silk, they looked like one creature, a living erotic sculpture.

Dorian coughed awkwardly. 'Sabrina.'

Nothing. The writhing continued.

'Sabrina,' he said more loudly. This time she heard him, turning around and disengaging herself from Jago with a half-irritated, half-embarrassed look on her face.

'You were due in wardrobe fifteen minutes ago,' said Dorian. 'What's going on?'

'Not much, now that you're here,' grumbled Jago. Grabbing Sabrina's hand, he murmured, 'Do you *really* have to work, darling?'

'Yes,' Dorian answered for her, 'she does. And I don't appreciate having to leave the set to come and find her and remind her of that fact. Would you give us a minute?'

Jago looked disgruntled, but left them to it.

Once he'd gone, Dorian closed the door and stood with his back against it.

'What the hell are you playing at?'

Sabrina frowned, straightening her hair and tying it back in a ponytail.

'What do you mean? I'm a few minutes late for wardrobe. Jesus. It's hardly the crime of the century.'

'I'm not talking about that,' said Dorian. 'I'm talking about you and Jago.'

'What about me and Jago?' said Sabrina defensively. 'It's not complicated. We're in love.'

'Right, and I'm Danny La Rue,' said Dorian bluntly.

Sabrina flushed indignantly. 'We *are*,' she insisted. 'You know what, whatever. I don't have to defend myself to you.'

Dorian looked at her, like a scientist studying a puzzling

specimen. After a few moments, he said, 'At first, I thought it was just Viorel you were trying to hurt. But now I get the feeling that this charade's for Tish's benefit too. Am I right?'

'It is *not* a charade!'

'Oh, come on, Sabrina. I *know* you. This ridiculous talk of marriage, threatening to sell Loxley.' He laughed scathingly. 'Don't tell me that isn't about hurting Tish. A girl who, as far as I can see, has never done a damn thing to hurt you.'

Sabrina lost her temper. 'My God, you're like a scratched record, defending her all the time without ever listening to my side of the story.'

'What "story"?' said Dorian, exasperated.

'I never said we were going to sell Loxley, OK? I said that we *might* sell. And that it was up to Jago, not *her*. I'm tired of her lording it over me, thinking she's so high and mighty. Just because you think the sun shines out of her saintly ass, doesn't mean the rest of us have to run rings around her precious feelings.'

Dorian shook his head. 'You're better than this, Sabrina.'

His disappointment was more than Sabrina could bear. Dorian was obsessed with class. Her engagement to Jago was supposed to make him think more of her, not less. Yet here he was, *still* going on about 'poor' Tish, *still* taking her side. The unfairness of it made her lash out.

'You're just jealous, because I'm getting married to someone who loves me, and you're saddled with a miserable wife who's so resentful of you I doubt she'd piss on you if you were on fire.'

Dorian reeled backwards, as if he'd been slapped.

Sabrina felt a stab of guilt. Perhaps she'd gone too far?

For a moment, they stood there in silence. Then Dorian

said, very quietly, 'You know nothing about my relationship, Sabrina. *Nothing.*'

'Fine,' shot back Sabrina. 'And you know nothing about mine.'

'I know a sham when I see one. If it's money you're after, there is none. Loxley's a black hole. I have a stately home of my own so I know what I'm talking about.'

Of course you do, thought Sabrina bitterly. Dorian might give off regular-Joe vibes, but the truth was he was an aristo just like Tish. No wonder they stuck together like limpets. *And I'm just a nobody who got lucky, right?*

'This has nothing to do with money,' she said icily, determined not to let Dorian rattle her. 'I'd marry Jago if he had nothing.'

Dorian smiled wryly. 'You know what? You probably would, too. *Purely* out of spite. You are a piece of work when you want to be, Sabrina. It makes me sad because I know how much more you are, how much more you could be.'

Sabrina pushed past him. There were tears in her eyes.

'Fuck you,' she said viciously. 'I don't need your approval. And I don't give a crap what you think. You are not my father. You're my director, and thankfully not for much longer. I'm going to marry Jago, and if you, or *Tish*, or anybody doesn't like it, you can all kiss my ass.'

She stormed out of the room.

'Where are you going?' Dorian yelled after her. 'We aren't done yet, Sabrina.'

'Wardrobe,' she shot back at him. 'And, for your information, we are done. We are totally and completely *done.*'

She fled down the corridor, willing him not to follow her. Whatever else she did, she must never, ever let Dorian Rasmirez see her cry.

* * *

Four days later, the film crew packed up and left for Romania. Tish, who couldn't bear goodbyes, watched them go from an upstairs window with Mrs Drummond.

'You'll be next,' said Mrs D wistfully, as the last of the trucks pulled away, with Chuck MacNamee waving cheerfully from the driver's window. 'I'll miss you and Abel. It's been lovely this summer, having a child in the house again.'

'You'll still have a child in the house,' joked Tish. 'You'll have Jago.' It was gallows humour, but she didn't really know what else to say. None of them knew what the future held for Loxley with Jago, and perhaps Sabrina, at the helm. Tish felt terrible about going and leaving poor Mrs D in the lurch again.

'He won't really put the house on the market, will he?' The tremor in the old woman's voice filled Tish with fury towards Jago. Loxley was Mrs Drummond's home as much as it was theirs. How could he and Sabrina play fast and loose with so many people's lives and emotions? They deserved each other.

'I doubt it,' she said, hoping she sounded more convinced than she felt. 'He hasn't mentioned it again since our row. And, whatever she says, I think Sabrina loves the idea of being lady of the manor. I doubt she'll give it up when push comes to shove.'

'You really think they'll marry, then?' Mrs Drummond sounded surprised. 'You don't think it's a flash in the pan?'

Tish shrugged. 'With Jago, who knows? It could be.' But deep down she feared that this was one flashing pan that might very easily turn into a forest fire. Sabrina Leon was trouble, a lighted match to Jago's fuse.

And all I can do is sit and watch.

PART THREE

CHAPTER EIGHTEEN

Chrissie Rasmirez arched her back and thrust her hips forward, greedily pulling her husband deeper inside her.

'Tell me you want me,' she whispered in his ear. 'Tell me you need me.'

'You know I need you,' replied Dorian automatically, nibbling Chrissie's earlobe, and marvelling again at her fit, athlete's body. He himself was in lousy shape, physically and mentally. So much so that he could feel his erection starting to fade, and tried doubly hard to focus on the job in hand.

Coming home to Romania had been bitter-sweet. As ever, Dorian's heart leaped at the sight of the majestic Transylvanian landscape, the verdant Carpathians jutting against the sparkling blue sky like a string of giant emeralds threaded on the golden Bistriţa river. Nestled amongst the jewelled countryside, the Rasmirez Schloss stood as tall and proud and ancient as ever, solid, unchanging and beautiful. Loxley was a romantic house, and the fields and villages surrounding it idyllic, but it was beauty on a miniature scale. Compared to the Schloss it felt like a perfectly rendered doll's house. But Dorian missed Loxley Hall nonetheless. Or, rather, he missed the sense of calm that he had come to feel there. Certainly, there was precious little calm and order to be found at home.

Since he'd got back, Chrissie had been as demanding and complicated as ever. Her neediness, combined with the stresses of filming, establishing a new set in the Schloss's East Wing and all the long hours of frustration that entailed, left Dorian permanently exhausted. And then there were the financial pressures. At Loxley Hall, Dorian had somehow been able to shut everything else out and focus on making the movie. The money, the distribution deal, that would all come later as long as the work was good. *Build it and they will come*, he told himself. But here, every day on set was a reminder of what he stood to lose if *Wuthering Heights* was not a success. The sleepless nights were back with a vengeance.

'What's wrong?'

The pace of Dorian's thrusts had slowed. Chrissie could sense his distraction, feel him wilting inside her.

'Nothing,' Dorian lied, speeding up but feeling increasingly hopeless. He'd reached the point where no amount of visualizing Brooklyn Decker minus her *Sports Illustrated* bikini was going to help – and if Brooklyn couldn't help him, no one could. Chrissie always took it personally when he didn't come, and any excuses Dorian offered – tiredness, jet lag, work stress – only served to fan the flames of her anger. Especially after being apart for so long, now that he was home, Chrissie expected sexual fireworks on a daily basis. Dorian felt the performance pressure like a lead weight on his chest; or, more accurately, a slow puncture in his dick.

It was no good. Pulling out of her, he rolled onto his side and tried to hold her close, but it was like hugging an ice cube. Her whole body was locked rigid with anger.

'I'm sorry, honey. It's not you. It's . . .'

'Work. I know,' said Chrissie contemptuously. 'Until the damn movie's finished, I should put up, shut up and forget about us having a sex life, right?'

This was hardly fair. It was eight o'clock in the morning and, although Dorian's morning glory had admittedly turned out to be less than glorious, he *had* made love to her last night, as well as the night before.

'You know, I think Princess Diana was lucky having three people in her marriage,' added Chrissie caustically. 'I only have one person in mine: me. I feel lonelier now than I did when you were in England.'

'Honeeeey,' Dorian remonstrated. 'Come on, that's not true. You know how happy I am to be home with you and Saskia.'

But even as he said the words, they felt wrong and contrived on his tongue. In fact, the overwhelming feeling Dorian had been aware of since he got back to the Schloss was nervousness. Quite apart from his work worries and bumpy re-entry into the marital atmosphere, inevitable perhaps after such a long stint on location, he was expected to become a father again overnight. Distressingly, he realized he had no idea what to do.

Yesterday, he'd taken Saskia to the local park on his own, after Chrissie insisted she needed 'a break' – oddly, given that Rula the nanny had worked the last four straight days since Dorian got back, with Saskia practically glued to her ample hip at all times.

'It'll do you good anyway,' Chrissie had added, reapplying her lipstick as she ran out through the door. 'You need to bond with Saskia again.'

How he hated that word, *bond*. For some reason it always made him think of the Airfix model aeroplanes he used to build as kid. *Bond the propeller to the wing.* . . . If only parenthood came with a similar set of easy-to-follow instructions.

But to Dorian's surprise, the playground expedition had actually been fun. Saskia had matured so much in the last two months, in her language, her expressions, her play; it was a delight to watch her. Dorian had enjoyed it thoroughly; right up to the part where an older child had pointed at him and asked Saskia if he was her daddy, and she'd looked pensive and said, 'Sometimes.' That was a long, cold glass of guilt in the face, and all the more hurtful because he knew he deserved it. He'd like to have confided his feelings to Chrissie, but he knew if he did she'd turn the incident against him and he'd never hear the end of it. Unbidden and unwanted, Sabrina's words in the kitchen at Loxley came back to him: *'Your wife's so resentful she wouldn't piss on you if you were on fire.'*

Was she right?

Lying stiffly in Dorian's arms now, twitching with frustration, what Chrissie actually felt was a maelstrom of conflicting emotions. What Dorian read as anger, at him for not keeping it up, Chrissie experienced as acute anxiety: she was losing her looks, her sex appeal, her *raison d'être*. *He doesn't want me any more. I don't excite him.* If she no longer did it for Dorian, her adoring lapdog of a husband, who else was going to look twice at her?

Certainly not Viorel Hudson.

Chrissie had spent the week before Dorian's return (which conveniently coincided with Viorel's arrival) in a flat-spin panic about her looks – she was terrified of appearing old and raddled next to Sabrina Leon, but knew Dorian would hit the roof if she flew her dermatologist over from LA. So she had had her Botox touched up by some local quack in Bucharest and was convinced he'd made her look like Meg Ryan. When the film crew finally showed up, it was all a bit of an anti-climax. While Sabrina glided about the Schloss looking predictably perfect as she bemoaned her separation from her newly acquired, aristocratic fiancé to anyone who would listen, Viorel flew in from LA looking drawn, and immediately withdrew to his room. He'd spent the days since in a flat, humourless mood; not aggressive, as Dorian complained he had been in England, but gloomy and sullen. Gone was the flirtatious, devil-may-care rake who'd so entranced Chrissie a few weeks ago. Gone also was the spark that she had felt between the two of them the whole time she had been at Loxley. This Viorel was polite, distant, professional and painfully uninterested, at least in her.

Chrissie challenged him about it on the second day. Running into him in the Schloss's magnificent library, where he was admiring the mind-boggling array of first editions and original folios, she'd slipped an arm coquettishly around his waist. Viorel withdrew as if he'd been stung.

Chrissie pouted. 'I don't bite, you know. At least, not unless you ask me to.'

But Viorel hadn't asked her to. Instead, he'd had the gall to apologize, feeding her some line about Dorian and feeling guilty for what had happened between them at Loxley. 'It's not that I'm not tempted,' he said smoothly. 'But it mustn't happen again.'

Chrissie tried to believe him, but the blow to her ego was severe. As always when rejected by one of her lovers, her knee-jerk reaction was to turn to Dorian for reassurance – but now he, too, seemed to be confirming her suspicions: *I'm old and dried up. I've been in this place so long I've desiccated, like a Christmas orange stuck under the sofa.* The high she'd felt in LA, with Harry Greene and the world's press paying her so much attention, felt light years ago now.

Part of her wanted to stop chasing it, that elusive bright

light, to be content in her marriage to Dorian and make it work. After all, they had been happy once, in the early days. And despite this morning's lacklustre performance, she was sure he still loved her. But Chrissie couldn't be expected to make all the effort. Dorian would have to try too. He'd only been home a week, and already his good resolutions about leaving the set on time every day and prioritizing family life were fraying severely at the edges. Last night, he hadn't emerged from his editing suite until almost ten o'clock. Angry at being neglected, Chrissie had squeezed herself into a sexy red Hervé Léger minidress and heels, secretly hoping that if she caught Viorel's eye it might reignite their flirtation over pre-dinner drinks. But, after forty-five minutes alone in the Grand Ballroom, one of the butlers told her that Viorel, Sabrina and the rest of the cast had all gone into Bihor to eat. Of course, nobody had thought to include *her* in the invitation. Sitting alone at the kitchen table, again, eating leftover chicken wings and salad for one, it was hard not to feel resentful.

Dorian's hands were around her waist, caressing the smooth hollow of skin between her belly and her hipbone. She softened, turning around and kissing him on the lips.

'How about I cook for us tonight?' she said, her voice low and sultry. 'I could do my special-recipe lasagna. We haven't had that in years.'

'That would be great.' Dorian tried not to sound as surprised as he felt. Since their first year of marriage, he could count the times Chrissie had turned on an oven on the fingers of one hand.

'I want it to be just us, though. Tell everyone we need some private time. I'll have Rula put Saskia to bed. What do you think?'

Dorian was touched. He knew he'd been neglecting

Chrissie and that things weren't right between them. He wanted to bridge the growing gulf more than anything. 'I think it's a terrific idea,' he said, pulling her closer so that her firm, apple breasts pressed against his chest. 'Things are gonna get better, Chrissie. I promise.'

By four o'clock that afternoon, Dorian was slowly losing the will to live.

It was the first day of shooting Cathy and Heathcliff's pivotal love scene. This was the moment when, after Cathy's death, Heathcliff begged her spirit to remain on earth – she might take whatever form she would, she might haunt him, drive him mad – just as long as she did not leave him alone. For Dorian it was the most moving scene in the book, the crux of Catherine and Heathcliff's tortured love affair. It had to be pitch perfect.

The day began badly. The temperature on set was unbearable, literally and metaphorically. The late Transylvanian summer was punishingly hot, almost a hundred degrees at noon and with the sort of humidity that drained the body of energy like a vampire sucking blood. Today's scene was being shot in one of the old bell-tower bedrooms, a stunningly romantic backdrop, but one whose only ventilation consisted of a small, stone mullion window. As this was also the only source of natural light, blazing halogen lamps had been strapped to the ceiling, increasing the heat levels in the room threefold. Dorian, like the lighting and sound guys and two cameramen, was working topless and barefoot in a pair of simple cotton shorts. But Viorel and Sabrina had no such luxury. Sweating like a horse after the Grand National in his dark wool trousers and ruffled shirt, Viorel's face was an oil-slick of smudged make-up. Sabrina, in full corset and crinoline, was even more overheated, although this didn't seem to stop her from expending what little energy she had left on provoking Viorel rather than focusing on the scene.

At one point she asked for a minute in which to 'find her centre'.

'I'm sorry,' she announced, looking directly at Vio, 'but I really can't project arousal unless I'm thinking about Jago. I need to get into the right head-space.'

'For fuck's sake,' muttered Vio, pulling at his sweat-drenched shirt.

They'd done the scene again and again. But the only two emotions Dorian was catching on camera were hostility and heat exhaustion.

'Cut!' he shouted, for the third time in as many minutes. 'What is this, amateur fucking dramatics night?'

Sabrina pouted petulantly and lit a cigarette out of the window. Vio merely stuck his hands in his pockets and scowled.

'Grow up, both of you,' snapped Dorian. 'I've seen more of an erotic charge between the three little bears at Saskia's nursery-school pantomime.'

'Maybe the three bears had air-conditioning,' grumbled Sabrina.

'Yeah. Or maybe they brought their "centre" with them and didn't need constant validation about their utterly uninteresting sex lives,' snapped Vio.

Debbie Raynham giggled and he winked at her.

'I don't need *validation*,' said Sabrina furiously, catching the wink. If there was one thing she couldn't stand it was being the butt of other people's jokes. 'Maybe if you played your goddamn part, I'd be able to play mine. Heathcliff's supposed to be smouldering with desire and distraught with insatiable need. He's grief-stricken. He wants to fuck

Cathy's ghost, OK, so we can assume he's got it pretty fucking bad. But all I see is a whiny little boy in a gay shirt getting pissy because he hasn't gotten laid in the last five minutes.'

'ENOUGH!' Dorian's voice boomed around the room, echoing off the stone walls like a ricocheting gunshot. 'Enough. Both of you take fifteen minutes, get some water, cool down. We roll again at five. And if necessary at six, seven, eight, two in the fucking morning. We roll until I see some passion.'

Chrissie poured the dregs of the béchamel sauce over the squares of fresh pasta, dipping her finger into the empty saucepan and licking it. *Delicious.* There was something intrinsically erotic about cooking, she decided. The enticing smells and textures; the primitive feel of a waxy onion against one's palms; the warm, creamy comfort of the sauces, rich and forbidden. She laughed at herself. *I've got sex on the brain*, she thought, pre-heating the oven and wiping her hands against the cook's apron.

The kitchen at the Schloss was a vast room built to prepare meals for a village, not for rustling up a romantic supper for two. In addition to the twenty-foot oak table running down the centre of the flagstone floor, there were numerous sideboards, two six-door cast-iron ovens that looked as though they belonged in a factory, and a ceiling punctuated with sinister four-inch metal hooks, designed presumably for hanging meat, but which would have been equally appropriate props for a bondage movie. But, despite the room's size and raw, functional décor, or perhaps because of it, it made the perfect setting for the night of seduction that Chrissie had planned. It was still light outside at the moment, but when the sun set and she lit the candles she'd scattered along the deep window ledges, the soft orange glow would transform the space, giving it a mellow, almost ecclesiastical feel. She and Dorian would eat, and laugh, and drink too much of the Châteauneuf-du-Pape '59 she'd brought up from the cellar. Then she would lie back on the table while he made love to her, too excited to wait until they got upstairs.

I'm getting carried away. Tearing off a few bay leaves from the sprig on the sideboard, she began chopping them up for a garnish. It was so long since she'd even had to boil an egg for herself, Chrissie was gratified to discover her culinary skills had not deserted her. Particularly since moving to Romania, where labour was so cheap and a large estate like the Rasmirezes' was expected to provide ample local employment, she'd lost touch almost entirely with the everyday tasks of normal life, and had forgotten how enjoyable they could be. Her lasagna was a thing of beauty, if she did say so herself, with or without the bay leaves.

Carefully pushing the dish forwards into the dark centre of the oven, she set the timer and closed the door with a satisfying thud. If the way to a man's heart was through his stomach, she and Dorian should be in hearts-and-flowers-ville in forty minutes exactly. But just in case it wasn't, Chrissie had double-bagged the situation this morning by unearthing a cheap, horrendously slutty French maid's outfit in a box at the back of one of her dressing rooms. *How incredible that I kept it!* She remembered buying it donkey's years ago at a costume store in Westwood for Halloween. She used to wear it occasionally in her UCLA days, whenever she wanted to drive Dorian even wilder with desire than usual. If they were going to do a trip down memory lane, they might as well take the scenic route. Slipping it on, she was delighted to discover that it not only still fitted, but made her legs look endless and pushed up her small breasts till they could have passed for a C-cup. *I'm in better shape now than I was in my twenties*, she thought smugly. *I can't wait to see Dorian's face when he sees me in it.*

She looked up at the kitchen clock. Seven thirty. Dorian usually finished on set by seven at the latest and had asked for dinner at eight. He'd be in his office in the East Wing now, making calls to LA; or in the editing suite, glancing over the day's footage. That gave Chrissie thirty minutes to shower, change and beautify herself while one of the maids set the table, after which *all* the servants were under strict instructions to make themselves scarce, as were the actors and crew.

Fuck you, Vio Hudson. I don't need you. My husband's twice the man you are, in business and in bed. Everyone in Hollywood believed the Rasmirezes' marriage was a fairytale. Starting tonight, Chrissie decided, it was time to write her happy ending.

Up in the bell tower, the air temperature had dropped but tempers were still at boiling point. Viorel and Sabrina had run through their scene more than fifteen times, but Dorian still wasn't satisfied.

Viorel groaned. Admittedly, the first nine takes were probably his fault. Sabrina's mention of Jago was setting his teeth on edge. He could easily have put a stop to it by giving her what she wanted (attention) but he couldn't bring himself to do it.

But the last seven takes were entirely down to Dorian's perfectionism. The light hadn't fallen quite correctly across Sabrina's face. Viorel's forearm had blocked a split-second's worth of shot. The ghost kiss was too long, too short, too contrived, too passionless. Grudgingly, Vio and Sabrina had bonded through adversity and finally started giving the scene their all. But nothing was good enough for Dorian.

'When you go in to kiss her, I want it faster, rougher, more sudden,' he berated Viorel. 'So from, "I don't care, Cathy, you can't leave me," move in and grab her forearms like so.' Stepping out from behind the camera, Dorian grabbed Sabrina by the wrists and pulled her violently towards him. 'We need to see the desperation.'

'You can't see desperation?' drawled Vio. 'Are you sure the camera's switched on?'

'You are *losing* her,' continued Dorian, ignoring him. He was still holding Sabrina so tightly by the arms that her hands had begun to throb. 'This is the woman that you love, the love of your life, and she is slipping through your fingers, literally. It's anguish, OK – raw fucking *anguish.*'

He looked at Sabrina and for a moment his stomach lurched. She'd got it. At last she'd got it! Staring straight back at him, her eyes brimmed with such sadness, such pain, it took his breath away. For a second, Dorian stood trans-fixed. The suffering in Sabrina's eyes was quite real, the line between her and Cathy Earnshaw erased utterly. *I was so right to cast her*, he thought triumphantly. How could Viorel not respond to that? How was he not howling and moaning and tearing at his hair when he saw that exquisite face so tortured, so wildly in need of rescue?

He ran back to his position behind the camera. 'Roll!' he shouted. 'For God's sake, roll!'

'I don't care, Cathy.' Grabbing Sabrina as Dorian had shown him, Viorel pulled her towards him. But the look she gave him was nothing like the poignant gaze she'd just used on Dorian. Instead, with her face only inches from his, Sabrina's eyes flashed with lust. And there was something else there too, a sort of bravado, almost a defiance. The look was unmistakably a challenge, a dare. Viorel rose to it, throwing Sabrina backwards and kissing her with a passion that bordered on hatred, grinding his lips against hers, pulling at her hair, her cheeks, the bodice of her dress. The kiss went on and on and on, a full three seconds longer than the previous take, which Dorian had nixed for 'dragging'. But there was no dragging here. The sexual tension was so explosive that none of the crew dared breathe. When Vio finally released her, Sabrina stared back up at him, too shell-shocked to remember her line. Panting, lips slightly parted, cheeks red and scratched from his stubble, she looked as if she'd spent the last twenty-four hours in bed.

'Hello,' she laughed.

Viorel beamed back at her. 'Hi.'

From the other side of the camera, Dorian felt his adrenaline pumping. It was a bizarre sensation. He ought to be delighted, and part of him was: that was the best piece of footage they'd shot so far, no question. But there was a distinct, bitter aftertaste to the sweetness of success. All day he'd been praying for the spark to ignite between his lead actors. But now that it had, now that he'd seen that look of purest passion on Sabrina's face, he felt panicked.

'Cut!'

Chuck, Debbie and the crew broke into spontaneous applause.

'Desperate enough for you?' Vio asked Dorian.

Pulling himself together, Dorian forced a smile. 'Yes, Mr Hudson, it was. Now while the two of you are on a roll, I want to go back and reshoot some of the earlier stuff.' A collective groan rose up around the room.

'You're not serious?' Sabrina spoke for all the crew, but with more urgency than the rest of them. She wanted to talk to Viorel, alone, now. That kiss was more than just Cathy and Heathcliff and they both knew it. How could she go back to work after that? Her heart was pounding away like a jackhammer.

'Sure I'm serious,' said Dorian. His earlier, irrational panic had subsided. This was good; it was all good. Looking around at the sea of hostile faces, he shrugged his shoulders innocently. 'What? Come on, guys. We can't waste this. Mike,' he turned to the exhausted runner, 'go get us some coffee and sand-wiches. You can't make cinema history on an empty stomach.'

They finished filming just before midnight. Dorian, who'd been running on raw energy since breakfast, suddenly stood up and found he was dizzy with hunger. Only after everyone had gone to bed and he walked back to the private, family wing of the Schloss did he go into the kitchen to forage for a sandwich and see it.

Candlelight.

Flowers.

The beautifully laid table.

Dinner with Chrissie. It was tonight.

Fuck.

The evidence mounted. One clean plate, one dirty plate. A half-drunk bottle of extremely expensive red wine. A cold dish of lasagna, hardening to a greasy crust on the stove-top.

She's gonna kill me.

Walking upstairs, he rehearsed explanations in his mind.

If we got it right today, I knew I'd have more time off to be with you and Saskia later.

No. Lame. She'd never buy it.

I wouldn't have been able to give you the attention you deserved if I'd missed what we shot tonight. Chemistry like that is once in a lifetime.

As an actress, Chrissie might at least understand that one. But would she forgive it?

When you see that scene, honey, you'll understand. This movie's for us. If it's a hit, we'll never have to worry about money again.

Not strictly true. But as the truth was, '*I forgot about dinner,*' probably a safer option.

Pushing open the bedroom door with a guilty creak, Dorian saw that the bedside lights were still on. Chrissie was lying face down on the bed, apparently asleep. Unless he was seeing things, a possibility after the day he'd just had, she appeared to be wearing a French maid's outfit.

Oh my God. Not 'a'. 'The'. That was the maid's uniform she used to put on for me when we first started dating.

Dorian's heart swelled first with love, then with remorse. Suddenly he knew there were no excuses he could offer. She'd made a titanic effort to please him, and he'd let her down.

'Honey?' Perched on the edge of the bed, he rested a tentative hand on the small of Chrissie's back. 'Sweetheart? Are you awake?'

Slowly, Chrissie turned around. Dorian winced. Her face was puffy and swollen, her eyes red raw from crying.

'Chrissie, I don't know what to say. I'm really sorry.'

He braced himself for the firestorm, the screaming, the insults, the hysteria. Instead, he got silence and a blank, empty stare. It was infinitely more chilling.

'I'll make it up to you, I promise,' he babbled, nervously filling the silence. 'Sabrina and Vio were so incredible tonight, I got caught up in it and I couldn't get away. I truly am sorry.'

'It's OK,' said Chrissie. 'I understand.'

Her words should have comforted Dorian, but they didn't. *It's the voice*, he thought. She sounded strange, different, as if she were a dummy into which some hidden ventriloquist was throwing his voice, reading from a pre-prepared script.

'The good news is we nailed it,' he said, trying to sound normal himself. 'We're actually ahead of schedule now, so I can take some time off. We'll go somewhere, just the three of us.'

For a moment, Chrissie emerged from her stupor, narrowing her eyes in puzzlement. 'Three?'

'Sure,' said Dorian. 'You, me and Saskia.'

At the mention of their daughter, the curtain fell back over Chrissie's features. 'Fine,' she said dully. 'I'm tired, Dorian. Let's go to sleep.'

Ten minutes later, exhausted from the day's exertions and relieved that the expected Hurricane Chrissie had not materialized, Dorian was in a deep sleep and snoring loudly.

Next to him, rigid-backed and wide-eyed, Chrissie stared at the ceiling.

If I had the strength, she thought, *I'd kill him. Right now. Put the pillow over his fat head and hold it down till he stopped kicking.*

She was so filled with hatred, it was hard to breathe. Hatred for Dorian, hatred for his cursed movie, hatred for Viorel, hatred for herself for caring so much. The worst part of all was that Dorian hadn't even wanted to make it up to her sexually. His idea of a 'do-over' for their romantic night together was a family outing with fucking Saskia. He might as well have come to bed with the words 'I don't want you' tattooed across his forehead. He'd said nothing about her outfit, about how sexy she looked. *He didn't even try to touch me, just rolled right over and went to sleep.*

She felt like a hooker, cheap and worthless. *Except men actually want to sleep with hookers. Dorian would rather pay to see me in a burka and a fucking chastity belt.*

Lying there seething in the still silence, something inside Chrissie Rasmirez snapped. To any outside observer, it was as if nothing had happened. The break was clean, quiet and irrevocable, like a silk scarf floating softly down onto a Samurai sword and splitting into two. Chrissie didn't stir, or speak, or blink. Instead, while her husband snored beside her, she softly sailed past the point of no return.

Back in the West Wing, Sabrina lay on top of her bed in just her bra and pants, breathless. Even at this time of night the heat from the day lingered, stored in the walls of Sabrina's whitewashed bedroom and seeped into the linen bedclothes. After three straight hours of erotic scenes with Vio, Sabrina felt hot and sultry, conscious of the damp saltiness of the sweat glistening on her thighs and running in a trail between her breasts.

Where the hell was he?

She'd expected Viorel to show up in her bedroom a few discreet minutes after she'd gone to bed, to pick things up where they'd left off. The thought of fucking him at last had her practically hyperventilating with excitement. But as the minutes passed, ten, twenty, thirty, anticipation turned to anxiety. Surely, she couldn't have misjudged the erotic vibes she'd got from him in the bell tower? Could Viorel actually be that good an actor?

Her cellphone rang. Maybe he was calling to check the coast was clear? She answered instantly. 'Vio?'

'No, darling. It's me.' Jago's voice sent a wave of disappointment flooding through her veins.

'Oh, hi. I was just going to bed.'

'Hmmmm,' said Jago dreamily. 'What are you wearing?'

Before Sabrina could tell him she was in no mood for phone-sex, her bedroom door opened. There was no knock. It just opened. *Bloody Romanian maids. Didn't they know what time it was?* Instinctively, Sabrina grabbed the edge of the sheet and pulled it up over her body. She opened her mouth to scream, then closed it again. Viorel stood in the doorway, staring at her intently. Sabrina stared back. In pyjama bottoms and a plain white T-shirt, his black hair still wet from the shower, sleek and gleaming like an otter's pelt, he looked as sexy as she had ever seen him. Better still, the look in his eyes was unmistakably predatory.

Jago was still talking. 'Tell me about your panties . . .' Yesterday, Sabrina might have been aroused by the dirty talk. But today, coming from Jago, it sounded ridiculous.

'Erm . . .' Sabrina cleared her throat. Her head felt heavy suddenly and her mouth had gone dry. It was hard to concentrate. 'They, er . . . I mean . . .'

Viorel walked slowly but deliberately towards the bed, his eyes never leaving Sabrina's, and removed the phone from her hand. 'She's busy,' he drawled into the receiver. 'Call back later.'

He clicked the phone shut, then switched it off.

'That was an important call,' said Sabrina, feigning outrage. It was difficult with Viorel standing over her, so close she could smell the Floris shower gel on his newly washed skin.

'No it wasn't.'

He pushed her back on the bed. Sabrina stretched out her arms above her head. Her hair fanned out across the bedspread like an arc of peacock feathers, iridescent in the lamplight, and her breasts rose and fell beneath the delicate lace of her bra like two ripe peaches quivering on a tree.

Viorel stroked her face, slowly tracing one finger along her jawline and down to her collarbone. She shivered.

'You're nervous.' He smiled.

'No,' she lied, reaching forward to grab his face in her hands to try to kiss him. Gently, Viorel removed her hands.

'Stop,' he whispered. 'Stop trying to be in control. That doesn't work with me.'

Bending his head lower, he kissed the tops of her breasts, his hands moving languorously down over her ribs and belly, his fingertips tantalizingly brushing the elastic of her panties, but not venturing beneath. Sabrina moaned, arching her body upwards against him.

'Relax,' he whispered in her ear. 'We have time. We have all night.'

And miraculously, Sabrina did relax, abandoning herself to him, to his touch, his voice, his tongue, to all the incredible, indescribable things he was doing to her body.

Jago was a good lover, unquestionably, and Sabrina had slept with plenty of sexually talented men in her life. But Viorel was on another plane altogether, reaching her in ways that she had never experienced before, arousing feelings that transcended physical pleasure and spilled over into something else, something far deeper, more intense, more frightening. Comparing Jago with him was like comparing a bicycle with a fighter jet, or an Olympic swimmer with a real, live shark. Pointless. Ridiculous.

For the next two hours, Sabrina surrendered herself completely to Vio, aware of nothing but the rush of joy that flooded her senses like a tsunami. She had no idea when his clothes had come off, or how. She lost track of how many times she came, how many positions he put her in, whether a specific sensation was being caused by his hands, his mouth, his dick. For the first time she understood what her character, Cathy, had meant when she said that she and Heathcliff were one person and described him as 'more myself than I am'. To Sabrina, sex had always been a tool, something she had used to exert power over others, over men. With Viorel, all of that fell away. She was naked, not just in body but in soul.

When they finally finished, she lay beside him, shaking violently. Pulling the bedclothes up over her, Viorel was shocked to see tears streaming down her face.

'What's the matter?' he asked, genuinely concerned. 'I didn't hurt you, did I?'

Sabrina didn't answer, but started sobbing more loudly.

Vio looked panicked. 'Oh, God, Sabrina, what is it?' He'd been so lost in his own pleasure – having denied himself Sabrina's body for three long months, and spent the last four weeks in agonies believing he would *never* have her, tonight had been the best, most explosive fuck of his life – he'd missed the emotional storm building up inside her.

'Please don't cry. I'm sorry. I thought it was what you wanted. You seemed, you know . . . into it.'

This was such an understatement, Sabrina laughed, much to his relief. But the tears soon returned.

'It was what I wanted,' she mumbled, between sobs. 'It is what I want.'

'So why . . .?'

'I'm *frightened*, you fucking moron!' she shouted at him, sitting up. Without thinking, she drew back her arm and swung a punch at his face. Vio only just ducked in time.

'Whoah!' he said, tentatively sitting back up. 'Easy. Frightened of what?'

The question seemed to enrage Sabrina. Letting out a frustrated yell, she lunged at him again, but this time Vio was too quick for her, grabbing her wrists and holding tightly till she at last stopped struggling and broke down in tears again. Finally, she looked at him, her face a picture of misery.

'I think I love you,' she said quietly.

Now it was Viorel's heart that began to race. The silence hung in the air after Sabrina's words like an unspoken death sentence. Gazing into her liquid eyes, still holding her hands in his, he caught a glimpse of the chasm of need and longing inside her and felt as scared as he had ever felt in his life.

She's the most beautiful, most desirable woman in the world, he told himself. *She's talented. She's sweet underneath all the bullshit. She's the best lay you've ever had. And she loves you.*

Say something, you asshole.

'I love you too.' The words were out of his mouth before he knew he'd thought them. Just as Viorel was thinking how uncomfortable they were, how wrong, like an ill-fitting suit, Sabrina collapsed into his arms like a demolished building, all the tension and terror magically released. Viorel held her, shooshing her like a child, murmuring meaningless words of comfort – *it's OK, it's all right, I'm here.* Very quickly she was asleep.

Laying her down on the bed beside him, he covered her again with the sheet and bedspread and turned out the light. For a long time, he lay there, staring at her. After today's scene, making love to Sabrina hadn't even been a choice any more. It had been a necessity. It felt right.

So why, watching her sleep peacefully beside him now, did he suddenly feel so wrong? Like he was playing a part; a part intended for somebody else. But then so much of his life had felt like that: England, Eton, Cambridge – maybe it had simply become second nature for him to question every-thing, or at least to question everything good.

I have to relax, he told himself. *Learn to enjoy it. Who knows? Maybe a challenge like Sabrina is exactly what I need?*

CHAPTER NINETEEN

Saskia Rasmirez rearranged the plastic Little Mermaid tea set on her play table, and wondered how long it would be before Rula, her nanny, came back. Saskia was a happy, uncomplicated child, and at three years old had not yet thought to question the sanity or otherwise of her existence. She had no memories of Los Angeles and was unaware that other children did not live in enormous, fairytale castles like she did with movie stars running around the guest wings and paparazzi flying helicopters overhead. She did not know that her daddy was famous, or that her family led an extravagant, privileged life. What she *did* know was that life was a lot easier and more fun when she was left alone with Rula to play mermaids, or princess nurses, or fairies and elves, and her parents weren't around.

Saskia viewed her father's presence in the nursery as a freak anomaly, mildly interesting but too fleeting to be of any real significance, like an unexpected storm. Her mother's presence, on the other hand, was more frequent and could be a serious problem. Watching Chrissie out of the corner of her inquisitive blue eyes now, Saskia noticed the vacant stare and the despondent slump of the shoulders. Mommy always had a turned-down mouth, like Nanny Plum from the Ben and Holly cartoons after a spell had gone wrong. And there was something wrong with her ears too. She'd sent Rula away so that she and Saskia could play together, but whenever Saskia asked her a question: which dolly she wanted to be, if pink biscuits were her favourite, whether the pretend tea was too hot and burn-ish, Mommy couldn't seem to hear properly and would say something that didn't make sense, like 'whatever you want, honey,' when Saskia hadn't wanted anything.

Occasionally, both her parents would hug her uncomfortably tightly and ask her if she loved them. Saskia had learned that the correct answer to this question was a simple 'yes'. Nine times out of ten, this made them smile, then go away, after which Rula would invariably reappear and start playing with her properly.

Today, however, Saskia's mother was not in a huggy mood. She was in a staring-randomly-into-space sort of mood. *Oh well.* Turning back to her tea party, the little girl rearranged her other guests on their pink plastic chairs (Ariel, Growly the teddy and Princess Feather Dress rarely complained about the seating arrangements), and was about to pour them all a second cup of fairy-dust tea when the playroom door opened and a very pretty grown-up walked in. Saskia had seen this grown-up before a couple of times, sometimes talking with her father, occasionally on her own, talking on the telephone or gliding down one of the Schloss's myriad corridors in fat, princess dresses. Saskia thought she was lovely.

'Are you Pocahontas?' she asked. 'You've got very Pocahontassy hair.'

The girl .laughed, a low, warm, throaty laugh quite

different from Saskia's mother's, or Rula's. 'Thank you,' she said. 'But I'm afraid not. I'm Sabrina.'

'Hello, Sabrina.'

'And you must be Saskia?'

The child nodded earnestly. 'We both begin with a "S".'

'We certainly do.'

'Have you come to play with me?' Saskia brightened. Maybe Sabrina would want to help her put clips in her hair? Or at least express a preference, biscuit-colour-wise.

'Actually, I was looking for your mom,' said Sabrina, still smiling. She seemed very happy, this woman. In a white floaty skirt and draped vest top, it crossed Saskia's mind that she might be some sort of angel, come to cheer Mommy up. If so, she was going to have her work cut out. Since her arrival in the nursery, Mommy's mouth had turned down even lower, till she looked a bit like Ketchup, Saskia's friend Monica's pet pug dog.

Chrissie looked at Sabrina with a combination of apathy and contempt that would have withered a less robust ego. In black baggy Ralph Lauren trousers and a thin-ribbed, cobalt-blue cotton T-shirt clinging to her bony frame, Chrissie looked pale and exhausted, as washed out as Sabrina was radiant. 'What can I do for you?'

'Oh, nothing for me,' said Sabrina. 'It's Dorian. I said I was coming back to this side of the house to get some vitamins from my room, and he asked me to check on you. You know, see how you were doing.'

'How I'm *doing*?' Chrissie repeated. What was she now, some sort of mental patient who needed to be 'checked up' on? 'I'm fine,' she said frostily. 'Why wouldn't I be?'

'Oh.' Sabrina looked bewildered. 'Well, Dorian mentioned you'd had a migraine this morning. I get them myself so I know how hideous they can be. But I guess you're over it.

I'll tell him.' She turned back to Saskia. 'Sorry to interrupt your tea party. Maybe I can get an invite to the next one?'

For a moment curiosity overcame Chrissie's anger. Was it her imagination, or was there something markedly different about Sabrina today? It was a combination of her demeanour, the way she'd practically skipped into the room earlier, and a general looseness that had not been there before. Her hair hung newly washed and slightly frizzy down her back; her make-up-free face shone with sweat but she didn't seem to care; her usual sexy jeans or shorts had been replaced by a skirt that bordered on the virginal. Then it struck her.

Of course. She's in love.

Chrissie knew that Dorian disapproved of Jago Crewe, though she'd never been interested enough to find out why. She was interested now. 'Don't rush off,' she said, her tone suddenly soft and inviting.

'I have to.' Sabrina looked apologetic. 'I'm needed back on set.'

'Oh, needed schmeeded,' said Chrissie, scooching over and patting the space next to her on the window seat. 'We both know my husband's a tyrant. He had you working till all hours last night. Come hang with the girls for a few minutes.'

The girls? Sabrina was just adjusting to the shock of Chrissie Rasmirez in 'nice mode' when Chrissie dropped the second bombshell, adding conspiratorially: 'You're obviously *dying* to tell someone about him.'

Sabrina blushed. Was it really that obvious?

'I don't know what you mean,' she muttered, unconvincingly.

'Yes, you do,' said Chrissie. 'There's no need to be shy about it. I was the same when I was your age. When you're in love, you just can't hide it. He must be quite a guy.'

'He is,' sighed Sabrina, then clammed up again.

'Listen, if you're worried about Dorian, don't be,' said Chrissie. 'I don't tell him everything, you know. And besides, you are entitled to a private life.'

Sabrina was torn. It *would* be nice to tell someone. Anyone. Last night had been so magical, so perfect, she'd had the urge to pinch herself all day. *Viorel Hudson loves me!* Had he really said those words? He hadn't repeated them this morning, but had been so gentle and tender with her when she woke up, and later on set, that she was sure she hadn't dreamed them. Or had she? Every few minutes, the irrational, gnawing fear returned that it had all been a dream, a figment of her fevered, overworked imagination. Perhaps telling the story to someone else would make it more real, more solid and true; less likely to slip through her fingers like a fistful of sand?

On the other hand, she knew Dorian would disapprove, an idea that bothered her more than it should have. She wished she didn't care so much for her director's good opinion, but her admiration for him had sort of crept up on her and now she was stuck with it. Neither she nor Vio wanted to look unprofessional, especially after she'd made such a big deal about Jago, and Viorel had told the whole set how he *never* slept with his co-stars.

'I wouldn't want Dorian to get the wrong idea, that's all,' she said eventually. 'I take my job very seriously, even though sometimes I know he thinks I don't.'

Chrissie laughed. 'Let me give you a little friendly advice about dealing with my husband. With any director, come to that. Give them an inch and they'll take a mile. Screw what Dorian thinks about your love life! It's none of his business. From what I hear, you're doing a stellar job as Cathy.'

'Thanks,' said Sabrina, genuinely touched. Not because Chrissie's opinion meant much to her, but because she could only have heard this from Dorian, and his opinion meant everything.

'So come on! What's he like?' Chrissie dropped her voice to a whisper. 'I hear Englishmen are the kinkiest lovers.'

Sabrina grinned. 'I wouldn't say kinky exactly. But he certainly gets an A plus in bed. And not just in bed, in everything.' And she was off, gushing out her love uncontrollably like water from a broken fire hydrant. 'He's different from anyone else I've ever met. I knew it the first time I laid eyes on him, although I guess I didn't want to admit it at first.'

Chrissie nodded understandingly.

'I know on the surface he can seem arrogant. But underneath it all he has *such* a good soul. He's talented, he's intelligent, he's educated . . .'

Educated? Chrissie paused. She was sure she remembered Dorian saying something about Tish's brother being some sort of New Age Neanderthal. What was the expression he'd used again? Ah yes: *'Thicker than a pile of horseshit but with half the charm.'* Then again, Sabrina Leon was vagrant white trash from Fresno not so many years ago, so it was all relative.

'You mustn't be intimidated by his family, you know,' said Chrissie, cutting Sabrina off mid-drool. 'You're as good as any of them.'

'Thanks,' said Sabrina. 'But I don't think that's an issue.'

'Of course not, my dear. You'll fit right in at Loxley Hall. All it takes is a little practice.'

'Oh!' Sabrina laughed nervously. 'No, no, it's over with me and Jago. I sincerely hope that I never have to set foot in Loxley Hall again.'

'I don't understand,' said Chrissie, her smile wilting at the edges. 'Then who?'

'Viorel!' said Sabrina joyously. 'It all happened last night, although to be honest we both knew it was coming for a while. Months, ever since we got to England really. I guess I was in denial or something. I wasn't sure if he felt the same, but now . . .'

Misinterpreting Chrissie's stricken face as moral disapproval, Sabrina paused, then backtracked.

'I didn't mean to hurt Jago,' she said defensively. 'I mean, I know we were engaged and all, but it *had* only been a few weeks. And the way I feel about Vio, well, it can't be compared. When Jago gets over the shock and sees how in love we are, I'm sure he'll understand. He will understand, won't he?'

But Chrissie was no longer listening. She didn't care about Jago Crewe, or Sabrina, or any of them. Viorel hadn't rejected her because he felt guilty. He'd turned her down because he had a better offer, from a girl fifteen years Chrissie's junior. He didn't want her because she was old.

'Mommy?' Saskia was pawing at her trouser leg, trying to get her attention. With a jolt, Chrissie realized that she'd switched off and been in a world of her own, for how long she wasn't sure. Sabrina was also looking at her strangely, her hateful, flawlessly youthful features knitted into an expression of faux concern.

'Are you sure you're OK, Chrissie? Is it the migraine again?'

Chrissie nodded, not trusting herself to speak. She needed to be alone, to think.

This was all Dorian's fault. Dorian and his obsession with this damn movie. Ever since he'd started work on *Wuthering Heights*, the problems between them had escalated. He'd been away more, neglecting her more, practically pushing her into Viorel's arms only for him to reject her too. In her mind, it was the movie itself that was the enemy, the catalyst for all her disappointment, anger and fear. But if Dorian thought she was going to lie down and take the humiliation quietly, if any of them thought that, they had another think coming.

Harry Greene sat on his therapist's couch looking angrily at his watch. *Forty-five minutes of my time, another two hundred bucks down the drain, and all this schmuck's got to tell me is I need to 'let go of my anger'? I know that, dip-shit. That's why I'm here. What I want you to tell me is* how.

Harry Greene had been coming to this bland, corporate-looking office in Beverly Hills once a week for the last eight years. Before that he'd gone to a chick therapist, Liana, in Bel Air. That had been a lot more fun. Liana had a terrific pair of tits, and a penchant for wearing very short skirts and semi-sheer underwear that had made the hour of self-analysis positively fly by. But the bitch had dumped Harry as a client after he'd asked her out for dinner – *dinner, for Christ's sake! It wasn't like I tried to rape her; although God knew she'd been asking for it hard enough, the little prick tease. Trying to tell me I've got 'issues' with women. Fuck you, doctor.* He'd been seeing Dr Brewer ever since.

A slight, balding man in his mid-sixties, with no distinguishing features other than his eyebrows, which were enormously bushy, like two hairy caterpillars intent on taking over his face, Dr Brewer shared his patient's frustration at the circular nature of their sessions. Harry Greene was a profoundly angry man, a hater-by-nature – of women, certainly, but also of anybody he perceived to have crossed him. This was a very long list, and one that, despite showing up every week on Dr Brewer's couch, Harry appeared to have no interest whatsoever in reducing.

'Professionally, things are going well?' Dr Brewer probed. 'You're happy with your current project?'

'Very happy.' Harry Greene smiled, as he always did whenever he thought about work. His latest movie was a departure from his normal fare of big-budget comedies or action flicks. A period drama, based around a fallen woman in eighteenth-century Paris, *Celeste* was a visually gorgeous feast of a film starring Marta Erikksen, currently Hollywood's highest-paid female star, thanks to her breakout success in the latest Tarantino movie. If anyone had told Harry that *Celeste* was a deliberate attempt to go head to head with Dorian Rasmirez's *Wuthering Heights*, he'd have denied it vociferously. Rasmirez didn't have a monopoly on artistic, critically acclaimed films. Why shouldn't Harry branch out? Besides, anyone could do that arty shit – anyone with an eye for the right script and the clout to cast his first-choice actors in every role, right down to the third fucking under-gardener. Harry knew for a fact that his production budget had been more than four times the size of Dorian's. He also knew that Dorian was going to have a hard sell trying to bring a distributor on board, what with the continued negative press buzzing around Sabrina Leon. Thanks to the veil of secrecy surrounding *Wuthering Heights*, the big studios' interest was piqued. But it was a long way from piqued interest to a multimillion-dollar cheque. Harry Greene knew that better than anyone. Celeste *is gonna wipe the floor with Rasmirez's piss-poor remake.*

But beating Dorian commercially was no longer enough for Harry. Even if he succeeded in bankrupting Rasmirez, it might not be enough to break the bastard. *I have to get to him some other way. Hit him where it'll really hurt, hit him so hard he won't be able to get back up.*

Harry's mind turned back to Dorian's wife. He remembered the night at the Starlight Ball a few months ago, when Chrissie Rasmirez had reciprocated in a little mild flirtation. Of course, she'd had reason enough to be mad at her husband that night. Would she be as receptive if Harry tried to seduce her now? Physically she was past her prime, of course, and her body was a little too overmuscled for Harry's taste. But Chrissie Rasmirez was still an attractive woman. How delicious it would be if Harry were to nuke Dorian's fairytale marriage the way Dorian had destroyed his! That was certainly one possibility, but of course much depended on the lady's willingness, her appetite for betrayal.

What are Rasmirez's other weaknesses?

Harry suspected that Dorian was one of the rare breed of film-makers who actually meant it when they told reporters they were 'all about the work'. Fame meant little to Rasmirez, and money was only important because it enabled him to make more movies, and to keep up that ridiculous Disney castle he had in some East European butthole country no one had heard of. Rumour had it that *Wuthering Heights* was his best work yet. Viorel Hudson's performance was said to be strong, and the infamous Sabrina Leon's stellar. Harry had even heard whispers that Dorian might be gunning for an Oscar.

Now *this* was interesting. Dorian Rasmirez had been nominated three times in the Best Director category, but had never won. Independent movies rarely took home the big gongs these days (there were only six that mattered: Best Picture, Director, Actress, Actor and the two Supportings). Without a big studio to finance your Oscar campaign, you stood next to no chance. Could Dorian woo a big studio backer, even this late in the day? Had that been his plan all along?

Harry had already begun his own, slow-burn campaign

for *Celeste* with the Academy months ahead of schedule. Was Rasmirez hoping to challenge him? Harry hoped so. If he could sink Dorian's movie in theatres *and* beat him to an Oscar, that truly would be revenge worthy of the name. Just thinking about it brought a smile to his face.

'Listen, doc, I gotta go. Speaking of work, you know. The back lot beckons.'

Dr Brewer thought about reminding Harry that the session had another ten minutes to run; that his unwillingness to commit to the full hour was almost certainly a reflection of his inner unwillingness to examine fundamental difficulties in his personality; but he wisely thought better of it. The last psychotherapist to irritate Harry Greene, his predecessor Dr Liana Craven, had been the victim of a whispering campaign so toxic and relentless, her practice had been decimated and she'd ultimately been forced to relocate to Texas. Dr Brewer had never warmed to Texas.

'Of course,' he said cheerily. 'Stay well. See you next week.'

Outside, in the blazing sunshine of Burton Way, Harry Greene immediately felt his spirits lifting. Goddamn shrinks. They always made you feel like a bag of crap. He only went because in Hollywood, *not* having an analyst was like admitting you had a problem. Like *not* having a driver, or a mistress, or a Thai masseuse who gave you all the extras without being asked. For a man in his position, it was unthinkable.

His dark blue Bentley gleamed outside the doctor's office, with Manuel, his uniformed driver, ready and waiting to take him back to Universal, but Harry Greene felt like a walk. Crossing the street past a line of lithe-limbed teenage girls outside Pinkberry, he headed south toward Wilshire Boulevard. It was Wednesday lunchtime, which meant that

Angelica, his ex-wife, would almost certainly be getting her pedicure done in the top-floor salon at Neiman Marcus. Now on her third husband since her divorce from Harry, Angie had become something of a friend in recent years, one of the few women Harry knew for a fact wanted nothing from him. *I'll surprise her. Take her to lunch. Maybe buy her something sparkly from Neil Lane to tick off that attorney husband of hers.*

He turned on his cellphone to check his messages (that was another irritating thing about therapists; they always wanted him to switch his phone off, which inevitably made him doubly tense). It rang immediately.

'Greene,' Harry answered, not breaking stride. A few seconds later a broad smile spread across his face. Now that he controlled every aspect of his life with military precision, it wasn't often he was surprised, still less pleasantly surprised. But this call had done it.

'Well hello, my dear,' he purred. 'Believe it or not, I was just thinking about you.'

CHAPTER TWENTY

Tish stood in the hallway at Loxley, not sure whether to believe her eyes.

Is that a grand piano? Good God. Is it a Steinway? Preceded by a good two thousand pounds' worth of Moyses Stevens flower arrangements, an enormous rug that took three men to carry it and looked suspiciously Persian and antique, and a hideous modern painting of two orange-clad Buddhist monks staring at each other, the piano was the latest (but apparently not last) in a procession of luxury goods being carried single file into Loxley's drawing room. It was like watching a line of leafcutter ants.

When the first Harrods van had pulled up outside twenty minutes ago, Tish had thought little of it. *Another of Mummy's extravagances. Probably some turn-the-clock-back face cream made of baby seal's bottom you can only get in London; or a few cases of overpriced Smythson's stationery with 'Vivianna Crewe, Loxley Hall' embossed in gold leaf on the top.* Vivianna was only ever 'Crewe' when it suited her, and at the moment it suited her down to the tips of her Bottega Veneta stilettos.

Tish's mother had flown in two days ago to 'comfort Jago',

who'd taken to his bed with a bout of melodramatic grief when Sabrina Leon suddenly broke off their engagement. He was still refusing to get up, despite the fact that he knew full well that Tish and Abi were leaving for Romania at the end of the week and that Loxley's bills were once again piling up.

It was only after the second van arrived, then the third, and the ants began their relentless march through the house weighed down with extortionate loot, that the severity of Vivi's latest spending spree began to hit home.

'Mummy!' Tish called hoarsely, following the workers in hopes of finding the queen. And sure enough, once she got into the drawing room, there was Vivianna, directing her minions to position their various treasures around the room, alternately pointing imperiously and clapping her hands with glee like an overexcited little girl. *Catherine the Great meets Shirley Temple*, thought Tish. *She doesn't change.* In a simple lemon-yellow sundress teamed with sky-high black Bottega heels and matching black sunglasses, Vivi looked as ravishing as ever. Her glossy black hair was piled, Sophia Loren style, on top of her head, and her slender, French-manicured hands gesticulated in that wild, Italian way of hers, as if somehow disconnected from the rest of her body. Not for the first time, Tish thought: *I'm nothing like you. Genetically, we're as disconnected as a pair of total strangers.*

'Ah, Letitia *cara*, there you are.' Vivi smiled. 'What do you think, darling? Would your brother prefer the piano in the corner of the room – more traditional – or per'aps beneath the window? It is more romantic, no? Looking out across the deer park.'

Tish shook her head despairingly. 'It'll have to go back, Mother. It'll all have to go back.'

'Back?' asked Vivi innocently. 'Against the wall, you mean?'

'I mean *"back"*,' snapped Tish. 'Back to London. Before you lose the receipts.'

Vivianna pouted. 'I can't possibly do that, darling. It's for your brother. He needs something to lift his spirits, something to focus on other than that 'orrible, fickle woman. This house feels like a morgue, no wonder 'e's so depressed. It must be decades since Henry redecorated.'

'It's decades since he could afford to,' said Tish defensively. 'How much did all this crap cost, anyway?'

Vivi looked momentarily sheepish. 'Who can put a price on your brother's happiness?'

Marching over to the piano, Tish picked up a dangling white paper label and read the number printed on it in bold black ink. 'Harrods, apparently,' she said bluntly. 'This is over a hundred thousand pounds, Mummy!'

'It's an investment.'

'In what? Penury? Jago doesn't even play the piano. And look at all these flowers! It's like Elton John's funeral in here.'

Vivianna's exquisite brown eyes welled up with tears, shining like two pieces of amber in a stream. 'Don't even joke about funerals,' she whispered sombrely. 'I don't think you realize how close to this poor JJ is. You have no idea of the pain of a broken heart, Letitia. You're too cold and English, just like your father.'

It took every last ounce of Tish's self-restraint not to slap her mother round her perfect, high-cheekboned face. How *dare* she criticize Henry! Not to mention preach about broken hearts, she who had shattered her poor husband's heart into a million tiny fragments, not to mention the damage she'd done to her children.

'I'm not cold,' said Tish through gritted teeth. 'I'm practical. Somebody has to be. At the rate you and Jago are spending, Loxley'll be bankrupt again before Christmas. If you had any idea of the work I've put into turning this place around, clearing our debts, starting the repairs . . .'

'You see?' said Vivi triumphantly. '*You* were spending money on improving the house. And that's all I'm doing, darling. I'm just trying to do it with a little colour, a little *life*. Would you really begrudge your poor brother that?'

It was pointless talking to her mother in this mood. If she hurried, Tish could probably collar one of the Harrods drivers outside and get hold of Vivianna's order number, so she could arrange to have the goods returned next week. By then, with any luck, the novelty of playing Jago's Florence Nightingale would have worn off and Vivi would have returned to Rome, where she could waft around looking glamorous and spend some poor besotted Italian count's money rather than her children's inheritance. Mrs D would have to oversee the pick-up, of course. Tish would be in Oradea by then, back in her normal rhythm: work at Curcubeu and the hospital, school runs with Abel, coming home to the morose, disapproving Lydia. *No, I really must give Lydia the boot.* The thought of returning to her old battleaxe of a nanny was almost as depressing as saying goodbye to Loxley.

Tish ran out into the driveway but it was too late. The Harrods vans had gone.

From an upstairs window, she could hear Jago moaning, like an actor in a bad B-movie practising his death throes. She didn't for a moment buy his heartbroken schtick. Sabrina had been an infatuation, a status symbol. Nothing more. At worst, Jago's ego had been bruised, although admittedly in his case that was probably akin to a vital organ. Not in a million years could Tish ever have seen her brother and Sabrina Leon making old bones together.

Viorel and Sabrina, on the other hand, made a far more

plausible match. There had been a chemistry between them from the beginning; they were like two sides of the same rare, beautiful coin. *It was only a matter of time before this happened*, Tish thought. But, try as she might to talk herself out of it, the truth was that the thought of Vio and Sabrina together made her feel depressed.

I've lost perspective, she told herself firmly. *That's all it is*. The drama of this summer and the film shoot had distracted her, consumed her when she ought to have been thinking about her own life, her own future. Viorel would go back to his world of premières and red carpets, and Tish would go back to her world of hospital wards and frozen pipes, and all would be right with the world.

Just at that moment, Abel came hurtling out of the house and coiled his arms around Tish's legs. He'd grown noticeably taller over the summer, Tish realized, and his face had matured too. It was less rounded, less generically babyish. He was more of a boy now. Suddenly Tish could picture him at eight and twelve and seventeen. She felt a wave of love engulf her.

'Hello, sweetheart. What have you been up to?'

'Nothing,' he shrugged. 'It's boring without Viorel. Has he called?'

'No, sweetie,' Tish said gently. 'He will though, I'm sure, once we get home to Oradea.'

It was strange that Vio hadn't telephoned since leaving England. Tish tried not to mind. Perhaps he'd decided it would be best all round if Abel forgot about him and they all moved on with their lives?

Perhaps he was right.

'Come on,' she said, her voice heavy with forced heartiness. 'Come and help me finish packing. You can jump on the suitcase while I try to zip it.'

* * *

Back at the Schloss, the entire set was abuzz with excitement about Viorel and Sabrina's new red-hot love affair.

It was tough to keep anything on the down low on location at the best of times, but when it was a romance between a movie's two stars, and when neither of them could keep their eyes off each other, never mind their hands, it was a lost cause.

Dorian wasn't sure how to react to the blossoming relationship. He was delighted Sabrina had called time on her fauxmance with Jago Crewe. He'd become very fond of Sabrina over the past few months, but Dorian also knew her faults and weaknesses intimately, and he was by no means sure that Viorel was the 'steady ship' Sabrina needed. On the surface, she and Vio Hudson might appear to be similar creatures: both preposterously beautiful, talented and vain, both ferociously ambitious. But Sabrina's ambition, like her arrogance, was powered by a deep-seated insecurity. Her confidence was an act. Viorel's wasn't. Hudson wanted adulation, but Sabrina needed it. Big difference.

Whatever misgivings he had about the wisdom of the romance, however, evaporated when he watched the chemistry between them on set. Sabrina and Viorel barely needed directing any more. All Dorian had to do was switch the camera on and leave them to it. Which was a good thing, given the huge amounts of mental energy he was expending on Chrissie.

Ever since he'd forgotten to show up for their romantic kitchen supper, Dorian's marriage had begun unravelling at a frightening pace, like a dropped reel of cotton bouncing uncontrollably down a mountainside. What worried him most was that it wasn't the usual fireworks. Dorian was used to Chrissie's tantrums, to her throwing things and acting out, either by reckless spending or by hurtling headlong into another disastrous affair. He hated the drama. The affairs, in particular, hurt him deeply. But it was an enemy that he understood and that he knew how to fight. This new Chrissie – sad, silent, uncommunicative – was an unknown entity, a shadowy figure in the woods. She wouldn't talk to him, wouldn't touch him, wouldn't engage in any way. When Saskia was with them, Chrissie would talk only to her daughter, referring to Dorian in the third person as 'Daddy'.

In the past, their marital arguments had given Dorian the stomach-churning adrenaline rush of charging into battle. This was more like guerrilla warfare: the slow, sickening fear of walking along an empty road, wondering when a home-made bomb might blow you to pieces. As a tactic it was highly effective, leaving Dorian in a permanent state of nervous exhaustion. He tried everything to snap Chrissie out of it – cajoling, pleading, bribing, ignoring; but it was as if she were in a trance, as calm and unmoving as a stone. In the end, he returned to putting in long days on set, simply because he didn't know what else to do with himself.

One baking hot Friday afternoon, two weeks exactly since Sabrina and Viorel had become an item, Dorian surprised the crew by opting to re-shoot a couple of the outdoor Heathcliff and Cathy scenes they'd done at Loxley Hall. If the camera got in close enough, the Derwent and the Bistriţa could easily be made to look like the same river, and the late summer Transylvanian light was so perfect, it seemed a shame not to attempt some re-shoots now that Sabrina and Vio had both raised their game.

Viorel for one was delighted to be out of doors for a change. The atmosphere inside the Schloss was so close and tense, it was a relief to look up and see sky. It was still incredibly hot, though, in the high nineties. Slipping off his boots and socks between takes, Vio dipped his feet luxuriantly in the cool river water, lying back on the bank and closing his eyes while he wriggled his toes in pleasure.

'Want some company?' A shadow fell over his face. Viorel opened his eyes and looked up at Sabrina. With the sun behind her, her features were dark and indistinct, but he could hear the smile in her voice.

'Sure.'

He tried not to feel annoyed. They were together 24/7 now, working on set all day and making love all night. He'd been enjoying a few, precious minutes to himself when she'd come over and found him.

'The scene works much better out here, don't you think? I feel like we were sleepwalking through those lines back in England.'

'Mmm.' Vio was still trying to focus on how incredible the cold water felt between his toes. 'I guess.'

Sabrina straddled him, blocking his sun. 'You were amazing, my darling, as always.' She bent low to kiss him, her tongue darting between his lips, passionate and hungry. 'You totally nailed it.'

Vio kissed her back, absently slipping a hand around the back of her neck. Sabrina lay her head down on his chest with a contented sigh. Since they first slept together, it was as if a switch had flicked inside her. Gone was the combative, prickly diva of old, the insecure Sabrina, always ready to hit back first, always spoiling for a fight. In her place was a serene, contented, actually really sweet girl. The change was reflected not just in her behaviour, but in everything: her expressions, the way she moved, even the way she dressed off set, all floaty flowing skirts and messy hair. Even her voice seemed softer somehow and more mellifluous.

Chuck MacNamee joked with Vio about it. 'Whatever you've done to her, man, keep doing it. I actually heard her say "thank you" to Deborah today, and to Monica in make-up. At least, I thought I did. Maybe my ears need syringing.'

There was no doubt Sabrina had changed for the better. But the suddenness of the transformation unsettled Vio. Partly because he did not relish the idea of being responsible for someone else's happiness. Pursuing his own happiness was a full-time job. But also because, part and parcel with Sabrina's new kindness and thoughtfulness to others, was a clinginess so at odds with the feisty girl he'd come to know that he wasn't sure how to handle it.

In bed, thank God, the wildcat Sabrina remained. Vio had a crisscross of livid scratch marks on his back to prove it, and sex was as explosive and exciting as he had ever known it. But as soon as they were out of the bedroom, Sabrina got that doe-eyed, stoned-with-happiness look, and Vio could hear the sombre thud of jail doors closing.

Unable to recapture his inner calm of a few minutes ago, Vio opened his eyes and looked around him. They were shooting in a wildflower meadow. An army of buttercups cascaded down to the river bank, shielded by swaying grasses and flanked on either side of the field by a tall row of shady oaks. He'd been determined to dislike Romania, the people, the countryside, even the Rasmirez Schloss. It was the country of his birth that had rejected him, after all, and Vio was passionate about how little he owed it. But it was hard to find fault with such an idyllic setting on a cloudless summer's day like today. While he was drinking it in, two figures appeared at the top of the hill, silhouetted by the blazing sun. It was a woman and child, and for a split second Vio's heart instinctively soared: *Tish and Abel!* Then he realized that of course it couldn't be them, and the bubble of joy burst like a pricked balloon.

I miss them, he realized with a pang. Four times since he'd been in Romania he'd picked up the phone to call Abel. But four times he'd chickened out, unable to face the sadness he knew he'd hear in the boy's voice. He and Tish would be leaving Loxley soon themselves, and Viorel was sure that as the date for their departure grew nearer, Abel's anxiety levels would be rising. *If I call, it might give him hope. He'll want me to help, to convince his mother to change her mind.* If Viorel had learned one thing about Tish Crewe over the last two months, it was that 'the lady was not for turning'. And certainly not for being turned by him.

The child on the hill was coming closer now, skipping towards the set. It was Saskia, Dorian's doll-like daughter, and the woman with her was the nanny. Throwing her arms wide, the little girl ran towards her father, staggering drunkenly down the steep hill before launching herself upwards into Dorian's arms for a hug. *Sweet*, thought Vio.

Over on the set, Dorian thought his daughter was pretty adorable too. Pressed against his, her cheeks felt as round and warm as two doughballs, and she smelt of sugar and sweat and general summer stickiness that instantly took Dorian back to his own childhood.

'Are you nearly finished, Daddy? I made a mermaid town; can you come and see it? Can you come and play mermaids?'

'I can very soon, honey,' said Dorian, straightening the pink silk bow in Saskia's hair. 'I'll take a break here in half an hour, and we'll play, OK? Promise.'

'Half an *hour*?' moaned Saskia. 'That's almost a whole day.'

'No, it isn't, princess.' Dorian laughed. 'Rula can play with you for a little bit, before I get there.'

'I'm bored of Rula,' Saskia pouted.

'Ask Mommy then. Mommy loves mermaids.'

'Mommy's asleep,' said Saskia.

Dorian frowned, handing his daughter back to her nanny. Chrissie was taking to her bed more and more during the days. She was clearly depressed, but refused to see a therapist or even talk about it with Dorian. Without Tish to confide in, Dorian had even turned to Sabrina for advice.

'You're a woman,' he began inauspiciously, cornering Sabrina after breakfast.

'How sweet of you to notice.'

'You know what I mean,' said Dorian awkwardly. 'I need some advice. How do I get Chrissie out of this funk? I know she's mad at me, but it's been weeks. I'm really worried about her.'

Sabrina's suggestion was to get her out of the Schloss. 'It can't be easy, having all of us hanging around like a bad smell for weeks on end. She probably feels she *can't* talk to you, like she has to schedule an appointment or something. That pisses women off.'

'It does?'

'Of course!'

It was funny: a month ago Dorian could no more have pictured himself taking love-life advice from Sabrina than flying to the moon. But now he'd done as she suggested, booking a cosy table at a romantic restaurant in Bihor for tonight. Alone, away from the *Wuthering Heights* circus, Chrissie would have to talk to him, or scream at him, or give him *some* clue what he could do to put things right. It was only a matter of days now till filming wrapped for good. Then he could devote his attention to her wholeheartedly. But in the meantime, the situation had already deteriorated to a point where it was affecting Saskia.

Tonight's going to break the deadlock. It has to.

* * *

The rest of the day's filming went well. After a thirty-minute mermaid-break with Saskia, Dorian returned to the set refreshed for the final scenes and delighted by his actors' performances, especially Sabrina's. Anyone who'd written Sabrina Leon off as a major movie star after last year's scandals – which was pretty much all the big Hollywood studios – was going to be eating their words when they saw the final cut of his movie.

Dorian fervently hoped that *Wuthering Heights* was going to be the film that saved them all. But for Sabrina it had been truly transformational. Directing her this afternoon, Dorian felt a deep glow of pride for whatever small part he might have played in helping her to grow, to become the actress and the woman she was truly capable of being. Viorel was increasingly becoming the bright centre of Sabrina's universe, her love for him burning up the screen like lava. But it was still Dorian she turned to for counsel and support.

Dorian got back to the Schloss at seven and headed straight for his and Chrissie's bedroom, praying she was at least out of bed as he climbed the grand stone staircase. These depression naps seemed to drain her of energy rather than revive her, and it always took her a good hour from waking up to get back into the swing of things. Dorian had booked Gianni's, one of the few local restaurants Chrissie actually professed to like, for eight o'clock. He desperately wanted to make the reservation.

Opening the bedroom door, his spirits lifted. Chrissie was obviously up. The bed was made. More than that, the room looked spotlessly clean, with all her clothes put away and the heavy, velvet drapes drawn back, a sure sign that her mood had lifted. At her most depressed, she left mess every-where and shuffled around in darkness like a mole. It was only when he opened the wardrobe to find a clean shirt and noticed that *all* Chrissie's clothes were gone that the first misgivings began to creep up on him.

Maybe she just reorganized some things.

Trying not to panic, Dorian walked through into her private dressing room. It was totally bare. Around the room, closet doors stood open, like giant mouths laughing at him as they revealed their emptiness. In the centre of the room, a few forlorn pairs of sneakers were the only remaining inhabitants of Chrissie's beloved 'shoe island'. With all the jewel-coloured pairs of Jimmy Choos and Jonathan Kelseys gone, it looked painfully depleted, a peacock stripped of its feathers, a rainbow faded to lifeless grey. *Like our marriage*, thought Dorian bleakly.

He walked into Saskia's bedroom like a zombie, already knowing what he would find there. With no toys or teddies, the pink-painted room looked stark, as if someone had died there and the staff had cleaned up afterwards with ruthless efficiency. A few hours ago, Saskia had been on set, in his arms. Now, in a single afternoon, all traces of Dorian's family life had been brutally removed. *Pouff. Gone.*

Without knowing how he got there, Dorian found himself downstairs in his study, staring at the phone on his desk. Propped up against it was a note, a single folded piece of paper with his name scrawled across it in Chrissie's spidery, angry handwriting. Bracing himself, as if for a physical blow, he picked it up and opened it.

'I left this note here because this is where you always are – working. And because without a note, I doubt you'd even have noticed we'd gone. I'm moving back to LA and I'm taking Saskia with me. That's all you need to know. Maybe I'll see you there some time, next time you're on business. Or maybe not. To be honest, I'm past caring. C.'

There was so much anger in those few lines. Clearly, the note had been designed to wound him, but reading it over and over, Dorian found he wasn't so much hurt as saddened. How awful that Chrissie felt reduced to writing something so small, so mean-spirited. He knew he was numbed by the shock. Eventually, in a few hours, or perhaps days, the enormity of what had happened would probably hit home and he'd feel all the desperation and anguish and horror that he knew he ought to. But right now there was nothing but a still, quiet feeling of loss. He felt as if he were watching a poignant movie scene, but about somebody else.

He picked up the phone, then put it down again.

Who am I calling?

Obviously, he ought to do something. His wife had left him and taken their child. It was a situation that called for action of some sort on his part. Crisis management. But when he stopped to think about it, Dorian realized he actually had no idea what to do. In an accident, you called an ambulance; after a crime, the police. But what did you do when somebody upped sticks and walked away with twenty years of your life, then left you a note that basically told you to go fuck yourself?

'Are you OK?'

Sabrina appeared in the doorway. In dark green Bermuda shorts and a sleeveless vest, with her long hair scraped up into a messy bun, she looked young and happy and in love. Just seeing her made Dorian's heart ache. It was so long since Chrissie had looked like that.

'I'm fine.'

Sabrina had been about to head into town herself for a drink with Viorel when she'd happened to pass by Dorian's study. Seeing him staring into space, she was concerned.

'Are you sure? You look as if the world's just ended.'

337

Dorian thought: *Part of it just has.*

'Chrissie's left me,' he said blankly. 'She's taken Saskia back to LA.'

Sabrina grimaced. 'God, Dorian. I'm so sorry.'

'But not surprised?'

She shrugged. 'Are you?'

Dorian thought about it. 'I guess not. A little. I don't know. I thought we might have made it to the end of the shoot. We're almost wrapped.' He ran a hand through his hair, suddenly aware of how incredibly tired he was.

'Maybe she just needs a little space,' said Sabrina, trying to sound optimistic. 'She's probably trying to make a statement, to teach you a lesson or something. She'll be back.'

'Sure.' Dorian smiled. 'She'll be back.'

But neither of them really believed it.

CHAPTER TWENTY-ONE

The final weeks of shooting at Dorian Rasmirez's Romanian Schloss seemed to rush by at the speed of light. So much had happened since they'd left England. Dorian's marriage appeared to have finally snapped. Sabrina had broken off her engagement to Jago. And of course, she and Vio had now plunged headlong into an intense relationship, igniting a spark that had transformed their on-screen chemistry, and consequently the whole feel of the movie. Yet, in a very real sense, it felt like yesterday when they'd arrived in Transylvania. By the time everyone had come to terms with the grandeur of Dorian's castle and the breathtaking majesty of the Carpathian Mountains, filming was done and it was time to go home.

As a result, there was a certain air of unreality about the wrap party. *Was this really the end?* This was intensified by the fact that most of the actors, including Lizzie and Rhys, had finished their scenes weeks ago, so it was only a hard-core group of Sabrina and Vio, Dorian, Chuck, and a skeleton gaggle of crew and extras, who'd gathered in the grand Victorian summerhouse for the traditional toasts and farewells. Some of the Schloss staff had rocked up to swell the numbers, making it even more of a motley crew.

The summerhouse itself looked and smelled incredible. The Greek Revivalist building had been filled with white lilies and freesias, and the artwork from the huge back wall had been temporarily removed to make space for a full-size movie screen on which images from the long summer of shooting were being projected. In the middle of the room, two long trestle tables had been placed end to end, laden with delicious salads, meats and desserts, and some of the best wine from the Rasmirez cellars, and around the edges of the oval room, white sofas strewn with silk cushions and throws provided comfortable retreats for those who wanted to talk in private.

Chuck MacNamee, who'd worked with Dorian on every film he'd made since *Love and Regrets*, kicked off the speeches with an emotional tribute to his mentor.

'As we all know, some of the most beautiful art in history has been forged through pain. This shoot hasn't been easy, the last couple of weeks especially. But Dorian, what you've achieved here is something truly incredible.' His eyes welled up with tears. 'You're awesome, man.'

Chuck's been at the Mojitos already, thought Dorian, not without affection, trying to look appreciative as the speech rambled on. He *was* proud of the film. It still needed to be edited, of course – the difference between a good movie and a great one often rested on what was left on the cutting-room floor – but he had no doubts that *Wuthering Heights* would be the crowning achievement of his career. As long as he could sew up a distribution deal and get the thing financed, of course, but with work of this quality that shouldn't be hard.

What Dorian doubted was whether he still cared. He'd made this film, at least in part, for Chrissie. To get them out of debt and back on track, so he wouldn't have to be working constantly, so he could spend more time with her, and give her all the things she wanted: the shopping trips to Paris, the vacations, the $20,000-a-head parties. Now Chrissie was gone, his marriage in tatters, did any of it really matter any more?

Mercifully, Chuck's speech was at an end. Glasses were refilled, Dorian mumbled a few words of thanks and, a few minutes later, Sabrina got to her feet. She and Viorel had spent the early part of the evening coiled up on a love seat in the corner, like an impossibly lithe and glamorous two-headed snake. Looking fresh and radiant as ever, her dewy, lightly tanned skin glowing beneath a simple grey silk maxi-dress, and her still-wet hair clinging to her shoulders and neck like tendrils of mahogany seaweed, Sabrina positively glowed with contentment and belonging.

'I'd also like to say a few, short words,' she began. 'Firstly, I wanna apologize to all of you if I was, you know, a little edgy when we first began shooting.'

'Edgy?' yelled one of the sound guys, to general laughter. 'You were a fucking razor blade.'

A few weeks ago, Sabrina would have shot the man down with a suitably pithy comeback, but now she took it on the chin.

'OK, OK, I get it. I was difficult. But that brings me on to the second thing I wanted to say. Which is thank you – to all of you, but especially to this man,' she pointed at Dorian. 'This man, who I was unforgivably rude to in a restaurant in Beverly Hills a year ago, but who offered me a lifeline anyway; this man who pulled me out of the flames, who gave me not just one chance but a whole bunch of chances when nobody else would.'

Dorian found he had to tear his eyes up from the ground and force himself to look at her. Since Chrissie left, merely looking at Sabrina's face could bring him close to tears. It was pathetic. *Am I really gonna become one of those misanthropic old assholes who can't bear to be around happy people?* he asked himself sternly. *Get a grip. This is Sabrina. You care about this girl. Be excited for her.*

'I hope, in the end, I've made you proud as Cathy,' Sabrina went on, beaming at him. 'Thank you. For everything.'

Skipping over to the trestle table where Dorian was sitting, she leaned down and kissed him, throwing her arms around his neck and hugging him tightly. It was unexpected. People were clapping and cheering. Dorian hugged her back awkwardly, stroking her back the way one might pet a dog.

'I mean it,' she whispered in his ear. 'You've changed my life. I won't ever know how to repay you.'

'Not at all,' said Dorian, finding his voice at last. 'You've worked hard, Sabrina. You've earned this. I've as much reason to be grateful as you do.'

Leaving Sabrina and Dorian to their mutual love-fest, Viorel chatted to one of the make-up girls. He was glad Sabrina seemed to have brought Dorian out of himself, stopped him from sitting there staring blankly into space like the ghost at the feast. When Chrissie did her disappearing act, Vio had confidently expected her to spill the beans about their night together at Loxley. As LA therapists were fond of saying, hurt people hurt people, and this was exactly the sort of information that a disgruntled wife on the brink of divorce might throw in her husband's face. When it hadn't happened he'd been relieved, but he still felt terrible, watching the effect Chrissie's departure had had on poor Dorian. It reminded him yet again what a good man Rasmirez was. *A better man than me.*

Yet again, Viorel found himself battling the strange feeling of dissatisfaction that had overshadowed his time in LA. It was really starting to bother him. *This should be the happiest time of my life. The movie's terrific, I just got a huge payday, I dodged a bullet with Rasmirez's wife and Sabrina's in love with me. Better still, tomorrow I finally get to go home.*

'We' *get to go home.*

Perhaps that was the problem, or part of it. Sabrina kept talking about their future as if it were an acknowledged fact. Which, by osmosis and a lack of action on Vio's part, it now pretty much was. 'They' were going home to LA. 'They' couldn't wait to go to Sushi Roku, to party together at Hyde, to go hiking up in Rustic Canyon, to celebrate Sabrina's birthday at Cecconi's. So far, Sabrina hadn't specifically brought up the idea of their living together. But she talked about Venice and Viorel's place there with an ease and familiarity that sounded distinctly proprietorial. Was he going to lose his fortress? If he let Sabrina in, it wouldn't be a fortress any more. It would be a home, their home. *Is that what I want?*

'More wine, dearest?'

Leah, the make-up girl with the most obvious crush on him, leaned in closer as she topped up his glass. She had spectacular tits, Vio noticed, pale and freckly like her face but as buxomly jiggly and fun-filled as a pair of water balloons. He couldn't think why he hadn't ever focused on them before.

'Thanks.'

The thought crossed his mind that if he weren't with Sabrina, he'd probably have slept with Leah tonight. And that if he *didn't* sleep with Leah tonight, he would almost certainly never see her again. Another chance lost forever. Another door closed.

'Is it really that bad, the life of a movie star?' Leah did a funny impression of his miserable pout. 'Down to your last pair of spun-gold boxer shorts, are you? Got the second-best seat on the private jet?'

Vio smiled. 'Sorry. Do I really look that tragic?'

'I'd say you had a good chance of making the Olympic sulk

squad, yeah.' Leah took a sip of her own wine. It was getting late and they were all distinctly tipsy. 'You know, you can tell me what's on your mind. I'm a good listener.' When Viorel didn't say anything, she added teasingly, 'Of course, I'd probably sell it to the *National Enquirer* first thing tomorrow morning. But a problem shared is a problem halved, right?'

Vio laughed loudly, taking her face in his hands.

'You're adorable. You know that, right?'

Leah froze. *I could kiss her*, thought Vio. *Right now, in front of everybody. Blow things up with Sabrina just like that. Blast open the doors and walk to freedom*. Then he glanced across at Sabrina. She was still talking to Dorian, throwing back her head and laughing at something he'd said, her long hair streaming out behind her like leaping flames, her angel's face a picture of happiness. She wasn't just beautiful. She was perfect. And she was all his.

What the fuck is wrong with me?

He drew back his hands from Leah's face.

'Sorry,' he muttered. 'I'm a jerk. I think I need to be on my own for a while.'

Without saying anything, Leah rummaged in a bag under the table, pulled out a packet of Marlboro Lights and a silver Zippo lighter and pressed them into his hands. Vio was touched.

'You really are adorable.'

'Yeah, yeah, I know,' said Leah. 'If you ever discover you've got a long-lost twin brother, be sure and give him my number.'

Back at Loxley Hall, Tish slumped down on one of Vivianna's new B&B Italia sofas, utterly shattered. Her flight to Bucharest was at eight tomorrow morning, and she desperately needed some sleep, but she was determined to finish the accounts and filing before she left. At least, she reasoned, if she left everything in a clear, organized state for Jago, there was a chance, however technical, that he might eventually get out of bed and start taking his responsibilities at Loxley seriously. At least she would know that she'd done her level best and that no one could blame her if the estate fell to rack and ruin. *I tried.*

In a minute, she would go back to Henry's study. *I'll just sit down for a few moments. Rest my eyes.*

She was woken by what was becoming one of her least favourite sounds in the world: the irritable buzz of her mobile phone. *Who on earth would call her so late?* She contemplated not answering. But then it occurred to her that it might be Carl calling about a problem with one of the kids at Curcubeu. He wouldn't call at this hour if it weren't something serious.

'Hello?' she said groggily.

Sitting on a wooden bench in the grounds of Dorian's Schloss, Viorel took a long drag on his cigarette. *I shouldn't have called. She sounds pissed off already.*

'Hi.' He coughed nervously. 'It's me.'

Silence.

'Viorel.'

More silence.

'I was just wondering how my friend Abel's doing?'

He tried to keep his voice light and casual, but was conscious of the agitated *thump thump* of his heart. Even from eight hundred miles away, Tish could make his heart beat faster. But not in a good way. More like the feeling you get when you see the cops in your rearview mirror.

'He's fine,' said Tish coolly. 'No thanks to you.' Inside she thought: *Why am I being so horrible to him? Is it force of habit?*

'What do you mean, "no thanks to me"?' Vio sounded irritated. 'What have I done now?'

'It's what you haven't done that's upset him,' said Tish. 'No letters. No calls.'

She knew she was being unfair. Breaking off contact with Abel was the kindest thing Vio could have done for him, under the circumstances. It was impractical to think he'd be able to visit them in Oradea or stay in any kind of regular touch, so why drag the thing out? But she couldn't seem to stop herself lashing out at him. Hearing his voice made her aware how much she missed him, which only angered her more.

'Oh, come on,' said Vio. 'I've been gone less than a month.'

'Have you any idea how long a month is to a five-year-old child?'

'Jesus,' snapped Vio, 'I was trying to be diplomatic, OK? After the whole Sabrina and Jago thing, I didn't know if a call from me would be welcome.'

'Diplomatic?' Tish scoffed. 'You? You're about as diplomatic as Russell Brand with Tourette's. Abel's got more tact than you.'

Viorel inhaled deeply on his cigarette. Why, why, why had he called? At the wrap party, flirting dangerously with Leah, watching Sabrina from across the room, he'd felt anxious and unhappy. He wanted somebody to make him feel better, and had found himself dialling Tish's number before he was really aware what he was doing.

I must be drunker than I realized.

'For your information,' Tish continued, 'Jago hasn't got out of bed since Sabrina broke things off with him. He's in a terrible state.'

'Pull the other one,' said Vio robustly. If he must, he would take a guilt trip about not calling Abel, but he wasn't about to shed any tears for Tish's drama queen of a brother. 'He's faking it. Jago never loved Sabrina.'

Tish, who'd privately thought exactly the same thing, was not about to take this from Viorel.

'How do you know?' she challenged him.

'Because it was bloody obvious,' snapped Vio. 'He wanted to get in her pants like everybody else.'

'Except you, of course,' said Tish sarcastically. 'You're deeply in love with her I suppose?'

'As a matter of fact I am,' Vio fired back, unthinking.

There was a pause of a few seconds, while they both retreated to their respective corners. When the bell went for the second round, it was Vio who landed the first punch.

'You know, you ought to be thanking me,' he said provokingly.

'Thanking you?'

'That's right. For putting an end to your brother's fantasy engagement. Admit it, you hated that relationship even more than you hated me.'

'I don't hate you,' said Tish, shocked.

'Whatever,' slurred Vio. 'I did you a favour, seducing Sabrina.'

'Oh, I see,' said Tish. *The arrogance!* 'A bit like the favour you did for Dorian, was it? By screwing his wife? You were actually helping a friend, putting an ailing marriage out of its misery.'

'That was different,' Vio mumbled. He was not proud of himself for what had happened with Chrissie.

'You know you're really quite saintly, when I think about it,' said Tish, warming to her theme. 'I can't *think* how I misjudged you so badly. You're like a sort of hands-on therapist, aren't you, Viorel? Not just a selfish bastard who follows his own dick around this world like a dog with a bone, never caring who he hurts.'

'You're impossible,' snapped Viorel. 'What are you going to blame me for next – the Middle East fucking peace crisis?' He hung up, the phone still shaking in his hand.

Back at Loxley, Tish sat stunned on her mother's

overpriced Italian sofa, listening to the long beep of the dial tone. The drawing room suddenly felt freezing. It also looked cold and unfamiliar, more like a furniture showroom than the shabby old home Tish had always loved, packed with all the expensive knick-knacks that Vivi had refused to return, despite Tish's pleading.

Viorel's call had upset her, not least because *she* was the one who'd turned it into a row. She'd been totally over-emotional recently, not to mention physically shattered, and she was taking it out on others. She put the tears welling up in her eyes now down to this, and the fact that she was leaving tomorrow, with no idea when she would see her beloved Loxley again. That was one of the biggest ironies about her falling out with Viorel. He seemed to believe that Tish found it easy to go. That it was only Abel who was upset to be leaving England. If he knew how much Tish was dreading it too, perhaps he wouldn't be so hard on her?

Opening up her wallet, she pulled out a picture of Michel and turned it over in her hands, rubbing the thumb-eared corners thoughtfully. Had it really only been one summer that she'd been away? When she'd first got back to Loxley, that picture had been her lifeline, an umbilical cord linking her with Oradea and her life there, a talisman that she could touch and that would transport her back to the place where she had left her heart.

But where was her heart now?

'You're never still up.' Mrs Drummond burst into the drawing room. 'Do you know what time it is, child? You've a flight in the morning. Get to bed at once.' In a long, fluffy pink dressing gown that had seen better days, and with her grey hair tightly wound in curlers, Mrs D looked more Nora Batty-ish than ever. The sight of her filled Tish with relief.

At least some things at Loxley would never change.

CHAPTER TWENTY-TWO

Los Angeles, two months later . . .

'No.' Chrissie Rasmirez's angular face hardened, her lips drew tighter and her ice-blue eyes narrowed. 'I don't accept this. You're not looking hard enough. Or you're looking in the wrong place.'

Larry Harvey observed his client with a depressing feeling of déjà vu. After thirty years working as a divorce attorney in Beverly Hills, he had seen the whole gamut of human emotion and frailty played out in his impeccably decorated corner office on Canon Drive: desperation, greed, grief, hatred, Larry had sat across the desk from them all. He'd represented tearful, wronged wives struggling to come to terms with their husbands' betrayals, and heartless Hollywood hookers intent on bleeding their rich, elderly husbands dry. And he treated those two imposters just the same: like open chequebooks.

Divorce had made Larry Harvey a very rich man indeed, and there were aspects of his job that, even after such a long and arduous career, he still enjoyed. But the business of divorce was changing. These days it was all about forensic accounting and jurisdiction shopping. Watching Chrissie

Rasmirez's hard, loveless face *demanding* that he wave a magic wand and miraculously uncover more money in her husband's bank accounts, Larry Harvey thought, *This isn't as much fun as it used to be.*

'I know Dorian has more money than that,' Chrissie insisted. 'He's hiding it somewhere. He has to be.'

'Mrs Rasmirez.' Larry Harvey's low, nasal voice wasn't loud, but somehow still managed to fill the luxurious taupe and cream room. 'I can assure you we have the best forensic accountants in the country scouring your husband's finances with a fine-tooth comb. If there were other monies, we would have found them.'

Chrissie shook her head defiantly, like a petulant child.

'We're still looking at several million dollars here,' the attorney went on. 'I'm confident I can get you a full fifty per cent settlement, and that's before child maintenance payments, which in your daughter's case would be . . . significant.' He pronounced this last word with relish, like a cat slurping a saucer of cream.

Chrissie didn't share his enthusiasm. *I'm paying this asshole a thousand bucks an hour because he's supposed to be the best. 'A Rottweiler,' that's what Linda Greaves called him. More like a fucking poodle. All he does is sit here and tell me that Dorian's money is stuck in Romania and there's nothing I can do about it. I can get Dorian's attorney to tell me that without paying for the privilege.*

'I'm not interested in "significant",' she barked, tapping her red-taloned fingers irritably on the desk. 'I'm interested in *fucking enormous.* My husband sleeps with a Velásquez over his bed, Mr Harvey. That painting alone is worth more than the number you've just shown me. I have girlfriends in this town with dry-cleaning bills bigger than what you're proposing. I'm the wronged party here, OK? I want my fair fucking share.'

You want your pound of flesh, thought Larry Harvey, *but you ain't gonna get it. Stupid woman, don't you think I would if I could? The more you make, the more I make. What part of the words 'national treasure' do you not understand? The Romanian assets cannot be liquidated and that's the beginning and end of it.*

Aloud, he said calmly: 'Are you instructing me to continue with the accounting investigation?'

Chrissie's face was by now so rigid with rage she looked as if she had lockjaw. 'Yes, I'm instructing you to continue,' she hissed. 'Continue until you find something. That's what I'm paying you for.'

Sweeping out of her attorney's office in high dudgeon, she emerged a few minutes later onto Canon Drive feeling ready to punch someone. In a new pale pink Hermès suit teamed with delicate blush calfskin pumps from Louboutin (she'd splashed out on clothes in her first few weeks in LA; after what Dorian had put her through, she deserved it, and she'd get it all back in the settlement anyway), Chrissie looked as rich, slim and carefree as any of the other wealthy wives and girlfriends out shopping in downtown Beverly Hills that day. *Only I'm not*, she thought furiously. *It's all a façade. And if I go through with the divorce, it'll all come crashing down around me. I'll be another middle-income housewife. A nobody.*

Since leaving Romania with Saskia and setting up home in LA (she'd rented a gorgeous, wisteria-clad English estate in Brentwood Park for six months, just to tide her over), Chrissie's emotions had seesawed wildly. She'd arrived utterly consumed with anger and hell bent on divorce. On her attorney's advice, she'd agreed to attend marriage-counselling sessions with Dorian – by phone, of course. Dorian was tied up in Romania editing the *Wuthering Heights* footage and couldn't come to LA full time till Christmas.

But Chrissie had no intention of taking him back. It was purely a tactical measure. Even if it hadn't been, the therapy would have been counterproductive. Each phone call with Dorian and the intensely irritating therapist, Billy, who would *insist* on remaining neutral, despite the fact that Chrissie was quite plainly in the right and Dorian quite fully in the wrong, only served to deepen Chrissie's resentment and resolve.

But since then a series of things had happened that had begun to eat at her certainty. Firstly, her social life dried up. After an exciting flurry of party, premiere and dinner invitations when she'd first arrived in town, her phone had suddenly stopped ringing and the glamorous dinners ground abruptly to a halt. It was a chilling wake-up call, and Chrissie had been around the block in Hollywood long enough to know what it meant. *As Dorian's wife, I have an identity here. As his ex-wife, I'm nobody. I'm Kevin Federline. I'm Cris fucking Judd.*

Secondly, there was Saskia. To Chrissie's surprise, the little girl kept asking after her father: where was Daddy, when was Daddy coming back, why hadn't Daddy come with them; and the questions had increased rather than lessened with time, becoming more and more charged with confusion and loss. Although self-centered and greedy, Chrissie was not entirely without human, maternal feeling. Saskia's unhappiness troubled her. Because Dorian had always been such a crappy, absent father, she'd assumed that her daughter's emotional ties to him would be weak and easily broken. Apparently, she was wrong.

And thirdly, and perhaps most crucially, there was the money. If Larry Harvey, and Dorian, were to be believed, Dorian's net worth was a fraction of what Chrissie had imagined it to be. The money they'd made from selling their LA home had all gone towards paying off debts on the last two movies, or into the bottomless, money-eating pit that was the Transylvanian Schloss. Could it really be that after a decade-long career as one of the most sought-after directors in Hollywood, Dorian had managed to wind up, if not broke, then at least no better off than an averagely successful dentist? *How could he have been so profligate?* Chrissie thought furiously, conveniently forgetting her own, Imelda Marcos-like retail habit. *Wasting all our money on uncommercial films and that damn stupid castle of his. Talk about throwing good money after bad!* The life of a rich divorcee was one thing. She could contemplate living without the attention and the glamorous friends if she could at least live out her days in luxury, fucking whomever she chose, shopping on Rodeo every day and lunching with the girls at The Ivy. But a poor divorcee? That had never been the plan.

All of a sudden, Dorian's promise to be back in LA by Christmas, for face-to-face therapy and to try to make things work, started to look less like an approaching storm cloud and more like a slowly reopening door. After her grand, dramatic exit, she didn't *want* to go back to him. But perhaps, if he grovelled enough . . . and in the absence of a better offer . . .

'Christina.'

Chrissie spun around. A gleaming silver Rolls-Royce with blacked-out windows and polished chrome hubcaps had pulled alongside her. It was one of the most vulgar, ostentatious cars one could imagine, the sort of vehicle favoured by rap stars or newly signed NBA players. So she was doubly surprised when a familiar blond head poked out of the window, smiling broadly.

'I heard you were in town. How incredible to run into you like this.'

'Crazy,' Chrissie agreed, smiling back.

Harry Greene looked as suavely handsome as Chrissie remembered him. Physically, he was the antithesis of Dorian: blond and slim and always immaculately dressed (today he wore a cream linen Armani shirt and matching jacket and classic vintage Ray-Bans) versus Dorian's dark, heavy-set scruffiness. In his manner, too, he was everything that Dorian wasn't: attentive, flirtatious, thoughtful. There was nothing wild about Harry Greene, nothing uncontrolled, yet he exuded power in a way that made Chrissie feel flattered, excited and nervous all at the same time whenever he looked at her.

'Are you busy?'

Trick question, thought Chrissie. *If I'm busy, that's his cue to drive away. If I'm not busy, I look like a loser, like a spare part.* She glanced at her watch. 'Not for an hour or so. My meeting finished early, and I'm not picking Saskia up from ballet class till three.'

'Great,' said Harry, jumping out and opening the passenger door of his pimpmobile. 'Hop in. I got something I wanna show you.'

Chrissie looked hesitant.

'Come on,' insisted Harry, 'It'll be fun. I'll get you to the ballet class on time, I promise. And on the way we can talk about how much we both despise your husband.'

Chrissie laughed. That *did* sound like fun. And God knew she had nothing else to do.

'OK. I'm game. But I can't be late for my daughter.'

Harry grinned, helping her into the car. 'Trust me.'

What Harry Greene wanted to show her was a house.

'House' was the technical term for the building. 'Single Occupancy Four Seasons Hotel' would have more accurately described the property, set behind the enormous stone gates of Coldwater Canyon on a five-acre plot of flat land. At the top of a half-mile drive lined with perfectly symmetrical poplar trees stood a mock-Tudor pile of well over 30,000 square feet. There were formal gardens with peacocks strutting around the lawns, koi ponds, multiple swimming pools complete with waterfalls and rock pools, and even a quarter-size golf course. Most impressive of all, though, were the views. Stepping out of the car, Chrissie could see right across the city to the Pacific and Catalina Island beyond. She felt like a queen, surveying her kingdom. *Harry's kingdom.*

'This is yours?' she gasped, genuinely dazzled.

'Not yet,' said Harry. 'It's on the market for ninety million dollars. I'm thinking about it, but I need a second opinion. Shall we go inside?'

Inside, the house was a tasteless riot of conspicuous consumption, as impressive as it was vulgar. You couldn't move for marble and gold, from the floors to the taps to the door handles. Ridiculously over-the-top chandeliers hung in every room, even the maids' kitchen, and flat-screen televisions emerged from the most unexpected places – inside closets, descending out of ceilings, rising up from floors, appearing ghost-like from behind two-way glass mirrors. The bedrooms, all fifteen of them, were laid with cream shag carpeting so thick and soft that if you took your shoes off it felt as if you were walking through custard, and the beds had all been dressed in vivid silks – purple, pink, orange, like a Miami nightclub owner's wet dream.

'What do you think?' Harry asked Chrissie, halfway through the tour. They were in the gym-and-pool complex, a gaudily mosaiced room that was evidently supposed to be Roman in theme, but which had nonetheless been plagued by the curse of the chandeliers.

'Honestly?' said Chrissie. 'It looks like Liberace ate too many sequins and threw up. Impressive but vile. You couldn't live here, not without redecorating the entire place.'

'Couldn't you?' Harry raised a quizzical eyebrow.

'I don't know,' Chrissie blushed. '*I* couldn't. I guess somebody must have liked it. Do you . . . is this to your . . . taste?'

Harry shrugged. 'I'm not sure I have a taste, as such,' he said honestly. 'With my movies, I care, I pore over every frame. But a house is just a roof over my head.'

'Pretty expensive roof,' said Chrissie. 'If *I* were paying ninety million bucks for a place, I'd want it to be perfect down to the very last lampshade.' She glanced around at the enormous gym complex and sighed. 'There's *so* much I could do to this place.'

'Great. Design it then.'

Chrissie looked at Harry. His face was impassive, unreadable. Was he serious?

'Me?'

'Why not?' Harry shrugged. 'You're in LA now; you have some time on your hands. You know about interior design, spaces and what-not.'

'Well, yes, but . . .'

'I'll knock ten million off my offer to pay for interiors, and I'll pay you fifteen per cent commission.'

'It's very kind of you,' said Chrissie, hugely gratified that a man like Harry Greene would trust her taste to that degree, and with something as personal and intimate as his own home, too. 'But I can't possibly accept. I'm not even a professional interior designer. It's just something I've done with my own homes, you know, for fun.'

Reaching into his jacket pocket, he whipped out a chequebook and a silver Montblanc pen and started writing. Ripping it off and folding it, he handed it to Chrissie. 'You're a professional now. Congratulations.'

He looked at her, his cold, grey eyes boring into hers, and Chrissie felt all the protestations die on her lips. *He's like Rasputin*, she thought excitedly, aware of the pulse of desire building between her legs. *He's so masterful, you can't deny him anything.*

'In any case,' Harry smiled, 'I don't think I would want to buy a house that *you* couldn't live in. That sounds awfully limiting.'

Chrissie's heart skipped a beat. *Is he suggesting what I think he's suggesting?*

'Come on.' Slipping a hand around the small of her back, Harry guided her back towards the stairs. 'We can talk more about the house tomorrow. Right now we should get you to that ballet recital.'

It was only later, once Harry had gone and she was back in Brentwood with Saskia, that Chrissie unfolded the cheque.

It was for $1.5 million dollars.

She wasn't sure what game Harry Greene was playing, exactly. But with this sort of prize money thrown in on day one, Chrissie Rasmirez was in. If it all came to nothing, she could always fall back on Dorian. For all that he'd insulted her and ignored her and rejected her sexually, she knew in her heart of hearts that Dorian still loved her. All she had to do was pull away, and he came running, like a little lost dog.

Yes, in an uncertain world, Dorian's devotion was the one thing of which Chrissie was totally, unwaveringly certain.

Outside Cecconi's on Doheny and Melrose, the usual gaggle of paparazzi gathered on the pavement, ready to snap celebrity diners on their way home. There were a number of starry restaurants on this side of town: Il Sole on Sunset,

Jen Aniston's favourite; Katsuya on La Cienega, where the Simpson sisters hung out. But Cecconi's remained the undisputed number one, at least in terms of genuine A-list. Simon Cowell called the restaurant his 'kitchen'. Tom and Katie were regulars, as were Posh and Becks, who'd both had their birthday parties at the unprepossessing corner building with its French bistro interiors, complete with tiled floors and vast ham hocks hanging behind the bar for charcuterie chic. Gwen Stefani, Jack Nicholson, LiLo and Sam Ronson, Kobe Bryant . . . the list of celebrity clients went on and on, so much so that it had been known for ordinary citizens to face waits of up to three *months* to get a dinner reservation that wasn't at 5.30 p.m. or 11.15 p.m.

On a Tuesday in October, however, and early in the evening at that, none of the paps had expected much action. So when word spread that Viorel Hudson and Sabrina Leon had arrived for an early dinner, the excitement was palpable.

In the six weeks since they'd been 'out' publicly as a couple, Sabrina and Vio had quickly risen to become the tabloid editors' most wanted. Their unexpected love affair, the most photogenic event since Brad and Angie got together, had transformed Sabrina's media profile overnight from Wicked Witch of the West to America's Unlikeliest Sweetheart, and raised Viorel's to undisputed A-list status. Together, they were a gold mine. *US Weekly* readers couldn't get enough of how the handsome Mr Hudson had 'tamed' wild child Sabrina Leon. In love, and visibly aglow with contentment, Sabrina had ditched her trademark miniskirts and black leather for a softer, more feminine look. The fashion editors adored it, and the tabloids gorged themselves on the 'Bad Girl Made Good' angle, until even Sabrina's agent, Ed Steiner, started to worry that the exposure might be *too* much and start to detract from her profile as an actress.

'You don't need to worry about that,' Sabrina told him, with a rare flash of her old arrogance. 'Once *Wuthering Heights* comes out, they'll start talking about my acting again. It's the best work I've done, I'm sure of it.'

From the paps point of view, the problem was *getting* a shot of them together. Sabrina, once the ultimate party girl and as easy to find out on the scene on a Saturday night as a gay man at a Barbra Streisand concert, had suddenly turned all homebodyish and reclusive. She and Vio were rarely out, and never in the clubs or up at the Chateau, their usual haunts. Sabrina's new-found shyness extended to interviews as well. Whereas before she would happily spout off, drunk, about her sex life to any reporter who asked her, now she refused to answer any 'intimate' questions about her and Viorel's relationship. 'All I will say is that we're very happy' was as far as she'd go, a mantra repeated endlessly to journalists and TV stations across the country with a sweet, guileless smile. And, of course, her reticence only whetted the public's appetite further. Just looking at Sabrina and Vio together, observing the body language, the way they leaned into one another and touched constantly, you could see that their sex life must be explosive. The fans couldn't get enough.

Tonight, dressed in a pale green Chloé gypsy skirt and flowing silk blouson top from Chanel, she breezed out of Cecconi's a few paces ahead of Viorel, looking ravishingly angelic as she handed the valet their ticket. The clicking of cameras was deafening and, despite the restaurant security's best efforts, a number of photographers broke ranks and ran towards Sabrina, pushing and shoving each other violently in their eagerness to get the closest shot. Sabrina looked panicked.

'Hey. HEY!' Viorel came forward, pulling Sabrina towards him and shielding her with his body. 'Back off,' he said angrily.

'This is out of line, guys. You're way too close. Leave her alone.'

It was a terrific image, Vio playing knight in shining armour in vintage Levis and a dark blue Turnbull & Asser shirt, the quintessential Englishman-in-LA look, his dark, brooding good looks heightened by his anger. And Sabrina was in shot too, clinging to him for protection like a baby bird nestling under its mother's wing. *Fucking adorable.*

Pop pop pop went the flashbulbs. Vio was tempted to lash out and punch one of the paps but, knowing how much mileage they'd get out of him losing his temper, he restrained himself. Happily, his Bugatti arrived seconds later. With the help of security he was able to bundle Sabrina safely into it before driving away at speed, scattering photographers like dead leaves as he roared off along Melrose towards Santa Monica Boulevard.

'You OK?' he asked Sabrina, once they'd finally shaken off the last of the stragglers.

'I'm fine.' She reached across and laid her hand over his as it rested on the gear stick. It was incredible how physical contact with him, however minimal, instantly calmed her. She could feel her pulse slowing and the adrenaline from their run-in with the paparazzi ebbing like a receding tide. Soon they'd be home, cocooned from the world in their private Venice fortress. Sabrina still owned her house in the Hollywood Hills, but had spent only two nights there since they got back to LA, and had come to think of Viorel's apartment on Navy as 'their' place. Last weekend they'd spent a blissful Sunday pottering around the furniture stores on Beverly and Robertson, picking out a new bed. Sabrina had never been the jealous type before, but with Viorel she found she couldn't stand the thought of making love in a bed where he'd been with other women.

'I know it's superstitious and crazy,' she told him, 'but I want a fresh start. I want everything to be perfect from now on, you know?'

Viorel did know. And it worried him. Love affairs were rarely perfect. *He* certainly wasn't perfect. With every passing day, Sabrina's expectations seemed to rise and rise like flood-waters at the levee. He tried hard to shake the feeling that eventually the flood would overwhelm him. That the intensity of Sabrina's love would drown him. He tried to find the words to express any of this to Sabrina, but every time he looked at her loving, trusting face, his nerve failed him. They bought the new bed.

'I've been thinking,' said Sabrina, as they arrived at their underground garage and the door swung open to welcome them. 'What are we gonna do about Christmas?'

'Do we have to "do" something about it?' asked Vio, parking and switching off the engine. 'Last time I heard, you couldn't stop Christmas from coming. Some guy called the Grinch tried once, but apparently it came all the same.'

'Ha ha, very funny,' said Sabrina. They stepped into the elevator. Seconds later they were in the apartment. 'I meant are we gonna stay here, are we gonna go away some place?' She kicked off her shoes. 'Cabo's real romantic at Christmastime, but part of me thinks we should stay home and do the whole shebang, you know? We can get a tree, we can bake pecan pies . . .'

We, we, we, thought Vio. 'It's not even Halloween yet, sweetheart.' Sinking down on the couch he reached for the TV remote. 'Let's see how we feel. Keep it spontaneous.'

'OK,' said Sabrina. She tried to sound unconcerned, but Vio could hear the disappointment in her voice. 'Sorry. It's just, I never really had a proper Christmas before.'

Vio put down the remote. 'What do you mean?'

'Well,' Sabrina sat down next to him, 'I mean, obviously I *had* Christmas. But the last few years I spent it with Camille and Sean, looped out of my mind.'

'Oh.' Vio frowned. Sabrina's vacuous hangers-on had called her ceaselessly the first week they got back to LA, to the point where Vio had had to persuade her to ditch her old phone and get a new number. The last thing she needed was those parasites back in her life.

'And before that I was always filming somewhere,' said Sabrina.

'On Christmas Day?'

'Sure. I made sure I was working Christmas Day.'

Vio looked puzzled. 'Why?'

Sabrina shrugged. 'I kinda always had a bad time with Christmas. When I was a kid, in Fresno, the Christmases in the children's home were so sad. The staff would make an effort, give you presents and all. But it was so fake, everybody trying real hard to act like a family, when in reality nobody there gave a shit whether you lived or died.'

'How do you know they didn't give a shit?' asked Viorel gently.

'How did you know your mother didn't give a shit about *you*?' asked Sabrina. 'You're a kid. You just know.'

Vio nodded understandingly. He couldn't argue with that.

'Plus, in my case, my "house father", the guy at the home who was kind of in charge of me, snuck into my room on Christmas Eve when I was twelve and tried to put his dick in my mouth. So that was like, you know, "Merry Christmas!"' She laughed, rolling her eyes, but Vio could see the pain underneath, the scar this bastard had left behind him. 'That kind of finished things off for me.'

'Poor baby.' He pulled her closer, slipping his hands beneath her silk Chanel blouse, stroking the bare skin on her back. *How could anybody treat a twelve-year-old kid like that?* he thought bitterly. *No wonder she's been so fucked up.*

As always when he touched her, Sabrina's response was instant, her back arching and her pupils dilating. She kissed him greedily, pulling his face closer with her hands, opening her mouth as she pressed her soft lips against his hard ones and wriggling out of her skirt like a snake shedding its skin. Within a few seconds she was naked in his arms, a smooth, caramel-limbed, exotic creature offering herself up to him completely. *No man could resist this*, Vio told himself. Sabrina's desire was a huge aphrodisiac, but at the same time it could be so powerful, so overwhelming that at times Vio felt out of his depth, like a leaf being dragged along in a fast-flowing current. Many women had wanted him, but Sabrina seemed to need him in a way he'd never experienced before. As if by their physical union she was somehow sucking the life force out of him, feeding from his desire for her like a mosquito gorging on blood. He wanted to pull back, to slow things down, to distance himself. But how could he when she was so ridiculously desirable, a complete virtuoso between the sheets? Not to mention the fact that, in the last few days especially, she'd started opening up to him about her childhood and the horrific experiences that had shaped her life. Sabrina Leon, who never showed vulner-ability – to anyone. *She trusts me*, thought Vio. *If I break that trust, I'm as bad as every other asshole who's abused her or let her down.* He desperately did not want to be another 'bad man' on Sabrina's lifelong list of losers and users.

Sabrina undid his belt buckle one-handed and straddled him on the couch, the palest pink nipples of her magnificent breasts on a tantalizing level with his mouth, brushing his lips with a feather-light touch, then pulling away as he opened his mouth to try to kiss them. Viorel groaned with pleasure, unbuttoning his Levis and releasing his rock-hard erection.

'Tell me you love me,' Sabrina whispered. She was leaning forward so her long dark hair hung over him like a silken curtain. He could smell the desire on her skin, feel the longing in the quiver of her breasts as she breathed.

'I love you,' said Vio, slowly easing himself inside her. And in that instant, feeling Sabrina's muscles tighten around him and hearing her gasp in pleasure, he did. Running his tongue across her breasts and his hands down her naked back, it was as if his whole body had become an instrument of worship. Because she *was* a goddess. Physically, sexually, she was perfection. They moved together like a single, frenzied animal, grabbing at one another's bodies like two monkeys grasping for purchase in the trees, but ultimately tumbling to the ground, locked in combat. Slipping off the couch onto the floor, Vio rolled on top of Sabrina, pinning her down, their fingers entwined. He tried to stop himself coming, but it was like an exhausted salmon battling its way against the fast-flowing river. He might be on top, but sexually, as ever, it was Sabrina who was in control. With a shudder of ecstasy, he exploded into her, every nerve in his body alive with pleasure.

Afterwards, still slumped on top of her, it took him a full minute to recover sufficiently to speak. 'I'm sorry,' he whispered in her ear. 'That was way too fast.'

'It was perfect,' sighed Sabrina contentedly. She loved it when Vio couldn't control himself. Every orgasm was a victory, a bond tightened, a bolt locked. Nothing gave her more pleasure than knowing that he wanted her.

It was strange, this feeling Vio gave her. Their sex life was so explosive because it was a respite from fear. Her fear. When they were fucking, Sabrina knew she had him, that

Vio Hudson was utterly, irrevocably hers. But at every other time – at dinner, on set, with his friends, while he slept – she doubted it. As a result, she found herself living in a permanent state of tension. Rationally, the experience was unpleasant. Sabrina needed the relationship like an addict needed heroin but, like most addictions, it brought her more pain than pleasure. Sometimes she hankered after the early days of filming *Wuthering Heights* at Loxley Hall, before they'd gotten together, and before Jago; the days of fun, easy flirtation. How long ago that all seemed now. For a moment, she wished Dorian Rasmirez were here with his father hat on, to guide her through these uncharted waters with Vio. But perhaps even Dorian couldn't help her now? *I'm in love. I guess this is what it's supposed to feel like.*

'So what do you think then?' Rolling onto her side as Vio eased out of her, she propped herself up on her elbow so they were face to face. 'Christmas here? Together?'

Reaching out, Vio stroked her cheek tenderly. 'Sure. Sounds like a plan.'

He smiled, banishing the sinking feeling deep in the pit of his stomach.

There was no way out.

CHAPTER TWENTY-THREE

Dorian Rasmirez gazed sadly out of the restaurant window and thought, *I have to get out of this funk.* It was late December, a few days after Christmas, and Santa Monica was still decked out in its festive finery. The store windows glittered with bright, enticing displays of toys and candy, and Montana Avenue was lit with snowflake-shaped streetlights and flashing red-and-white candy canes. The post-Christmas sales had already started, and even though it was 7 p.m. and already dark, the pavement outside Luigi's was still busy with bargain hunters.

Normally, just being at Luigi's was enough to put Dorian in a good mood. A modest, low-key Italian place on Montana and Seventh, it was one of his favourite LA restaurants. The Cioppino in front of him now smelled mouthwateringly good, wafts of saffron and white wine and garlic floating up from his bowl. But he couldn't seem to enjoy it. Not with tomorrow's marriage counselling session hanging over him like a brooding thundercloud.

He'd been in LA for three weeks now, and with every passing day his depression had deepened. This was despite the fact that, last week, he'd finally pulled it off and signed a lucrative funding-and-distribution deal with Sony Pictures. His strategy, of building up the hype around *Wuthering Heights* by keeping it under wraps, could not have worked out more perfectly, with Sony and Paramount ending up bidding against each other to take a slice of the movie. The deal was large enough to pay off all Dorian's immediate debts. More importantly, it meant that *Wuthering Heights* definitely wouldn't suffer the same fate as *Sixteen Nights,* and sink into acclaimed but unwatched oblivion. Sony would promote it and would make sure it found its way into theatres all over the world. They'd also promised to set a good chunk of change aside for an Oscar campaign, putting Dorian head to head with Harry Greene's *Celeste,* the year's other big-budget period movie. This was the White Knight deal he'd been praying for every night since he signed Viorel Hudson's first pay cheque. But had it come too late to help him work things out with Chrissie?

At the moment, it sure seemed that way. Dorian had flown to LA to see his wife and spend some time with his daughter over the holidays. But a reconciliation now felt further off than ever. Christmas Day itself was a disaster. They'd agreed to spend the day together, at Chrissie's rented place in Brentwood Park, to try to keep things as normal as possible for Saskia. But in fact it was anything other than normal. Dorian and Chrissie had not been together under one roof since Chrissie had walked out four months earlier, and both of them were tense. Feeling guilty about Saskia, Chrissie had gone over the top with the decorations, shipping in a tree that wouldn't have looked out of place in the Rockefeller Center and weighing it down with enough lights and tinsel to deck out a small Midwestern town.

'Jesus!' said Dorian, arriving at nine a.m. with sacks of

presents under his arms. 'Eat your heart out, Charlie Brown. That's the biggest Christmas tree I've ever seen.' He meant it as a compliment, but Chrissie immediately took offence, assuming it was just another of his barbed criticisms of her spending and lifestyle.

She shook her head bitterly. 'Incredible. You even resent paying for your daughter to have a decent Christmas.' And things pretty much spiralled downhill from there. As usual, Dorian couldn't put a foot right. Saskia, overtired and picking up on the tension between her parents, behaved dreadfully, crying at the slightest thing, breaking the expensive, hand-made doll's house Dorian had bought her in under an hour, and finally eating so many candies at lunch that she threw up all over Chrissie's new, white-mink-trimmed Ralph Lauren sweater.

'She never behaves like this when you're not here,' said Chrissie accusingly. 'It upsets her, seeing you again after so long.'

Dorian tried not to show how wounded he felt by that comment. Or how panicked, because he suspected deep down it was true. He knew he'd stayed in Romania longer than he should have, finishing *Wuthering Heights*. But, as usual, the editing process had proved longer and more arduous and complicated than he'd expected. It had also been addictive. Sabrina's performance as Cathy was utterly electrifying. It had been good in the scenes shot at Loxley, but it had improved so much since she'd gotten together with Vio, it was actually a struggle to edit the footage together without the difference being too noticeable. Hudson shone, too, as Heathcliff, but his work was more consistent throughout. Overall Dorian was immensely proud of the movie, and more excited by it artistically than he had been by anything he'd done in the last ten years. Early preview audience reactions to the film had been rapturous. It was that, more than anything, that had clinched the desperately needed Sony deal. But personally, the extra time Dorian had devoted to post-production had come at a cost.

What did I expect? thought Dorian, as he drove back to his poky rented apartment late on Christmas night, alone. *To show up after three months and have Saskia welcome me with open arms?*

Chrissie's hostility had been less of a surprise, although perhaps oddly Dorian found he was less hurt by it than he'd expected. He put this down to battle weariness. After trying and failing to make his wife happy for at least the last decade, he felt numbness and resignation where once he would have felt acute misery. Since he'd got to LA, they'd been attending twice-weekly couples therapy sessions. These were a marginal improvement on the phone therapy, but still seemed to boil down to Dorian writing an astronomical cheque each week for the privilege of sitting on a grubby sofa in Venice opposite some dirty-fingernailed hippy, listening to Chrissie recite his failings as a husband. Every session, she seemed to get angrier. And yet she still hadn't filed for divorce, leaving him hanging on a precarious thread of hope that, perhaps, the therapy *was* worth it; and perhaps, in some unseen way that he didn't understand, these sessions *were* bringing her back to him.

'You didn't like the fish soup, sir?'

Dorian glanced up, startled. His Cioppino sat before him, stone cold and untouched.

'Sorry, Luigi. I thought I was hungry, but I guess I lost my appetite.'

'Not a problem at all, sir.' The elderly restaurateur smiled kindly. Dorian Rasmirez had been a regular for over ten years, the kind of regular every restaurant dreamed of:

famous, rich, a generous tipper and with no attitude. He looked exhausted, and miserable, and the old man felt sorry for him. 'I'll have the kitchen bag it up for you. We'll throw in a plate of tiramisu as well. If that doesn't revive your appetite, I'm afraid you may need to see a doctor.'

'Thanks.' Dorian smiled, but he felt exhausted. If tomorrow's trip to Venice was as unproductive as the last eight sessions, he was going to say something to Chrissie. At some point she had to tell him which way she was going to jump. She'd seemed mildly pleased when he told her about the Sony deal, and the fact that *Wuthering Heights* was at least now set fair to be a huge commercial success. But she had yet to commit to their future together, and all the therapy in the world couldn't make the decision for her. Did she want him back or didn't she? If she didn't, at least he would know where he stood. And if she did . . . to his surprise, he found thinking about this prospect more mentally exhausting than joyous. If Chrissie took him back, there were a million and one hurdles to jump over, things that they needed to start talking about now. Like, was she expecting him to move back to LA? And, if so, what would happen to Romania and his family home? He couldn't just leave the Schloss. It was his duty. But if he didn't agree to move . . . His head began to throb.

It was a five-minute walk back to his apartment, and the cold night air did him some good, blowing away the worst of his anxieties. *We'll find a way through this. We've weathered so many storms together already. Once the movie comes out and is a hit, our money worries'll be over. I can write my own cheque on the next picture, spend more time with the family. It'll all be OK somehow.* By the time he got home, he almost believed it. Sinking down on the couch with a bag of Kettle Chips and a Budweiser – *appetite's back; things are looking up already* – he flipped the TV on to E!, hoping to catch the Sundance previews. Instead, an image of Sabrina Leon's face filled the screen. At first, he felt oddly startled, having his living room taken over by her larger-than-life features: that familiar, soft, wide-set mouth and those mint-green eyes looming over him like some sort of sexually charged Big Brother. Then the image faded, and was replaced by a rapid-fire montage of shots of Sabrina's love-interests, past and present, culminating with a picture of her at The Ivy restaurant on Robertson with Viorel Hudson last month. The two of them were holding hands over the table, radiating happiness, the look of love between them unmistakable.

'The E! *True Hollywood Story*, Sabrina Leon and Viorel Hudson, will be right back after these messages.' The announcer's voice woke Dorian as if from a trance. *Are they really running couples-shows on those two already?* It was astonishing how quickly the press fever had built over Vio and Sabrina's relationship. Of course the PR was terrific news for Dorian's movie. It ought to have thrilled him that *THS* was already profiling his co-stars as a Hollywood power couple, a younger, edgier Brangelina for the new generation of movie fans. So why didn't it?

The commercials over, Sabrina was back on screen, this time talking to Diane Sawyer about her infamous meltdown of last year and how different her life looked now.

'I've been working pretty much constantly since last spring,' she said, her voice softer and more mellow than Dorian remembered it. 'I'm really grateful for that, and grateful to Mr Rasmirez for believing in me.'

Mr Rasmirez? Dorian frowned. She made him sound old. Like her high-school principal or something.

'But I actually think being in love and so happy in my personal life is what's changed me the most.' Leaning forward, looking pretty and low key in a white cotton Donna Karan shirt and Ksubi jeans, Sabrina treated Diane to a megawatt smile. 'I'm happier now than I've ever been.'

'And you have a certain Englishman to thank for that, I assume?'

A still of Viorel as Heathcliff appeared on the screen. *Jesus, the guy's got it*, thought Dorian. Not since Johnny Depp had any serious leading actor had that combination of good looks, depth and raw, sexual arrogance that radiated out of Vio like heat from the sun. Dorian could see what Sabrina saw in him – what all women saw in him. He'd heard the rumours about a possible dalliance between Vio and Chrissie last summer in England. Movie sets were notorious hotbeds of gossip, not all of it accurate. Dorian didn't know if the whispers about his wife and Hudson were true, but looking at Viorel's handsome, smouldering features now, he could imagine they might be. Perhaps strangely, the thought didn't make him hate Viorel. It would be like hating an earthquake or a flood. The sort of sexual energy Hudson possessed was a natural phenomenon, wild and unstoppable.

The camera cut back to Sabrina, puppy eyed and adoring. 'I do, yes,' she told Diane Sawyer. 'It's early days, but we're very much in love.'

All of a sudden Dorian felt sick. The beer and chips curdled in the pit of his stomach like sour milk. And it hit him with a lurch, right there, as if someone had cut an elevator cable and left him plummeting into the abyss: *I'm in love with her.*

I'm in love with Sabrina.

It wasn't just exhaustion stopping him from making progress with Chrissie. It wasn't frustration, or despair, or his inner perfectionist shackling him to an editing suite. It was more than that. He wasn't in love with her any more.

I don't love my wife.

The thought was so shocking, so unexpected, he tried to dislodge it physically, shaking his head from side to side like a dog drying itself after a swim. He even tried the words out loud, to see how ridiculous they sounded.

'I don't love Christina.'

The ring of truth was so deafening, Dorian burst out laughing. *Holy shit.* For a moment he felt liberated, filled with something close to elation. But then reality kicked back in. It wasn't all about Chrissie, about whether he loved her or not. There was Saskia to consider. They were a family. You didn't just jack in a twenty-year relationship because your heart no longer skipped a beat every time you saw one another. Not unless you were a teenager. Or a jerk. As for being in love with Sabrina, that was just crazy. *She's young enough to be my daughter. Not to mention the fact that she's utterly besotted with Viorel.* Again, he tried the words out loud for size.

'I love her. I'm in love with Sabrina Leon.'

The phone rang. Dorian jumped out of his skin, like a guilty adolescent caught with a copy of his dad's *Penthouse* magazine. His heart was pounding and his palms sweating when he picked up the receiver.

'Hello?'

'Dorian?'

'Yeah, it's me.' He didn't recognize the voice on the line, but it was male and sounded clipped and businesslike. 'Who is this?'

'Jonathan Lister.'

Lister, Lister, Lister . . . the name rang a vague bell.

'Sony Pictures.'

Oh yeah. Lister. Tall. Blond. Very white teeth. Mike Hartz's number two. About as much sense of humour as an undertaker with haemorrhoids.

'Hey, Jonathan. What's up?'

'We need you in our offices first thing tomorrow. Eight a.m.'

Dorian bridled. He disliked being dictated to, even by someone as powerful as Johnny Lister.

'I'm afraid that's not possible. Not tomorrow. I—'

'Make it possible. We've run into some significant problems. We may have to withdraw our offer.'

Now Lister had Dorian's attention. He muted the TV, struggling to quell the feelings of panic pressing against his chest. 'What do you mean "withdraw"? You can't withdraw.'

'Certainly we can withdraw.' The voice on the other end of the line was as emotionless and blunt as an android's. 'It may not come to that, but significant problems have arisen . . .'

'What sort of problems?' demanded Dorian. 'I don't understand.'

Jonathan Lister began his next sentence with two words that struck dread into Dorian's heart. 'Harry Greene's come forward at the last moment with a proposal that we have to look at seriously, OK?'

'*OK?*' Dorian repeated, incredulous. 'No it is not "OK". We agreed a deal, Johnny. We signed a deal. You and Mike can't just fuck me over because Harry Greene says "boo". You know the guy has a personal vendetta against me.'

There was a pause.

'Be in our office at eight a.m., Dorian. It's in your own interests.'

Dorian felt his anger mounting. 'I told you. I can't make a meeting tomorrow. I'm in an all-day therapy session with my wife. Couples counselling. So whatever bullshit you're trying to pull, you're just gonna have to tell me over the phone. Or, better yet, get Mike Hartz to do his own dirty work and call me himself.'

Another pause, longer this time. When Jonathan Lister spoke again, his tone was different. If Dorian hadn't known him to be an emotionless drone devoid of shame, he might almost have thought the man was embarrassed.

'I think your counselling session may have been cancelled.'

Dorian frowned. 'What? What are you talking about? What the hell do you know about my marriage counselling?'

'I saw your wife tonight. At a BAFTA fundraiser downtown.'

More silence. This time Dorian didn't fill it, but waited for the creep from Sony to go on.

'She was with Harry Greene. They were together.'

Dorian rubbed his eyes. His head was spinning. 'Don't be ridiculous.'

'I was at their table,' said Jonathan.

Dorian tried to process this information. 'No, that's not possible,' he mumbled. 'Chrissie knows . . . Uh-uh. She would never date Greene. You must have made a mistake.'

'I'm sorry.' The automaton voice was back. 'I thought you knew. Apparently, he's asked her to move in. She has a diamond on her hand the size of the Hollywood Bowl.'

Dorian was speechless. For a few seconds the line was silent. Then Jonathan Lister said brutally, 'Look on the bright side. Your schedule just cleared for tomorrow. Mike and I'll see you at eight.'

CHAPTER TWENTY-FOUR

'We had a deal, Mike. You shook my hand, in this fucking room. We had a deal!'

Dorian could hear the desperation in his own voice and hated himself for it. All he wanted to do was to tell these two-faced pricks from Sony to go fuck themselves. But while there was any chance at all, he had to try to control himself. Without this deal, he could see his beautiful movie disappearing into the black hole of oblivion. He needed them, and everybody in the soulless, seventh-floor meeting room knew it.

Michael Hartz shrugged with the nonchalance of a man who knew he held every last card. 'Come on, Dorian. We've both been in this business a long time. When you get an offer like this one, it's a game changer. It's nothing personal.'

'"Nothing personal?"' Dorian wanted to reach across the table and throttle the bald, bug-eyed Sony MD until he turned as blue as his Ralph Lauren shirt. 'Of course it's fucking personal! Harry Greene's out to destroy me. He started fucking my wife so she'd spill the beans on my agreement with you and he could use that information to fuck me over. My *wife*, Michael. How personal would you say that is?'

The MD stared back at him impassively. 'Greene's given us a written agreement to deliver *Fraternity IV* and *V* on the condition that we do not distribute *Wuthering Heights* for another twenty-four months. The *Fraternity* franchise is worth, conservatively, over eight hundred million dollars, Dorian.'

'Don't lecture me!' Dorian lost his temper. 'I know how much Greene's shitty movies are worth. But you signed a deal with me.'

'A deal to take an eighty per cent revenue share in *Wuthering Heights*, and to promote and distribute it. Which we're honouring.'

'*Honouring?*' Dorian spluttered. 'How do you figure that? You're sitting on the movie for *two years*. You're signing its death warrant.'

'Don't be so defeatist.' Mike Hartz smiled infuriatingly. 'It's a classic. People'll still come and see it in two years' time.'

Like hell they will, thought Dorian. Even if, by some miracle, they did, it would be too late for him. Coutts weren't going to wait another two weeks for their money, never mind two years. And of course he could wave goodbye to his Oscar hopes. Not just his but Viorel's and Sabrina's. *Oh God, Sabrina*. She needed this deal almost as much as he did.

'If you're not going to release it, I'll find someone else who will,' said Dorian defiantly. 'Not everybody in this town's prepared to bend over just because Harry Greene's got a hard-on.'

Jonathan Lister, who thus far had sat in complete silence throughout the tense meeting, suddenly cleared his throat. 'Ah, but that's the thing you see, Dorian. As you rightly pointed out, we signed a deal. We're under no obligation to release you from your contract.'

'Bullshit!' Dorian erupted. 'You haven't paid me a cent. The contract's not valid until you pay me—'

'Ten per cent of the overall deal value before January the fourteenth,' Lister interrupted, reading directly from the deal memorandum in front of him. 'I believe those funds were wired to Dracula Productions . . . was it yesterday, Mike?'

'Uh-huh,' Hartz nodded callously. 'That's right. Yesterday afternoon.'

'You bastards.' Dorian shook his head. How could he have been so stupid, leaving a clause like that in the paperwork? He'd been so distracted trying to save his marriage, and so happy about the Sony deal, he hadn't thought through the possible implications.

'Look, Dorian, this deal could still work out well for you,' Mike Hartz continued. 'You'll still get paid, eventually. The movie will show at Sundance as planned. And you know, if you don't want to wait two years for a full theatre release, we're open to exploring other options.'

Dorian hated himself for asking, clutching at straws, but he had to. 'Such as?'

Jonathan Lister smirked. 'Mr Greene has said he'd be more than willing for us to take *Wuthering Heights* straight to DVD. If you were agreeable of course.'

Dorian stood up, shaking with anger. 'Fuck Greene. And fuck you. I hope you rot in hell, together.'

As he stormed out of the room, Mike Hartz called after him. 'Like I say, man. It's nothing personal.'

Downstairs, sitting behind the wheel of his Prius, Dorian willed himself to try to think.

Focus. There must be a way out of this.

He looked at his watch: 9.17 a.m. Five o'clock in London.

He called Coutts. It was a long shot, but there was just a chance . . . 'Did a large payment from Sony Pictures hit my account yesterday?'

'Let me check, Mr Rasmirez.' The six-second pause felt like a decade. 'No. We're not showing anything on the system yet.'

Dorian tried to contain his excitement. 'What about today?'

Another pause. Then the teller's voice again, apologetic. 'Not as yet, sir, no. Sometimes our systems can be a bit slow.' The girl didn't know she was giving Dorian the best news he could possibly have hoped to hear. 'I expect it'll come in overnight. Would you like us to let you know when—'

'Can you put a stop on it?' Dorian asked, breathlessly. 'Can you refuse to receive it?'

'I'm afraid not,' said the girl. 'Not if it's an automatic transfer.' Dorian's heart sank. 'We can return the money once we receive it, but we can't prevent it from landing in your account.'

Dorian hung up. At least it wasn't in his account yet. There was still time, but every minute counted.

At 9.22 a.m. he was on the phone to his business manager.

David Finkelstein was sympathetic but blunt. 'It can't be done. Not in twelve hours and probably not at all.'

'It can be done,' said Dorian stubbornly. 'It has to be. If someone signs a distribution deal before Sony's money hits my London account, I can save my movie.'

'Dorian, listen to me. No one's gonna buy you out of this.'

'Why not?'

'Because they'd be taking a huge risk, that's why. Who wants to make an enemy of Harry Greene *and* Sony Pictures? No one, that's who. And even if they did, they'd have to do due diligence, have their legal team draw up a contract. That takes weeks, days at a minimum. You've got hours. Don't make an ass of yourself running all over town like a rat on a wheel. Don't give Harry Greene that satisfaction.'

Dorian winced, but said nothing. He knew David Finkelstein

was right, but what was he supposed to do? Sit back and watch while *Wuthering Heights* died a slow, anonymous death?

'Take Sony's money and try to cut a deal with your creditors,' said David. 'I know it's tough, but that's the best advice I can give you, as your business manager and your friend. Chalk it up to experience and move on.'

'I can't,' said Dorian. 'I have to try. I want you to get on the phone, David. Call in every favour you've got, at every studio, big or small; independents, foreign houses, I don't care. Get me some face-time with the decision makers. This morning. Now.'

The sigh on the other end of the line spoke volumes.

'I'll do my best. But Dorian . . .'

The line had already gone dead.

His first meeting was at noon, with Paramount, the original underbidder to Sony.

Richard Bleaker, the Head of Distribution, looked pained. 'I'm sorry, Dorian. I've seen the movie and you know I think it's terrific. Stellar work, super-commercial.'

'So what's the problem, Rich?'

'You know what the problem is. Legal would laugh in my face. You really think Sony wouldn't come after us? And Greene?'

'But that's just it,' said Dorian. 'If we sew this up now, they'd have no legal claim against either of us.'

'Come on, man,' said Richard Bleaker reasonably. 'You're not a lawyer and neither am I. I can't do this on a handshake. It's a mess.'

'The paperwork's a mess. I'll admit that. But look at the big picture here. The movie's gonna be a classic, Rich. One of the great love stories of our time. You'll see, after it shows at Sundance, it's gonna be huge. We're talking about

Academy Award-winning performances by two of the most bankable stars in Hollywood.'

Bleaker shifted uncomfortably in his seat. He felt bad for Rasmirez. Harry Greene was a bastard. But he knew a dead movie when he saw one. 'I'm not arguing with you, Dorian. It's great work, I told you that already.'

'And this is your chance to get your name on it. You'll regret it if you let this go, Rich.'

'Probably,' said Richard Bleaker magnanimously. 'But my hands are tied. I'm sorry.'

Dorian's next meeting, at MGM, was at 2 p.m. It was the same story.

'We'd love to take a look at it. We'll need at least a couple of days.'

At 3 p.m. he was at Miramax, at four with an independent in the Valley, at six with the Asian giant Kunomo and at seven with Red Line Productions. Over and over came the inevitable responses.

'I'm sorry.'

'It's out of the question.'

'We love the movie, but our hands are tied.'

In between meetings, Dorian made repeated, increasingly frantic calls to Chrissie, to her cellphone, to the rented house in Brentwood, even to Saskia's school in a desperate attempt to get hold of her. None of his messages was returned. Clearly, it was Chrissie who'd betrayed him to Harry Greene. She'd told Harry about the Sony deal and given him the leverage he needed to blow *Wuthering Heights* out of the water. The thought of Chrissie sleeping with Greene was still too much of a head-fuck for him to contemplate. David Finkelstein had confirmed what that bastard Lister had told him last night: that the two of them had moved in together, but Dorian still couldn't quite believe that it was real. Was Chrissie really that stupid? Couldn't she see that Greene was using her, for one reason and one reason only – to destroy him? Perhaps, if he could make Chrissie see sense, she could undo some of the damage. Persuade Harry to drop this insane vendetta, or at least to allow Dorian time to buy back his movie and make a new deal.

Then again, perhaps not. If Greene didn't care about Chrissie, why would he listen to her?

Even so, it had to be worth a try. Only Dorian couldn't try it because, not content with ruining his life, Chrissie was now refusing even to take his calls.

By eight thirty, physically and emotionally exhausted, he staggered into Toscana on San Vicente Boulevard to meet David Finkelstein for dinner. His white James Perse shirt was yellow and soaked with sweat, and his hair was wild and matted from running his fingers through it so many times.

'You look like hell.' David Finkelstein passed him a glass of Sangiovese. Sitting down, Dorian took a long, thirsty sip.

'I feel like hell.'

David pushed a plate of garlic crispbread across the table. Dorian attacked it greedily, washing it down with the wine. He hadn't eaten all day and, despite his mental turmoil, he was ravenous. For a minute, neither of them spoke. Dorian broke the silence first. 'They killed my movie.'

'I know it feels that way,' said David.

'It is that way. By tomorrow morning, I'll have Sony's thirty pieces of silver. It'll never see the light of day.'

The waiter arrived and recited the specials. Sensing his client was in no mood to make decisions, David ordered for both of them: beef carpaccio followed by a poached sea bass with spinach and garlic fries. Noticing that Dorian had already finished his wine and was pouring a second glass, he ordered another bottle of Sangiovese.

'Look, the critics at all the private screenings loved it,' he said, trying to think of something encouraging to say. 'Who knows? If it goes down well at Sundance, it could be a sleeper hit on DVD. Stranger things have happened.'

Dorian laughed bitterly. 'Right. The straight-to-DVD movie that made it. C'mon.'

The events of the last twenty-four hours had myriad consequences, none of them good. David was still talking, and Dorian tried to focus on what he was saying, but the negative thoughts kept creeping back in, like seawater seeping through the cracks of a slowly sinking ship. *I'll have to give up the Schloss. There's no way I can afford it now.* He thought of his father, of how disappointed he'd be, and felt sick. *But that's not even the worst of it. I have no assets, nothing I can sell to pay off my bank loan with Coutts. Maybe I should file for bankruptcy?* he thought bleakly, although he had no idea how one went about such a thing. He felt as though he were in a mental maze. Every way he turned he faced another wall, another dead end.

'I've let everybody down,' he said aloud, although his blank stare made it plain he was talking more to himself than to his business manager. 'My parents, Chrissie and Saskia, everyone who worked so hard on *Wuthering Heights.* Viorel, Sabrina . . .'

'That's crap,' said David Finkelstein robustly. 'Your parents are dead, Chrissie left *you*, let's not forget, and your actors got paid. Right now I'd say they're the only ones who've actually done well out of this whole fiasco.'

'Sabrina didn't get paid,' said Dorian, absently. He was thinking back to last night, watching Sabrina on television proclaiming her love for Viorel to the world, and realizing with sickening clarity that he loved her. He'd been too busy today trying to salvage his precious film to give this revelation much thought. But it hit him again now, like an ice-cold glass of water in the face. Could his life possibly get any more hopeless?

'How am I gonna tell her the movie won't be released?' he said aloud to David Finkelstein. 'This was her big come-back. She worked so hard for it.'

'Jesus, man, would you stop beating up on yourself?' said David, taking a bite of the succulent, wafer-thin beef the waiter had just brought them. 'You should try this by the way, it's seriously delicious. Look, Sabrina Leon was on the scrapheap when you cast her. Now she's halfway back to being America's sweetheart. She's gonna be the toast of Sundance next week, whatever else happens to that movie. She's "in love".' He pronounced these last words as mockingly as two syllables would allow. As a Hollywood manager for over twenty years, David Finkelstein had an understandably jaded view of celebrity romance. 'Sabrina Leon's the last person you should feel sorry for.'

Dorian ate his food in stony silence. Everything David said was true. But he knew Sabrina would be crushed by today's news, as crushed as he was. They all would.

'If you want, I'd be happy to let the cast know,' said David, reading his client's gloomy thoughts. 'I'll call a meeting at Dracula in the morning. Or I can call people one by one, if you think that's more appropriate?'

Dorian shook his head vigorously. 'No. I'll do it. But it can wait till morning. There's someone else I need to talk to tonight.'

Chrissie Rasmirez put her feet up on the antique French footstool with a feeling of deep contentment.

This is right. This is where I'm supposed to be.

As Harry's interior designer, she'd already transformed

the Coldwater Canyon estate that he'd picked up for the knockdown price of sixty-five million dollars back in the autumn. But now, as his live-in girlfriend, she finally got to enjoy the fruits of her labours. It was amazing what could be achieved, and how quickly, when one had unlimited money to throw at a project. All the gold and marble had been ripped out, along with the Liberace chandeliers and the Austin Powers shag-pile carpeting. In their place, Chrissie had laid antique, reclaimed wood floors, installed exquisitely delicate hand-made English taps and porcelain bath tubs, and picked up an eclectically tasteful mix of antique and modern furniture pieces and Persian rugs to brighten up the newly Farrow & Ball-painted living areas. The house had always been spectacular. But now, Chrissie congratulated herself, it was *classy*.

Reclining in one of the overstuffed Ralph Lauren armchairs she'd bought last week, wearing a full-length, fire-truck red evening gown from Carolina Herrera, Chrissie finally felt she'd made it. Already the struggle and conflict of her life with Dorian was starting to feel like the past, like part of another life. And it was all thanks to Harry.

Chrissie's relationship with Harry Greene had taken off far more quickly than she'd ever expected or imagined. Of course, he'd been flirtatious with her for years. But once she started working for him on the house, things had moved from flirtatious to sexual to committed at an exhilarating, whirlwind pace. Even Chrissie had hesitated when Harry suggested she give up her Brentwood rental and move in with him after less than a month of dating.

'If it were just me, it'd be one thing. But I have to think about Saskia,' she told him, laying her head on his chest after another session of surprisingly erotic, athletic love-making. That was another plus about Harry. He had the sexual energy of a teenager, and was never so caught up with his work that he didn't want to fuck. Unlike Dorian.

'What about Saskia?' he asked, stroking Chrissie's hair. 'She'll love it here. What's her favourite toy? What's she into at the moment?'

'Barbie,' said Chrissie. 'But that's not the point, honey. She's been through so much change this year already. What if—'

'I'll get her a Barbie room. It'll be like FAO Schwarz in there! Her own pink, plastic palace.'

Chrissie smiled. 'That's so generous of you, sweetheart. But I mean, what if things don't work out between us? You know, in the long term.'

Harry rolled on top of her, taking her face in his hands. Gazing deep into Chrissie's eyes, he told her: 'They will work out. You worry too much.'

They made love again, and Chrissie could feel her resolve start to weaken. But it wasn't till the next day that it crumbled utterly.

'Oh my God!' she gasped, as Harry led her proudly into the His 'n' Hers dressing rooms off the master suite. 'What did you *do*?'

Along all four walls, newly built closets had been stuffed with the most beautiful preview pieces from the spring collections. Chrissie saw three Stella McCartney trouser suits, a beaded midnight-blue Bottega Veneta evening gown and a stack of exquisite taupe silk La Perla negligees before she'd so much as turned around. In the centre of the room, the *pièce de résistance* was a shoe 'island', stacked to shoulder height, and filled with every imaginable pair of shoes from all her favourite designers: Jimmy Choo, Jonathan Kelsey, Manolo, YSL, Zanotti, Louboutin, Chanel. There were pumps, boots, stilettos, wedges, in every conceivable colour and style. 'It's like Bergdorf's in here!' she exclaimed gleefully, picking up pair after pair with all the wonder of Dorothy touching her ruby slippers. 'I feel like I walked into Carrie Bradshaw's dream.'

'It's your dream now,' said Harry. He seemed genuinely delighted to have pleased her. 'Do you like it? Will you stay?'

It's time I put myself first for a change, thought Chrissie. *Just because Dorian let me down and took me for granted, it doesn't mean every man will.* In Chrissie's book, nothing said commitment quite like $50,000-worth of shoes.

'OK,' she said, wrapping her arms around his neck and kissing him. 'I'll give notice on my lease in Brentwood this afternoon.'

Tonight was the first night Harry had gone out without her since she moved in. Chrissie had pouted dutifully when he told her he had a business dinner, but secretly she was relieved. As much as she enjoyed his company and the constant spoiling it entailed, she felt as though she hadn't had a moment to herself in weeks. Once Saskia was in bed, she'd spent the early part of the evening playing dressing-up, finally trying on all of the exquisite evening wear Harry had bought her, and mixing and matching accessories with all the unrestrained delight of a little girl in her mommy's dressing room. The red Carolina Herrera was her absolute favourite, sultry and dramatic, but not an overtly young woman's dress. Jumping down from the armchair to take another look at herself in the mirror, Chrissie suddenly let out a bloodcurdling scream. A male figure was standing in the hallway behind her, half hidden in the shadows.

'Get out!' she shouted, fear and shock making her aggressive. *How the hell had an intruder got in? Every inch of the grounds was tracked by security cameras. There must be some sort of fault with the system.* 'My boyfriend will be back any second. He won't wait for the cops; he'll set the dogs on you and let them rip you to shreds.'

'Sounds painful.' Dorian stepped forward into the light. 'Your "boyfriend" doesn't sound like such a nice guy.'

'Dorian.' Chrissie exhaled, adrenaline still coursing through her veins. 'You scared the life out of me. What the hell are you doing here? If you're looking for your daughter, she went to bed hours ago. Oh, sorry, silly me,' she added spitefully, 'of course you're not looking for your daughter. Why would you be?'

Dorian walked past her into the drawing room. It was a beautiful space, grand without being cold, luxurious yet simple. He recognized Chrissie's style instantly.

'You did the room?'

She nodded. 'I did the whole house.'

'It looks great.'

'Thank you.'

Dorian turned to look at her. How weird it was to be making small talk with the mother of his child, the woman he'd loved and lived with his entire adult life. But the weirdest part of all was, Chrissie didn't feel like that woman. She felt like a total stranger. A beautiful stranger, he had to admit. In the clinging red taffeta, with her blond hair freshly coloured and cut in a gamine bob, with diamonds glinting in each newly exposed ear, she looked radiant. As happy and rested as Dorian was exhausted and defeated.

'You look good, Chrissie.'

Chrissie's eyes narrowed suspiciously. 'What do you want, Dorian? I'm serious about Harry coming back. I'm expecting him home any minute.'

'Home?' Dorian shook his head. 'You think this is home?'

'It is home,' said Chrissie defiantly. 'Saskia and I are very settled here.'

'Settled?' Dorian laughed mirthlessly. 'My God. You really think Harry Greene's gonna marry you, don't you? That the two of you will live happily ever after?'

'The *three* of us,' Chrissie corrected him. 'And, yes, I do think that. For your information, Harry happens to be crazy about me.'

'How stupid are you?' Dorian paced the walnut floorboards in frustration. 'Can't you see he's using you, to get at me?'

'Right,' sneered Chrissie, 'because everything's about you, isn't it, darling?'

Against his better judgement, Dorian walked over and grabbed her by the wrists. As if by physically restraining her, he could force her to listen to reason. 'Greene's been out to ruin me for years. He knew how much I had riding on this movie. He wanted to kill it out of spite, and you, *you*, my own wife, told him how he could do it.'

'Don't be so melodramatic,' said Chrissie. 'I did nothing of the kind.'

'You told him about my Sony deal!' Dorian exploded. 'You may as well have handed him my head on a plate!' He let go of her wrists. 'But you know what the bad news for you is?'

'Enlighten me.' Chrissie yawned.

'Harry's already got what he wanted. He doesn't need you any more.'

'Oh really?' said Chrissie. 'Then why do you suppose I'm still here?'

It was a good point. For a moment, Dorian couldn't think of a rejoinder.

'You're right,' Chrissie went on. 'Harry doesn't need me. He *wants* me. I'm having the best sex of my life, and I'm having *fun*, and so is Harry. And *you* can't stand it.'

Bitch, thought Dorian. Despite everything, the sex gibe still hurt.

'He played you, honey,' he shot back. 'He could see how needy you were and he exploited that weakness.'

This was too much for Chrissie. How dare Dorian show up here and patronize her?

'Did it ever occur to you that maybe it was *me* who wanted to bury your goddamn movie, not Harry?' she seethed. 'The movie that you chose over our marriage, our family? What if it was Harry who helped *me* to keep *Wuthering Heights* on the cutting-room floor, and not the other way around? Because he cares about me. Because he loves me. D'you ever think of that?'

Dorian paused. Something in Chrissie's face, the flash of fury in her eyes, made him think. Was she telling the truth? Was this whole thing *her* idea? Seducing Harry Greene deliberately so he could use his influence to nuke the *Wuthering Heights* distribution deal? All through today's nightmarish round of meetings, Dorian had pictured Chrissie as Harry Greene's gullible dupe: guilty, certainly, but only by association and only out of weakness. Greene had played on her insecurity. He had used her, groomed her, like a paedophile cynically befriending a wayward, needy child. *But what if it was the other way around? What if Chrissie was the mastermind, and Greene the accomplice, albeit a more than willing one? Did she really hate him that much?*

'You're very quiet all of a sudden.' Chrissie walked over to the window. 'Don't you want to tell me some more about how Harry doesn't love me?'

'Would you listen?' asked Dorian.

'Of course not, and why should I? After what you put me through, belittling my career, flirting with your actresses, leaving me alone for months on end in that dump of a country you come from. If you're here to tell me you want me back, then I'm sorry. You're too late.'

'Actually, that's not why I came,' said Dorian quietly. He'd come here to make Chrissie see the light, to try to get her to undo the damage she'd caused, if that were possible, or at least to see her new lover for the conniving snake that he was. But he realized now it was he who'd been labouring under a misconception. And not just about the collapse of his deal for *Wuthering Heights*. About his entire, twenty-year marriage.

'I don't love you, Christina. Not any more.'

'Right.' Chrissie rolled her eyes sarcastically, flopping back down into the armchair and making a big show of admiring the eight-carat diamond ring on her finger. 'Of course you love me. You're just bitter because you lost me to a better man.'

'You're wrong. I don't love you,' said Dorian. Looking her in the eye, without anger or fear, he realized fully that it was true. It was so liberating, he almost felt like laughing. 'As for Harry Greene, the man isn't capable of love. But I guess that's something you're gonna have to figure out for yourself.'

He turned and walked out of the room. Furious, and determined not to let him have the last word, Chrissie followed.

'It won't work, you know,' she screeched after him. 'You aren't going to poison things between me and Harry.'

Dorian kept walking.

'You're finished in the movie business, you do realize that?'

He was almost at the front door now. With every step he took, Chrissie became more and more enraged.

'Your precious fucking "masterpiece" will be lucky to make it to DVD. Are you listening to me? That whore Sabrina Leon can forget about her so-called "comeback". She'll be crawling back to the scrapheap where she belongs!'

Dorian was outside now, walking towards his car. At

the top of the hill, he saw the flash and sweep of Ferrari headlights. Harry Greene, no doubt, heading home.

'And you can forget about seeing Saskia,' Chrissie shouted, in a last-ditch effort to get Dorian's attention. 'Harry's already twice the father that you've ever been.'

It worked. Dorian spun around on his heel. He stepped towards her, so close that Chrissie panicked for a moment that he might be about to hit her. Instinctively, she shrank back, like a disturbed rattlesnake.

'Nobody's going to keep my daughter from me,' muttered Dorian darkly. 'Do you understand? Nobody. I'll fight you for that child with my dying breath.'

'What's going on here?' Harry Greene's whiny, nasal voice cut through the night air like razor wire. Slamming his car door, he marched up behind Dorian. 'Rasmirez. What the hell are you doing on my property?' He put an arm around Chrissie, the picture of conjugal concern. 'Are you OK, sweetie? Did he hurt you?'

'Of course I didn't *hurt* her,' said Dorian indignantly.

'Not yet,' said Chrissie, returning Harry's embrace. 'I'm so happy you're home, darling. Dorian was just leaving. Weren't you?'

'Sure,' muttered Dorian. He wanted out of there as badly as anyone. Ignoring Harry, he walked back to his car without a word and started the engine. 'I mean it about Saskia,' he shouted out of the window at Chrissie as he pulled away. 'You try anything and I will fight like you've never seen.'

'Yeah, yeah,' she called back, emboldened again now that Harry was here to protect her. 'I guess I'll see you in court then. If you can afford it.'

But her words were drowned out by the angry roar of Dorian's engine.

He was gone.

CHAPTER TWENTY-FIVE

Three weeks later

'Give me twenty more bicycle crunches. Go!'

'*Twenty?*' Sabrina rolled her eyes. Was he kidding? She'd hired Diego Vera because he was renowned as one of the toughest, most effective personal trainers in the business. And when it came to looking hot for Viorel, nothing less than perfection was gonna cut it. But after a solid hour of physical torture on the roof terrace of Vio's Venice apartment, Sabrina's stomach muscles were already spasming as if someone had injected her with arsenic. Her face was flushed an unattractive tomato red and and her sexy new Stella McCartney workout shorts and vest were as sweat drenched as an old dishrag. Diego seemed to have confused her with the Terminator, or Lara Croft, or some other superhuman, immune-to-pain cyborg.

'I can't, Diego. I'm serious.'

'So am I,' the stocky little Mexican grinned down at her, arms folded. 'No such word as "can't". Now move before I change my mind and make it fifty.'

As much as she hated exercise, Sabrina couldn't seem to shake the deep well of happiness that overflowed inside her.

The irony was, for once she had plenty to bitch about if she wanted to. Three weeks ago – two weeks after their triumphant showing at Sundance – Dorian Rasmirez had broken the news to her and the rest of the cast that *Wuthering Heights* was not going to get a general theatre release. The movie that had consumed the last year of Sabrina's life, and for which she'd been paid nothing but the promise of a career comeback, would never be seen by a moviegoing audience. Just like that, Sabrina's come*back* had turned into a come*down*, and there was nothing she could do about it. Six months ago, this was exactly the sort of disappointment that would have sent Sabrina straight off the deep end, back into drugs and partying and all the self-destructive behaviour that had fucked her up so spectacularly in the past. But now – now that she was with Viorel, now that she was in love – it was amazing how easily she found herself able to shrug it off.

Sure, it was a shame *Wuthering Heights* wouldn't make it. It was good. *She* was good. It would have been gratifying to have her performance recognized, to have an audience beyond the Sundance critics see what she was capable of as an actress. But there would be other opportunites. And even if there weren't, she had more important things to think about now. Namely, herself in the leading role of her life, as Mrs Viorel Hudson.

I'm going to be a wife, she told herself joyfully. *We're going to be together forever, the most happily married couple in Hollywood.*

She'd even begun to think about the possibility of children – not now perhaps, but a few years down the line: a troupe of perfect little Vios. As a teenager, Sabrina had made a private vow to herself that she would never become a mother. The thought of repeating her own mother's mistakes was too terrifying, and the practical demands of a baby far too distracting from her all-important career, her relentless pursuit of fame. But now she felt differently. With Viorel's love at home, she no longer needed the love of an adoring, faceless public with the same desperate violence that she had before. *Wuthering Heights* would be a commercial failure, but it remained the movie that had completely changed Sabrina's life. For that she would be forever grateful.

'Are we done?' Hauling herself up to a sitting position after the final crunch, she looked at her trainer pleadingly.

He glanced at the clock on the wall. 'Done,' he said. 'Except for stretches.'

On a sun-lounger at the far end of the roof terrace, Sabrina's cellphone buzzed loudly. 'Saved by the bell,' she grinned. Ignoring Diego's look of disapproval, she ran over to answer it. It was Ed Steiner, but he was talking so fast and so breathlessly that at first Sabrina couldn't make out a word of what he was saying.

'Slow down,' she said, holding the phone a few inches from her ear, 'and stop yelling. I can't understand you.'

After a couple of attempts, Ed finally calmed himself enough to string a coherent sentence together. 'The Academy released their nominations this morning,' he panted.

'That's it?' laughed Sabrina. 'That's what you called to tell me? Jesus, Ed, I know it's nomination day. I live in LA and I have a TV. Who cares?'

'You do, sweetheart,' said Ed. '*Wuthering Heights* got four nods. *Four!*'

Sabrina hesitated. This had to be a leg-pull. But Ed wasn't the practical joking type. 'It can't have,' she said sensibly. 'You must have made a mistake.'

'No mistake. Four nominations, including Best Picture and *you* for Best Actress.'

Sabrina's heart started to race. 'But . . . but . . . Harry Greene held our distributor to ransom.'

'I know.'

'But Ed, we're going straight to DVD. Nobody's even seen the movie.'

'The Academy saw it. And it *did* get a theatre release, so technically it qualifies.'

'You mean Sundance? That was nothing!'

Ed Steiner laughed. 'Well, I guess it was enough for the critics. Look, trust me, I was as bowled over as you are. Who knows how it happened? We all thought the movie was as dead as a dodo's dick. Maybe someone close to Oscar got pissed at being dictated to by Harry Greene? Or maybe it's the Chinese Year of the Period Drama. *Celeste*'s also up for Best Picture.'

'Who am I up against?' said Sabrina on autopilot, her ambition kicking in as she began to realize this was actually happening.

'Annie Hathaway, Emily Blunt for *Mad Dogs,* Laura Linney for that spy movie, and some Belgian chick I never heard of. The picture's up against the Pixar Frog movie, Eastwood's war film, *Celeste* and some obscure French shit that Woody Allen co-produced.'

'*Embouteillage,*' said Sabrina absently.

'Yeah, whatever. But can you believe it?' Sabrina had never heard Ed this excited. 'We are back from the dead, sweetheart! We are fucking Lazarus!'

Sabrina looked up and saw that her trainer had packed up and left, leaving her alone on the rooftop of Vio's apartment in blissful shock. She couldn't wait to tell Viorel. He'd had a casting this morning but should be on his way back by now. For a split second it crossed her mind that he might be jealous, upset that she had been nominated rather than him. But she quickly dismissed the idea. Vio wasn't like that.

'What did Dorian say?' she asked Ed. 'He must be over the moon. Has he made a statement?'

'Ah,' said Ed. 'I was hoping you might be able to tell me. Dorian's been AWOL for the last two weeks apparently.'

'What do you mean "AWOL"?'

'He packed up his LA apartment and took off. No one knows where the hell he is. His agent called me twenty minutes ago. Asked me to ask you and Hudson if either of you'd heard from him.'

'Sorry,' said Sabrina. 'I'm sure he'll call soon though. If his agent can't reach him, he'll see it on the news.'

She imagined Dorian's shock and delight and felt a rush of affection and happiness for her director. *He's such a good man. He deserves this more than any of us.*

It seemed as if the curse of *Wuthering Heights* was well and truly broken. Everybody's luck was finally changing.

'How is this possible? HOW the FUCK is this happening?'

Harry Greene paced around Mike Hartz's office like a caged tiger, banging his fist on the walls so that his rage could be heard reverberating down Sony Pictures' corridors.

'You told me you would kill that movie. And now it's up for a fucking Oscar? Oh, excuse me, my mistake, *four* fucking Oscars? Including Best fucking PICTURE? For that schmaltzy pile of crap?'

'With respect, Harry,' Mike Hartz swallowed hard, 'we don't have any influence over the Academy. It's extremely rare for something like this to happen, especially at such a late stage. A fluke, if you will.'

'If I *will*?' Harry Greene erupted, his face reddening like an engorged baboon's backside. 'I FUCKING *WON'T*, Mike, you supercilious son of a bitch. You told me you would bury

Rasmirez. With what? A giant pile of Academy fucking Awards?'

'Harry, be reasonable. The fact that *Wuthering Heights* has been nominated doesn't mean it stands a hope in hell of actually winning. Rasmirez doesn't have a buck for a coffee, never mind funding for a serious Oscar campaign. *Celeste* will take Best Picture.'

'It had better,' Harry muttered murderously. 'Because if it doesn't, I swear to God I will take *Fraternity IV* back and burn it before I'd let you assholes release it.'

Mike cleared his throat nervously. 'I must remind you that you are under contract. If you—'

He didn't get any further. Lunging across the desk, Harry grabbed the terrified producer by the lapels. 'If you ever, *ever*, say the word "contract" to me again, I will shred the fucking contract and ram the pieces down your throat until you choke to death, you useless, corporate fuck. Do you understand? I will slice off your balls and use them for earrings.'

Outside in the lobby, Mike Hartz's secretary Linda listened to her boss being eviscerated by Harry Greene and felt a small, illicit rush of pleasure. Mike was a bully, greedy, sexist and vile. All his staff loathed him.

Linda Googled the odds on Dorian Rasmirez beating Harry Greene to take home Best Picture.

A hundred to one.

Not encouraging. But then this was Hollywood.

Anything could happen.

Viorel waited at the traffic lights at Doheny and Sunset, oblivious to the stares of the tourists on the pavement. Normally, he enjoyed the attention, although he was never totally sure whether people were ogling him or his Bugatti, the slick, matt-black Batmobile of every small boy's dreams.

But today, he didn't care. Nothing could lift his spirits, not the street audience, not the blazing LA sunshine overhead, not the knowledge that this morning's audition had gone as close to perfectly as he could have wished. All he could think about was the tape playing over and over in his head:

I have to tell her.

I have to break things off with Sabrina.

He'd been meaning to do it for weeks now, but every time she looked up at him with that adoring, trusting, beautiful face of hers, his nerve failed him. He despised himself for his own weakness, for allowing things to go as far between them as they had. But it was so hard, what with the press making such a huge deal about their relationship, and how his love had 'saved' Sabrina. Viorel enjoyed being a saviour. It had a better ring to it than 'heartbreaking asshole'. The pressure of knowing that the whole of America was debating the details of a wedding you knew in your heart you would never have – would the service be outdoors, would they do a magazine deal, would Sabrina go traditional with the dress or opt for something edgier? – crushed him like a dead weight, and sapped all of the courage out of him like a giant mosquito gorging on his blood. But nothing compared to the pain he was about to cause Sabrina.

Poor kid. The irony was that he cared about her far more deeply now than he had when they'd first got together. Back then it had been purely sexual, a pride thing as much as anything else. He had to have her, to conquer her, to make her his own. But now that he knew her, now that he had seen her vulnerability and sweetness, all the sexual impetus was gone. She was as beautiful and desirable as she had ever been, but it was no good. Viorel wasn't in love with her. He could never be the husband that she needed him to be, and he was terrified of what she would do when he told her.

The lights finally changed and he sped west on Sunset, past the grand mansions of Beverly Hills and the kitsch pink magnificence of the famous Beverly Hills Hotel. For once the traffic was actually moving. Lost in his own thoughts, Viorel drove on through Holmby Hills, past the Playboy Mansion and the East and West gates of Bel Air and on into the suburban tranquillity of Brentwood, unaware of anything except the heaviness in his heart. He *had* to do it today. If he didn't he'd be well on his way to a nervous breakdown.

Turning left onto Ocean, as the condos of Santa Monica gave way to the ramshackle Twenties cottages of Venice, he tried out opening phrases.

'We need to talk.'

'I don't think things are working out.'

'I don't think I'm right for you.'

Jesus. It was all so clichéd, so trite, like a bad episode of *In Treatment*. But could there ever be a right set of words to tell someone who expected to marry you that you weren't in love with them after all?

As so often recently, Viorel found his thoughts turning to Tish Crewe. Tish would know what to say, how to let Sabrina down gently. She was so wise about stuff like that. He wished their relationship was at a point where he could call and ask her for advice, but after their last disastrous phone conversation, he was by no means sure that he and Tish would ever speak again. The thought depressed him still further.

Turning into the back alley behind Navy, Viorel saw that the entrance to his parking garage was blocked with a throng of paparazzi. Ever since Sabrina moved in, a small group of die-hard paps had taken to hanging around the apartment daily, an intrusion into his privacy that Vio violently resented. It was tough for them to get any kind of a decent shot, though, thanks to the apartment's fortress-like walls and high metal gates, and most had given up the stakeout. A group this large – fourteen or fifteen photographers all jostling for position around the garage – was distinctly unusual. As the Bugatti pulled closer and the garage door opened, they descended on Viorel like locusts, shouting his name as their flashbulbs popped.

'Congratulations!'

'Have you talked to Sabrina yet? Is she home?'

'Were you surprised by the news?'

Vio said nothing, driving inside with his Ray-Bans still on and his Lakers cap pulled low over his face. He could still hear the cameras and the muffled shouts as the electric doors wheeshed shut behind him. *What the fuck was going on?*

He took the lift up to the apartment. The second the doors opened, a naked Sabrina, still wet from the shower, leaped into his arms and started showering him with kisses.

'Ohmygodohmygodohmygod!' she squealed, grinning from ear to ear like a kid on Christmas morning. 'Did you hear?'

'No. Hear what?' Vio laughed awkwardly. Her slippery, naked skin was sending unwanted, automated messages to his dick, which was the last thing he needed right now. Setting her down on the floor, he opened the hall closet and pulled out a towel. 'Here.' He wrapped her in it. 'Don't die of cold.'

'I won't die of cold,' she beamed. 'I might die of excitement though. And *you* might die of shock. *Wuthering Heights* got four nominations today.'

'Nominations for what? Shortest cinema release in history?'

'I'm serious!' said Sabrina. 'We're up for four Oscars, including Best Picture.'

Vio frowned. 'That's impossible.'

'I know, that's what I said,' laughed Sabrina. 'But you

should call Ed Steiner if you don't believe me. It's all over the news too – just turn on the TV. Four nominations, that's the second most after *Celeste*. And . . .' she took a deep, dramatic breath, 'I'm up for Best Actress.'

Viorel read the joy in Sabrina's face. Turned up hopefully towards him, her wet hair still dripping, she was awaiting his approval, his praise, his love. With no make-up on, smelling of toothpaste and soap, she looked younger and more innocent than he had ever seen her. So trusting, wanting only to share her triumph with the man she loved. He felt his resolve crumbling to nothing, like a sandcastle in the rain.

'That's wonderful, baby.' He hugged her tightly. *Coward, coward, coward.*

Sabrina breathed into his chest. 'I love you so much. Let's go to bed.'

Dorian was dreaming the first time the phone rang.

He was standing on the bridge over the river at Loxley. It was pouring with rain. On one side of the bridge, Chrissie was playing hide and seek with Saskia, who was slipping down the bank towards the water. Dorian ran to try to save her, but found himself being pulled back to the other side of the bridge. Turning around to see who was pulling him, he saw it was Sabrina Leon. 'What are you waiting for?' she asked him.

She was wearing a white dress and smiling a strange, angelic smile. 'Come back inside the house. It's raining.' Dorian looked up at Loxley Hall, and suddenly it began to crumble to the ground, bricks and masonry crashing down all around him like giant hailstones. Then he heard sirens wailing. The emergency services must be coming. The sirens grew louder and louder, shriller and shriller, dragging him groggily back to consciousness . . . *my phone.*

Fumbling on the bedside table for his cellphone, by the time he picked it up it had stopped ringing. Heart racing, he slumped back against the pillow of his grimy motel room bed. *Stupid. I must have left it on last night by mistake.* He'd been drunkenly scrolling through his photos before bed, staring at pictures of his daughter. Since he'd fled LA two weeks ago, he'd made a point of keeping his phone switched off. Last night was the first time he'd looked at it in over a week, ignoring the hundred-plus missed calls and groaning mailbox and going straight to his media file.

Saskia, holding up her grey cat and yawning.

Saskia, laughing on a swing in a Santa Monica playground.

Saskia sleeping in the car, her chubby, baby's head lolling to one side of her car seat, a picture of innocence and peace.

I've been a shitty father. I was never there for her. Harry Greene can't do a worse job than I did. The dark, depressing thoughts kept coming back, one after the other, like waves in a sea of pain.

After he'd broken the news to the cast and crew that a year's hard work and commitment had been for nothing, Dorian had kept driving on up the coast, stopping only for gas and some basic supplies before he reached the skuzzy motel on the outskirts of Big Sur. A stunning stretch of the California coastline, just south of the quaint tourist town of Carmel, Big Sur was a popular romantic vacation spot for couples, or for artists or nature lovers seeking inspiration from the dramatic seascapes and majestic ancient redwood forests. The Sea View Motel was one of the rare ugly buildings to be found there, a low 1960s breezeblock box with dirty windows, set back from the road amongst some scrubby pines. But for Dorian it was perfect. Remote. Anonymous. Cheap. He had no idea how long he intended to stay, or what his future plans were. All he knew was he couldn't be around people. Not yet. His family life was in tatters. His career was over. He was financially ruined. And yet none of these things haunted him as much as one bleak, unalterable fact.

Sabrina Leon was going to marry Viorel Hudson.

They'd shown up at the meeting at Dracula together, hand in hand, two poster children for youth and hope and romance. Sabrina was obviously disappointed, though she tried not to show it. Dorian saw the way she leaned into Viorel's chest for support, how he had wrapped a comforting, possessive arm around her shoulders. Like a passer-by staring at a car crash, he couldn't seem to tear his eyes away. But the pain was exquisite.

God only knew he didn't *want* to be in love with Sabrina. It was ridiculous, a man of his age and a young girl like that. Of course she was in love with Hudson. Why on earth wouldn't she be? If Dorian were half a man, he'd be happy for them.

The phone rang again, an irritating, insistent buzz like a trapped bumblebee demanding release. Dorian picked up.

'Go away.'

'So you're alive, then.' David Finkelstein sounded more annoyed than relieved. 'Where the *hell* have you *been*, D? I've been trying to reach you for more than a week.'

'I'm sorry David. I don't want to talk to anyone,' said Dorian, and hung up.

Before he could switch the phone off, it rang again.

'I mean it,' said Dorian, getting angrier now. His hangover was starting to kick in after last night's solitary downing of a bottle and a half of Cabernet. It was still early – at least, he thought it was early – and he wanted to go back to sleep. 'Leave me alone.'

'*Wuthering Heights* got a Best Picture nomination from the

Academy,' Dorian's manager blurted out, before he got hung up on again. The line went deathly quiet.

'Dorian? Are you still there?'

'I'm here,' said Dorian.

'Well, aren't you gonna say something? This is the Oscars, man. This is the big one. You got four nominations. Sabrina's up for Best Actress.'

The mention of Sabrina's name seemed to rouse Dorian from his stupor.

'Have you spoken to her?'

'Jesus, D, no, I haven't spoken to her. She's not my client. You are. I've been *trying* to speak to you. Surprise, surprise, Sony suddenly want to talk to you.'

'I have nothing to say to those bastards,' said Dorian with feeling.

'Be that as it may, you need to get your ass back to town. Every media outlet this side of the fucking moon wants an interview.'

'OK,' said Dorian. 'I'll call you back.'

'No, D, wait! Don't hang up!' begged David. But it was too late. The line was already dead.

Throwing back the bedclothes, Dorian dropped his phone back on the bedside table and staggered unsteadily across the room to open the blinds. Glaring sunshine poured in through the window. He winced. *Shit.* It must be noon at least. How long had he been asleep? He turned on the coffee machine next to the unused television set, and opened a packet of Oreo cookies, mindlessly chomping through them as his mind slowly lurched back to life.

The Oscars. Four nominations. Best Picture.

It was a fantasy. The kind of stuff that Hollywood dreams were made of, but that never actually *happened* in Hollywood. At least not to him. He'd been saved by some mysterious guardian angel, right at the very moment when he'd stopped believing. He ought to be ecstatic. Giddy with happiness. Instead he felt . . . what? He felt nothing. Blank.

Maybe I'm losing it. Maybe I need some psychological help.

The coffee was brewed. Dorian poured a cup and drank it, black and strong, the bitter liquid reviving him even as it burned his tongue and throat.

He had to go back. To make a statement. A Best Picture nomination meant he would have to talk to the press, to travel, to promote the film until the soles of his feet ached and his voice was hoarse. Although quite how he was going to pay for a PR tour he had no idea. Sony almost certainly wouldn't fund it, Harry Greene would see to that. Not that Dorian would have taken a cent of Mike Hartz's money, even if it were offered.

More importantly, an Oscar nomination meant he could no longer hibernate and lick his wounds. He would have to see Sabrina again. With Viorel. To stand next to the pair of them and smile while they proclaimed their love to the world, hand in hand on Oscar night, looking on like an avuncular cupid, the man who'd brought Hollywood's new golden couple together. Suddenly, embarrassingly, Dorian's eyes welled with tears.

Get a grip, he told himself angrily. *You're Sabrina's director and her friend. Nothing more.*

He would go back to LA, congratulate Sabrina, master his emotions and pretend to be happy. But inside, Dorian wondered whether he would ever be truly happy again.

CHAPTER TWENTY-SIX

Sabrina sat down at the corner table at Mastro's, aware that every eye in the upstairs restaurant had followed her as she walked across the room. Perhaps she shouldn't feel so gratified by the adulation. But then again, it wasn't every day one got nominated for an Oscar. Why shouldn't she enjoy it?

After a blissful afternoon spent making love to Viorel – as always, sex had been a virtuoso performance, with Vio as lost and intoxicated in the moment as she was – she'd driven over to Ed Steiner's office on the Wilshire and Beverly Glen and given a press conference. The last time Sabrina had faced the press in her agent's office, she'd been grudgingly delivering a pre-scripted mea culpa to a sea of hostile, bloodthirsty faces. This time, the love in the room was so thick she could have eaten it with a spoon.

How did it feel to be back on top in her career? Was she surprised by the nomination, given the movie's very limited release? Had she spoken to Dorian Rasmirez, or the rest of her co-stars?

Dressed simply in a white Michael Stars T-shirt and Ksubi skinny jeans, with her long hair tied back in a ponytail and no accessories other than a smile that could have powered the whole of Los Angeles, Sabrina answered every question with patience and humility. 'I know how lucky I am,' she told the reporters. And she meant it. If happiness was wanting what you have, this evening Sabrina Leon was as truly happy as any human being on earth had ever been.

After her meet-the-press, she'd called Vio and arranged to meet for dinner at Mastro's steakhouse, a popular celebrity haunt in downtown Beverly Hills and one of their favourite restaurants for its old-school atmosphere, Sinatra-themed piano bar and privacy-ensuring low lighting. He was already there when she arrived, sitting in a black blazer and blue Ralph Lauren shirt and fiddling absently with his napkin.

How exquisitely, ridiculously handsome he is, thought Sabrina for the millionth time.

'Hi,' she beamed, leaning over to kiss him as she sat down. 'Sorry I'm late. Things ran over a little at Ed's.'

She started to tell him about the press conference, chattering away excitedly about who'd asked her what and what her responses had been. It was five full minutes before she realized he was no longer listening, but staring past her to the piano bar in the back.

'Hey,' she said, frowning. 'Am I boring you?'

'Hmm? Oh, no. Sorry. I was just—'

'I know what you were just doing,' said Sabrina reproachfully. Looking back over her shoulder she saw a pretty, elfin-faced blonde alone at the bar, directly in Viorel's line of vision. 'Do you know her? Is she an ex?' She winced at the insecurity in her own voice. But really, it was a bit much for him to sit there ogling other women, tonight of all nights.

'No,' said Vio guiltily. 'She reminded me of someone, that's all.'

Given his past reputation, both their past reputations,

ghosts of their former relationships inevitably popped up from time to time, especially in a town as small and gossip-ridden as Hollywood. Sabrina tried not to be jealous, but it was hard. She loved him so much.

'Who?' she asked, wishing she didn't care so much. 'Who does she remind you of that's so distracting?'

God, I sound like a nag. Let it go. You don't want a row tonight.

'If you must know, she reminds me of Tish,' said Vio.

'Tish Crewe?' Sabrina laughed, instantly relieved. So it wasn't an old lover he was thinking about. Turning around, she studied the girl again. 'You know, you're right. She does have a look of her. God, Tish Crewe.' She shook her head, turning back to Vio and sipping her sour apple martini thoughtfully. 'She was a funny one. I wonder what she's up to these days. Saving the world somewhere, no doubt, off adopting more kids, trying to outdo Angelina.'

'I doubt it,' said Vio curtly. But Sabrina didn't notice his frosty tone.

'Do you think she's heard the Oscar news? I guess they're not that interested in Merry Old England. Or Romania or wherever she is. Hey, I wonder if she'll come to the Academy Awards?'

'Why would she?' said Vio crossly.

'I don't know,' said Sabrina, looking slightly hurt. 'Maybe Dorian'll ask her. He's single now, and he always did think the sun shone out of her ass. I bet she'd fall over herself to date him now his career's on a roll again.'

'Rubbish,' said Vio. 'Tish was never remotely interested in Rasmirez romantically. Besides, not everybody's as obsessed with fame as you are.'

Sabrina's eyes welled up with tears. 'That's not fair.'

Viorel looked away. He knew he was being an asshole, not to mention a hypocrite. He wasn't exactly immune to a bit of camera-chasing himself. And Sabrina was only trying to make conversation. It wasn't her fault he'd been too much of a coward to say no to sex this afternoon; or that he was furious at himself for enjoying it as much as he had.

'Sorry,' he muttered guiltily. 'Can we talk about something else?'

'Sure,' said Sabrina, instantly forgiving now that the unexpected storm had passed. She hated it when they fought. It made her feel out of control in a way that terrified her. Pushing the fear aside, she munched away happily on rare fillet steak and shoestring fries, and did her best to steer the conversation away from *Wuthering Heights* and Oscar talk and onto the safer subject of Hollywood gossip, and who was reputedly fucking whom behind who's back. But like a moth drawn back to the light, she soon found it impossible to avoid the subject of her nomination completely. By the time their key lime pie arrived for dessert, she'd moved on to the all-important matter of her dress.

'It's not just the Academy Awards themselves,' she gushed excitedly. 'There'll be the nominees' dinner, the Independent Spirits a few weeks before, plus we're pretty certain to have a premiere now for the US release at least, and I guess something in London too. Don't you think?'

'Sure.' Vio feigned enthusiasm. 'We're all gonna be busy promoting now, but you especially.'

'*Us* especially,' Sabrina corrected him. 'No one wants to see me on my own, babe. The world wants the love story.'

Oh Christ, thought Vio helplessly. *She's right. I'll be sucked in deeper than ever now.*

'I thought I'd go short for the Independent Spirits and the US premiere. Probably Marchesa, although Jason Wu's doing some awesome stuff for spring . . .'

'Uh-huh.' Vio nodded vaguely.

'You pretty much have to go long for the Oscars. But I don't want anything too frilly or romantic.' She reached across the table and took his hand. 'I'm saving the big princess dress for our wedding.'

Viorel took back his hand and ran it through his hair.

'Oh God, Sabrina,' he said desperately. 'There isn't going to be a wedding.'

Sabrina hesitated for a moment. Then she laughed and said, 'Well, no, not this year obviously. With all this Best Actress circus going on, we won't have time to plan for—'

'Not any year. Not ever,' said Viorel. He didn't want to look at Sabrina, but he had to. He knew each word hit her like a hammer blow, but he had to keep going. 'I'm not in love with you. I'm sorry. I wish I were but I . . .'

'Is there someone else?' Sabrina's voice was quiet, thin and reedy like a young child's. It didn't sound as if it had come from her, and indeed she wasn't aware of having thought of the question before her subconscious had blurted it out.

'No,' said Viorel truthfully.

'Then maybe . . . maybe there's a chance?' Sabrina quavered. Viorel winced. The heartbreak in her face, the desperation in her words . . . it was unbearable.

'There isn't,' he said. He felt like a murderer.

'But, how can you know that?' she pleaded. Tears were streaming freely down her face in the darkness. Quiet tears, not the hysterical, angry tears that would have been so much easier. She wasn't making a scene. All the pain on her face was raw and genuine. Viorel felt sick. 'You loved me before.'

'I didn't,' murmured Vio, soundly barely less anguished than she did. 'I mean, I do love you, Sab. But not in the way you mean. More like a . . . a sister.'

For the first time, Sabrina sounded angry, although the

anger was all but lost beneath the pain. 'A sister? Jesus, Vio, you didn't seem too *brotherly* this afternoon. When you were in my bed, begging me to come for you. Remember that?'

'I know.' He looked down at his lap, more ashamed than he could ever remember feeling in his life. 'I know. Sexually things have always been so good between us. That's part of the problem.'

Sabrina laughed, but it was a laugh without a shred of joy.

'It's not that I don't want you,' said Viorel.

'Just that you don't want to marry me.'

He nodded miserably. 'I'm so sorry, angel. But I wouldn't be able to make you happy.'

'You would!' she insisted, the tears flowing faster than ever.

'No. I wouldn't. And I can't stand up in front of millions of people and keep living this lie. I'm sorry.'

'So you keep saying,' said Sabrina. Burying her head in her napkin, she sat still for a few moments, breathing deeply, trying to compose her emotions. Finally, she looked up, her tears dry, her voice even. 'I appreciate you telling me the truth,' she said calmly. 'It can't have been easy for you.'

'Oh God, please don't be kind to me,' said Viorel. 'I'm a total arsehole. You deserve so much better.'

Sabrina stood up. Gently, she reached over and stroked his cheek. 'You're lovely,' she said softly. 'But I think I need to be on my own right now. I'll stay at a hotel tonight.'

'No,' Vio insisted. 'Please. *I'll* stay at a hotel. For a few weeks, or as long as you need. The apartment's yours, forever if you want it.'

Sabrina hesitated for a moment. 'OK,' she said eventually. 'Thanks.' And without another word, she turned and walked away.

Viorel didn't know how long he sat at the table alone, staring at her empty chair. He'd expected to feel relief, now that the deed was done. Instead he felt horribly depressed, as if all the hope had been sucked out of him. By the time he was aware that a waiter was talking to him, the bar was all but empty.

'Is there anything else I can get for you, Mr Hudson?'

Vio shook his head. 'Just the check.'

There was something missing in his life, he decided. Or perhaps it was missing in *him*. Some crucial piece of the puzzle that had been misplaced, and without which he could not be truly happy. *Poor Sabrina*, he thought, rubbing his eyes tiredly. *I hope she's OK.*

Dorian hesitated at the stop light on Wilshire and Ocean.

Should I turn back? Do it tomorrow? Is ten thirty too late to drop by unannounced?

He was on his way to Viorel's apartment – Viorel and Sabrina's apartment – to congratulate Sabrina in person. It was the right thing to do. The *normal* thing to do. Somehow he had to try to get his life back to some form of normality, to accept things as they were. Sabrina and Vio were together. He was their director. They were all of them standing on the cusp of a career-defining moment. This was a time for graciousness, for professionalism, for maturity. Both Sabrina and Hudson were little more than kids. Dorian was the old Hollywood hand. They would look to him for guidance and leadership in the media frenzy that an Oscar nod always generated.

The light turned green. Above Dorian's head, the moonless California sky was lit not by stars but by the light pouring up from Santa Monica's commercial district, Third Street Promenade, and the gaudy, flashing neon glow of the pier. He thought about Transylvania, with its nights so clear and stars so diamond bright you almost felt you could reach up and touch them with your fingertips. How wildly, preposterously different it was to Los Angeles. And yet how he loved both places with such passion. Both were part of his life, his blood, his history. He hadn't yet gotten around to the paperwork, officially transferring the Schloss back to the Romanian government. Maybe now, with this Oscar news, he wouldn't have to? Maybe he could afford the place after all.

Pulling over on the Venice end of Main Street, he switched off the engine of his rented Prius and sat alone in the driver's seat, debating with himself.

Do I not want to go in because it's so late? Or because I can't face seeing them together, all loved-up and excited?

Once he'd got back to LA and taken a room at the Beverly Wilshire, he'd shaved, showered and eaten in an attempt to make himself look less like a hollow-eyed madman. It had worked, on the outside. But inside he still felt a despair that threatened to transmute itself into embarrassing tears at any moment. He'd put off the inevitable for as long as he could, taking business calls in his room, walking out into Beverly Hills to pick up a newspaper and a new packet of razors and a bottle of very essential acai berry vitamin water – *when in LA, right?* But at last he'd realized that if he didn't face Sabrina today, he would have to do it tomorrow, or the next day. And that one more night with that axe hanging over his head was more than even he could bear.

Just do it, you big pussy. Ring the buzzer, go on up, have a glass of champagne with them and leave.

Somehow the 200-yard walk from Main to Navy managed to take him fifteen minutes. But eventually, Dorian was standing at the apartment gate. *It's now or never.* He was about to ring the buzzer when he noticed that the gate was actually ajar. Stepping inside, he locked it behind him and took the stairs up to Viorel's apartment. That, too, had its front door open, although inside it was ominously silent and dark. Dorian felt his pulse quicken.

Jesus. There's been a break-in.

Straightforward burglaries were not uncommon in this part of the West Side. But with a celebrity home, you always had to wonder whether some unscrupulous tabloid journalist wasn't involved, or a would-be blackmailer, hoping to find some compromising material, drugs or a sex tape or . . . *please, not a sex tape*, thought Dorian in agony.

'Hello?' he called nervously into the blackness. 'Is anybody in there?'

Silence.

He fumbled for his cellphone, hoping to use its screen as a makeshift flashlight. *Perhaps I should call the cops?* he thought, *just to be on the safe side.* But he was already stepping into the apartment, shining the Nokia's dim light on the walls, hunting for a switch. Eventually, he found it and turned the lights on. The entire open-plan living room lit up like a movie set, so brightly that for a minute Dorian half closed his eyes against the glare. Nothing appeared to have been touched. The place looked immaculate, like a feature for *Dream Homes* magazine. Hudson always had fancied himself as design guru *manqué*.

'Viorel?' Dorian called again, growing less jumpy now that he could see. 'Are you in here? It's me, Dorian.' He walked down the hall towards the bedroom. 'The gate was wide open. I almost . . .'

He stopped mid-sentence. Sprawled naked in the bedroom doorway lay Sabrina. Looking past her into the bedroom, Dorian saw a slew of empty pill bottles littering the bed and floor and nightstand.

No.

'Sabrina!' He turned her over and slapped her face, shaking her limp body like a rag doll. No response. Desperate, he pressed his face to her mouth, trying to feel if she was breathing. She wasn't. Panicked, he froze for a few seconds, trying to remember anything about CPR and failing utterly. Finally, he remembered the cellphone in his hand and dialled 911.

'Emergency. Yeah, I'm with a friend, she's overdosed. 11991 Navy Boulevard Venice. She . . . she's not breathing.' He could hear his own voice breaking. 'I think she might be dead.'

CHAPTER TWENTY-SEVEN

St John's Hospital on Santa Monica and Twentieth was comprised of two gleaming-white towers connected by a lower glass building, and everything about it spoke of modernity, efficiency and wealth. Everything except the Emergency Room, a stinking, windowless basement filled with homeless drunks, incontinent junkies, screaming, bleeding children and their distraught parents and three of the most obese, joyless and unhelpful registrars it had ever been Dorian's misfortune to encounter.

'Overdose?' asked the charge nurse, in the same bored monotone with which a McDonald's waitress might have asked him if he wanted fries.

'Yes,' he panted frantically. 'Her notes are right here. She's stopped breathing again. The paramedics have been trying to revive her in the—'

'Uh-huh. Wait here please.'

'"Wait here"? I don't think you're hearing me. She is *not breathing!*'

'I hear you, sir,' the nurse sighed heavily. 'Your friend is

417

the third overdose we've had in here in the last two hours. We'll get her intubated just as soon as we can.'

'It's Sabrina Leon,' one of the paramedics blurted breathlessly.

The nurse looked more closely at the wan, masked face on the gurney. 'It is?'

'Uh-huh. The one and only.'

'Well why didn't you say so?' Instantly, the fat woman's face changed from hostile to pleasant. 'Follow me, please. Room six, triage. Doctor Emanuelle'll be right with you.'

And from the moment Sabrina's name was mentioned, Dr Emanuelle *was* right with them, as were a veritable legion of white-coated voyeurs, all of them swooping down on the triage suite like a flock of fame-hungry doves. *Only in LA*, thought Dorian bitterly, although for once he was grateful for the special celebrity treatment, stepping back to let them do their work, his own identity apparently unnoticed as they descended on Sabrina's lifeless form with tubes and needles and an astonishing array of monitors, paddles and wires.

'What's happening?' He tapped one of the nurses on the shoulder, no longer able to see Sabrina at all through the throng. 'What are they doing to her? Is she breathing again?'

'Are you family?' asked the nurse.

'No. I'm a friend. I'm the one who found her.'

'Then I'm sorry, sir, but I'm gonna have to ask you to wait outside. We can only share information with immediate family or partners, and even they aren't really supposed to be in here.'

Unlike the harridan on reception, this nurse was kind and polite in her tone. But she was also firm. Dorian pushed through the double exit doors and stood in the corridor stunned, like a man who'd just been bombed and dug his way out of the rubble into the sunlight. The hallway had been full twenty minutes ago, but now it was empty, save for one blue-scrubbed orderly folding gowns on a trolley. The quiet added to the eerie sense of unreality, but it was soon broken by a familiar voice.

'Dorian?'

At first glance, Viorel looked his usual suave, immaculate self, the black wool of his jacket and lapis blue of his shirt reflecting perfectly his oil-black hair and azure eyes. But as he came closer, Dorian made out the circles of stress under his eyes, and the haunted sunkenness of his cheeks. *He looks almost as miserable as I do.*

'Where is she?' Vio ran his hand through his hair frantically. 'I drove here like a fucking maniac. Someone called me twenty minutes ago. I guess I'm listed as her next of kin or something. Is she OK?'

'She's alive,' said Dorian bleakly. 'But she isn't breathing. At least she wasn't a few minutes ago. They've got a hundred doctors in with her now.'

'Oh God.' It came out as more groan than words. Leaning back against the wall, Vio literally slumped to the floor, like a paraplegic whose wheelchair had suddenly been whipped out from under him. 'It's all my fault.'

'Nonsense,' said Dorian. There could be no doubting that Viorel's anguish was genuine. His weakness triggered a return of Dorian's own strength. He mustn't be allowed to blame himself. 'Sabrina took those pills, She made that decision.'

'Yes, but only because I drove her to it.' Viorel let out a shout that was half grief, half rage. 'I swear to God,' he sobbed, 'I thought she was OK. When she left the restaurant she seemed fine. Oh Jesus, what have I done?'

Dorian sat down on the floor and wrapped a paternal arm around Viorel's shoulders. Slowly, piecemeal, the story unfolded: how Viorel had felt trapped by the relationship, by Sabrina's terrifying need and the growing media fantasy; how he'd been too scared, too weak to break things off sooner; but how tonight, finally, he'd snapped and ended their relationship at a corner table in Mastro's.

'I knew she was upset, obviously. She cried, you know, when I told her. But by the time she left she seemed really calm and,' he searched for the right word, 'I don't know. Accepting, I guess.'

'What time did she leave?' asked Dorian.

'Around nine,' said Vio. 'Why?'

Dorian did a quick calculation. It must have taken her thirty minutes at least to drive home, and maybe another ten to undress, find all those pills and swallow them. Say nine forty-five at the earliest, probably more like ten. What time had he found her? Eleven? And she threw up in the ambulance twenty minutes later. Which meant the drugs couldn't have been in her system for *that* long.

'No reason.'

The orderly squeezed past them, his trolley piled high with neatly folded gowns.

'If she dies, it'll be on my hands,' muttered Viorel despairingly.

Dorian looked Vio in the eye. 'No it won't,' he said, firmly. 'You did the right thing. You had to tell her. You couldn't have known she was gonna do something as crazy as this.'

He meant it too. If anyone ought to feel guilty, it was him. When Viorel told him that he and Sabrina had broken up tonight, Dorian's first feeling had been one of elation, of hope. *With Sabrina fighting for her life behind those doors? What kind of a narcissistic, self-centred excuse for a man am I?*

'She will be OK, won't she?' Vio asked, desperate for reassurance.

'I'm sure she will,' lied Dorian.

A few moments later, Dr Emanuelle, a tall Latino with a mocha complexion and a faintly off-putting, movie-star white smile, emerged through the swing doors looking stony faced. Viorel practically grabbed him by the lapels.

'What's happening?' he asked. 'Is she OK? I'm her . . .' he hesitated. 'I'm her next of kin.'

'I know who you are, Mr Hudson,' said the doctor, kindly. 'She's alive. And she's breathing. Not on her own, though. With help.'

Dorian felt the room start to spin. 'With help?'

'Yes.'

'You mean a ventilator?'

'Yes. Miss Leon is in a coma.'

Viorel gasped. Seeing his legs start to shake again, Dorian put an arm around his waist to hold him up. 'Oh please no. She can't die.'

'I know it's very distressing,' said Dr Emanuelle. 'But try to keep calm. The fact that she's comatose doesn't necessarily mean she's going to die. Sometimes the body shuts down in this way so that it can repair itself. A bit like shutting down all the open programmes on your computer so you can restart,' he added helpfully.

Both men stared back at him blankly.

'Look, we'll know more in the next few hours. We're running a brain scan, a CT, everything. For the moment she is stable. We're moving her to Critical Care. You can wait up there while they run the tests. It's a lot more comfortable than this hole.'

Outside in the parking lot, the orderly cupped a hand furtively around his cellphone, making sure he wasn't overheard.

'Yes, I'm sure it's her. I heard Viorel Hudson with my

own ears, man. But I'm not telling you nothing else till I see some money.'

The rest of that night was one of the longest in both Viorel and Dorian's lives. Camped out in the Critical Care family waiting room, they were drip fed information throughout the small hours as Sabrina's test results came back. Some were positive. Her liver, lungs and heart all looked healthy. Others were agonizingly inconclusive. It wasn't clear whether or not she would suffer permanent brain damage. Much would depend on when – and if – she emerged from the coma.

'It could be in an hour,' Dr Emanuelle told Vio. 'It could be tomorrow. It could be weeks or months from now. Obviously, we're hoping that that's not the case. But you need to be prepared. There truly isn't much point to your waiting around here. She's stable, and if that changes, we'll call you. But you should both go home and get some rest.'

At first, Viorel had refused. But by dawn, the press pack gathered outside the hospital had swelled to close to a hundred, some of them with full camera crews. From the waiting-room window, Vio could clearly see the Channel 9 news team as well as the hated *Extra*.

'You should get out of here while you still can,' said Dorian. 'It's you they want to see, not me.'

'Either me or some doctor telling them Sabrina's dead,' said Viorel bitterly. 'Fucking parasites. How can they make entertainment out of something like this?'

'Seriously, Dr Emanuelle's right. There's nothing you can do here. You need some sleep.'

'What about you?'

Dorian shrugged. 'I'm a vampire, remember? We're not

big on sleep. Besides,' he added wryly, 'I have nowhere to go.'

Viorel hesitated. 'You promise you'll call me if there's any news at all?'

'I promise. Go.'

Outside, a spectacular orange-and-pink sunrise was spreading across the Santa Monica sky. Camera crews and paparazzi anxiously corrected their light meters, while reporters and presenters double checked their mikes, in preparation for either Viorel's emergence or an official statement from the St John's press office on Sabrina's condition.

With the hospital staff's help, Viorel was able to choreograph this so that he was smuggled out of the trade entrance at exactly the same time that Dr Emanuelle walked out front to address the media.

'Ladies and Gentleman,' he shouted, raising a hand for silence as the noisy rabble closed in around him. 'I'm going to read a short factual statement detailing Miss Leon's current condition. And I will not, repeat *not*, be taking any further questions at this time.'

With the flashbulbs popping and boom mikes thrust at him like so many padded spears, the handsome doctor read out his prepared statement. Sabrina had been brought in at eleven thirty yesterday evening, after an apparent overdose of prescription medication. Her condition was critical but stable. Test results so far had given grounds for optimism, but there could be no further comment made at this stage as to her ultimate prognosis.

As he lowered his paper and turned to walk back into the hospital, the furore that erupted behind him was deafening.

'Can you confirm this was a suicide attempt?'

'Is it true that Sabrina tried to take her own life because Viorel Hudson left her?'

'Is Viorel with her now?'

'Is Hudson being charged with any offence? Have the police been involved?'

'Will Viorel be making a statement?'

Only with the help of three burly security men was Dr Emanuelle physically able to extricate himself from the baying crowd and make it safely back inside.

'What the fuck's wrong with these people?' he complained to one of the nurses. 'That girl's fighting for her life up there, and all they're interested in is getting the Hudson kid's head on a plate.'

The nurse raised an eyebrow. 'That surprises you?'

Dr Emanuelle sighed. 'I guess not.'

'You live by the sword, you die by the sword.' The nurse shrugged. 'That's the nature of fame.'

The doctor shook his head sadly. Sometimes he hated this town.

Over the course of the next two weeks, *Wuthering Heights'* cast and crew prayed to the gods of Hollywood that the old adage was true, about all publicity being good publicity. All over America, all over the world, headlines were screaming.

This year's Oscar underdog was the movie that had wrecked the once famously solid Rasmirez marriage. That had brought together two photogenically star-crossed lovers, only to break them apart. That would, very possibly, result in the death of one of the brightest, yet most troubled stars of her generation, just *weeks* before she might have won an Oscar and turned her life and career around.

Like all good soap operas, the *Wuthering Heights* train wreck had the crucial ingredients of hope and despair, of fame, fortune and glamour side by side with tragedy, misery and disaster. It had a heroine – the newly forgiven and once again adored Sabrina, lying fighting for her life in a hospital bed – and now it had a villain: Viorel Hudson.

Ignoring Dorian's protests, Vio had funded *Wuthering Height's* pre-Oscar PR campaign out of his own pay cheque. 'I'd have done it for half the money anyway,' he reasoned. 'And I want to beat that bastard Harry Greene as much as anybody. Besides, I owe it to Sabrina. And it's not like I can promote it myself.'

This, unfortunately, was true.

Viorel had refused to release a statement defending himself over his break-up with Sabrina. 'Why should I?' he told his agent angrily. 'I don't owe the world an expla-nation.' With nothing concrete or factual to go on, and with Sabrina irritatingly refusing either to die or dramatically to recover, the tabloids and TV stations filled the dead air with increasingly vitriolic and poisonous character assassinations of Viorel, fuelled by information from anonymous 'insiders'. The hospital orderly who had overheard Vio's guilt-fuelled outpourings to Dorian Rasmirez had cheerfully abandoned his $20,000-a-year drudge job at St John's in exchange for a string of lucrative interviews with every syndicated entertainment show going. Like the others, he painted Vio as a heartless lothario, who had deliberately driven poor innocent Sabrina to suicide with his infidelity, cruelly aban-doning her in public on the very day she had learned of her Oscar nomination, crushing her fragile spirit and wantonly annihilating her recent, brave recovery from her 'demons'.

'You have to sue.' Viorel's attorney, George Lewis, finally managed to get through to his client after the most splenetic and libellous of all the stories so far ran in the *National Enquirer*. 'At the very least, let me demand a retraction.'

'Why?' Vio responded wearily. 'What good will it do? It'll only stoke the flames of this stupid circus. Let them print and be damned.'

They printed. But it was Viorel who was being damned.

Meanwhile, Dorian was emerging as the unlikely hero of the piece, much to his own bafflement, and his soon-to-be ex-wife's annoyance. It had been Dorian who had found Sabrina 'just moments from death!' as *US Weekly* breathlessly intoned. Her devoted mentor had not left her bedside since.

'*Rasmirez, described by insiders as a father figure to the young star, continues his lonely vigil in Sabrina's hospital room,*' the magazine reporter wrote. '*He is said to have refused to allow Viorel Hudson any access to the gravely ill actress and is, friends say, "distraught" by recent events.*'

Well, the last part's true, thought Dorian. He had, in fact, been back to his room at the Beverly Wilshire twice in the last week, once to pick up some clothes and supplies, including his PC, and once for a series of Oscar campaign strategy meetings with the PR firm Vio had paid for. Both times he'd come and gone in a yellow cab and both times remained unnoticed, perhaps because the press believed their own bullshit about him being shackled to Sabrina's bed, watching her every breath. It was true that Viorel had not returned to St John's since Sabrina's admission. But this was purely because of the media intrusion, and the doctors' insistence that his presence there would do more harm than good, and nothing to do with a 'banning order' from Dorian. Indeed, it was Viorel who had given permission for Dorian to be allowed to stay with Sabrina. The two men were in constant touch.

But Dorian *was* distraught. He knew that with every day that passed, the chances of Sabrina waking up at all, never mind waking up unimpaired, dwindled. Stroking her hand, he would talk to her for hours, reading out every new review of her outstanding performance as Cathy, as well as poetry, novels, even new scripts in an attempt to rouse her, however momentarily, from her dreamless sleep. The doctors were adamant she could not hear him. But Dorian had read hundreds of stories about coma victims waking up after decades and announcing that they'd heard every word said to them. In any case, the talking was for him as much as for Sabrina. To stop talking would be to stop hoping. And he couldn't do that.

It was a Wednesday morning, and unusually dull and grey outside, when it happened. Clutching his usual morning latte, Dorian was standing at the window of Sabrina's room, trying to get cellphone reception, when he heard a voice from behind him.

'Hey.'

It wasn't a faint voice, it wasn't hoarse or weak or querulous. It was just an everyday, 'Hey, how are you?' kind of voice, and he turned around expecting to see a nurse. But there was no one there. Only him and Sabrina. His heart pounding, Dorian walked over to the bed. Sabrina appeared unchanged, eyes closed, chest rising and falling in its usual rhythm, apparently sleeping peacefully. *I must be imagining things*, he thought. *I've been cooped up in here too long.*

Just as he had this thought, Sabrina's eyes opened wide, like a doll's, and she said, 'I'm thirsty. I need water.'

Dorian jumped up and ran into the hall. His screams could be heard reverberating all the way to the maternity ward. 'Get Doctor Emanuelle! Get someone! She's awake!' Running back to Sabrina he hugged and kissed her, only with difficulty resisting the temptation to squeeze the life back out of her. When he spoke, to his own surprise he sounded angry.

'Goddamn it, Sabrina, how could you be so stupid? Do you know how fucking scared we've all been?'

'Water,' repeated Sabrina weakly. 'Please.'

'Oh shit, sorry.' Dorian hurried to the sink, returning with a paper cup of tap water. He held it to her lips and she drank it greedily, nodding to him for a second cup and then a third.

'Well, hello!' Dr Emanuelle walked in looking elated, as well he might. 'We weren't sure if you were going to make a reappearance. It's good to meet you, Miss Leon.'

Sabrina looked at him uncomprehendingly, then turned back to Dorian. He could see, physically see, the memory of what had happened slowly and painfully returning to her, the pain of it spreading like a storm cloud across her features, from her furrowed brow down to her trembling lower lip.

'I didn't die,' she murmured.

'No, my darling,' said Dorian gently. 'You didn't.'

Sabrina's eyes filled with tears. 'I wanted to.' Slumping back against the pillow, she closed her eyes again.

'Sabrina!' Dorian panicked. 'Do something,' he shouted at Dr Emanuelle. 'Help her!'

'She's fine,' said the doctor, looking at the red lines on the monitor measuring Sabrina's brainwaves. 'She's tired, that's all. Let her rest. I'll leave the nurse with you. When she wakes up again, we'll run all the tests, but you should try to relax now, Mr Rasmirez. She made it.'

He was right. It was astonishing how quickly, once she'd come around, Sabrina bounced back to normal. Well, perhaps 'bounced' wasn't quite the right word. Throughout the day her mood remained listless and subdued. She herself did not seem to share the general delight at her survival. But physically, her recovery was as fast as it was miraculous. By the end of that first day she was sitting up in bed, eating and drinking and catching up on the television news. When an item came on about the Oscars, she turned up the volume. But when the commentary turned to her own dramatic recovery – evidently, Ed Steiner had wasted no time releasing a statement – and included footage of her and Viorel together, she became visibly distressed.

'Turn it off,' she told Dorian, who was still seated in his usual armchair beside her bed. 'I can't watch.'

Dorian did as he was asked. He hated to see her so upset, fighting back the tears.

'He wasn't right for you, you know,' he said gently.

It was the wrong thing to say, like opening the floodgates on an enormous dam of emotion. 'He was!' sobbed Sabrina. 'He was right for me. I wasn't good enough for him, that was the problem.'

'How can you say that?' said Dorian. 'You're *too* good for him. You're too good for any man, for that matter. You're perfect.'

Sabrina was so surprised, she stopped crying for a moment. Was this the same Dorian Rasmirez who'd spent the best part of last year telling her what a spoiled, selfish, obnoxious little madam she was? 'Perfect?'

'Well,' Dorian grinned, 'perhaps not perfect in the strictest sense of the word. But you're perfect to me.' Taking her hand, he said solemnly, 'I love you, Sabrina. I'm in love with you. Will you marry me?'

Sabrina lay still for a long time, saying nothing. *I should have known*, she thought to herself. *He's been here in the hospital all this time, waiting for me. That's more than friendly concern*. But at the same time she struggled to reconcile the Dorian she knew in England, the dictatorial director, with the man clasping her hand now, proclaiming his love for her.

'I can't marry you,' she said, her voice as soft and kind as she could make it. 'I know there's no hope for me and Viorel.

If I didn't know that for sure, I wouldn't have . . .' She left the sentence hanging.

'I know,' said Dorian quietly.

'But that doesn't change the fact that I still love him. I'm sorry.'

As she said the words, she thought: *What am I sorry for, exactly? That it's over for me and Vio? Or that I've just rejected an offer of marriage from one of the most wonderful men in the world?* The truth was that there had always been something between her and Dorian. That night when he'd defended her outside the pub at Loxley and they'd ended up having a screaming row; or after he bailed her out of a police cell in Manchester and they'd shared that totally unexpected kiss; or in Romania, when he'd confided in her about the end of his marriage. There was a spark between them, a connection that ran deeper than friendship or even than the notoriously volatile actress/director relationship. She just wasn't prepared to have it verbalized here, now, in hospital, only days after Viorel had left her. What else could she say but 'no'?

Sabrina's answer wasn't what Dorian wanted to hear. But he could hardly claim to be surprised. Even if she weren't still obsessed with Hudson, what reason on earth would a girl like that – a world-class beauty with her whole life ahead of her – have to be interested in an ageing, past-his-prime retread like him? How foolish must he have sounded, proposing out of the blue like that?

'No,' he said, embarrassed. 'I'm sorry. It was foolish of me.'

'Not foolish,' said Sabrina truthfully. 'I'm flattered.'

'Look, can we just forget this?' said Dorian gruffly. 'Let's talk about something else.'

'OK.' For the first time since she'd opened her eyes that morning, Sabrina smiled. 'Let's talk about our strategy then.'

'Strategy?' Dorian raised an eyebrow.

'For the Oscars,' said Sabrina impatiently. 'I'd have gotten Best Actress for sure if I'd done the decent thing and died.'

'Jesus, Sabrina, don't say that!'

'Why not? It's true. But now that I've pulled through, we're gonna have to fight for it.'

'All you need to be fighting for is your strength,' said Dorian soberly, marvelling for the thousandth time at Sabrina's apparently limitless ambition. Even with a broken heart, and having just emerged from a coma, she was thinking about her next career move.

'Screw that,' said Sabrina robustly. 'Harry Greene fucked your wife. Then he fucked your Sony deal. Are you really gonna sit back and let him fuck your Oscar chances too?'

Dorian smiled. 'Well, when you put it like that . . .'

'Great,' Sabrina grinned. 'So we're agreed. No more weeping and gnashing of teeth. Let's annihilate the slimy little fucker.'

Dorian didn't think he had ever loved her more.

Two weeks later, Viorel Hudson was trying to get out of his car in Beverly Hills when he accidentally opened the driver's door into a paparazzo's face, knocking the man into the gutter.

'Fuck you!' the photographer snarled, clutching his nose, which was spurting blood like a faucet. 'I'll sue you for assault, asshole.'

'Good luck with that,' drawled Viorel, stepping over the injured man whilst weaving his way through a crowd of his compatriots. 'Perhaps your lawyer would let me know where I can send the bill for my car? I think you may have scratched the bodywork.'

He'd decided a few weeks ago that if people were going to paint him as a villain, he might as well live up to his new, dastardly reputation. *They want a heartless bastard?*

I'll give them a heartless bastard. Sabrina had left hospital a few days ago and given a press conference in which she completely exonerated him of any wrongdoing, but it had made no difference. 'BRAVE SABRINA FORGIVES EX', ran the headlines. 'HUDSON SHAMED BY LEON'S COMPASSION.' Viorel had broken the heart of the nation's on-again sweetheart. Sabrina might be prepared to forgive him. But nobody else was.

As a result, Viorel had emerged from his self-imposed hiding and begun to live his life in public again, eating out at well-known restaurants, unashamedly attending industry parties in the lead-up to the Oscars, and generally behaving like a man who didn't care that half of America seemed to view him as on a par with Saddam Hussein. Perfecting his best, Jeremy Irons, villainous British accent, he deliberately taunted the hostile media, ignoring photographers and delivering as many pithy, ironic one-liners as he could think of to every earnestly condemnatory journalist who approached him. In private, he had spoken to Sabrina twice since she'd recovered from her overdose. Neither of them were easy conversations, but Viorel was happy that she sounded healthy and focused on work. She was staying at the private guest-house on Ed Steiner's property. He'd offered to visit her there to talk things through in person, but she'd declined.

'Truly, I can't face seeing you. Not yet,' she said, her voice breaking. 'I've told Dorian I'm not up to doing promotion yet, at least not jointly.'

'That's OK,' said Vio wryly. 'Nobody wants me anywhere *near* the promotional events. I'd be about as popular as Hitler at a Bar Mitzvah.'

'Yeah. I'm sorry about that,' said Sabrina.

'Not your fault, angel.'

'It'll pass. You'll be yesterday's news before you know it.'

Viorel laughed. 'Thanks a lot!'

'Come on, you know what I mean. I've been there, remember? Maybe you should try taking some pills? It worked for me.'

'Don't joke,' said Vio angrily. He cared about Sabrina far, far more than people knew, or cared to admit. But, stubborn to the end, he was damned if he was going to show it to the press who were so determined to destroy him.

A pretty, peroxide blonde in a vintage denim miniskirt and cleavage-bearing, Gucci silk shirt thrust herself in front of Vio as he crossed the street.

'Is it true you're quitting Hollywood and moving back to England?'

'No,' snapped Vio. 'It isn't. It's utter crap, but I suspect you'll print it anyway.'

Ironically, he found he'd been thinking about England a lot lately. He'd always adored LA. In the last six years he couldn't bring to mind a single occasion on which he'd felt homesick. But recently the allure of Hollywood's bright lights had soured, even for him. Cooped up alone in his apartment under self-imposed house arrest, his mind kept returning to Abel and Tish, to Loxley in all its glorious tranquillity, to Tish's maddening, self-righteous, pull-your-socks-up attitude and clipped, upper-class tones, which had irked him so much last summer, but which now seemed to call to him with all the nostalgic pull of a sea siren's song.

'Will you be going to the Academy Awards with the rest of the *Wuthering Heights* cast?' The peroxide girl was no sea siren. Her voice was nasal and grating, the aural equivalent of lemon juice in the eyes. 'How do you feel about seeing Sabrina again?' She smelled even worse than she sounded. Her perfume – Kai – was so strong that Vio felt as if he'd walked into a freshly air-sprayed loo.

'I'll support the movie in whatever way I'm asked,' he said curtly. 'And I couldn't care less about seeing Sabrina again.' Cue horrified gasps from the passers-by in earshot. 'Now be a good girl and fuck off, would you? I'm busy.'

Pushing past the girl as she gleefully wrote down his last gift of a quote, Viorel hurried into the nearest store. Talk about being hounded. That was truly what the paps were like, a pack of bloodthirsty dogs intent on ripping the flesh from his body. It was a relief when the gold-plated door of Louis Vuitton swished closed behind him, and he found himself on the cool, air-conditioned side of the tinted glass storefront windows, alone at last.

Or so he thought.

'Well, well. This *is* a surprise. Mr Viorel Hudson, as I live and breathe.'

Chrissie Rasmirez stepped out from behind a row of fur coats and fixed him with a coquettish smile. Vio's first thought was: *Christ, she looks good*. Dating Harry Greene obviously agreed with her. With her hair newly cut and dyed a softer shade of honey blonde, and her skin glowing like a teenager's, she looked ten years younger than when he'd last seen her in Romania. The red Hervé Léger minidress she was wearing was probably a bit too young for her, but with her taut size-two figure she managed to pull it off.

'Are you shopping or hiding?' She gestured towards the photographers lined up outside the shop window like a firing squad.

'Neither,' said Viorel. He was in no mood to make small talk with Dorian's bitch of an ex.

'Well, it must be one or the other,' said Chrissie, either missing his *froideur* or ignoring it. 'Perhaps you're looking for a peace offering for poor little Sabrina? If that's the case,

I can recommend the mink stole. A very *comforting* fur, mink, I always think.'

Viorel looked at her, struggling to think of anything to say. Every time he saw Chrissie he felt guilty about Dorian, although their afternoon of lovemaking at Loxley felt like a lifetime ago now. 'I'm sorry,' he said brusquely. 'I have to go.'

'Wait, don't be like that,' Chrissie called after him. 'I'd like to talk to you.' There was genuine pleading in her voice. Reluctantly, Viorel turned around.

'How's Dorian? I know the two of you must be seeing a lot of each other, what with the Oscars coming up and everything.'

'He's fine,' said Viorel frostily. 'Very good in fact,' he couldn't resist adding. 'Excited about the movie's chances. We all are.'

'I wouldn't get too excited if I were you,' said Chrissie, running her fingers lovingly over a full-length fox-fur coat. '*Celeste* is odds-on to sweep the board.'

'We'll see,' said Vio. 'What do you care about Dorian anyway? You've clearly moved on.'

Chrissie pouted. 'We were together for almost twenty years, you know. I still care.'

Yeah, right, thought Vio. *You want to keep your options open in case he gets that Oscar after all, or Harry leaves you for a younger model.*

'I read that he'd been at Sabrina's bedside for weeks like a lovesick puppy,' Chrissie said archly. 'I always knew there was something going on between those two, though of course he denied it.'

Viorel laughed. Her hypocrisy was truly stunning.

'There's nothing going on. There never was. Sabrina's young enough to be his daughter.'

435

Chrissie laughed loudly. 'Oh, darling, please. This is LA!'

'Look,' said Viorel, 'Dorian's a friend of mine, OK? He's doing well, and he'll keep doing well if you just stay the hell out of his life. Haven't you done enough damage?'

The simpering smile died on Chrissie's lips. 'Me?' she hissed. 'What about you? What kind of friend sleeps with someone's wife behind their back? Not to mention your cruelty to poor Sabrina. You don't care who you hurt, so don't you *dare* presume to judge me.'

'Leave Sabrina out of it,' said Vio, angry because he knew Chrissie's accusations were justified. 'And you know what, leave *me* out of it too. If you want to know how Dorian is, ask him yourself. Goodbye, Chrissie.'

He stormed out of the store. This time he didn't look back.

CHAPTER TWENTY-EIGHT

Tish knelt down and held out her arms as the little boy staggered unsteadily towards her.

'Bravo!' she smiled encouragingly. 'Bravo, Sile!'

The two-year-old beamed. He'd been born with clubbed feet, and had undergone a series of painful operations to correct them. This morning, after months of physio, he was walking unaided for the first time across the brightly carpeted playroom at Curcubeu, toddling proudly into Tish's arms as the other children looked on, clapping and cheering.

'You *did* it!' Tish hugged him, holding him up in the air and tickling him till he could hardly breathe for laughter. It was moments like these that made it all worthwhile. *I have to remember that*, she told herself. *I have to remember why I'm here*.

It wasn't easy to keep one's spirits up in Oradea in February. The cold was so bitter, so biting, one's limbs seemed to be constantly aching, the same ache that shot through your skull when you bit into a too-cold ice cream. And although the snow undoubtedly made the drab concrete streets of the city more picturesque, covering the communist bleakness with a blanket of dazzling white, it also clogged up the roads, froze the pipes and mounted up in endless drifts outside Curcubeu, drifts which had to be shovelled away by hand on an almost hourly basis. The central heating at Tish's children's home had broken down twice since Christmas, and in her apartment she, Abi and Lydia spent their evenings huddled around two fan heaters and went to sleep in bedsocks and fingerless gloves.

The freezing weather was not the only thing bringing Tish down. Like the rest of the world, she had followed the 'Curse of *Wuthering Heights*' drama on television and in the papers, from the movie's out-of-the-blue Oscar nominations, to Sabrina and Viorel's shocking split, and of course Sabrina's suicide scare. Although they'd never seen eye to eye, Tish felt awful for Sabrina. She'd had a small taste of heartbreak herself last year, over Michel, and could imagine the anguish the poor girl must have felt to do something so terrible. Part of her wanted to call when she heard the news, to send her good wishes at least. But since she'd moved back to Romania, Tish had had no contact at all with any of the LA contingent, not even Dorian, who'd been hounding her with calls at Loxley. That period in her life, last summer and the filming back in England, almost felt like a dream now. And though at times she felt wistful or nostalgic for it, she told herself that the severing of those ties was for the best. Particularly for Abel, whose fondness for Viorel Hudson had begun to reach dangerous proportions. The last thing Tish's son needed was any more disruption in his life, in the form of an unreliable, on/off father figure. No. It was time to move on. Clearly Viorel thought so too, or he would not have stopped calling.

Despite the radio silence, or perhaps because of it, Tish often found herself wondering about Viorel, and how he was dealing with all the horrible comments written about him in the press, after Sabrina's highly public overdose. Badly, she suspected. Viorel bucked against criticism, even when he knew it was fair. Blaming him for Sabrina's suicide attempt, Tish suspected, was unfair, or at the very least grossly oversimplified. She remembered well her last conversation with Vio on the phone at Loxley, when he'd accused her of selfishness for bringing Abel back to Romania. Sometimes, seeing her son's cold breath hanging in the air as he tried to do his homework in their freezing apartment, his words came back to her. It troubled her. The truth was, everything about Viorel Hudson troubled her. She'd be glad when the Oscars were over and the stories about him and Sabrina ran out of steam. Perhaps then she would finally escape him, and draw a line under that part of her life for good?

Once she'd handed Sile back to his carer and finished her rounds checking on the other children, Tish got into her trusty *(or should that be 'rusty'?)* Fiat and headed back into the city. More in hope than expectation, she turned the fan heater up to full blast as she bumped along the dirt roads out of Tinka. A faint whisper of heat seeped through the ventilation slats, accompanied by a noise like a plane taking off. Shivering, Tish reached across to the passenger seat and pulled a dirty green fleece blanket over her knees. By the time she arrived at the children's hospital, she was so cold the tips of her fingers were blue and her nose glowed red like an old drunk's.

'I thought you weren't coming.' Michel Henri met her at the fourth-floor elevator. In jeans and an open-necked cornflower blue shirt – it was arctic outside but inside the hospital the wards were kept on perma-roast – he looked as handsome and unruffled as ever, but Tish no longer felt her pulse quicken painfully at the sight of him. She couldn't pinpoint when, exactly, her feelings for Michel had changed. But she was hugely relieved that they had. *The only thing more satisfying than falling in love*, she reflected, *is falling out of it.*

'Sorry,' she panted, peeling off the top three layers of her clothing. 'The roads were lethal.'

'Your car's lethal,' chided Michel. He worried about her. Not just about her physical safety, but about her unhappiness, the distance that he'd seen in her eyes ever since she came back from England. Tish wasn't happy in Romania any more, not the way she used to be. 'Couldn't you have used some of your movie money to buy something with a few more mod cons? Like a functioning engine, for example?'

Tish laughed. 'Sadly, no. That money was spent before it was earned.'

'On your brother's house.'

'On the *family* house,' Tish corrected. 'Besides, I like my car.'

'It's a deathtrap,' said Michel. 'You should ask your friend Viorel Hudson to buy you a new one. He probably has dry-cleaning bills bigger than the cost of a new Punto.'

'My car's fine,' said Tish, suddenly keen to change the subject. They strode down the corridor towards the Critical Care unit. 'How's Fleur? Any cravings yet?'

Michel grinned. 'Other than for me, you mean? *Non.*'

His fiancée, the gorgeous Canal Plus reporter, was four months pregnant, and Michel couldn't hide his delight. Tish was delighted for him.

'She's moody though, my *God*,' Michel complained. 'Last weekend my flight into Paris landed twenty minutes late. She practically clawed my eyes out when I got back to the apartment.'

'You *would* be late for your own funeral,' Tish teased him.

'Yes, but this wasn't my fault!' said Michel. 'Plus, she

refuses to even discuss the wedding. She thinks she looks fat.' Pulling out his mobile phone, he showed Tish a picture of a slender, smiling woman in tight jeans pointing at a barely perceptible rounding of her belly.

'She's stunning,' said Tish, truthfully.

'I know. I've told her a hundred times. I get a bigger gut than that after a couple of beers, but she won't listen. What is it with you women?' He threw his hands up in the air dramatically. 'Crazy, all of you.'

Tish's phone rang. Vivianna's number flashed up on the screen. *Not now, mother.* She switched it off. Ever since the *Wuthering Heights* drama became front-page news, Vivianna had taken to calling her daughter regularly, 'just for a chat, darling', fishing for inside information on Vio or Sabrina with which to impress her vacuous ex-pat girlfriends in Rome. The fact that Tish knew nothing, and had told her nothing, did not seem to have put her off. Another reason to look forward to the end of the Oscars season.

Tish spent the rest of the afternoon with Michel and the children, playing and talking with them and making notes of complaints to pass on to child services. It wasn't until much later, after she'd got home and put Abi to bed that she remembered to switch her phone back on.

'You have six missed calls,' an automated voice told her. 'First missed call, received today . . .' Tish scrolled through the numbers. Four of the six calls were from her mother. Two were from Loxley Hall.

Another of Jago's dramas, thought Tish wearily. *I wonder what the problem is now? His morning caviar wasn't sufficiently aged? He found a wrinkle in his cashmere sock, and Mummy wants me to fly over and iron it for him?*

She called the house and was relieved when Mrs Drummond answered.

'Hullo, Mrs D,' she said, automatically smiling at the sound of the housekeeper's voice. 'What's going on? I had a hundred and one messages from Mummy, so I can only assume it's some nonsense about Jago.'

'Oh, Letitia. You don't know.' The quiver in the old woman's voice sent a tingle down Tish's spine. This was no joke.

'Know what?' asked Tish, praying that Jago hadn't hurt or killed himself or something awful, and already regretting her earlier snide thoughts about caviar. 'Is he OK? Is Mummy . . .?'

'He's fine,' said Mrs Drummond bitterly. 'Your brother and mother are both quite well.'

'Oh. Then what . . .?'

'It's Loxley Hall. I'm so sorry to be the one to tell you this, my darling. But Jago's sold the estate.'

CHAPTER TWENTY-NINE

For three hundred and sixty four days a year, the Kodak Theatre, at 6801 Hollywood Boulevard, is just another routine stop on the LA tourist trail. Part of a large complex of restaurants and stores at Hollywood and Highland, it is best known as the venue where *American Idol* is filmed, although it also hosts various concerts and stage shows throughout the year, playing second fiddle to the larger, more prestigious Nokia Theatre. But for one night in March, the Kodak shines, not just as the brightest star in Hollywood, but as the guiding light of the entire global entertainment industry. A mecca for stars great and small, for one, magical night hundreds of millions of pairs of eyes are drawn to its famous, curved façade and the red carpet leading up to its grand entry. On Oscar night, the Kodak Theatre becomes the center of the world.

The Academy of Motion Picture Arts and Sciences – the Academy, for short – actually rents the theatre weeks in advance of Oscar night. From security arrangements to lighting, acoustics to plumbing issues, everything must be checked and double checked, tinkered with, polished and improved, so that on the night itself the fantasy remains fantastic, unsullied by mortal imperfections, a true gathering of the gods. As with the Great Pyramids of Egypt, the toil and sweat of countless lowly, unseen hands are in fact responsible for the miracle that seems to unfold effortlessly out of nothing. Work starts early and finishes late. Meanwhile, the city of Los Angeles becomes gripped with a sort of fever, a frenzy of anticipation so widespread and sweeping that it transcends the industry itself. A light, fairy dust of excitement falls over everyone, from bank tellers to waitresses, drug dealers to cops. In this most disparate and heartless of towns – as Dorothy Parker famously put it, 'Fifty-two suburbs looking for a city' – for one night in March, everybody's heart beats as one. They call it Oscar Magic, and it is bottled at the Kodak.

Every year there is one big story, the compelling narrative of Oscar week around which all lesser dramas revolve. Heath Ledger's death was one such story. The birth of Brangelina's romance was another, Mel Gibson's drunken rant against the Jews a third. This year, at the Eighty-Fifth Academy Awards, industry insiders were focused on the Best Director/ Best Picture battle between Harry Greene and Dorian Rasmirez. But, for the world at large, the big story was Sabrina Leon and Viorel Hudson. Neither had been seen in public together since before Sabrina's suicide attempt. And so the question on everybody's lips was: *Would Viorel Hudson show up?*

No one doubted Sabrina's attendance. As odds-on favorite to win Best Actress, and with public love and affection for her running at an all-time high, this year's Oscars were set to be Sabrina Leon's ultimate comeback.

No pressure, then, thought Sabrina, flipping through the five couture dresses her stylist had laid out on the bed. She was staying at The Peninsula, in a vast penthouse suite. Right now her bedroom resembled a bustling corporate office, full of scurrying minions all looking harassed and with cellphones glued to their ears.

The gowns on Sabrina's bed were the final five. She'd been offered, and rejected, scores of outfits by every designer under the sun, Marchesa, Lanvin, Carolina Herrera, Jason Wu, Marc Jacobs, and had thought she'd settled on a silver sequined Armani gown; but then this morning one of the make-up girls said she thought it washed her out, plunging Sabrina back into a frenzy of indecision.

'Forget the short ones.' Katrina, the bossy British stylist Ed Steiner had foisted on Sabrina the day she was nominated ('*You're a nominee now, sweetie. Best Actresses do not dress themselves*'), picked up two exquisitely embellished Versace cocktail dresses and flung them unceremoniously onto the pile on the floor. 'That leaves the Gucci, the Lanvin and the Victoria Beckham.' At the mention of this last name, Katrina crossed herself. She'd always sworn it would be a cold day in hell before she dressed one of her clients in something dreamed up by a footballer's wife from Essex, but even she had to admit that the clinging, wine-red silk column with its subtle draping across the collar bones and sensual, deep V in the back was utterly ravishing.

Sabrina looked at the dresses again, picturing herself on the podium at the Kodak, the same fantasy she had had every day for the last seven years, since she first stepped on stage at Sammy Levine's theatre in Fresno. Except today, it wasn't a fantasy. Today, it was happening for real. And she had no idea which Sabrina she wanted to be. The Lanvin was virginal, white and pretty and feminine, perfect for the innocent, wronged Sabrina that the press seemed so eager for her to be. The Gucci was more mature, more businesslike, a beautifully cut gunmetal grey satin that would announce to the world she had finally grown up, thrown off her demons and evolved into the great actress she was always meant to be. But the Beckham dress was an enigma. Sexy without being slutty, dangerous yet controlled, dark and tempting and complicated.

I wish Dorian were here, thought Sabrina. *He'd know which dress I should wear. He'd know everything.*

It was strange how much closer she'd grown to Dorian since the awful awkwardness of his bedside proposal. She'd expected to feel uncomfortable around him afterwards, or for him to feel embarrassed, too crippled by wounded pride to be around her. But in fact during the interminable round of promotions and pre-Oscar press junkets that had become Sabrina's life since she got out of hospital, their relationship had blossomed quite unexpectedly. With Viorel voluntarily removing himself from all *Wuthering Heights* promotion, Dorian had taken on a more prominent role. As a result, he and Sabrina were thrown together constantly, giving interviews to every network talk show in America. There was a new dynamic to their relationship now, a jokey banter that had been entirely absent during the long months of filming. It was Dorian's friendship that had kept her sane through this whole crazy roller-coaster ride, and stopped her from dwelling too much on Viorel.

'You've got *so* much ahead of you,' he would tell her, day after day. 'So much good work, so much love. This is the beginning, Sabrina, not the end.' Eventually, Sabrina began to believe him.

'I'll go for the VB dress,' she said, suddenly decisive.

'Great,' said Katrina. 'I agree. Now, accessories.'

'No accessories,' said Sabrina.

'Don't be ridiculous,' said the stylist brusquely. 'This is

the Oscars, not prom night in Bethlehem Pennsylvania. You need diamonds. Now, the question is, do we go Fred Leighton?' She flipped open a dark red box to reveal an elaborate diamond and ruby choker and matching drop earrings, 'or keep it classic with Cartier?'

'No,' said Sabrina firmly. 'No jewellery. No clutch.'

'But Sabrina—'

'And I want my hair up.'

'With no earrings?' The stylist gasped incredulously.

Dorian always says I do my best work when I stop trying so hard. If he were here he'd tell me to keep it simple.

'No earrings.'

Sabrina smiled. She could feel her confidence surging back. Just thinking about Dorian made her feel calmer. She could picture him now, fixing his cufflinks with no more drama than if he were going out for a casual dinner with friends. *If only I could be a bit more like that.*

'I can't do it. I can't go.'

Dorian lay back on his therapist's couch, eyes closed, wondering if he were going to throw up.

'Why do you say that?'

Damn fucking therapists. Always asking questions, never giving you a straight answer.

'Because, I can't do it! What if Viorel shows up?'

'What if he does? I thought the two of you got along?'

'We do,' said Dorian miserably. 'But Sabrina will look at him, and then she'll look at me, and I'll have to watch the –' he winced – 'the love in her eyes and I'll have to comfort her. And I can't. I can't do it. I can't go. Oh, Jesus.' He put a hand on his chest, willing his heart rate to slow down.

It was so ironic. Everybody had him down as the steady one, the mother ship, cool, calm and collected through all the dramas. For the last month, he'd devoted every ounce of his energy to hiding his true feelings from Sabrina. But tonight, with the whole world watching, he didn't know if he could keep it up. What if Sabrina and Vio got back together? What on earth was he going to do then?

'You can go,' said the therapist gently. 'The question is, do you want to?'

And the answer is no, thought Dorian. Win or lose, tonight would mark the end of something he had come to treasure. The end of him and Sabrina spending time together, day in and day out. What excuse would he have to be around her after this?

But the truth was, he had to go. *Who am I kidding? Of course I have to be there. I'm up for Best Director and Best Picture. Me against Harry Greene. This is it. The Showdown.*

It was already almost two o'clock. If he was to make it to the Kodak on time, he needed to get back to his hotel right now, change, and jump in the limo with his game face on.

'Sorry Doc.' He sat up, rubbing his eyes as if he'd just woken from a deep sleep. Which in a way, he had. 'I gotta run.'

'Good luck,' said the therapist, shaking him by the hand. 'And remember, you're not a fortune-teller. The truth is you don't know what Sabrina's thinking, or feeling, or what her reactions might be. But whatever they are, you can't control her. You can only control yourself.'

Hopefully, thought Dorian. He felt as sick as a dog. But it was time to go.

Harry Greene looked around the packed auditorium and smiled.

So far, the evening was going swimmingly. As his limo had pulled up, he'd been practically deafened by the screaming fans. *Celeste* was a phenomenon. It had broken every box-office record for a period drama, was almost as big a hit with audiences as *Fraternity*. Oscar or no Oscar, the movie was a runaway success. Indeed, if it hadn't been for his obsession with thwarting Dorian Rasmirez, Harry couldn't have cared less about his Oscar chances. Who gave a fuck what a bunch of self-important old farts at the Academy thought of his directing skills? The public were the only critics who had ever mattered to Harry Greene. But he knew Rasmirez felt differently. That he actually cared about the opinions of his 'peers', as he'd pretentiously called them on Katie Couric's talk show yesterday, the self-important douche bag. Dorian *really* wanted those Oscars, Best Picture and Best Director. Harry Greene couldn't wait to see the look on his face when he lost. But first he would savour the pleasure of walking the red carpet with Dorian's wife, cuckolding him in front of hundreds of millions of people around the world.

Chrissie looked great tonight in a scoop-necked flesh-colored Carolina Herrera cut on the bias, with a classic, Old Hollywood fishtail train. As befitted any date of Harry's, she also wore half her bodyweight in diamonds. No point having a trophy if you couldn't make it sparkle. At home, behind closed doors, Harry had already started to find Chrissie's neediness tiresome. She kept pressuring him about a date for the wedding, which was difficult as Harry had not yet decided if he intended to go through with it or not. In many ways it would be the icing on the cake of his annihilation of Dorian. But, on the other hand, it meant being married. Matrimony had never been Harry Greene's strong suit.

Chrissie, meanwhile, was having the time of her life. Photographers were shouting at her from all sides. 'Congratulations on your engagement!'

'Thank you,' she replied graciously, clinging demurely to Harry's arm.

'Can you show us the ring?'

'How do you feel about seeing your ex-husband again tonight? Are you nervous?'

'Not at all,' Chrissie preened, turning from side to side so that the cameras could catch the best angle on her dress. 'Dorian and I are still great friends. I wish him well.'

'We'll be sure to stop by and commiserate with him after the show,' added Harry, to general laughter.

Inside the theatre, things got even better. Harry had been given a seat a full six rows in front of Dorian. But, as the auditorium began to fill up, Dorian's seat, and those of the rest of the *Wuthering Heights* nominees remained empty. For a moment, Harry's heart lurched. Surely, it wasn't possible that he would do a no-show? Not tonight. Harry had dreamed of this night for eight long years. Beating Rasmirez wasn't enough. He wanted to *watch* him being beaten, to see the pain in his eyes. But, to his relief, a few minutes before the lights went down, Sabrina Leon arrived, swiftly followed by a dishevelled and stressed-looking Dorian.

You'd have thought he'd get his suit pressed for the fucking Academy Awards, thought Harry disparagingly, taking in Dorian's crumpled tuxedo jacket and amateurishly tied bow tie. His face looked dreadful too, so pale it was almost green (*nerves?*), the eyes lined and puffy with exhaustion.

'Is he here?' Chrissie spun around, following Harry's gaze. 'Oh my goodness,' she gasped. 'He looks ill.'

He's lovesick, she thought smugly. *Pining for me. Maybe, when all of this is over, I'll take him back after all? I should marry Harry first, of course, get a decent divorce settlement . . .*

After the double rejection from Dorian and Viorel last year, it felt fabulous to have two men fighting over her. And not just two men, but two of the biggest power players in all of Hollywood. For a washed-up soap actress over forty, she wasn't doing too badly.

Lifting a white-gloved hand, she waved regally at Dorian, but he stared straight through her.

Leaning over, Sabrina whispered in Dorian's ear. 'Two o'clock, Wicked Witch of the West, waving.'

'Hmm?' said Dorian. 'Oh.' He waved absently back at Chrissie. It was like acknowledging a vague acquaintance. All he could think about, all he could see, was Sabrina.

Sitting beside him in her wine-red dress, she radiated beauty and sophistication, as well as that trademark vulnerability that had helped transform her into the perfect Cathy. Her bare neck and wrists shone infinitely more brightly than Chrissie's diamonds, at least in Dorian's eyes. How was he ever going to let her go?

But that's ridiculous, he told himself firmly. *You never had her in the first place.*

At least Viorel's seat to Sabrina's right remained resolutely empty. He knew he shouldn't, but Dorian thanked him for that, for staying away. It wasn't until the lights dimmed and the opening refrains of 'Hollywood' rang out from the orchestra that it struck Dorian.

This was the Oscars. Best Picture. Best Director. Technically speaking, he might actually win, although according to every industry pundit, *Celeste* was the runaway favourite for both gongs.

Sabrina squeezed his hand. 'Good luck.'

'Thanks,' said Dorian, reluctantly releasing her fingers. 'You too.'

As ever, the ceremony dragged on for what felt like an eternity. The interminable litany of thank-you speeches were enough to make anybody lose the will to live. Best Dubbing Mixer, Best Animated Short – *Why was it all the animation people were always bald, wore knitted ties and 'zany' wire-rimmed glasses and couldn't seem to speak without mumbling?* thought Sabrina – it was torturous. She tried to shake the feeling of unreality that seemed to have settled over her. She, Sabrina Leon, from Fresno California was nominated for Best Actress. Best Actress. At the Oscars. Surely, any moment now, she was going to wake up. If she did, and this were all a dream, would Viorel wake up beside her? Would she want him to?

Glancing at his empty chair, she wondered why she didn't feel worse. Had she hoped he'd show up tonight, or feared it? She didn't even know any more. All she did know, feeling the warmth of Dorian's body next to hers, was that she was glad her friend was here to support her. Glad too that she was there for him, especially with that cow Chrissie here twisting the knife, and Harry Greene clearly determined to destroy him. If *Wuthering Heights* got Best Picture, Sony would be forced to do a U-turn and release the film in cinemas after all. Either that or allow another distributor to buy out their contract, at an extortionate profit, of course. Not even Harry Greene carried enough clout to keep an Oscar-winning classic out of theatres indefinitely.

At the same time, Sabrina knew it was the Best Director honour that Dorian really, secretly coveted. *I owe him so much*, she thought, noticing for the first time how green and unwell he looked. *Please, God, let him get Best Director. He so deserves it.*

Just as she had the thought, Clint Eastwood walked onto the stage looking old and stooped. This was it then. Too nervous to look at Dorian, she grabbed his hand silently.

'And the nominations for Best Director are . . .' Eastwood's familiar cowboy drawl rang out through the auditorium. 'Jason Reitman for *All God's Children.'*

On the enormous plasma screen behind him, a montage of Reitman's war film began playing. To Sabrina it was little more than lights and colours. She was so tense she could barely breathe.

'Harry Greene for *Celeste.'*

A loud ripple of applause swept around the room as the *Celeste* footage began rolling. Sabrina had deliberately avoided watching it till now. After Harry Greene had effectively cut them off at the knees, the whole *Wuthering Heights* team had boycotted his much-hyped period epic. But, looking at the highlights now, even Sabrina had to admit it was a sumptuous piece of work, the cinematic equivalent of a red-velvet cupcake, rich and textured and so delicious you wanted to slow it down, to savour every second. *He's an asshole*, she thought, staring at Harry's ramrod-straight back next to Chrissie Rasmirez, *but he's a talented asshole.*

Clips from the other nominees followed, but Sabrina found it hard to focus. Judging by the ever-tightening grip of Dorian's hand in hers, he was struggling too.

'And last but not least,' Clint intoned, 'Dorian Rasmirez for *Wuthering Heights.'*

There was no applause for the *Wuthering Heights* montage. Just a rapt, breathless silence. Sabrina, who hadn't watched the movie herself since before the night Viorel broke up with her, now saw his face again on screen, six foot high and as perfectly formed as any Michelangelo sculpture.

Fuck, he's beautiful, she thought, squeezing Dorian's hand more tightly. But the pain in her heart was less brutal than she'd expected. Even when they showed the bell-tower scene, the moment that had marked the beginning of her and Viorel's affair, Sabrina found she could detach enough to appreciate the quality of the work, and Dorian's outstanding achievement as a film-maker. There was Loxley Hall, looking magical and haunting in the dawn light. Lizzie Bayer was practically unrecognizable as the dying Isabella. How tirelessly Dorian must have worked with her to get that raw a performance out of her. He truly was a genius.

As the screen faded to black for the last time, a stunned hush fell over the room. After what felt like an eternity, Clint Eastwood cleared his throat. 'And the award goes to . . .'

'Congratulations,' Chrissie breathed huskily into Harry's ear.

'Thanks.' Harry Greene smiled, imperceptibly moving forward in his seat.

'. . . Jason Reitman for *All God's Children*.'

CHAPTER THIRTY

Three thousand people gasped as one.

Harry Greene slumped back into his seat as if he'd been shot. Chrissie Rasmirez's incredulous face was panned and beamed all around the globe. Dorian, who was equally surprised, managed to keep his game face on.

'I'm so sorry,' Sabrina whispered through half-closed lips, aware that somewhere, a camera would be watching them both for their reaction.

'Don't be,' said Dorian, applauding loudly as Reitman made his way onto the dais. 'He's a terrific director. And nobody likes a bad sport.'

'He's not a patch on you,' said Sabrina loyally.

'Thank you, sweetheart,' Dorian smiled at her broadly. 'To be honest, I'm glad it's over with. And at least Greene didn't win.'

By this point, Harry Greene was also smiling for the cameras, quickly regaining his composure after the initial shock. Inside, however, he was fuming. *Jason Reitman? Who the fuck is Jason Reitman?* When Harry found out which members had voted against him – and he *would* find out

– he would make them wish they'd never heard Jason Reitman's name.

With one of the Big Six out of the way, another round of more minor Oscars began, and the excitement of Jason Reitman's shock triumph over both the night's big-name directors died down. The next major award was Best Actor, which predictably went to *Celeste*'s Roger De Gray. It was the third gong of the night for Harry Greene's movie, after Best Costume Design and Best Original Soundtrack, where it had beat out *Wuthering Heights*. Harry's inside sources had assured him that Best Picture was one hundred per cent in the bag, as it should be after what he'd spent on the campaign; but then they'd been pretty confident about Best Director too, and where had that got him?

When Julia Roberts walked onto the stage, Sabrina said audibly, 'Not now! It can't be now!'

A ripple of affectionate laughter rang out as the cameras all zoomed in on Sabrina's face. It *was* unusual for the Best Actress nominations to be announced directly after Best Actor. But Sabrina's shock was endearingly naive. The audience loved it.

'So much for playing it cool,' she whispered apologetically to Dorian.

'And making the world a little colder?' he whispered back. 'Who cares? They're all rooting for you anyway.'

The montages rolled. Competition was fierce this year. *Wuthering Heights* and *Mad Dogs* were both terrific, complex movies with beautifully written female leads, and Anne Hathaway and Laura Linney were two of the best-liked stars within the industry, as well as with the public at large. Sabrina was the favourite to win it, but that in itself could often play against you, as Dorian knew all too well. He felt far more nervous for Sabrina than he had for himself. As the nominations were announced he said a silent prayer. *She's been through so much, Lord. Let her get this. Let her believe in herself.*

'And the Oscar goes to . . . Sabrina Leon, for *Wuthering Heights.*'

For a moment, Sabrina froze, aware of nothing but a loud buzzing in her skull, accompanied by the insistent *thud thud thud* of her heart. It was the oddest sensation, as if the entire Kodak Theatre had been submerged underwater and everything was happening in slow motion. In the back of her mind she was aware of the smiles and cheers, the heads turned in her direction . . . and Dorian. Dorian hugging her, lifting her up out of her seat and into the air as if he were the winner and she were the trophy. Of his face, just one huge smile, and the smell of his skin: soap, Floris aftershave and something else, something comforting and familiar and strong. It was Dorian who pushed her forward, ushering her towards the podium. Dorian whose voice somehow made it through the buzzing.

'You've won, sweetheart. You did it. Go on up there.'

Blindly, Sabrina put one foot in front of the other until she found herself shaking hands with Julia Roberts and holding the surprisingly weighty golden statuette in her hands. The carefully crafted speech that Ed Steiner had prepared for her flew instantly out of her head. Instead, she blurted out a few short words of thanks – to Dorian, to Tarik Tyler, to Sammy Levine back in Fresno and to Viorel, whose name drew muted boos from much of the audience.

'Oh, no,' Sabrina looked hurt. 'Please don't. He's my friend. If it weren't for him I wouldn't be here.'

She wasn't even aware how she got back to her seat until she felt Dorian's congratulatory arm around her, enveloping and protecting her the way he always did.

'My, my. Don't those two look thick as thieves,' said Chrissie snidely to Harry.

'What do you care?' he snarled back at her.

Chrissie shivered. Harry had never used that tone with her before. It was ugly, vicious. Dorian never would have spoken to her, or to any woman, that way.

'I don't.' She tried to keep her voice light. 'I was only making an observation.' But inside she felt an unpleasant lurch of nerves in the pit of her stomach. Watching Dorian and Sabrina together upset her more than she knew it ought to.

She felt worse when, turning back to Harry, she caught him openly flirting with Carey Esposito, the stunning eighteen-year-old star of Disney's latest teen hit, *Love Bytes*. Was she losing his interest already?

There was only one more major award to go now, the one that everyone in the auditorium – and all those glued to their TV screens around the world – had been waiting for. Best Picture.

Martin Scorsese was presenting the Oscar this year. He shuffled onto the stage, looking as short and stooped and nondescript as any Italian grandfather.

'You'd have thought he'd have more presence,' muttered Sabrina, but Dorian wasn't listening. Everything rested on the next few moments. If he won, *Wuthering Heights* would be released and Dorian would be riding high, his faith in the movie that had cost him his marriage, his home and his professional reputation vindicated. If he lost, he faced financial ruin. His film, his beautiful film, the best thing he'd ever made, would sink without trace.

Was it worth it? he wondered, as the Best Picture clips appeared on the screen. Making this film had changed his life – in all tangible senses for the worse. His family was in tatters. His ancestral home was about to be repossessed by the state. He was tragically, pathetically in love with a girl who had no romantic interest in him whatsoever. Would an Oscar really make it all worthwhile?

Six rows in front of him, he watched the tense, tuxedo-clad shoulders of his rival, Harry Greene, and wondered what was going through *his* mind. He was the favourite to win, of course, for *Celeste* – this strange man who had whipped up such a ferocious enmity out of nothing at all; who had slept with Dorian's wife and tried to keep him from his daughter; who had sabotaged his deal with Sony Pictures out of sheer spite. It occurred to Dorian that he didn't really know Harry Greene at all, just as Harry didn't really know him. And yet some strange, toxic gravitational force had brought their lives and careers together, propelling them towards this moment, this ultimate ruling on . . . what? Which of them was the more talented? Hardly. Everybody knew that it was studio money that won you an Oscar these days. Studio money that Dorian simply didn't have.

Even so, tonight would settle Harry Greene and Dorian Rasmirez's eight-year feud once and for all. In a few short seconds, one of them would win and one of them would lose. *A coin-toss for my whole life's work.*

'And the Academy Award for Best Picture goes to . . .'

CHAPTER THIRTY-ONE

All over Los Angeles, people were throwing lavish, glitzy parties to celebrate the Oscars. But everyone who was anyone knew that there were only three events that mattered. Madonna's party. *Vanity Fair*'s. And the Governor's Ball.

Winners of the big gongs usually put in an appearance at two of the three at least, with the Best Actor and Actress being the single most-coveted guests at each after-bash. This year that was Roger de Gray and Sabrina Leon, but as De Gray had already announced that he and his heavily pregnant wife would only be going to the Governor's, the hysteria when Sabrina showed up at *Vanity Fair*'s was quite unsurpassed. It took security a full five minutes to help her get safely inside the Chateau Marmont through the throng of pre-approved press swarming her like locusts.

'Sabrina! How do you feel?'

'Have you spoken to Viorel?'

'Did you know he wasn't going to attend tonight?'

'Has he offered his congratulations?'

Sabrina smiled at everyone, but inside she was irritated.

Why won't people stop talking about Viorel? I just won an Oscar, for God's sake. Can't tonight be about that?

'It must be tough for you tonight, not having someone here to share your triumph with.' The comment came from a spiky-haired brunette whom Sabrina recognized as a stringer from *People* magazine.

'I have someone here,' said Sabrina, sweeping past her into the hotel. 'I have my friend, Dorian Rasmirez.'

Only she didn't. Where *was* Dorian?

Celeste taking Best Picture would have been reason enough for Dorian to want to disappear and lick his wounds. But he'd seemed pretty stoical about it at the time, sitting calmly through Harry Greene's gloating acceptance speech, politely accepting commiserations from the many friends who came up to him after the ceremony. He and Sabrina had left the theatre together, but somewhere in the melee of well-wishers and old friends, Sabrina found herself being swept away and the two of them had lost each other. In the end she'd gone on to the *Vanity Fair* party alone, hoping to find Dorian there. But as she scanned the sea of famous faces in the Chateau's famous rose garden, she couldn't see the only one she cared about.

'Sabrina.'

She spun around. Tarik Tyler, looking older than Sabrina remembered him but with the same kind eyes and crooked smile, was right behind her. Sabrina hadn't seen her old director in person in over two years, not since before the ungrateful 'slave driver' comment that had marked the beginning of her fall from grace.

'Congratulations, kiddo.' He smiled warmly. 'And thanks for the mention in your speech. I appreciated that.'

Sabrina found herself momentarily lost for words. But eventually she found the right ones. 'I'm so sorry, Tarik. Really.'

'I know you are,' he said, hugging her. Embarrassingly, Sabrina felt her eyes welling up with tears.

'Hey, c'mon, are you kidding me?' said Tarik. 'You can't cry tonight. This is your night, and you so deserve it.'

Sabrina shook her head. 'I don't deserve it.' She held up her Oscar. 'Dorian deserves this. He's the one who gave me a chance when no one else would. If it hadn't been for him . . .' Her words tailed off.

Tarik Tyler looked at her for a long time. Sabrina remembered how he used to do this on set, stare at his actors as if looking for some sort of key, some clue in their faces that would unlock whatever emotion it was he was trying to get out of them. It was disconcerting then, but it was even more so now.

'What?' She laughed nervously. 'Do I have spinach in my teeth or something?'

Tarik kept staring. Finally, he said, 'Why don't you just tell him?'

Sabrina frowned. She'd never been any good at riddles.

'Just tell him that you love him.'

Sabrina sighed. 'Sorry, Tarik, but you're way off target. Viorel's a part of my past and I'll always love him for that. But it's over. I'm not thinking about him, honestly.'

'Nor am I,' said Tarik. 'I was talking about Dorian Rasmirez.'

Dorian sat on the bed in his hotel room, staring out at the lights of Beverly Hills, tears streaming down his face. He hated himself for feeling so depressed. *There are people starving in this world,* he told himself. *Right now some poor bastard's being told his cancer is terminal, and you're sitting here crying because you didn't win Best Picture? Because you lost some money and you can't live in a castle any more? What the fuck is wrong with you?*

What he didn't want to admit to himself, but what he knew deep down, was that he wasn't crying because he hadn't won Best Picture. Nor even because Harry Greene had, and had been so loathsomely triumphant and graceless about it. In fact, Dorian realized with absolute clarity as he walked out of the Kodak Theatre that he didn't give a rat's ass about Harry Greene, or about Chrissie, who'd called his cell twice in the last hour offering what sounded like genuinely heartfelt commiserations. He hoped she'd see the light about Greene eventually. Maybe then they could become friends. For Saskia's sake, that had to be a good thing. He tried to picture his daughter's sweet, smiling face, but not even that could lift him out of his despair. The only person who could do that was a few miles across town, hopefully having the best night of her life.

He'd felt guilty ducking out of the after-parties. Having officially accepted both the Governor's Ball and *Vanity Fair*, he ought to have been there, to support Sabrina if nothing else. He knew that his *not* showing up made him look like a sore loser, and the thought bothered him. No doubt the media would crucify him in his absence, just as they had poor Viorel, who'd been found guilty of cowardice for not showing up tonight but would no doubt have been hung, drawn and quartered for insensitivity if he had.

But a man had to know his own limits. Dorian didn't know if he could hide his emotions tonight, if he could act happy around Sabrina. *And if I can't be happy around her, I have no right to be there. This is her moment, not mine.*

'Room service.'

A knock on the door brought him back to reality. The service at The Peninsula really was excellent. Dorian had only ordered the bourbon a couple of minutes ago and already someone was at his door.

'Coming.'

Kicking off his shoes and dropping his crumpled jacket on the bed, he shuffled across the room. 'That was quick. I . . .'

He caught his breath.

Leaning against the doorframe, her beautiful body curved like a Greek statue and her head tilted shyly to one side, Sabrina looked more perfect than she did in his dreams.

'Can I come in?'

'No.'

She frowned. 'No? It was kind of a rhetorical question. Why not?'

'Because,' Dorian looked at his watch, 'it's only eleven fifteen. You should be at the Governor's Ball, enjoying yourself.'

Sabrina shrugged. 'So should you.'

Dorian shifted awkwardly from foot to foot. 'I wasn't in the party mood.'

'Anyway, I did enjoy myself. You should have seen Chrissie's face when Harry Greene stuck his tongue down Carey Esposito's throat on the dance floor.'

'No!' Dorian gasped. 'Really? Jeez. I feel bad for her.'

'Why?' Sabrina pushed past him into the bedroom. 'She treated you like shit.' But she hadn't come here to talk about Chrissie Rasmirez. Kicking off her own shoes, she hitched up her dress and stepped out onto the balcony. Not knowing what else to do, Dorian followed her.

'You know,' said Sabrina wistfully. 'When I saw Viorel's empty chair tonight, I felt sad.'

'I know,' said Dorian, automatically. 'I understand.' But inside, his heart sank. *Oh God. She wants to talk about Hudson. She's gonna start crying and telling me how she'll never get over him, and I'll have to stand here and listen and comfort her.*

'I felt sad because it was over.'

'That's normal, sweetheart,' said Dorian. 'These things take time.'

'No.' Sabrina spun around to face him. 'You don't understand. I felt sad because it was over, and I realized that what we had wasn't love after all. It never had been.' Unsure as to how to respond to this, or whether he'd even heard her correctly, Dorian said nothing. 'Oh, it was obsession and need and a lot of other things,' Sabrina went on. 'Attraction, I guess. But it wasn't love. Guess who I saw tonight?'

The abrupt change in subject threw Dorian off guard. 'I'm sorry?'

'Tarik Tyler.'

'Ooo.' Dorian looked anxious. 'How'd that go?'

'Actually,' said Sabrina, her sombre expression evaporating suddenly as she broke into a dazzling, full-faced smile, 'it was very enlightening. He made me see something I should have seen a long time ago.' Leaning forward, she put both hands on Dorian's cheeks, gently cupping his face, and kissed him full on the lips.

Dorian tried not to respond, telling himself sternly all the reasons why he shouldn't. Sabrina was drunk. She was confused about Viorel. She was high on the night's events and not thinking clearly. Unfortunately, neither his lips nor his groin seemed to want to listen to reason. It was like telling the wave not to hit the shore or the moon not to rise. Pulling her so close, he kissed her back with such passion and force that Sabrina had to reach out for the balcony rail for support.

'I love you,' he said helplessly, when at last they broke for air.

'That's a coincidence,' grinned Sabrina. 'I love you too.'

Scooping her up into his arms, Dorian walked back into

the bedroom, laying her down on the bed. Slowly, desperate to savour every second of the miracle, he pulled himself up on his elbows till his face was above hers. Peeling down the red silk of her dress, he pressed his lips to the smooth skin just above her breasts and closed his eyes, breathing in the scent of her, the glory and the magic. When he looked up, his eyes met hers, and he knew for certain that he would never, ever let her go again.

'So, does the offer still stand?' she whispered.

'Offer? What offer?'

'You know. The one you made at the hospital. The "till death do us part" one.'

Harry Greene was welcome to his little gold statuette. In fact, he was welcome to every Oscar and every box-office record in the world. Dorian had just won the only prize that mattered. 'Oh yes,' he told Sabrina softly. 'That offer definitely still stands.'

CHAPTER THIRTY-TWO

Viorel stared out of the grimy taxi window at the bleak, frosted landscape and wondered how long he would be able to live here before topping himself. *A week? A month?* How the hell had Tish stuck it out here for six years?

His flight had landed in Budapest, Hungary, a few hours earlier and he had just crossed the border into Romania, chauffeured by a man with quite the worst body-odour problem Viorel had ever encountered, in a car whose windows, he soon discovered to his dismay, didn't open. Nose pressed to the filthy glass, Vio tried to distract himself from the stench by focusing on the 'scenery'. *Man, what a shit hole.* This was a far cry from the Romania of Dorian Rasmirez's Schloss, the verdant paradise of the Carpathian Mountains, the romantic home of vampires and noble princes. The Bihor region was flat and desolate, its muddy, single-lane roads stretching ahead endlessly through a featureless landscape, punctuated only by dilapidated gypsy tenements, grandly termed 'villages' but actually little more than rancid slums. Every ten miles or so they passed lay-bys at the side of the road where lorry drivers could stop and rest. At each of these rest stops, prostitutes shivered in cheap faux-leather miniskirts, hoping to sell them-selves to one of the truckers for a few leu, or in some cases a couple of shots of vodka. Alcoholism was everywhere here, in the ruddy faces of the indigent Roma men, in the bloated bodies of the women, in the birth defects of their hopelessly impoverished children who lined the streets like so much litter, unwanted, filthy and ignored.

I could have been one of those children, thought Vio with a shudder. *I was one of those children*. As much as he resented her coldness as a mother, he was grateful to Martha Hudson for removing him, physically, from this nightmarish, hopeless place.

Now it was his turn to do the rescuing.

While the world speculated about the demise of his romance with Sabrina Leon and his motives for shunning the Oscars' red carpet, the truth was that Viorel hadn't given the Academy Awards a thought. Ever since he'd received Abel's phone call, a week ago now, his mind, heart and soul had been here, in Romania. It had taken him seven days to get here – he had some urgent business to attend to in England first – but now, at last, he was here in body too. He knew what he had to do. But would he succeed? He thought about Tish, how stubborn she was, how infuriat-ingly self-righteous, how unwilling to listen to reason; he wasn't sure.

'How much longer?' he asked the driver, pointing at his watch. He was answered with a shrug so lethargic it might not even have been a shrug. Moments later, a large herd of cows ambled onto the road, followed by an arthritic-looking herdsman in a smock who could have walked straight out of the Middle Ages.

Viorel sighed. It was going to be a long day.

* * *

Tish Crewe had also had a long day. First, the heating had packed up yet again at Curcubeu, and she'd been forced to empty the charity's bank account to install a new boiler. Carl and the other foreign volunteers would be willing to forgo their salaries for a month or two to cover the cost, but the local Romanian workers needed their pay-cheques. As of today, Tish had no idea how she was going to pay them. Then she'd been called by Abel's teacher and told to come and pick him up early. Apparently, he'd been appallingly badly behaved all morning, quite uncharacteristically for him, and had ended up destroying another child's workbook and pouring ink into the loo cisterns.

'It's classic attention-seeking,' said his teacher, 'but I'm afraid we really can't tolerate that sort of acting up at school. You'll have to come and get him.'

Tish quizzed Abi in the car all the way home, but, again uncharacteristically, he decided to plead the fifth, remaining silent or monosyllabic for the entire twenty-minute journey. For a child who usually only drew breath once an hour, this was disconcerting.

When at last she made it home, Tish found a note from Lydia, Abel's grumpy but indispensable nanny, announcing that she could no longer tolerate Tish's erratic hours and had left; followed by an answerphone message from her mother, whom Tish had been trying and failing to reach all week, in which Vivianna said cheerfully that she had no idea where Jago was, nor did she have any details of the sale of Loxley Hall, but that she was relieved 'poor JJ' had sold 'that depressing old pile'.

'He needed a fresh start, darling. I'm sure you can understand that.'

As usual, Vivianna left no number.

'Abi, what are you *doing*?' Tish asked crossly. Abel's

dinosaur picture had strayed off the paper and indelible green ink was oozing all over the kitchen table. 'What's the matter with you today?'

'Nothing.' Abel smiled, glancing over at the door for the third time in as many minutes. He really was acting very strangely today. After all the playing up at school, Tish had expected to find him in an angry or sullen mood, but instead he seemed to be an odd mixture of happy and distracted.

'Aren't you feeling well?'

'I'm feeling fine, Mummy.'

There was a knock on the door. Abel practically leaped out of his seat.

'Are you expecting someone?' Tish asked him. *Perhaps it was Lydia coming back with a change of heart?* 'You didn't invite a friend over without telling Mummy, did you?'

'Sort of,' said Abel sheepishly.

Another knock.

'Aren't you going to open it?'

Suspiciously, Tish answered the door.

'May I come in?'

Before Tish could answer, Abel ran across the kitchen and flung himself bodily into Viorel's arms. 'I knew it,' he squealed delightedly, 'I knew you'd come!'

In dark brown corduroy slacks and a thick fisherman's sweater, with white snowflakes still melting into his oil-black hair, Viorel looked every bit as stomach-churningly sexy as Tish remembered. Before Tish had time to figure out whether he was real, or a figment of her overwrought imagination, Abel's eager eyes lit on a gaudily wrapped package poking out from Viorel's bag. 'Is that for my mummy?'

'Er . . .' Viorel hesitated.

'That's *such* a good idea of you to bring her a present because she actually really does like presents, don't you

Mummy? But if you do her a card she only likes the home-made ones, not the ones people buy in a shop because those kind are a waste of money and if people waste money d'you know what my mum says?'

Viorel grinned. 'What does she say?'

'She says, "What a damn fool!" And damn is a swearword so that is actually extremely serious and you should never ever do it. Go on, give the present to her now so she can fall in love with you.'

It was hard to tell who flushed redder, Tish or Viorel.

'Actually, mate, the present's for you.' Putting Abel down, Vio handed him the box. The boy ripped it open in seconds.

'A dinosaur!' he yelled joyously. 'It's remote-controlled!'

'Do you like it?'

'I LOVE it. Look Mum.' He held it up proudly. 'A electric, remote-controlled Acrocanthosaurus. I never had anything remote-controlled before that was extinct!'

'Nor me,' Tish smiled. 'What do you say?'

Dropping the dinosaur, Abel hugged Viorel's legs tightly. 'Thank you.' He breathed ecstatically. 'I love you.'

'I love you too, mate,' said Vio, his voice sounding choked.

Instinctively, Tish winced. What had she done? She should never have allowed Abi to get so attached.

'Now go and open the box in your bedroom,' Viorel continued. 'I need to talk to your mummy.'

'OK,' said Abel, adding in a stage whisper as he skipped off, 'I hope you got her a present too. She'll definitely like you more with a present.'

Once he'd gone, Tish and Viorel stood and stared at one another, like two actors with stage fright who'd forgotten their lines.

Tish broke the silence first.

'He's missed you.'

'I've missed him,' said Vio.

Tish looked pained. 'You shouldn't be here.'

It wasn't the response he'd been hoping for, but Vio figured it was as good a place to start as any.

'Why not?'

'Because!' said Tish exasperatedly. 'You *know* why.'

Vio cocked his head to one side. 'Do I?'

Oh, God, thought Tish helplessly. *Why does he have to be so attractive? It makes it so hard to think.*

'Yes,' she said, sitting down on the sofa and gesturing for him to sit beside her. 'You do. Because you coming in and out of his life when the mood suits you isn't fair on him.'

'I quite agree.'

'You're a movie star,' Tish went on, ignoring his acquiescence. 'You live in a totally different world from Abel and me. And of course it's exciting when you show up out of the blue.'

'Are you excited?'

Viorel's deep blue eyes locked onto Tish's. She felt her stomach turn to jelly.

'I'm . . . I'm happy,' she stammered. 'Look, we're talking about Abel, all right, not me. He needs stability, not to continually have his hopes raised and then dashed.'

'As I said, I agree.'

'Well stop saying "I agree"!' said Tish crossly. 'If you agree, then why on earth are you here?'

'I'm here to rescue him,' said Viorel.

Tish instantly bridled. '"Rescue him"? From what?'

'From this,' said Vio, looking around the freezing, ugly apartment. Above his head a brownish drip fell from a damp patch on the ceiling. Tish opened her mouth to protest, but Viorel cut her off. 'Stop arguing with me for a minute, woman, and listen.'

Tish was so startled, that for once she did as she was asked.

'Abel's miserable here and you know it. And if you don't know it, I'm telling you. He telephoned me last week in tears and told me how much he wanted to come home.'

'This is home,' said Tish stubbornly.

'Bollocks,' said Viorel. 'Loxley's his home and you know it. It's your home too.'

'Not any more it's not,' said Tish sadly, thinking of Jago and the sale.

Gently but firmly, Vio put a finger to her lips. The physical contact was like an electric shock. Tish was horrified to find she had an urge to take his hand and kiss it, but she resisted.

'That wasn't the only thing Abel told me.'

'It wasn't?' She barely trusted herself to breathe, never mind talk.

'No. He told me you've been sad. And that he thinks . . .' Viorel took a deep breath. 'He thinks you miss me.'

His hand was still on Tish's face. The silence was unbearable.

'Do you miss me?'

Imperceptibly, Tish gave the faintest of nods. She hadn't fully realized it herself until he'd shown up on the doorstep. But it was true. She had missed him. Day by day, almost without her noticing, Viorel had inveigled his way into her thoughts like ivy breaking through an old stone wall. She'd missed his face, his voice, his humour. She'd missed the thrill she felt, even when they were arguing, when Vio walked into a room.

'I've missed you too,' he said gruffly. 'Both of you. More than I thought possible.'

Stretching one arm along the back of the couch, he stroked

the back of Tish's hair. Tish placed her right hand over his and their fingers locked together.

'I didn't just come back for Abel,' Vio went on. 'I came to rescue you, too. Because I'm pretty sure you're the only woman on earth who can rescue me.'

Disengaging his hand he eased himself off the sofa, sliding down onto one knee.

'Will you marry me?'

It was all so sudden, Tish's emotions were having difficulty keeping up. 'What about Sabrina?' she heard herself asking.

'What about her?' Vio's gaze was unflinching. 'I never loved Sabrina. I always loved you.'

'You had a bloody funny way of showing it!' Tish laughed. 'You were completely obnoxious to me for most of the time you were at Loxley.'

'Yes, well, you reminded me of my mother,' said Vio, still on one knee. 'At the time,' he added hastily. 'You don't now. I think I was a bit confused.'

'I think you must have been!' said Tish, but she was too happy to fight about it. This was Viorel. *Her* Viorel. Hers and Abi's. *He's come to rescue us.*

'So?' His voice cut into her daydream. 'Will you?'

'Will I what?'

'*Marry* me,' Viorel frowned. 'Honestly, don't you ever listen?'

A voice in her head was practically screaming. *Yes, yes, for God's sake just say yes!* But old habits of practicality died hard, and the next words out of Tish's mouth were: 'But where would we live? You wouldn't move to Romania.'

'Damn right I wouldn't,' said Vio with feeling.

'And I could *never* live in Hollywood.'

'No,' Vio agreed with a smile. 'I don't suppose you could.'

'So?'

'So we'll live in England. Lord save us, Letitia, this is all just geography. You still haven't answered the question. Will you marry me or won't you?'

Tish released the smile that had been trying to escape her lips since the moment Viorel walked through her door. 'I will. Yes. I actually think I will.'

'You *think* you will?' Grabbing her hand, Viorel pulled her down onto the floor so suddenly Tish gasped. Then he kissed her so passionately and for so long she thought she might be going to pass out.

'Let me tell you what's going to happen,' he said, finally tearing himself away from her delectable lips. 'First, we're going to put Abel to bed.'

'Oh, are *we*?' Tish protested. This co-parenting thing was going to take some getting used to. 'I see. And then what?'

'Then,' said Vio grinning, 'I'm going to make love to you until you can barely stand.'

'Vio*rel*!' Tish blushed.

'And after *that*, tomorrow, I'm taking you both home to Loxley. Whether you like it or not.'

Tish sat up. Slowly, depressingly, reality began to seep back in.

'I love you,' she said, kissing Vio again. 'I do. But we can't just ride off into the sunset together.'

'Of course we can.'

'I'm being serious,' said Tish.

'So am I,' said Vio.

'I can't just up and leave Curcubeu. They need me.'

'Au contraire,' said Viorel. 'What they need is to become financially sustainable over the long term, and managed by a full-time, professional staff. Carl Williams will be running the charity from now on. As your primary donor – actually, let's be honest, as your *sole* donor – I've decided to make a few executive decisions vis-à-vis management.'

'What?' stammered Tish. 'Since when are you a donor?'

'Since I agreed to wire your foundation a million dollars.'

'Oh my God!' Tish gasped, then frowned. 'You haven't really?'

'I certainly have. I've also agreed to invest a further million for long-term income generation,' said Viorel. '*On the condition* that you and Abel move back home to England. For good.'

Tish sat back and thought about it for a moment.

'That's blackmail,' she said at last. 'You're holding me to ransom.'

Viorel's smile broadened. 'Yup.'

He kissed her again then, carrying her into the bedroom and laying her down on the bed. Sliding his hands up under her T-shirt, he finally caressed those gorgeous, round apple breasts through the cotton of her Gap bra. Reaching around her back, he'd almost managed to unclasp it when Tish sat up again, so quickly that she almost head-butted his nose.

'There's something else. I can't believe I forgot.'

Viorel sighed heavily. 'Good grief. What now?'

'It's Loxley,' said Tish. 'We can go back to England if you really want to, but I'm afraid we'll have to find somewhere else to live.'

'Oh?'

Tish nodded sadly. 'It's been sold. Jago sold the place off to some American buyer and did a runner with the proceeds. Poor Mrs D's been beside herself, and the Connellys. The new owner's moving in next week, so they'll all have to be gone by Sunday.'

'Shit.' Viorel jumped to his feet. 'That reminds me.' Walking back into the living room, he picked up his discarded coat and started rifling through the pockets, looking for something.

'For you.' He handed Tish an envelope.

She looked at it suspiciously. 'What is it?'

'It's anthrax,' said Viorel.

Tish raised a sarcastic eyebrow.

'Open it up and find out.'

Still frowning, Tish pulled the single, folded sheet of paper out of the envelope. She read it once, then twice, then a third time.

'Aren't you going to say anything?' said Vio.

'It's . . . it's the deeds to Loxley,' whispered Tish.

'Well, you did say we needed somewhere to live.'

'*You* bought it? The lawyer told me it was an American.'

'It was. You don't think Jago would have sold to me, do you? He still hates my guts over the whole Sabrina thing. No, he sold it to a charming Texan named John Dwight. I should warn you, it took some persuading to convince Mr Dwight to pass the place on to me and I'm afraid he didn't let it go cheap. Which means I'm going to have to do an awful lot of movies to pay off our debts. Do you think you could tolerate Hollywood in short bursts?'

'*Our* debts?' said Tish. 'Funny, I don't remember borrowing anything.'

'What's mine is yours, Mrs Hudson.' Vio grinned wolfishly, his eyes moving down unashamedly over Tish's glorious but – *How had it happened?* – still-not-yet-naked body. 'And what's yours is about to become mine.'

'Excuse me,' came a familiar, reedy little voice, just as Viorel was reaching for the fly buttons on Tish's jeans. 'My dinosaur's not roaring properly. I . . . Oh!' Noticing suddenly Tish and Vio were mid-embrace, Abel smiled contentedly. 'Good. You're married then.'

'Not exactly.' Tish giggled.

'Nearly,' said Viorel.

'Cool. Well, anyway, my dinosaur definitely has something not proper about it and I think it needs new batteries. Can you come and fix it, Viorel?'

Vio looked at Tish longingly.

'Pleeeaaase?' begged Abi.

Tish grinned. 'Welcome to fatherhood. Go ahead. Fix it. I'm not going anywhere.'

Watching Viorel follow her son into his bedroom, Tish thought happily: *He's already fixed it. He's already fixed everything.*

Tish Crewe was going home at last.

Turn the page
to read an exclusive Q & A
with

Tilly
Bagshawe

Questions
& Answers

**What particularly appeals to you about *Wuthering Heights*
and its themes?**

As a novel it really has everything. Romance, excitement, a gripping plot,
complex characters and a stunning setting. It's as fresh and readable today
as it was when it was written – plus it has probably the sexiest anti-hero of
all time in Heathcliff.

**People love reading about celebrity scandals at the moment.
What do you think has made society so fascinated by celebrities?**

I'm not sure, but I'm as guilty as the next person in this respect. For me it's
like a soap opera, a melodrama you can lose yourself in without taking it
too seriously. It's fun.

**If you could be any celebrity for one day, who would you
be and why?**

Probably Simon Cowell. The man has a permanent glint in his eye that
seems to say "I'm having so much fun." I hate angst ridden celebrities.
If you're rich and successful, enjoy it.

**Have you ever related to any of the characters you've portrayed?
How so?**

Not in the direct sense of actually basing them on myself. But there are
aspects of most of my characters, certainly my heroines, that I relate to.
In *Fame*, there are elements of Sabrina's ambition and need for approval that
I remember feeling acutely when I was younger. Whereas Tish's closeness to
her family and struggles as a mother feel closer to my own life today.

If you weren't writing, what would you be doing?

Sleeping? I have no idea. Maybe I'd ask Simon Cowell for a job.

How do you go about researching your books?

It depends. *Fame* is set in places that I already know well, Derbyshire,
Los Angeles and Romania, which made it easier. But of course there are
unfamiliar areas, which do need research. I talk to people in the film
business – most of my friends in LA are actresses – and like every other
writer I know I would be lost without Google.

Where do you draw your inspiration from for your plots?
Everywhere. From life. The Romanian aspect of this book and the focus
on Roma orphans came from my involvement with F.R.O.D.O, a charity my
husband founded to help disabled, institutionalized kids in that country.
It's an incredible place but my plots grow from my characters, and those
are drawn from all the different aspects of my life.

Do you find that being a writer enables you to travel a lot?
For me it's more the other way around. We travel so much as a family,
I'm lucky to have a job that I can take with me everywhere, and so many
different people and places to inspire me.

**What advice would you give to someone wanting to
become a writer?**
Read, as much as you can, in the genre you hope to write. Be disciplined.
Write something every day and don't stop until you type 'The End'. Ideas
are ten a penny, it's the execution that counts. Anyone who finishes a novel,
whether it gets published or not, deserves a lot of credit.

**If you could visit anywhere in the world where would it
be and why?**
India and Egypt are both on my wish list. I would love to see the pyramids
and am fascinated by ancient history.

What are your three travel essentials?
A good book, gin and tonic and a nanny.

Where has been your favourite place you have visited so far?
Impossible to nail it down to just one. I adore Nantucket, an island off
Boston. We have a holiday home there and my youngest child
was born on the island. It's magical.

What's the most adventurous thing you've done when abroad?
I once went white water rafting in Indonesia. That was pretty wild.

What items do you always take with you on an airplane?
Aspirin, an ipod and my glasses. I can't wear contact lenses on planes so
I'd be blind as a bat without them.

SEXY

Sasha Miller goes to Cambridge University with a dream, and leaves a broken woman. After losing her heart to sexy professor Theo Dexter, she departs in a scandal.

SHOCKING

Meanwhile, as Theo becomes a television heart throb, his long suffering wife Theresa realises that trust and fidelity are two words her husband doesn't understand. His betrayal is deeper than any cut.

SCANDALOUS

Years later the two women will unite in a daring scheme to bring down the man who almost destroyed them both. It took them years to realise how one man could cause so much pain, but now they are determined he will regret the day he entered both of their lives…

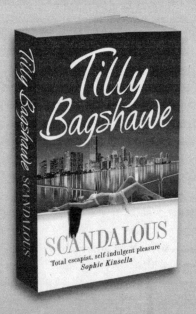

'Total escapist, self-indulgent pleasure'
Sophie Kinsella

SCANDALOUS

At eight on the dot, Sasha walked into the bar at the Ritz Carlton. Jackson was nowhere to be seen. I'll give him two minutes, she thought crossly. I'm not hanging around for that vain, self-important . . . 'You came.' In the twenty minutes since she'd last seen him, Jackson had showered, shaved and changed into a pair of cream linen Armani trousers and a coffee-coloured Interno 8 shirt that perfectly offset his butterscotch tan. For a split second his handsomeness, combined with his broad, apparently genuine smile, disarmed her. 'I can only stay for a drink. It's my parents' last night in town. But I figured I'd hear what you have to say.' Jackson frowned. He'd been planning on getting her tipsy in the bar, excited about Wrexall over dinner, then sealing the deal in bed. Now he would have to move straight to phase three. Languidly stretching out his arm, he stroked Sasha's hair. 'Let's cut to the chase, darling, shall we? I can tell you about Wrexall when you have more time. There's a job for you with us if you want it. But right now I think we both know it's not the job you want.' Before Sasha had a moment to protest, Jackson swooped in and kissed her passionately on the mouth. He smelled of lemons and soap and toothpaste. Feeling his body pressed against hers, for a moment Sasha felt a stab of longing. Old feelings flooded her body, familiar yet strange, like a frozen river cracking in the first spring thaw. Then, out of nowhere, an image of Theo Dexter naked and making love to her popped into Sasha's mind. She pushed Jackson violently away. 'Get off me! Are you out of your mind?'

'I don't think so.' Jackson was maddeningly unperturbed. 'I want you. You want me. We're both adults. You're not attached, are you?'

'That has nothing to do with it!' said Sasha furiously.

'Good. Neither am I.' He leaned in for another kiss.

'Stop it! What are you, some kind of sex pest? I saw you on the street half an hour ago. With the blonde? So for one thing, you are attached.'

Jackson grinned. 'Ah. You're jealous.'

'I am not jealous. I came here to talk about a job, you jerk. Clearly I made a huge error of judgement.'

'Look me in the eye and tell me you're not attracted to me. That when I kissed you just now you weren't imagining the two of us in bed together.'

'You're deranged.' Sasha turned on her heel and stormed out of the hotel. As she came out of the revolving doors onto Newbury Street, she saw Jackson's blonde. Clearly the girl couldn't keep away from him. 'Excuse me,' said Sasha on impulse. 'I'm sorry to intrude. But are you the girl dating Jackson Dupree?'

A look of pride spread over the blonde's face.

'That's right,' she smiled. 'I'm Rachel Cooper. Do you know Jackson?'

'Not at all,' said Sasha. 'But that didn't stop him trying to get me into bed right now. He asked me here to talk about a job with his company, then he stuck his tongue down my throat and begged me to sleep with him.'

Colour drained from the blonde's face. 'Look, I'm sorry to be so blunt. But you seem like a nice girl. You can do a lot better than that arsehole.'

SEXY. SHOCKING. SCANDALOUS.

Start the summer in style
with Tilly Bagshawe's FAME

If FAME's glitz and glamour has inspired you to indulge in some much needed pre-holiday pampering, now's the time to get started! We're offering every reader a FREE manicure, or other treatment, in association with this scorching new bestseller.

Available treatments include: Manicure, Pedicure, Aromatherapy Massage, Back Massage, Facial, Indian Head Massage.

To claim your treatment, and for more information, simply visit
www.harpercollins.co.uk/fame

T3L7B4N29J